Praise for *The Prime Minister's Affair*

'A compelling story of power, passion and intrigue based on
real events . . . A terrific read'
Nick Robinson

'A wickedly entertaining tale of political chicanery'
Daily Telegraph

'Ticks all the boxes . . . An historical spy thriller which
springs to life due to the complexity and humanity of its
characters, both public and private'
Crime Time

'Compelling and full of rich portrayals of both real and
fictional characters from the period . . . A wonderful read'
Sarah Ward

'A tense and intricate story that shows politics has always
been a brutal business'
Sun

'Spy tradecraft of the old school, with no computers, fast cars
or mobile phones, but not a whit less exciting for that.
Highly recommended as both a spy story and a piece of
social and political history'
Shots Magazine

Also by Andrew Williams

The Prime Minister's Affair

ANDREW WILLIAMS

HODDER

First published in Great Britain in 2022 by Hodder & Stoughton
An Hachette UK company

This paperback edition published in 2023

2

Copyright © Andrew Williams 2022

The right of Andrew Williams to be identified as the
Author of the Work has been asserted by him in accordance
with the Copyright, Designs and Patents Act 1988.

A CIP catalogue record for this title
is available from the British Library

Paperback ISBN 978 1 529 36830 7
ebook ISBN 978 1 529 36829 1

Typeset in Celeste by Palimpsest Book Production Limited,
Falkirk, Stirlingshire

Printed and bound in Great Britain by Clays Ltd, Elcograf S.p.A.

Hodder & Stoughton policy is to use papers that are natural, renewable
and recyclable products and made from wood grown in sustainable
forests. The logging and manufacturing processes are expected to
conform to the environmental regulations of the country of origin.

Hodder & Stoughton Ltd
Carmelite House
50 Victoria Embankment
London EC4Y 0DZ

www.hodder.co.uk

Why is every grievance put on our shoulders?
We have implacable enemies who sleeplessly lie in wait
   to damage our reputation.
But why?

Prime Minister Ramsay MacDonald,
Diary 16 January 1930

For Kate, Lachlan and Finn

Prologue

1 May 1929

1

THERE WAS A time before the Great War claimed the lives of millions when Frenchie wanted to be a carpenter like Jesus. There was a time when he was proud to serve his country. Then its politicians broke their pledge to create a land fit for heroes, and Frenchie began to believe those who had done most to rouse the people to service and sacrifice had only been serving themselves. So now Frenchie was simply happy to have a job when so many were without one. Sometimes it was work for Special Branch, sometimes for Mr Maxwell Knight, and tonight it was a shitty little outing to Brecon for both. Mr Knight tried to characterise it as work of 'national importance'. He must have thought those fine words would appeal to an old soldier and spy who had been decorated in the trenches for his 'devotion to duty'. Not Frenchie; he kept his Military Medal in a kitchen drawer with the spoons, a scratched and tarnished reminder of wasted years, before the slaughter at the Front gave way to the scrape-a-living peace. Frenchie was a bread-and-butter spy now, no more honourable than the crooks, pimps and hucksters Mr Knight and his fascist pals paid for half-baked gossip and rumour. Principles were for the well-to-do, and duty for those foolish enough to believe they owed their country some – not for old soldiers, not for Frenchie.

But when spies bugger about in bars too long or loiter for hours on the shadow side of the street, they brood, they scratch, and food for the family table can seem like a poor code to live a life by. That was Frenchie as the sun dipped below the hills to the west of Brecon. He was standing on the last corner in a week of corners in dirty little Welsh towns he was unable to pronounce, his chase near its end, and on May Day, Labour Day, when working men and women were expected to demonstrate class solidarity. That was bloody fate for you, and as a working man he felt quite bad about it. During the war they said, 'if the bullet has your number you're done for': May Day in Brecon the number was up for a couple of ordinary blokes called Owen and Eyre; and it was Agent Frenchie's job to make it so.

Owen and Eyre were across the street in a little boozer called the Dragon. Frenchie had ghosted in and out of the pub and seen Owen at the bar buying beer for Tommies; Eyre at a table persuading them to mutiny. How many pints would it take to convince them? And when their glasses were empty, Owen and Eyre were to walk to Brecon barracks to hand out flyers urging the rest of the garrison to do the same.

Frenchie reached behind his right ear for the dog-end he had left there. Desperate times. He would buy some more fags at the station kiosk. He knew it sold cigarettes because he had telephoned Mr Knight from the call box opposite.

'It's tonight, M.'

'I'll make the arrangements,' had come the reply. 'Ring me when the deed is done. Dudley 4832.'

Knight would be at a political meeting. The country was four weeks from a general election that the workers' party – the Labour Party – was expecting to win. Owen and Eyre were workers – or they would like to be. Owen was an ex-miner, a father of four, Eyre an unemployed furnace man, and the talk at their pints and politics meeting in the Dragon would be of jobs and of workers uniting everywhere. Wrong shade of Red, lads! Poor sods. They were labouring under the misapprehension they lived in a free country: not for communists, boys, not for commies. They wanted to sweep away the old order in a Russian-style revolution – well, the old order was not going to stand for it. Those that *had* were terrified of those that *hadn't*, terrified they would rise up and turn the pyramid upside down, that their grand houses would become hospitals, their estates collective farms, that aristos would be forced to pick up a shovel, and the colonies would revolt. That was why hounding unemployed butties like Owen and Eyre was work of 'national importance'. Frenchie gave a wry smile. Think! The spark of revolution, lit on a chilly May Day in Brecon. Only, if the country was run well and fairly, how could it happen?

The fag-end burned his fingers and he flicked it into the gutter. 'Here they come.' On the pavement in front of the pub: Owen, 43, sturdy as a pit pony, his arm about a Tommy's shoulders; Eyre, from Essex, 32, tall, sinewy, six feet of colliery winding cable, blathering to two more soldiers, a hessian sack of flyers over his shoulder. *Unite to free the heroic workers and peasants of India, Soldier! If you are sent to serve in India, you must refuse to shoot down workers fighting for their freedom. Our guns must be turned on our real enemy – the thieving, robbing, British ruling class.*

Their appeal to the soldier-workers of Brecon was printed on thin grey paper. Frenchie had followed the Communist Party's courier from London to iron and steel Merthyr, and to a meeting of local comrades in a temperance hall. Then to a crowded pub called the Patriot, where he had watched the courier pass the flyers under a table to Eyre.

'Who are you, butty?' the barman had enquired.

Union rep and a stevedore from London was Frenchie's story, and he had shown anyone who asked him a transport workers'

3

union card. A comradely visit – 'let me buy you another' – and he'd talked about the general election and a Labour government, and it was time for the people to seize control of the means of production. Yes, Frenchie had been a bloody bore, but his new Welsh comrades seemed ready to forgive him for being a Londoner and a little la-di-da because he was an old soldier and a worker too, with scars and calluses and money for beer. He had bought Owen a pint and listened to the story of how he was blacklisted for leading a strike. At closing time his new comrades had found him a bed for the night with an old grey woman who lived in a terrace beneath a slag mountain she called her old grey man. That was how the paperchase had begun. Dowlais to Aberdare, Pontypool to Mardy, he had followed the distribution of the flyers up and down the smokestack valleys of Wales, until the train pulled into Brecon, a different sort of town, a town with cow shit in the high street – and a barracks.

The comrades were walking towards the lights at its main gate now, Owen and Eyre on one side, Frenchie covering them on the other. They were taking their time about it too. Sober enough perhaps to recognise it was reckless, even suicidal, like storming a machine gun post without covering smoke, like Jesus riding into Jerusalem on a donkey. Brecon was home to regiments that were famous for fighting natives with spears. Stitched into their colours were battle honours awarded for actions in hot places. An appeal by the comrades for solidarity with the peasants of India was bound to end badly. With luck the police would break up the ensuing melee before too much blood was spilled.

They crossed to Frenchie's side of the street, the tall one, Owen, shortening his stride to keep in step with his companion. An old Vulcan lorry grumbled towards them, Mr Anthony Lewis, Grocer painted on a board above the cab. The whine and percussion of its engine filled the street with memories: a road through no-man's-land, a procession of ambulances carrying wounded from a shell-shattered city, the crump of high explosives, and the stop–start roar of a lorry that would carry Frenchie in and out of the line for the rest of his life. A few seconds later, MR ANTHONY LEWIS, GROCER and his Vulcan turned left and the war retreated along the side street with him.

Soldiers were drifting back from the pubs and a score or more were chatting and smoking beneath the tower to the right of the barracks' gate, enjoying their last minutes of freedom from barked orders and the clatter of the dormitory. Frenchie's own Tommy years had begun in a grey stone mental hospital very like Brecon barracks. The army had commandeered the place for use as a training camp and its new inmates had charged across its grounds to stick a bag with a bayonet. The recollection of it made him wince. Eyre had missed the war somehow; Owen had done his bit. 'Made me see the truth,' he had confided to Frenchie at the Patriot. 'Workers on both sides was doin' the dying, see, and for what?'

Eyre handed Owen some flyers and one of them must have shouted a greeting because the soldiers turned towards them. Frenchie staggered like a local with a skinful of beer and came to rest against the rough stone wall of the barracks. Chin on his chest, he gazed beyond his peaked cap at the terrace of shops and houses on the opposite side of the street. Someone was twitching a curtain at an upstairs window, a member of the local constabulary, no doubt.

There was trouble at the gate already. A burly-looking Tommy was trying to wrestle the bag of flyers from Eyre. One of his companions waded in with his fists. Owen tried to haul him away. The soldiers would be under orders to kick up the dust. A tussle in front of the barracks was all the excuse the police needed to scoop up Owen and Eyre and charge them with affray. A crowd was pressing round them and more punches were thrown.

'Christ!' Frenchie murmured. 'Arrest them, why don't you?'

Perhaps the officer commanding the barracks had decided to teach them a lesson: the shit. His 'chaps' were sticking in the boot, in and out like a village hall dance.

'Bugger it.' Frenchie looked away.

Owen was a decent bloke, and Eyre didn't deserve a beating. Flyers were spilling from his bag and scuttering along the street like the leaves of a fabulous tree.

'Come on now, come on.' Frenchie was willing it to stop, because the circle was tightening, the soldiers' dance at fever pitch. One of Owen or Eyre was going to die while he stood there watching. Then with a surge of relief he heard a blast on a whistle and policemen poured from the house opposite and shouldered their way into the ring. Comrade Owen was hauled to his feet; Eyre was lying motionless. A plainclothes copper knelt beside him. They were going to have to carry the poor sod into custody. To add insult to his injury, they would charge him with 'resisting arrest'.

Frenchie turned away. He felt empty, he felt numb, he felt as he used to feel at times in the big bombardments when he had ceased to care where the next shell would fall.

2

Knight said, 'Speak up! You'll have to speak up.'

For some reason known only to the municipal functionary responsible for planning these things, the public telephone at Dudley Town Hall had been placed on the wall outside its principal assembly room.

'A second! Will you wait, Frenchie,' he shouted into the receiver.

Inside the hall eight hundred Labour Party supporters were clapping, cheering, stamping their feet for Mr Ramsay MacDonald. 'Our next prime minister,' Sir Oswald Mosley boomed from the stage, and the hall rose as one to greet him. To witness so much passion spent on someone so ordinary was baffling. Hats off to Mosley because the warmth of the reception for Mac owed a good deal to his talent for whipping a crowd into a frenzy. Proof, in Knight's opinion, that for all their talk of equality and fraternity the socialist comrades were in thrall to the natural authority of a strong and confident fellow like Mosley. An aristocrat, a baronet married to the daughter of a marquis, he was born to play a leading role in society. What a rum lot the ladies and gentlemen of the podium party were, really. First, Mosley, the socialist member for Smethwick; then his dear lady wife, standing in the Potteries, and to cap it all, Oliver Baldwin, the son of the prime minister – a Conservative prime minister – the candidate for the shoo-in Labour seat of Dudley. The communists would call them 'class enemies,' and while Knight despised Reds of all shades, he was inclined to acknowledge they had a point.

'Mr Knight?'

'Patience, Frenchie, please.'

As Mosley resumed his seat the noise in the hall ebbed to an expectant murmur. The leader of the Labour Party was ready to speak.

'What do you think of Ramshackle, Frenchie?'

'Who, Mr Knight?'

'Never mind.'

'The coppers were waiting at the barracks, as you said.' Frenchie paused. 'Owen and Eyre took a beating.'

'That was to be expected.'

'It wasn't necessary.'

'Well,' said Knight, casually, 'send me your expenses and I'll leave an envelope at the usual place.'

No reply.

'Well done, Frenchie,' he said.

Again, no reply. Bloody man! Frenchie had hung up on him: damned cheek of the fellow. Courageous, clever, resourceful, but not a gentleman. But his 'casuals' wouldn't be of use to him as informers if they were gentlemen. Most of them didn't give two hoots for the country and the threat it was facing from the Red menace, just as long as they had money for beer and whores. They were scum. Frenchie was different. Frenchie was an old soldier and army spy. Pity he showed no inclination to set an example to the rest.

3

In the hall Ramshackle Mac was speaking of his recent visit to Canada.

I asked the Canadian people what message I should bring home and the answer was, 'carry on with your Labour work for Britain and the Empire.'

Knight returned to his seat and in his cheap tweed suit and collarless shirt, newsboy cap in lap, he looked indistinguishable from his neighbours. A foundry man perhaps or a panel beater – he liked to think he had the shoulders – no one would know he bought the Brilliantine he used in his hair at Harrods.

Canada's great electrical development is being accomplished by socialism. The people have cut out private enterprise. Here in Britain, the Tories depend on private money and in return they hand out contracts to their friends in business. They dip their hands in the public wealth of this country and assets that ought to belong to the community are given away to just a few.

The men on either side of Knight clapped and stamped to wake the dead and there was nothing for it but to join them. That Ramshackle Mac had presence was impossible to deny. The timbre of his voice and his soft Scottish accent, his grey locks and thick 'your country needs you' moustache, his fine chiselled features and poetic brow; he was a distinguished-looking fellow, more handsome than a man had a right to be in his sixties. He spoke with passion and apparent sincerity and while Knight abhorred the message, he had to admit to a grudging respect for the figure cut by the messenger. Mosley was a fine speaker but head over heels in love with Mosley, and were the workers going to trust a rich man who needed to do nothing to earn his keep, only profit from the salt of their labour? What was more, he was a turncoat: first a Conservative, then an Independent and now Labour. Where next? Knight had heard a rumour he was unfaithful to Lady Cynthia, too. No, grizzled old Ramshackle was the one to watch. Goodness, he oozed sincerity. A Red Elijah, urging his people to turn away from the false gods of capital and the market.

The nation is rich, he boomed, *and yet millions of pounds are squandered each year. Those who have, have not earned their keep, while the multitude who have not, toil all their lives and end them with nothing. This is a moral issue, the greatest of our time. The Labour Party will create a system in which the wealth producers – the working people of this country – may enjoy the rewards of their labours.*

The fifty-something man sitting to the right of Knight brushed away a tear. These people . . . they were lapping it up. The fervour in the hall reminded Knight of a Non-Conformist revivalist meeting. Ramshackle need only give them the order to take to the streets and they would go. Small comfort he was not prepared to, because he was paving the way for more ruth-less men who were – communist revolutionaries. Look at them, still on their feet! This was how it had begun in Russia! Ramshackle was paving the way for someone whose politics were a deeper shade of red, one of the wild men in his party – a British Lenin.

Knight rose and eased his way along the row to the aisle. At the door he turned to gaze back at the comrades as they launched into a rendition of their socialist anthem, 'The Red Flag'. Mosley and Lady Cynthia were singing with gusto too. The podium party was looking very smug, and if newspaper reports of public opinion were correct its members had good reason to be. The public seemed ready to put Ramshackle Mac in Downing Street for a second time. The public! Those people in the hall singing their sentimental song of *martyred dead* and of raising their *scarlet standard high*.

A muddy echo of it chased Knight into the street. Major Morton was expecting him to make a report at half past nine. Punctilious, the major, every inch the soldier, war hero, patriot. 'I have only one enemy in this life,' he had confided to Knight at their first meeting, 'and its name is international communism.' They shared a conviction that the country had to be protected by any means necessary from that insidious foreign creed. Within a few weeks of their first meeting the public had made the mistake of electing a Labour government, the first in the country's history. Ramsay MacDonald had become prime minister – but for only a matter of months. Major Morton and his associates in the Secret Service had seen to that.

4

Knight waited for the door of the kiosk to swing to, his pennies on the shelf beneath the telephone.

'Operator? London Abbey 3624.'

Labour would be harder to dislodge a second time, but it

was beginning to look as if those who loved their country and cared about its independence were going to have to try.

'Abbey? Put me through to 3624 please.'

Major Morton had a dedicated line. 'Abbey 3624.'

'Major, it's Max.'

'How are you, Max?' His voice was top-notch, Eton and army. 'News from Wales?'

'Just as we planned, only too late to make the morning papers, I fear.'

'I'll speak to our friends in the press, see what they can do. We want people to sit up, take notice.'

Knight bit his lip. *Reds Urge British Soldiers to Mutiny* wasn't going to swing the election in favour of the Conservatives. The voters expected commies to foment trouble. A couple of Welsh comrades in custody would cause no more than a ripple in the press. No, Ramshackle Mac was the real enemy. Ramshackle was able to make socialism sound like a religious obligation. God forbid the electors return him to government. He would barely have time to plant his big feet beneath the cabinet table before Labour's wild men, the real Reds, made their move.

'Knight?'

'I was at Ramsay MacDonald's meeting in Dudley tonight.'

'Ah.'

'It was impressive, Major.'

'Those town hall meetings . . . long on promises. He knows how to whip up a crowd. All passion and prejudice. Did he mention re-establishing diplomatic relations with the Soviet Union? If he wins, the commissars will be back in London.' He paused. 'You know, we're going have to manage things again. It won't be easy a second time, but we will. Don't doubt it, Max. For the country.'

'Yes.'

'Let's hope the Conservatives are able to pull a rabbit out of the hat and surprise us all. Goodnight, Max. Goodnight.'

That's that then, thought Knight. It was too late for a train to London. He was going to have to spend the night in Dudley. Ramshackle's people were pouring out of the town hall and washing round the telephone box, laughing, chatting, some still singing, as if they were on a church outing, only their hymn was to equality and the redistribution of wealth. Working men in flat caps and hobnail boots, young women, permitted to vote for the first time, tradesmen, shopkeepers, hurrying for a bus or a pint in a town centre pub. Gazing through the grimy glass of the telephone box, Knight wondered at their ignorance. They could see no further than the bottom of the street. The trouble with democracy was that the many were as capable of making a catastrophic misjudgement as the few. The country needed men of wisdom and experience – guardians – to protect it from public ignorance and alien influences. Guardians you could trust to do what was necessary, even if it meant breaking the law. MacDonald was promising to raise taxes and nationalise entire industries. To what end? A socialist paradise? Another Soviet socialist republic? Putting power into the hands of Labour was to run the risk of a revolution. Trade union Bolshies had done their best to foment one during the general strike; and in the three years since, their ranks had grown. Damn MacDonald for being such a plausible devil: he was wooing voters with an insidious brand of soft pulpit socialism, and he was winning.

But all was not lost: Knight had been wrong to doubt the resolve of the major and his Secret Service associates to do what was necessary. They had moved decisively against the socialists five years ago and if the people were foolish enough to elect another Labour government on the thirtieth of May they would do so again.

PART ONE

Beginning to feel work getting the better of me.
Creeps up over me like the tide over a man tied to a stake.
Insomnia also appearing with its consequential depression.
Regrets cloud and stay – the dead – my loneliness.

Prime Minister Ramsay MacDonald,
Diary 27 November 1929

1

27 November 1929

1

SOME EVENINGS THE prime minister counted his freedom from the noisome cares of the nation in the few minutes it took him to walk from parliament to Downing Street alone – on many evenings of late. Days when his troubles seemed to march in battalions. On this particular Wednesday in November, the echo of a stormy sitting of the House of Commons pursued him from the lobby to the members' entrance and into the cobbled yard below Big Ben. Shares falling; investment falling; production falling; unemployment rising. 'Do something, prime minister,' Conservative backbenchers had shouted across the floor at him, because 'something' was the privilege of opposition. He needed no reminder from the party of the well-to-do that working men and women who had trusted him and voted Labour were suffering. My God, he felt it deeply. They had invested prodigious hope in his government and after only six months their faith was faltering. Mr Ramsay MacDonald had put the cup to their lips and the cup was empty.

A fresh breeze was stripping the yellow memory of summer from the trees in New Palace Yard and chasing him to the gate. He paused to turn up the collar of his coat. An easterly wind always reminded him of home and, oh, how he longed to be there. In the night hours to come the wind would purge filthy London of its smoke, if only for a while.

A cab carrying an honourable member he did not recognise

– there were so many – swept past him into Parliament Square. Before him as he turned out of the gate, the imposing white stone government building that was shared by Trade, Education and Health. There were lights on in no more than a dozen of its windows. Most of the servants of an empire where the sun never set had left their posts hours ago, most of his ministers too.

A motorcar honked its horn at him as he scuttled across the square into Parliament Street. The doorman at the Ministry of Health tipped the brim of his bowler hat and wished him a good evening. On the pavement outside the Foreign Office, three young men in evening dress were flapping at a taxi. One of them noticed him and whispered to his companions, 'Alone and carrying his own case!' Well of course! He was the leader of the Labour Party: what did they expect? Goodness, they must have read his story, the papers were constantly dredging it up: bastard son of a ploughboy and a girl in service; born in a but and ben cottage north of nowhere; and not too high and mighty to labour in a field or as a warehouse clerk. Now that 'faitherless bairn' was the tenant of 10 Downing Street – although not an entirely happy one. He missed his home, his corners, their ghosts, and his wife most of all. He was still grieving for her after eighteen years – he always would be.

The wind was ruffling the poppies at the foot of the Cenotaph, where a fortnight before he had helped to lead the country in mourning for those lost in the Great War. The newspapers had accused him of being a 'traitor' – he had been against the war from the start – but people respected him now for taking a stand and because he knew what it was to lose a loved one and soldier on with an aching heart. Turning into Downing Street, his pace quickened, driven unconsciously after years of campaigning by the need to appear vigorous and purposeful in a public place.

Duty porter Barnes opened the door. 'Good evening, Prime Minister.'

'Good evening, Barnes.'

'Will you be going out again, sir?'

'No, no.' The porter helped him with his coat. 'Miss Rosenberg, is she still here?'

'I believe so, sir. Shall I tell her you're back?'

Rosa would know because nothing passed her by. She would be answering correspondence and screening visitors to his private office at a time when most women her age were ministering to children and a husband, or making it their business to find one. *Rosa of Number 10*, the newspaper correspondents called her: she had them wrapped around her little finger.

'And Ishbel?'

'Miss MacDonald is home, yes, sir.'

'Then would you ask her to join me?'

There was work to be done but first he would spend time with his daughter and his son, Malcolm. They lived with him on the second floor of the house. The grand rooms with crystal chandeliers, magnificent plaster ceilings, polished floors with Persian rugs, the paintings of his predecessors and of lords and ladies he didn't recognise and didn't care to, were on the ground and first floors. They were state rooms for the foreign dignitaries and visitors from the empire he received every day. The second floor was for the family and some of his own things, a place for quiet moments and memories. Step by step up the elegant cantilever staircase from glittering state to private felt like climbing from one part of his personality to another. Because there were times when he revelled in the company of grand society ladies and gentlemen, in wearing fine clothes and flirting, but more often he craved the quiet intimacy of his family life. He was the tenant of the entire house.

2

'You look exhausted, Father.' Ishbel was waiting for him at the door of the family's drawing room.

'Is Malcolm home, dear?'

'Yes,' said Malcolm, appearing at her shoulder.

'You were in the Chamber?'

'You spoke very well, Father.'

Malcolm was on the backbenches behind him in the House, and still only 28, while Ishbel was his housekeeper and hostess, as capable as her mother and just as bonny.

'Would you fetch me a whisky, dear?'

'The unions are up in arms about the Unemployment Bill.'

'Leave Father alone, Malcolm.'

Feet to the fire, he let his head fall back, his gaze settling naturally on a landscape by Turner over the chimneypiece.

'There's a letter from Sheila,' said Ishbel, setting the whisky on the table beside his chair. 'She's having a ball.'

Sheila was the baby of the family and in her first term at Oxford University. Middle daughter, Joan, was training to be a doctor in London. Three independent young women; his wife would have been proud of them all.

'I have the auction house catalogue you requested, Father.' Malcolm was moving behind his chair.

'Later.'

'And something from Lady Londonderry. At least, it has her husband's crest on the envelope.'

'Her crest too.' He picked up his whisky. 'Show me.'

Malcom was trying to suppress a smile, because he knew they were close. 'Here, Father.'

'I'll read it later. We have cigars, don't we? On the desk, in the Egyptian box.' The box his wife had used for things their children counted precious, like first teeth and fossils and party ribbons.

'Cigars but no matches,' said Ishbel.

'It's not just the unions, Father, members of the parliamentary party are unhappy with the wording of the Unemployment Bill too.'

'Yes, Malcolm, I *do* know that.'

'Malcolm, would you *please* tell me where you've hidden the matches.'

'What are you going to do, Father?'

He closed his eyes. 'Wheesht, Malcolm, not now.'

His secretary was at the drawing room door. He knew it was Rosa because she made a point of tapping lightly, then more firmly to be sure. 'Would you, my boy?'

'Good evening, Rosa,' he heard his son say.

'I'm sorry to bother you, Prime Minister,' she replied.

'Coming, coming,' and, gripping the arms of his chair, he rose stiffly and turned to smile at her. Petite, swarthy, dark-brown hair in a bob and dark eyes, she was dressed as always in something fashionable, even exotic: Rosa was Jewish, unmistakably so, at least to his mind.

'I haven't come about the papers you wanted, Prime Minister.' She was ill at ease. He could tell because the East End of London had slipped into her voice. 'A lady wishes to speak with you. She's very insistent. Her card . . .' Rosa produced it from the folds of a sleeve, like a music hall magician. 'I told her to speak to your parliamentary office, but she says it's personal. She's refusing to leave, Prime Minister.'

The card was duck-egg blue and bore the name KRISTINA M. FORSTER in Gothic type. No address, no note or explanation: KRISTINA M. FORSTER clearly believed none was necessary. He frowned. Goodness. How embarrassing. His family knew nothing of his friendship with Kristina M. Forster. What was she thinking? Really, it was too bad. He was angry with her for presenting herself at the door of Number 10 at half past ten at night, and he was angry with himself for the poor judgement he had shown in befriending a woman who was prepared to.

'Are you all right, Father?'

Ishbel looked concerned, Malcolm too.

'Who is she?'

'Frau Forster,' he said, slipping her card in his pocket. 'A friend of the Mosleys. We met last year on the driving tour we made together. Bern, or perhaps it was Vienna, I forget.' That was a lie. He remembered perfectly well that it was Vienna, then Bern, and then Berlin. A few months later he had invited her to join him in Cornwall.

'Then why isn't she knocking at Mosley's door?' said Malcolm. 'Tell her to visit Sir Oswald, Rosa, or she might write to the prime minister in the usual way.'

Rosa looked doubtful. 'I think it would be best if you spoke to her, sir.' Rosa was very capable of recognising trouble even when it came dressed in fancy frills and bows.

'I'd better see what she wants,' he said, 'to satisfy Mosley, you understand. Where is she?'

3

Mosley was on Frenchie's mind, too. To the south of parliament and only a short walk from Number 10, Sir Oswald was approaching a taxicab that was idling outside his home. Frenchie was feet away and stepped forward to open the passenger door. 'My good man, thank you,' said the baronet, and smiled his politician's smile. He was dressed in white tie and tails for champagne and cocktails and dancing, no doubt: the bugger. Frenchie watched his taxicab turn about the church in the centre of Smith Square and disappear. Mosley, the minister for employment in the people's party government: what a joke –

and his patronising, 'my good man' . . . Why, Sir Oswald, if only you knew. Because Frenchie was on another job for Mr Knight and the casual agent he was to contact was employed in the red-brick building across the square that served as the headquarters of the Labour Party.

Knight had characterised it as 'a simple pick-up', which was simple bloody balls. There was nothing straightforward about an exchange of stolen documents on the doorstep of a government toff like Mosley. For one thing, coppers kept a close watch on the square. If they nabbed him in possession of Labour Party documents he was going to be in heaps of trouble, and no turning to Knight for assistance. The police weren't in on this one, that much was clear. Was it a job for Knight's fascist comrades or his Secret Service controller? Knight didn't say and Frenchie didn't care to ask. No bloody business of mine, he thought, as he crossed the square in the direction of the church. Damn it, nice neighbourhoods were always well lit. A fat patch of shadow beneath a tree at the east end of the church was the best he could find. Ten minutes more and he would leave, or the boys in blue would be round to feel his collar.

4

The prime minister liked to conduct awkward interviews at the cabinet table and the interview with Frau Forster was certain to be one of those. He needed to impress upon her the delicacy of his situation. If the newspaper jackals learnt that an Austrian lady had been admitted to Number 10 at that late hour they would have a field day. My God, the headlines!

Rosa Rosenberg was waiting for him at the bottom of the stairs. 'Frau Forster is in my office, Prime Minister.'

'Show her into the Cabinet Room will you, Rosa.'

The grate was cold and the sharp easterly wind he had

imagined purging the city was working its way through the high windows and under the doors. He had spoken to his staff about heating and lighting many times. The chandeliers were uncomfortable to work by. Excepting the table, the room was furnished like an eighteenth-century gentleman's library with bookshelves at both ends and on either side of the fireplace. A painting of Walpole, the first prime minister, hung in pride of place above the chimneypiece.

Rosa would show Frau Forster in through the imposing coupled columns that separated the anteroom from the body of the Cabinet Room, and the great mahogany table. Prime ministers had gone to war, made peace, settled the fate of countries and peoples at that table. He would stand behind his chair – or would he do better seated, pretending to work? He could hear Kristina Forster berating poor Rosa for keeping her waiting, her English precise and unmistakably German.

'Oh, Mr MacDonald,' she said, sailing into the room. 'James, they 'ave kept me vait-ing so long.'

She was wearing her hat, which was black with a broad brim and a purple feather, a calf length skirt, also black, a white blouse and old-fashioned button boots. She fluttered towards him, hands raised, fingers splayed – he had forgotten how many rings and beads she liked to wear – and glasses on a long chain at her waist. She was in her late forties or early fifties (he hadn't asked her and she was careful not to say) with a fine figure – no children, he presumed – five feet six or seven inches tall. She had an oval face, full lips, a large nose and deep wide-set green eyes. Wisps of fading blond hair had escaped from pins and slides beneath her hat.

'James,' she said again. 'James, it is so good to see you.'

In other circumstances he might have felt the same. She was attractive and a most agreeable companion – more than agreeable: a thrilling companion at times. But in the Cabinet Room her accent, her forthright manner, her passionate nature – things that had drawn him to her – alarmed him, even repelled him a little.

'You are well, Frau Forster?'

'James—'

'Please, Frau Forster,' he said, raising a hand to check her passage round the table. 'You shouldn't have come here.'

'But James,' she said, the pitch of her voice dropping a semi-tone, 'I am your Kristina. Your pussy.'

'Frau Forster, please!' His skin prickled with embarrassment. My God, how could he have been so foolish? 'Frau Forster, *please* remember where you are. You must see—'

'What am I to see? Your letters were so loving, James. They mean so much to me. You remember the wonderful, passionate things you wrote to me?'

'Arriving here unannounced . . . My position has changed, you must see that.'

She put her hands together and touched them to her lips. 'You did not answer my letters, James. You became prime minister, then you stopped writing.'

That was true. She had written many times, love letters, intimate letters, increasingly desperate letters. 'Help your *liebchen*'; 'my poet'; 'my strong Highlander'; 'my master': the recollection made him wince.

'My situation, madam, I cannae risk a scandal.'

'The things you wrote, they were not true?'

'I . . . I did feel that way. Now . . .' He had been lonely, he was always lonely, and an attractive woman not so different in age, a grand foreign lady, cultured, interesting, well, he was fascinated by her. He wanted to possess her, and while the Labour Party was still in opposition there seemed no reason why he shouldn't.

'But now you are not in love with me? You no longer desire me?' Plucking a handkerchief from a sleeve of her blouse, she touched it to her nose and then her eyes. '*Ich glaube es nicht.* The things you wrote to me.'

'I'm sorry. It was . . .' He wanted to say 'a mistake.' It was a stain he wished to wipe clean. 'Ma situation, Frau Forster. Ye ken . . .' If only she would leave without a fuss. 'I have a duty to my country and ah won't neglect it!'

'Why don't you say what you mean, Mr MacDonald?'

'Then I'll thank you not to come here again.'

'You were ready to accommodate me when I was rich.'

'This has nothing tae do with money,' he said, even as it dawned on him that it had *everything* to do with money. Hadn't she hinted in a letter that she was in 'difficult' circumstances? Dear, dear, it wouldn't have happened, *never*, but for the death of Margaret. His behaviour in the last year . . . he was besmirching his wife's memory, and, my God, it made him sick to think on it.

'Things have not gone well for me since our time in Cornwall,' she said. 'The stock market crash . . . I lost everything. Everything. I must have some money.'

'How much?'

'A loan.'

'How much?'

'I thought you would offer to help. You said you loved me! I would not ask, but there is no one else I can turn to.'

He laughed but not in a pleasant way.

'Please, James.'

'Well?'

'Seven hundred and fifty thousand.'

'Seven hundred and fifty thousand! What? Washers?'

'Francs.'

'That's . . .'

'Six thousand pounds.'

'Ah don't have it . . .' stupid woman, he wanted to say. My God, he was so angry he was shaking.

'You have the whole Treasury of your country,' she said, caressing the table with her fingertips. 'You are the prime minister.'

'It isn't my money!'

The handkerchief had disappeared, the lines at the corners of her mouth were tighter. 'You have hurt me, Mr MacDonald. You forget . . . I have sacrificed for you.'

'Madam, ah cannae gie ye the buckie.' He took a deep breath. 'The money, madam. The money. I don't have it. Now, I must ask you—'

'But I am desperate, James. I do not know what I will do. I am so . . . in German, *arm* . . . poor. I am poor. I must have money.'

Damn her! She was so brazen. 'You're threatening me.' He wouldn't stand for it. 'You have no more business here. Leave, madam. Leave now!'

She had taken two steps and there were only two chairs between them. She was close enough to grab and drag to the door, only he had never laid hands on a woman like that before. Never. Perhaps the porters, perhaps the police.

'I do not want this,' she said, 'I do not want to hurt you, but newspapers . . . they will pay me.'

Oh, they would pay any amount to destroy him. How hard they had tried already, printing the story of his bastard birth, calling him a coward and an agitator during the war, and if Frau Forster sold her story they would paint him as something worse – a liar and a hypocrite. The prime minister who wrote a book about his love for his wife, then dishonoured her memory with a Viennese vamp: oh, what a story that would be. His story. Because when the fury was over and final words were written, it would be all anyone would remember of James Ramsay MacDonald: the prime minister chased from office after an affair with an Austrian gold-digger.

'You're going to ruin me.'

And the children? Everything he had built reduced to ashes because his poor romantic soul had trusted a woman who was capable of demanding money with menaces. He turned away from her. Perhaps he groaned. She was speaking but he was too confused to listen.

'Mr MacDonald, are you un-vell?' was the next thing he heard her say.

'How long has he been like this?' Ishbel was in the room. 'What is it, Father?' She touched his hand – 'Father?' – and her face was so like her mother's.

'A misunderstanding, my dear. Frau Forster is leaving now.'

Frau Forster had stepped away from him to stand at the civil service end of the table. She was tense with simmering anger, her lips a sour pout, her right hand balled in a fist. She was going no further until her business with the prime minister was satisfactorily concluded.

'Your father and I are old friends,' she said. 'Did he speak to you of me? I have helped him in the past and now I am in need of his help.'

'Get out!' He couldn't contain his anger. 'Out! Get out, madam!'

'Father!' Ishbel placed her right hand on his chest. 'Please don't shout.'

Frau Forster had turned pale but she stood her ground. 'Dis is not necessary or fair, or even like a gentleman.'

'Go now,' Ishbel whispered to him, 'please, go, Father. Rosa and I will see Frau Forster out.'

Rosa had slipped in through the anteroom door and was standing between the pillars like Samson's sister, her arms folded across her chest.

'Ah'm oot o'elbows wi the world, Ishbel,' he muttered and the hand he raised to cover hers was shaking. That a prime minister should behave with so little dignity was unforgivable. Turning his back on Frau Forster, he walked to the end of the table and the corner door to his parliamentary secretary's office. 'Madam,' he said, gripping the door handle; 'come here again and I will ask the police to arrest you. Do not doubt it.'

Then he left Frau Forster, her black hat and black skirt, rings and purple feather, he left her in the Cabinet Room, her fingers snaking across the top of the table, a fine trail of perspiration on its mirror surface.

5

Where was the bugger? They would be pushed to make the exchange before closing time. Was it possible Mr Knight's Labour sneak had got cold feet? Perhaps someone had caught him dipping into a file. Frenchie resolved to wait only five minutes more then he would be on his way. He was bloody lucky not to have been nabbed already. With his shoulder to the burl of the plane tree, he was able to gaze across the square into Labour's well lit lobby. A couple of blokes were exchanging a handshake and the shorter of the two carrying a briefcase. Mid-forties, sad grey fringe round a tonsure, his eyes like the donkey in the book Frenchie was reading his daughter: yes, that was code name Bill. Burly Bill was on the move at last. Lumbering through the door of Transport House, south-west around the square, his shoulders rocking as if one of his legs was shorter than the other. At the bottom of Dean Bradley Street, left on to Horseferry, his broad frame lit by passing cars, their red and amber tail lights trailing down to the River Thames.

Frenchie made the Bear with just seconds to spare. The hum of the last orders bell, the smoke and murmur of voices, lent the pub the air of a grubby temple. There were a dozen or so local working men in the bar. Pinned to one of its smoke blackened beams, a notice gave warning of the old Bear's final days. The brewery had sold her to a developer who was intent on building a very large office for men in bowler hats.

Knight's Labour sneak was sitting with his back to a tobacco-stained wall. Frenchie put down his beer and pulled out a chair.

'Seat's taken mate,' said the sneak. He spoke with a thick Black Country accent.

'By me. I'm Max's friend.'

'Yow?'

'Yes, me.'

'Me name's—'

'Don't tell me your name.'

'All right. It's 'ere.' He reached under the table for his brief-case. 'Sooner I get rid—'

'No! Drink your drink.'

The landlord had wedged the pub door open and was clearing empty glasses from the tables. 'Time gentlemen,' he growled, 'home to wives and sweethearts.'

'You've done what Max told you to?'

'Yes, and it's worth more.'

'How much more?'

'Ten pounds.'

'Take it up with Max next time you see him. I'm going to the lavatory. Leave the stuff in your newspaper. When I return, wait a minute then get up, shake my hand and go. Got it?'

The contact's jowls quivered as he nodded assent. 'Got it.'

There were half a dozen men in the shit palace and the floor was awash with piss. Someone farted loudly and laughed, someone else answered with one of his own. 'A tribute to Thorne's Brewery,' he said and there was more beery laughter.

Back in the bar, Burly had finished his pint and was fidgeting impatiently with a packet of cigarettes. A copy of the *Daily Herald* was lying on the table next to his empty glass.

'I'll be off then,' he said, rising and easing his stomach round the table. His expression was ludicrously furtive. The silly bugger was plainly trying to pull a fast one. But the landlord was at Frenchie's shoulder and all he could do was stare.

'What about you mate?' said the publican, clearing the empties from the table. 'Your carriage awaits.' He pointed to the folded newspaper. 'Want to keep this rag?'

'This fine organ of record?' said Frenchie. 'The only one that cares about the working man? Yes, I want to keep it.'

There was nothing inside its pages.

Burly Bill was rolling as fast as his little legs would carry him. He chose back streets, dark streets, where taxicabs were hard to come by. Frenchie chased him into a mansion block doorway and caught him by the lapels of his trench coat. The bleeder squirmed and squealed.

'Friend, you don't want to make an enemy of Max. He knows some very ugly people. Where is it?'

'Not until I'm paid,' whined Burly.

'You have been.'

'Twenty. I'm taking a big risk.'

'You are, yes.' Frenchie grabbed a scrap more of his coat and pulled until he could feel the toerag's breath on his face. 'I'm not askin' you again. Goin' to make me shake it out of you?'

'All right.' Burly's face fell. 'In the bag.'

Frenchie let go of his coat and took a step back. 'Very wise.'

'But tell Max twenty quid next time,' he muttered, his head bent over his briefcase.

There were a couple of dozen close-typed sheets in a cardboard file. Names, personal details, a lot of stuff about suspected communists in the Labour Party, and a position paper on its relations with the Soviet Union. 'That's everything?'

Burly Bill snorted. 'I need 'em back, you 'ear? And twenty

next time.' He turned and walked away: the contemptible shit. Yes, contemptible, a contemptible mercenary shit like me, thought Frenchie, stuffing the file into his coat.

6

'Mac-Don-ald!' she shouted as they put her out the door. They shut it so firmly in her face the boards beneath his feet seemed to shudder. He watched her stumble into Downing Street; he saw her reach between her feet for her lorgnette glasses – the chain had snapped – he saw her rise and walk into the light of the lantern that hung over the doorstep. He saw her tidy her hair, adjust her hat, then he saw her smile. Yes, smile, damn her! Because she could sense him watching at a window. '*Yah, weibliche intuition,* James,' she had boasted to him once; 'I am a woman.'

'And I am prime minister,' he muttered, as he turned away. What a dreadful business. That woman, her face so white in the lantern light and so determined . . . One way or another she was going to make him pay. 'Oh, how foolish I've been.' Was it possible that the passion and poetry he thought they had shared had been nothing but a web of deceit? The worst of it was his naivety, his stupidity, his cupidity: he had as good as spun the web for her. He had been – in the words of his national bard – *A whim-inspired fool.* And the family ... Making his way down the stairs, he heard voices in the anteroom, and Malcolm's raised above the rest. 'What did she want?' His son sounded so English these days. 'Should I speak to Mosley? Will you ask Father, Ishbel?'

But that would never do! He was not prepared to discuss it with his children, and stepping lightly to his study he closed the door on their schemes. Rosa had left the last red box of the day open on his desk. On top of the pile was a note from the Treasury on its plans for an economic advisory council to tackle the crisis; bottom of the pile, a sheaf of letters from Labour malcontents appealing to him to withdraw the Unemployment Bill. After ten minutes he had to own that he had read the same few sentences a dozen times and could recall nothing. His gaze kept lifting from the page to his wife. He had placed her opposite his chair, between a telephone and a silver inkwell. Their children were pictured on a bench beside her, looking to the left of the camera. Margaret's head was turned a little too, but she was watching him at the corner of her eye, staring straight into the lens. He had chosen the photograph for the quick wit and intelligence in her face, only he thought he saw something else there now – sadness. It was as if in their small family drawing room in Lincoln's Inn Fields twenty-two years ago she had seen an episode in his future like this one and was reproaching him from the frame: 'Oh, Ramsay, how could you?'

He stepped away from her and over to the chimneypiece. In her last days she had declared to him, 'If you find consolation in the silences of the night or of the hills, say to yourself that it is I being with you.' It had chilled him to the marrow. She should have been in bed – he said so – but she was sitting by the fire in the family drawing room, the minutes of a Women's Labour League meeting on the floor at her feet. She had said another thing that evening he would never forget: no matter the obstacles, the hostility, the humiliations he was obliged to endure, Labour's cause was his destiny. 'You must never desert it,' she had said. Seared into his memory, the solemn timbre of her voice. 'Never desert it, Ramsay. Never!' Well, he never had. He had been sorely tested by her death and by the war, but her faith in him and her conviction that it was their work for people and the party that gave their lives meaning had seen him through the dark times. His fate was bound to Labour's: she had believed that, and he believed it still.

He placed the page he had been clutching too tightly on his desk and smoothed out the creases. *Confidential! For the prime minister!* To his surprise the letter wasn't a badly written complaint from the backbenches, it was from the foreign editor of a left-leaning newspaper in Berlin. He had met Victor Schiff at a conference in Paris. The journalist had sidled up to him and whispered, 'Comrade, I know who forged the Zinoviev letter.' Always at socialist gatherings there was talk of *the* letter, rumours, suppositions, theories. Why? Because the Conservatives had used it to steal the 1924 general election from him. A'body kenned it. The Conservative Party's friends in the press had made hay with it in the run-up to polling day. They called it the Zinoviev letter because it purported to be from the head of the Communist International in Moscow to its members in Britain. Comrades were instructed to work with 'sympathetic forces' in the Labour Party to further the interests of the Soviet Union, and to wage a campaign of sedition in readiness for a revolution. And how had this extraordinary letter emerged? The British Secret Service claimed one of its agents had intercepted it – that was a lie. What's more, no one in the Secret Service was able to explain how its contents had ended up on the front of page of the *Daily Mail* four days before a general election. **Civil War Plot by the Socialists' Masters**, the newspaper's headline had screamed at voters, **Moscow's Orders to Our Reds; Great Plot Disclosed**. Only, the letter had been a fake. A swindle. An attempt to dupe the electorate. The plot was aimed at his government and it found its mark: Labour had lost the 1924 general election. The secret state and the press had connived with their allies in the Conservative Party to wrestle power from him. His French socialist friends called it a *coup d'état*; Schiff and his German comrades, a *putsch*.

'Father?'

'Ishbel!' She startled him. 'My dear, I didn't hear . . . I was reading.' Her concerned expression was disconcertingly like her mother's. 'Herr Schiff has written to me, my dear. Have I spoken to you of Schiff?'

'What are you going to do, Father?'

'Herr Schiff has new evidence about the Zinoviev affair. The Berlin police have arrested a Russian refugee called Orloff.'

'I mean Frau Forster—'

'It seems this man, Orloff, and his associates have been involved in forging many documents for anti-socialist purposes. Listen—'

'Father!' She was inching her way into the room. 'What did Frau Forster mean?'

'Not now, Ishbel!' His tone made her start. 'I'm sorry, I didn't mean to be sharp, but please listen,' and he raised Schiff's letter. 'He writes, "Orloff and his friends have confirmed that they have supplied the British Embassy in Berlin with forged anti-socialist documents on several occasions." You see? This fellow Orloff can prove the Zinoviev letter was a forgery and the Secret Service and the Foreign Office *knew* it was a forgery.'

She looked puzzled. 'And Frau Forster is involved in this in some way? I don't . . .'

'Schiff doesn't want me to make it public, not until he's finished his investigation.'

Ishbel was playing with her necklace – the black pearls he had given her mother – she looked very low. 'My dear girl, I don't want you to worry. I am going to speak to Sir Oswald Mosley.'

'Malcolm's going to ring him.'

'No! This is my affair . . . my *concern*. She is unwell. Frau Forster is unwell. *I* will ask Mosley to speak to her.'

His daughter must have heard the edge in his voice and knew it would be unwise to press him further. 'Is there anything you would like, Father? I can bring you some tea?' She stepped closer to his desk and picked up the photograph of her mother.

'Do you remember? We wouldn't keep still. Mother looks so . . . I don't know. Just . . . I wish she were with us.' She gave a sad little laugh. 'That's so silly! Of course I do. She would be so proud of you, Daddy.'

'I hope so,' he said, mechanically. Mention of his wife would have stung him again, only he was distracted by something else his daughter had said. It was the connection she'd made inadvertently with Zinoviev. 'Frau Forster is involved in some way?' she'd said. Could it be . . . was there a connection? Was Frau Forster working with his political enemies 'in some way'? Well, maybe, maybe.

'My dear, I must work,' he said. 'Will you kiss your father?' She came quickly to him and kissed his rough cheek, and held his hands, and as she walked to the door he called after her: 'Don't worry about your old papa. A misunderstanding, that's all it is.' Foolish of him to say so. She knew her father and could sense his hurt, and she would have been distressed to learn that in unwittingly proposing another motive for Frau Forster's shocking behaviour she had made it more acute.

Turning again to Schiff's letter, he ran his eyes down the neat lines until he found a passage that sent a frisson of anger and anxiety coursing through him:

We consider it our international socialist duty to call your attention to this matter having regard to the possibility of a new bombshell of the same kind as in the autumn of 1924.

A new bombshell! A bomb had exploded in Downing Street that very evening. Frau Forster had burst into Number 10, sowing confusion, demanding money, undermining his integrity, and humiliating him in front of his family and staff. Appalling! Their secret affair was just the sort of thing his enemies would use to cast doubt on his suitability for the highest office in the land – perhaps that was her intention. They had brought down his first government with a forged letter and if they were able to lay their hands on his private correspondence with that Austrian creature it would spell the end for his second government too, and his part in Labour's great cause. Stanley Baldwin and the newspapers, big money capitalists and the landed interest, the snakes in the Secret Service – Conservatives all – they wouldn't scruple to make a low woman their vehicle. But he would fight, fight back for the sake of the people.

He had promised them jobs and that those who could afford to pay more tax would pay; he had promised to nationalise land, coal, power, transport and life insurance; he had promised to cut spending on arms and increase it on welfare, he had promised a 'socialist commonwealth', because cooperation was the law of life. This he had promised to do without haste, but without rest; and the people had put their faith in him – in Ramsay MacDonald. There were hotheads in Labour who accused him of being too cautious; *they* didn't understand the power of the forces ranged against him. He had been fighting for socialism all his life and if it took a little longer to bring about peaceful change then so be it. 'Never desert the cause, Ramsay, never,' his Margaret had said. 'Well, my dear Missus,' he replied, addressing her photograph, 'I know my enemies. I promise you, I won't let them cheat us out of government a second time. No my dear, no. There is work to be done.' Sitting to his desk, he picked up a pen and a sheet of Downing Street paper and began to write.

7

'The gentleman wouldn't give his name.' Jimmy Cooper was unimpressed.

'One of my chaps, Jimmy.'

35

'I thought that must be the case, Mr Knight.'

Ex-army, Jimmy Cooper, ex-sergeant major, and you could tell by the swagger in his step as he marched across the entrance hall to the porter's room that he was proud of it too. A useful fellow to have on the door of a club for senior officers. A fascist and potty about animals, which made them kindred spirits of sorts. Jimmy was discreet about his politics, of course, but a willing postman, and from time to time he passed on snippets he picked up in the club. Most of it was gossip, but Knight made a note of it all the same; some important people were members of the United Services Club. Morton was a member, and it was over dinner at the U.S.C. that they had agreed upon his terms of employment with the Secret Service.

Jimmy Cooper was advancing across the hall with the fruit of their arrangement on a silver plate.

'Well, Jimmy, thank you. An invitation to the Palace?'

The porter smiled. 'Not in manila, Mr Knight.'

'No, perhaps not.' The envelope lay creased and curled on the tray like an autumn leaf.

'It's been in the wars all right.'

Ripped from the hands of his informer perhaps. Some of the casual agents he paid for intelligence couldn't be trusted to play by the rules. Burly Bill was a mercenary fellow. No scruples. Scum, really. But Frenchie knew how to deal with his sort.

'Now, Jimmy, do you know where I'll find Major Morton?'

'Smoking room, sir. If you'd like to follow me.'

Cooper escorted him from the entrance hall to the grand staircase, its white marble steps rising in tiers like an expensive wedding cake; and then on into the coffee room corridor. Knight paused: 'Jimmy, my dear fellow, do you mind waiting?'

Inside the cloakroom, an elderly gentleman was drying his hands on a linen towel. Knight stepped into one of the cubicles: simply, he had a right to know. The major had recruited him and paid his 'expenses' when a connection with a senior member of the fascist party would have landed him in hot water with the government. Of course, Knight was grateful. But he was more than a bagman, a housebreaker, an enforcer now, he was on the Secret Service payroll with the blessing of its chief – he was agent 'M'. Crouching in front of the lavatory, he spread the contents of the envelope on the seat. His informer had lifted fifteen pages from Labour files, including a report on the restoration of diplomatic relations with the Soviet Union. The prime minister's name was the first on the circulation list. A note on Communist Party infiltration of the trade unions was of interest too. Knight skim-read both, slipped them back into the envelope, then pulled the lavatory chain.

The smoking room was magnificent but tired, like an old battleship, its burgundy leather furniture scraped and worn, its burnished gold curtains dusty and frayed, its Persian rugs colourless and a little threadbare. Admirals and generals resplendent in blue and red, gazed down from the walls upon the grey heads of warrior pensioners nodding off in their chairs. Cigar smoke hung in the room like a whiff of cannon fire. Morton had chosen a seat at an open window with a view of the grand houses on Carlton Terrace.

'There you are,' he said, rising to offer his hand. 'Whisky? Cooper, would you speak to the steward? Sit, sit.' He directed Knight to a low-slung couch opposite.

'How are you, Major?'

'Very well, thank you.'

He looked fitter than a man in his late thirties had a right to be, a man with a bullet close to his heart, only an inch from death.

'I'm a little late.'

'Knight, my good fellow,' he said, tight smile, wave of the hand. 'How are you?' Morton could be charming and garrulous, but more often than not he was tense and drawn and struggled to appear affable. He was always immaculately dressed in a dark suit that he wore with the surety and bearing of a former staff officer, and he was most at ease in the company of his army tribe. But sentiment had played no part in the choice of the club for their meetings. It was the somnolent atmosphere of the smoking room that suited his purpose.

'Do you have something for me?' he said.

Knight placed the envelope on the low table in front of him.

'You've examined the contents?'

'No.'

Morton scrutinised him critically for a moment. 'Who else knows about this?'

'Our informer, of course, and my man, Frenchie.'

'Frenchie? The fellow responsible for the arrest of the agitators in Wales?'

'Yes. First-class agent. Military intelligence during the war.'

'Ah, here we are . . .' The steward was approaching with their whiskies on a tray. 'There, if you please, Thomas,' said Morton, lifting the envelope from the table.

'Can I get you anything else, sir?'

Morton's gaze slipped beyond him to a party of four that was drifting across the smoking room in search of a leather mooring. They found one at the fireplace.

'Sorry, Thomas.' Morton lifted the drinks chit from the tray and was making his mark when a burst of laughter like gunfire filled the room. For a second his pen froze. One of the new arrivals had spilled his drink and was dabbing his trousers with a handkerchief, his tipsy companions urging him to resume his seat. 'That's Fletcher,' said Morton, a chill in his voice: 'Lieutenant Commander Fletcher RN. No, don't look!'

Knight bridled. 'I had no intention . . .'

'My dear fellow, I'm sorry,' Morton raised his right hand apologetically, 'but I don't want to catch his eye. He's one of us now.'

'You mean he's . . .'

'With the Service, yes,' he said in a low voice. 'He used to be naval intelligence but he went into politics, and into parliament as a Liberal. Lost his seat in the 'twenty-four election. Then he did something very strange . . .'

'Oh?'

'He decided he was a socialist and joined the Labour Party.'

'Labour!'

'I'm sure he's a perfectly decent fellow, and he's with us now, but still . . . He's Labour.'

'I see.'

'The Chief thought it wise to recruit one of their people. Build bridges with the new government. There's bad blood . . . Well, you can imagine. Labour sees us as the enemy.'

Knight picked up his whisky and held it to his nose – 'hum' – then he lowered it back to his knee. 'We are the enemy, aren't we? I don't suppose you'll be sharing that intelligence with Commander Fletcher,' he said, gesturing to the envelope.

Morton smiled weakly. 'No.'

Fletcher and his companions were laughing heartily and members' chins were lifting from their chests. One old fellow got unsteadily to his feet to stare disapprovingly.

'The florid chap with the cigarette at the corner of his mouth,' said Morton.

Knight shifted on the couch to cast a glance in Fletcher's direction. Florid, yes. Forty-something, solid, weather-beaten: an old salt in a suit.

'This will have to be our last meeting at the club,' said Morton. He was poised to rise. 'We need to be more careful. Let's meet at St James's Underground station. Send a message in the usual way. Now . . .' He sighed. 'I'll speak to Fletcher and you can slip away.'

Knight waited for him to cross the room before getting to his feet and making for the door. He was leaving in a bad humour. Morton did not appreciate the time and trouble that had gone into acquiring the first-rate intelligence he was carrying under his arm. He took it for granted he could depend on good old Max. That sort of cavalier ingratitude was enough to make him wistful for a cosier billet in the City of London. The thirty-five pounds a month he was paid by the Service was a poor return for the risks he was running for his country. Still, he believed his mission, his crusade, was for the soul of the nation, as worthy as the battles fought by the soldiers in red coats that hung on the walls of every room in the club. Spying for his country was his calling.

In the entrance hall he stopped to consider a bust of the Duke of Wellington. 'The business of war is to find out what's at the other side of the hill, sir. That's what the Iron Duke said.' The ever-dependable Cooper had joined him and was carrying his coat. 'Let me help you, Mr Knight.'

'You're right, Jimmy,' he said, shrugging his coat on to his shoulders, 'the Duke was right.' He turned to the porter with a smile. 'I think he would approve, don't you?'

'I'm certain of it, sir.'

They had joined the British fascists to safeguard the country from revolution, Red despotism, a reign of terror – there was still work to be done.

THE PRIME MINISTER's note was delivered by hand to the home of Sir Oswald Mosley on the morning of Thursday, 28 November. Lady Mosley was at her breakfast table, Sir Oswald still busy with his toilette. Their home was an elegant early-eighteenth-century red-brick town house with a simple white architrave over the door. Five storeys from basement to attic, the children and Nanny on the third floor, the servants on the fourth. Too small for a family, in the honourable member for Smethwick's opinion, though it was twice the size of its neighbours in the terrace and much coveted by party comrades in the Commons. From his drawing room Sir Oswald was able to gaze across Smith Square to Labour headquarters, and when the division bell rang in parliament it jangled in the hall of Number 8 too. Time enough for Lady Mosley – the new member for Stoke-on-Trent – to hand the children back to Nanny and join him in the Commons for the vote.

Cynthia Mosley had been in the Chamber until late the evening before and had heard her leader and friend, 'Ramsay', speak in the dole payments debate. Her husband had been there for a time, but he had left without a word to her. She had been woken by his footsteps as he stumbled round his bedroom in the early hours. Drunk not only on wine but on sex and self-love too, he would have slept soundly, while his wife lay awake wondering which of his mistresses he had been entertaining. A member of their set, no doubt, because 'Tom' – as he was known to his family and friends – liked to make love to famous beauties and the wives of important men. Vote Labour, sleep Tory, he liked to say, perhaps to hurt her – he would often go out of his way to. Repentant and loving or resentful and bloody? Cynthia Mosley could never be sure which of her husbands was going to appear at the breakfast table. She could hear him talking to a servant and was encouraged by the humour in his voice to hope it was the former. Fine china cup and saucer in hand, she waited for his entrance. I could die for Tom, she thought, or I might kill him one of these days.

'My own blessed Moo Moo, forgive me?' The dining room door opened; loving Tom was joining her for breakfast, his chin raised, eyelids lowered, haughty little-boy smile. Footling, her sister called it, like a second-rate matinee idol, but handsome, all the same. Byronic in a way: thick wave in his black hair; gigolo moustache. He was looking very dapper in the brown wool suit he called his 'Labour suit', which was Savile Row trying not to be.

'Last night . . . Aneurin Bevan!' he said, stepping over to the sideboard. 'I couldn't escape, Cim, darling, I couldn't, really. He wanted to discuss my programme for public works.' He lifted the cover of a silver serving dish. 'What on earth does Cook do to the eggs? Have you spoken to her?'

'Cook doesn't prepare breakfast, Tom, I've told you a dozen times.' Cynthia put her cup down and reached for the envelope she had propped against a toast rack.

'Well, why don't you speak to whoever does prepare it, darling!'

'Really, Tom, can't you do something for yourself? Look, there's a letter here from the prime minister.' She lifted it between two fingers. 'He's written "Personal" on the envelope.'

'Ah. Good. I sent him my public works proposal,' he said, spooning scrambled egg on to a plate.

'*Personal*? At breakfast? I can't imagine Ramsay is that excited by your programme!'

Mosley frowned. 'Darling baby bleater, you're trying to provoke me.'

'No, Tom, merely stating what I know to be the case. I'm sure I know Ramsay better than you!'

Placing his plate clumsily on the sideboard, he turned to her with his right hand on his hip. 'Cim, there's the devil in you this morning. My programme may be the thing that saves this government, saves the country—'

'Please, Tom,' she snapped, 'it's too early for that.' My God, he was threatening to make one of his speeches, something musical, primitively emotive, and almost completely empty of substance. 'Would you like me to open Ramsay's letter for you?'

She could see she had stung him: wife-mother wasn't showing sufficient devotion. The day was going to start with another row – and why not? Trampling her feelings. Thankfully, before he could think of something biting to say to her there was a knock at the door. Sir Oswald was wanted on the telephone. 'A lady, sir,' said the maid. 'A Mrs Forster.'

'Mrs Forster?' he said, turning to his wife. 'Cim?'

'Tom!' Was he expecting her to remember the names of his women? Oh, she was sorely tempted to ask, only it wouldn't do in front of the staff. 'I don't know anyone of that name.'

'Does she sound foreign, Jane?'

'Yes, sir.'

'Ah. Thank you, Jane, I'll be through directly. Well, surely you remember?' he said, turning back to Cynthia. 'You who profess to know our prime minister so well. Frau Forster . . . Ramsay's little Austrian friend, the one he met on our tour. Vienna, wasn't it? She showed him the galleries and he invited her to Cornwall. He read poetry to her.'

'I remember.'

'Bit of an old tart, but agreeable in her own way. Can't imagine what business she has with me.'

'Well, you better ask her, Tom.'

'I suppose I must, for his sake.'

She barely had time to pour another cup of tea and unfold *The Times* before he was back in the room, his face tight with ill humour. 'Well,' he said, picking up a serving spoon, 'I think I know what that's about.' He waved the spoon at the prime minister's letter. 'You can't imagine what the old girl said to me.'

Cynthia sipped her tea.

'She wanted to come here. I said, "I'm delighted you're in London, Frau Forster, but I'm incredibly busy." Then she said she had important intelligence. To wit: *"I must tell you, Sir Oswald, I'm worried that the government will fall".*'

'What on earth does she mean?'

'Too sensitive to tell me on the telephone, she says. She's living in a flat around the corner from us, on Horseferry Road.' He leant across the table and touched the coffee pot – 'Oh dear, really' – then pressed the bell to the right of the chimneypiece. 'Read Ramsay's letter, if you like.'

'Shall I?' Taking a knife from the table, she slit the envelope. 'He wants to see you this afternoon. He writes, "*My Dear Mosley, I need to speak to you on a personal matter of great urgency. My dear fellow, I need your help.*" He wants you to meet him at four o'clock in his room at Westminster.'

Mosley pulled a chair from the table. 'It's plain enough,' he said, raising a forkful of egg to his mouth, 'the personal matter that concerns him is Frau Forster: the old tart wants paying.'

2

The jury was out for an hour. Charge one: guilty of inciting soldiers in Brecon to mutiny. Charge two: guilty of assaulting a police officer in the lawful execution of his duty. Owen and

Eyre were going to prison. The newspaper people were ready with their pieces. Foregone conclusion: everyone said so. The Old Bailey judge had as good as convicted them on day one of the trial. Free speech was not the issue, free speech was not on trial, he said. The accused admitted distributing seditious propaganda to soldiers at Brecon barracks and that was a crime. Nor was Mr Justice Roche prepared to listen to evidence of their good character and a plea for clemency. There were questions in the House but no answers, and when the court heard from the police that the mutiny campaign was funded by 'a foreign power', members of parliament who had expressed some sympathy for the defendants ran for cover.

Dick Stewart was with their communist comrades in the street when a runner burst through the doors of the Bailey and shouted: 'Eighteen months!' Owen and Eyre were going down for eighteen. The crowd greeted news of the sentence with a collective sigh, like pebbles drawn across a beach by the tide. There were cries of 'shame.' Someone near Stewart shouted, 'British justice!'

'What's the point of a Labour government?' said someone else.

'No bloody point,' the reply. And a comrade from Wales reminded them that Owen was the father of four.

Then Pollitt, the union leader, climbed on to a soapbox to address the crowd. Freedom meant nothing if it wasn't freedom for all, he said. Lords and ladies and members of parliament could say what they pleased but when working people spoke out in support of their comrades in the colonies they were imprisoned and beaten. 'We won't stand for it,' he said. 'Justice for our comrades!' The crowd cheered, and because Dick was supposed to be just one of the crowd he cheered too. Feelings were running high. Pollitt was serving a heady brew of passion and prejudice. Piss and wind. Justice? No chance. That boat had sailed. As for the colonies, well, in the streets around the docks where Dick lived families were too preoccupied with keeping food on the table to care much for the peasants of India. But that bugger Pollitt was a fanatic. Just out of prison after serving his own sentence for inciting soldiers to mutiny and straight down to the Bailey for more trouble. The mad sod. The coppers were there to oblige. Like flies to shit the boys in blue were gathering at the bottom of the street with their truncheons at the ready. Poor Mrs Pollitt, poor baby Pollitt, and the families of Owen and Eyre; it was the wives and bairns that Dick felt sorry for. Yes, he felt bad about the bairns.

What a rotten fucking country. Run by the few for the few in the name of the Crown. Know your place, that's what children learnt in church and school. Know your place children and all things will be bright and beautiful. His own children, Florence and Pierre, had come home singing it:

> The rich man in his castle,
> The poor man at his gate,
> God made them high and lowly,
> And ordered their estate.

Well, the war had taught him that the poor man's place was face down in a shell hole, and Labour . . . the communist comrades were right: what use was Labour? What fucking use were any of them? Pollitt: what fucking use was he? Getting by for the bairns was all that mattered to Dick these days, and with his hands deep in the pockets of his coat he shouldered his way through the crowd and down the street towards the coppers.

3

A perfect family, Connie used to say, before she left them for six feet of earth in Camberwell cemetery. Three years now, and the simple white marble cross Dick had purchased for her from an undertaker on the Lower Road had been joined by so many the same little Pierre was struggling to locate his mama's grave. The inscription read: CONSTANCE MARY STEWART, AGED 25, LOVING WIFE AND MOTHER. She had been both of those, but Dick was sorry that in a fog of grief he had chosen something so cemetery-trite. Better to have carved nothing. No words could do justice to the depth of his love for her – and to his despair.

They had met at a dance in the Rotherhithe Town Hall. Connie lived around the corner in Albion Street with her sister. Seven years younger than Dick but as bold as brass. 'Sergeant Stewart, the war hero, I'm Constance McKee. You can call me Connie.'

'No hero,' he'd said, 'and good riddance to the army.'

'Plain Dick then,' she had replied. 'Going to ask me to dance, plain Dick?'

There had been a great healing in their married life together. Connie would wake him with a cool hand on his brow and hold him until the heat of battle receded and he was able to close his eyes again. 'Lest we forget,' politicians and poppy sellers liked to say on Armistice Day. A well-to-do woman had tried to sell him a poppy at London Bridge station with just those words: 'Lest we forget'; and he had laughed at her. 'You *are* a rude man,' she had said, which was true. Poor Mrs La-di-da, she had meant well, only he resented the way the war they said would end all wars was being reduced to a single act of remembrance. The politicians had signed the peace treaties and moved on, 'but I'll be fighting the war until I die,' he had observed to Connie after one of his nightmares. 'Not here, not with me,' she had replied, laying his head upon her breast. But then she had left him job half done, still shattered, a shell, even as the world was rebuilding and ready to forget.

As always, she was in his thoughts as he turned out of Rotherhithe Station into the soot-stained terrace streets between the river and the docks where they had made a home. They were seamen's streets, dockers' streets, densely packed around the old parish church on the western side of the Rotherhithe peninsula. Connie had lived her life inside the trails of the River Thames, between the Lower Pool of London and Limehouse Reach. For more than two centuries engineers had been excavating acres of earth from the peninsula to create a vast network of docks, float ponds and cuts for merchant ships importing timber and food from Scandinavia and Canada. Connie's father had broken his back carrying timber; Dick's old man, a deckhand on a lumber ship, had ended his days as evil-smelling jetsam on the floor of a local boozer.

The Stewarts lived middle terrace in a house that was the envy of their neighbours because it boasted an extra bedroom. Dick's mother had moved into 15 Clarence Street the day they laid Connie to rest and had assumed responsibility for the care and education of his children. Florence was eight now, and Pierre six. On clear blue days they played marbles and hopscotch on the pavement and kicked a football against the gasworks wall, and Clarence Street and all the neighbouring streets rang with the laughter of children and sometimes their tears. But this was a chill day in November and the children were at school, and it was the grinding of the cranes in the Albion and the thump of timber unloaded dockside that echoed in the street.

Mother greeted him in the hall with a kiss on both cheeks. '*Est-ce que tu as pensé à acheter les choses dont j'ai parlé?*'

She had asked him to buy eggs and flour and tea but it had slipped his mind.

'I'll go out again,' he replied in French, because French was the language they spoke at home. Connie would not have approved, but Connie was dead. Marguerite Stewart was responsible for the house now and he was very fortunate to have her. Sometimes she talked of returning to Belgium to live with her bachelor brother, but only to conjure a wistful memory of how things had been before her bullying, drunken, idle husband had cast his shadow on her life. Mother and son were as close as it was possible for a mother and son to be. John Stewart had resented their bond but had been too ignorant to recognise that he was responsible for cementing it when he raised his hand to his wife.

A copper pot was simmering on the stove, the kitchen rich with the aroma of a chicken casserole, vegetables and herbs. Marguerite Stewart's cooking was the talk of Clarence Street. 'Frenchified,' said the women, who knew nothing of Belgium, though their menfolk had spent blood and four years fighting for its freedom. Marguerite's cooking was as much of a mystery to their neighbours as the money Dick made to pay for it.

'The trial's over?' she said, when he was seated at the table.

'Yes. They're going to prison.'

'That's sad,' she said without feeling. That the accused were communists, she had read in the newspaper. Poor misguided men! Communism was a wicked creed condemned by her church. 'Here,' she said, pushing a cup and saucer across the table.

'Honoured, I'm sure.' They were the only pieces of her china wedding service to have survived his father's rages.

'Do they have families?'

'Yes.'

'That *is* sad.' Then after a solemn pause, she said, 'Have you thought about a piano? I think Florence should have lessons. I wanted you to learn, but your father . . .'

Poor John Stewart: to have seduced an educated and cultured woman who expected him to be better than he could be. He drank for the courage to look his clever wife and his clever son in the eye. Gazing across the table at Marguerite, slim and elegant in a simple black dress, her thin face careworn by marital strife, Dick felt a surge of love and sadness and shame. She had endured so much for his sake, only for her hopes to be dashed in the first week of the war when he joined the army. She had wept and pleaded with him to stay but the deed was done. 'Let me buy you a drink, son,' his father had said, to celebrate the agony of his wife. Dick had left her alone with a brute. But she had written to him almost every day and accepted what was left of him when the whole lousy business was over.

'Will you be here when the children come home?' she said, covering his hand now with her own small dry hand. 'You could talk to Florence about the piano then.'

Yes, Dick would be at home.

'She's refusing to let me read to her. She says *The Little Princess* is Papa's story.'

He smiled.

'That's better,' she said.

'*Maman* . . .' He gave her hand a squeeze, then bent to kiss it. Words of love and thanks were not necessary, but he should speak them nevertheless. Only, where to begin? She was his guiding star. The members of his platoon used to tease him, call him 'Mummy's boy' and 'Frenchie' because she wrote to him in French. French was the language they had used to shut out his father. Wounded twice and decorated for bravery, 'Mummy's boy' had been forgotten; not 'Frenchie' – that nickname had stuck.

'So, just the things on your list?' he said, pushing his chair from the table.

'Just those, Richard, yes.'

'I'll be out for about an hour.'

Marguerite frowned: The Albion Street shops were only a short walk away. 'But you will be home for—'

'*Maman*, I promise, but there's something I must do first.'

He had an errand to run to the tip of the Rotherhithe thumb. The Ark was a hard-drinking seamen's boozer; the landlord, one of Mr Knight's fascist cronies. In a drawer behind his bar there was an envelope 'For Frenchie.' Dick called it his Judas money.

4

Members of parliament were gathering in the lobby of the Commons for the Widows and Old Age Pensions Bill. The low sun was casting cathedral shadows across the heraldic floor tiles and speckling their sober suits with the colours of the glass in the high Gothic windows. From time to time the voice of Lord Privy Seal Jimmy Thomas could be heard addressing the Chamber on the importance of brick-making. Slumped beside him on the government front bench, junior minister Sir Oswald Mosley, his chin bobbing on his chest like a fishing float.

''Ere, wake up, Mosley.' The Lord Privy Seal nudged him with his elbow.

A rough diamond, Jimmy Thomas, a good fellow, a card, an ex-railwayman, ex-trade union leader, and an utterly hopeless minister. Mosley had more confidence in the judgement of his gardener. But Jimmy was one of the prime minister's political muckers, with deep roots in the party. 'Salt of the earth,' Mac had said to Mosley when he offered him the job of Jimmy's Number 2. 'Yes, Prime Minister,' Mosley had replied; but 'what rot, Ramsay' was what he had thought. The PM had trusted him with responsibility for creating employment, which was a grand job, only not grand enough to merit a seat at the cabinet table. It hardly seemed fair when there was room there for men of the calibre of Jimmy Thomas. If 'salt of the earth' was a qualification for high office then why go to the trouble of an education? Why not turn the empire over to its taxi drivers and market traders?

'Jimmy, you'll have to excuse me,' said Mosley, 'but the prime minister has asked to see me.'

Thomas looked at him suspiciously. 'Anythin' I should know about?'

'No, Jimmy, I don't think so,' he said, and rising from his place on the front bench he made his way into the lobby. Among the members gathered there, his young firebrand friend, Aneurin Bevan, was in conversation with his parliamentary private secretary, Strachey. At the door of the clerks' office, Cynthia was laughing a little too heartily with dear Bob Boothby – a piece of scandalous gossip, no doubt – and in a corner by the Commons post office frightful frump Margaret Bondfield was preparing her ministerial team for the pensions debate. He passed her without a word: my, what a mess she was making of her brief.

Beyond the door keepers, beyond the clerks' office and the members' tearoom, the prime minister's office. As he approached it, the convivial hum of voices was drowned by the percussion of many typewriters played *prestissimo* and with a ferocity that induced his heart to beat with the anxious energy of a satrap summoned by a sultan, and not by good old Ramsay. Inside his office, Mosley tried to raise a smile, but the secretary typists played on, seemingly insensible to the charm of a gentleman the cheap press liked to call 'a heartbreaker'. At last, one of them raised her gaze from the keys of her machine long enough to inform him the prime minister was still in conference with his parliamentary private secretary. That was a pity. Mosley thought next to nothing of the PM's PPS. Weir was a lazy toad, a Scotsman, the sentimental choice of a sentimental prime minister.

The trouble with Ramsay was the deep element of hysteria in his nature. Goodness, the fuss he was making about this Austrian tart. He was a widower and quite free to take her as a mistress, and yet he was plainly in a state of moral panic about the press and the tut-tut puritans in the Labour Party. Statesmen were made of sterner stuff, they were men of destiny, masters of action: on this point Mosley was quite clear. The stock market crash in America had sent shares tumbling everywhere. Output was falling, investment in business and industry dwindling, the number of jobless rising: the country was sliding into a deep depression that would cause great hardship and despair, and dear old Ramsay's heart was in the right place, but he was old and vague, and the crisis called for fresh thinking, for youth and vigour.

'Mosley' – Weir was at the door to the prime minister's private office – 'He will see you now.'

'I imagine he will, Weir.'

Ramsay Mac was standing arms crossed at a mullioned window, gazing into the courtyard below. On the gold flock wallpaper behind him was a portrait of that wily old Tory bird, Disraeli, in a black tailcoat and tie. Now there was a statesman! Ramsey was dressed in a brown suit.

'Prime Minister,' said Weir, 'Mosley's here.' Mac didn't move a muscle. Perhaps he was thinking of his Viennese cocotte. 'Prime Minister!' This time he turned with a start – 'Tom, Tom, hello' – and stepped forward to offer his hand; 'How are you?'

'Busy with my employment scheme, Prime Minister. I was hoping we might have time to talk about it.'

'Aye, well, let's see how we get on Tom. Thank you, Lauchlan . . .' he said, turning to his PPS; 'if you don't mind . . .'

Weir *did* mind: what an expression; what a churl! Why did Ramsay put up with it?

'As you wish, Prime Minister.'

They watched him turn and walk to the door.

'Please, sit, Tom.' The PM gestured to a chair at his conference table. 'How is dear Cynthia?'

Mosley said his wife was well and enjoying her new role as the honourable member for Stoke, and that she had charged him with responsibility for persuading the prime minister to visit them in the country again soon.

'How kind. She is the perfect hostess.'

Weir closed the door with a petulant clunk, and straightway, the prime minister's countenance changed. 'Ah, Tom, this is an awkward business.'

Resting his left hand on the chair at the head of the conference table, his right hand in his jacket pocket, he gazed at Mosley through his round tortoiseshell glasses, his dark eyes narrow.

'You said in your letter that you wished to see me about a personal matter, Prime Minister.'

'Yes. I would appreciate your advice. It is rather a delicate matter, and you know about these things.'

'This delicate matter . . . it concerns Frau Forster?'

MacDonald stiffened. 'You've heard something?'

'Only from the lady herself.'

'I see. You've spoken to her then.'

'She telephoned me this morning, Prime Minister. She said she had information that I should act upon at once and that if I didn't the government would fall.'

MacDonald snorted. 'The damn cheek of the woman. She's after my money, Mosley! She wants my money. She came to see me at Number Ten and made a terrible scene.'

'You let her in?'

'A mistake.'

'Yes. My advice, Prime Minister—'

'What shall I do?'

'You can't pay her. Out of the question. Call her bluff!'

'She's threatening to go to the press!'

'Please, Prime Minister, calm yourself. You're a widower, free to make love to whomever you wish. Tell her to do her worst!'

'I didnae ken the sort of woman she was, Mosley. I fear she has a will to ruin me and bring down the government. What's best? If only it were a matter of her word against mine.'

'Isn't it?'

'She has letters.'

'I see.' Mosley took his cigarette case from his pocket and offered it to the prime minister.

'No, thank you.' He waved the case away. 'They are . . . intimate letters. Our enemies would make great mischief.' Head bent and hunched over a chair, it occurred to Mosley that the leader of His Majesty's government resembled his ploughboy father making penance for fornication in one of those puritan churches where the Scots practise their bleak religion. Mosley wanted to shake him.

'I blush to think how foolish I've been, Tom,' he said. 'Will you speak to her, reason with her?'

'Certainly,' said Mosley, tilting his head back to send a stream of smoke to the ceiling. 'I've arranged to meet her this evening – at her request, you understand – and I can tell you, Frau Kristina Forster will learn she is playing with fire.'

'It's been an awful shock.'

'Of course.'

'Do you think someone has put her up to it?'

'Whom do you have in mind?'

'The same people. The Zinoviev people. Our enemies on the Conservative benches opposite and their friends in the intelligence services.'

'I think it is much more likely to be a simple case of blackmail. To be blunt, Prime Minister, the tart has shown her true colours. I wouldn't be in the least surprised to discover she has done something like this before.'

'*Aye*, well, you may be right,' he said, dejectedly. 'Thank you, Tom, it's good of you.'

'The least I can do.' Leaning forward a little, Mosley squeezed his cigarette into an ashtray. 'And now, will you permit me to tell you about my employment scheme? It's very much in line with your personal pledge to the electors to make jobs the first responsibility of the government.'

'Have you spoken to Jimmy about your proposals?'

'With respect, Prime Minister . . . An awfully nice fellow, but he isn't up to the job. Completely out of his depth. An excellent shop steward, no doubt, but quite incapable of rising to the challenge of mass unemployment that the country faces. No, what is needed now is a bold and imaginative programme of public works, nationalisation of key industries, and a new organisation with the personal authority of the prime minister – your authority – to make things happen quickly.'

'Well, Tom, that sounds very interesting. Let me have a note,' he said, gazing pointedly at the papers on the conference table in front of him. 'And you'll see Frau Forster tonight? Will you let me know as soon as you've spoken to her?'

5

No one could remember why it was called the I.P. Club. Some of its several hundred members claimed I.P. was short for 'Important Persons', others that it stood for 'Intelligence Persons', while a third group – foot-in-the-door juniors – whispered that it was really the I.B. Club for 'Insufferable Bores'. They were proud to belong to it, nonetheless, and crossed mountains and deserts to attend its dinners, which in just ten years had become something of an institution. The biannual feast was held in gilded splendour, in the grand dining saloon of the Hyde Park Hotel. There were finer tables in London and more elegant surroundings, but in the judgement of the club's president, Colonel Kell, there was nowhere more suitable. The Hyde Park was trustworthy and circumspect – he endeavoured to make it so. And because the colonel was the director general of the Security Service and the members of his club were intelligence officers and spies, it was so.

Major Desmond Morton was a founding member. He had arrived late on this occasion and was hovering on the periphery of the assembly with only a glass of champagne for company. He could see his old commanding officer, Macdonogh, the wartime director of military intelligence, at the centre of an admiring circle; and in another group by the grand dining room doors, arch-schemer and irascible old eagle Admiral Hall, the former head of naval intelligence. Members of the old guard were dressed in white tie and tails as always, but some of the younger chaps had turned up in dinner jackets for the first time, which was a pity. One of their number, rising star Stewart Menzies was in conversation with old Freddie Browning; and the Secret Service's most illustrious spy, Paul Dukes, was recounting the story of his daring mission to Russia to the Conservative Party leader, Stanley Baldwin. The I.P. had invited the former prime minister to become an honorary member in recognition of the support he had always offered the Service. Former cabinet colleagues Mr Churchill and Mr Chamberlain were members too; and on the opposite side of the saloon, the I.P.'s president was in conversation with Major Ball, the head of the Conservative research department. Ball was ex-Security Service, a member of the club in his own right. By George, he had impressed them all with his handling of the Zinoviev letter affair. He was just the sort of battle-hardened veteran the country needed in the fight.

'Ah, Morton! There you are!' Admiral Sinclair was at his elbow. 'What a gathering! Baldwin's here, you know. An opportunity for us to bend his ear, what! And my dear fellow' – pinching Morton's sleeve – 'I *would* like a word in yours. Follow me, would you.'

The admiral plotted a steady course through the assembly with the quarterdeck confidence of one who has commanded a battleship in a storm. Junior officers were quick to step aside so their chief could pass. In his six years at the helm of the country's Secret Service he had earned a reputation as a forbidding character. Tonight was different, tonight he was at his most avuncular, ready with a few words for everyone, especially the 'young ruffians' of his own service.

'Splendid, splendid, isn't it?' he shouted over his shoulder.

One more hand to shake and he was free and through the doors into the hotel's pink marble lobby. As the doors closed on the party, Sinclair's convivial expression turned to something darker, like a cat's paw sweeping a sunlit sea. 'Desmond, you *are* being careful, aren't you?'

'Sir?'

'Maxwell Knight.'

'I thought we'd agreed—'

'We did, but—'

'He's discreet, sir.'

'Are *you*?' snapped Sinclair.

Morton's face twitched. 'You're not satisfied?'

'No, no, Knight's intelligence is first rate, but we're skating on thin ice with Labour. If he's caught, if any of his men are caught . . . You know I've asked Reggie Fletcher to head up Europe?' He paused as a waiter passed them with a tray of glasses. 'And you know why,' he said when he considered it safe to.

Of course, Morton knew! All the Service's senior officers knew. Why, even Fletcher recognised he had been appointed as a sop to the socialists. Labour held the Service and its 'friends' responsible for forging and leaking the Zinoviev letter to the press. There was talk of an inquiry, witnesses, evidence.

'They want heads, Desmond,' said Sinclair, 'we can't give them an excuse to sink us! What would happen to the country?'

'Is he here?'

'Fletcher? Don't be ridiculous.'

The babble of voices on the other side of the door was growing fainter as the party made its way into the dining saloon.

'We must join the others.' Sinclair bent closer. 'You will thank M for me, won't you. Bloody good job. Can we expect more from the same source?'

Morton nodded.

'Good, good, only, no slips. Now . . .' Hand on Morton's shoulder, he turned to the door and the party, his face a picture of breezy bonhomie again.

6

Madam was broke. Well-to-do once, she said, rich enough to give money to the leader of the Labour Party, she said, but Mosley knew the type who took lodgings on Horseferry Road because his scullery maid rented a room there; and an honourable member with whom he was on good terms met his tart in one of the public houses. 'Oh, Tom,' he had said with pride, 'you should hear her, how she abuses me.' What foolishness. Mosley had no time for puritans, to be sure, but hypocrites he despised even more. Bored and burdened by pressure to set an example, some of his colleagues preached family values in the Chamber and gambled with their reputations out of it like moths at a flame. Shopkeepers were ready to forgive the upper classes carrying on with their own class but not with ordinary girls and tarts. That was cocking a snoop at the voters, and one couldn't rely on one's friends to keep it from the papers any more. But Ramshackle was not that sort of fellow. He was a romantic, he was dreamy, he was lonely. Easy prey for an old cocotte. Yes, Frau Forster was showing her true nature now – and the damn cheek of her to rent only a stone's throw from his own home in the square. Well, Mosley was going to deal with her. He would call on here on the way to his friend Bob Boothby's for dinner.

Clouds were scudding across the night sky, the wind chasing the last leaves from the plane tree at the east end of the church. Strange conceit, but its baroque towers put him in mind of a ship's masts and the painting of a ghostly windjammer that had hung in his grandfather's library when he was a boy. An audience was arriving at St John's for another rendition of the

Messiah. As he turned out of the square into Marsham Street, fat raindrops began to speckle his coat. There had been a shift change at the gasworks and a dozen or so workers were smoking their first fags since lunchtime at the gates.

Someone shouted, 'You're Mosley.'

'That's right,' he said. They wanted to shake his hand and pressed him to join them for a drink. 'Another time, comrades. Another time.'

116 Horseferry Road was around the corner from the Sacred Heart church and the coroner's court, in the middle of a sooty brick terrace. A Jewish tailor had the shopfront and the door to the left of it was for his tenants in the rooms above, one of whom was Ramsay's *Frau.* Mosley rang the bell twice and rapped on the door for good measure, and after a few seconds he heard her approaching on the stairs.

'Ah, Sir Oswald,' she said, stepping across the threshold to present him with her cheek.

'Madam,' he replied, taking half a step back.

She looked crestfallen; she looked older too, as if the eight months that had passed since their gay party in Cornwall were eight years. She was dressed in black like a widow and perhaps that was how she felt now that Ramsay had cast her aside.

'You wanted to speak to me, madam,' he said, 'but not here, not on the street.'

She gazed at him defiantly for a moment, then, lifting her long skirt a little, she turned and led him up the stairs to her lodgings.

'You see, Sir Oswald,' she said, flinging her arms open like a diva at the Vienna State Opera. 'Dis is what I have become.' Indeed, it was a shabby room, dimly lit by a dusty chandelier in which two of four bulbs had died. There was a faded lime-green couch, matching chairs, two sun-bleached coffee tables, and on the wall to his left an ugly mustard-tiled chimneypiece with a small fire in the grate. The curtains were drawn across both windows and there was a rip in the one to the right of the boudoir. The window glass was thin and the noise of the traffic on Horseferry Road suddenly seemed to fill the room. 'So,' she said, turning to face him, her hands clasped at her waist. 'I'll come straight to the point, Sir Oswald.'

'That would be best.'

'Ah. You . . .' She was struggling for a word. '*Selbstgerecht*,' she said at last. 'So righteous. But you are not a fool, I think. You are a man of the world, no? You must understand, I have known James MacDonald a long time. We used to meet in Switzerland. He was poor in those days, and I helped him. Did he tell you that?'

'What do you want?'

'I want him to help *me*. I am poor now and he is the prime minister. He has the Treasury of the country at his disposal—'

'My dear lady, really!'

'You laugh. Why?'

'A prime minister can't just dip into the public purse to settle his affairs or those of his friends.'

She frowned and raised a hand to her temple. Was she so naive? He had taken her for an intelligent woman.

'Will you sit,' she said.

'I don't think that's necessary.'

'Do you think it is unreasonable of me to ask for help, Sir Oswald? He was in love with me. He wrote me letters.'

'That's as may be, but it's over. I understand he was quite clear on that score. Look, you can't roll up at Number Ten and demand to be paid for old times' sake. It isn't on, you know. Now, take my advice, catch the next train home.'

'No!' She turned away from him with her right hand raised, as if she were beseeching heaven for a judgement. He had to smile. What a part; what a performance!

61

'That is not just, Sir Oswald,' she said. 'Not just. This man, who wrote many words of love to me . . . His porter threw me on to the street!'

Like a commander choosing her battleground she had put the green couch between them, and it was plain to see she had no intention of giving up without a fight. 'I fall down on the step. My lorgnettes . . . Broken. My eyes . . . blind with tears. Is this the way to treat a lady you have made love to?'

Lady? Yes, at that moment he had to acknowledge she was a lady. A formidable lady. Delicate features, green eyes, the graceful sweep of her hand, and a finer figure in her fifties than his own dear Cimmie, who was twenty years younger. Roused to anger, Frau Forster was a lady, *une femme passionnée*, and it was easy to see why Ramshackle had been captivated by her.

'Shocking, I'm sure,' he said, 'and the prime minister wishes me to apologise on his behalf. You must understand, these are difficult times. The pressure of work . . . The poor man is exhausted.'

She gave a wry smile. 'And he asked you to offer me some assistance?'

'No, madam. He wants you to leave.'

'Ha! So, he wishes to throw me on the street again.'

'No.'

'I have letters. He cut off the address, but—'

'Madam—'

'. . . the newspapers will recognise his handwriting. And your prime minister, Sir Oswald, what an imagination! La!' Her eyes fluttered to the tobacco-stained ceiling. 'Even you would be shocked by some of the things he wrote. Some people – you English – you would consider them pornographic.'

'Are you trying to blackmail a prime minister, madam? No British newspaper will publish your letters, and if you try to sell them you will go to prison for fifteen years.'

'Then Paris,' she said, gripping the back of the couch. 'I will go to Paris. The whole thing will be ablaze in the French newspapers.'

'No, you won't, my dear lady. The British government won't permit it. A sordid attempt to blackmail a prime minister . . . Let me tell you, the British intelligence services will arrest you before you reach Dover. You will disappear. Poof,' and he clicked his fingers. 'Believe me. Take the advice of a friend: go home. Return to Vienna today or tomorrow, as quickly as you can.'

A lot of politics is bluffing – lying if you like – and that was something he knew he did well. It was with some satisfaction that he noticed the hand she lifted to her brow was trembling.

'I do not want to hurt him,' she said, plaintively.

'Then forget this nonsense.'

'The time we spent together, Sir Oswald . . . we were happy. I cannot understand why . . .' Fumbling in her sleeve, she produced a lacy handkerchief and pressed it to her eyes. 'I cannot understand why he will not help me. Sir Oswald, I am desperate. It is so . . . so, *peinlich. Demütigend.*' She shook her head in frustration. 'So humiliating!'

'My dear lady, please.' Her tears were drip staining the back of the dusty green couch. The proud and sophisticated cocotte he remembered in Vienna and Berlin and Cornwall, the seductress, the siren, the prime minister's femme fatale was weeping, her face blotchy and unattractive. She was a very different woman now, old and weak and demanding sympathy he was unwilling to give her. In fact, he was disappointed and irritated by her distress. 'Really, Frau Forster, control yourself!' It was very unbecoming.

'I want to leave,' she gasped, 'but Sir Oswald, I don't have money for the fare.'

'How much?' He reached into his jacket for his wallet, took out a ten-pound note and placed it on the table. 'There, Madam. There.'

She nodded and dabbed her eyes.

'Don't go near the Quai d'Orsay,' he said. 'Don't go near the French newspapers. That would be a very dangerous thing to do.'

'Do you think it fair,' she said, 'do you, Sir Oswald? Do you think your prime minister has behaved like a gentleman?'

Mosley stared at her contemptuously, then walked to the door. 'The prime minister,' he said, half-turning, 'the prime minister, madam, has behaved *exactly* like a gentleman.'

7

By common consent the chef at the Hyde Park Hotel served the finest club dinner anyone could remember. Morton chose the *selle de pré-salé a la broche* and the *caneton de Rouen vendôme*, with cheese and two glasses of his favourite dessert wine from the Vaucluse. There were no speeches, only a few warm words of welcome for Mr Baldwin and the loyal toast to the king. At the tables, the talk was of share prices and the market crash, the state of the nation's finances and of the government's decision to restore relations with the Soviet Union. Morton listened to Menzies entertain his neighbours with a colourful account of riding to hounds; Browning was excited about a boxing match at the Albert Hall in front of the Prince of Wales; and 'Woolly' Woollcombe said he was taking his wife to see Mrs Patrick Campbell in a play at the Royalty. A few of the younger fellows were a bit boisterous but there were no ladies present, and they had been schooled to say nothing of a confidential nature in the presence of the staff.

It was only after coffee, the cigar smoke heavy in the room, that those with confidential matters to discuss felt they could speak more freely. Members drifted from the tables to form conversational groups in the shadows at its edge. Morton was one of the last to rise and the moment he did so a waiter appeared at his elbow with a note from Admiral Sinclair: *Would you join me, Desmond.*

'Where will I find Admiral Sinclair?' he enquired.

'Reception saloon, sir. At the fire,' came the reply.

From the first savage days, men and women have been drawn to the light and warmth of a fire at gatherings. Gazing across the crowded reception room, Morton could see this one was commanded by the heads of the intelligence services and that they were in private conversation with Mr Baldwin. Everyone else was maintaining a discreet distance. As Morton approached, the Conservative Party leader shook hands with his hosts and made to leave.

'Ah, Desmond,' said Sinclair, 'enjoying the evening?'

'The club has done us proud,' said Morton, turning to its president. 'Thank you, sir.'

Colonel Kell acknowledged the compliment with a slight inclination of his head. In their long acquaintance Morton had never seen him smile. If anything, the myopic frown that hovered constantly on his brow had deepened with the passing of the years.

'You remember Major Ball?' said Sinclair.

Yes, Morton remembered Ball very well.

'He's with Central Office now, striving to get Mr Baldwin back into Downing Street.'

Morton was aware of that too.

'The thing is, Mr Baldwin thinks Ball can still be of use to us, that we have interests in common.'

'Well of course we do!' said Kell. 'I say, Morton, would you like a brandy?' He caught a waiter by the sleeve. 'Sinclair? Three glasses of the Hardy, if you please.'

The waiter glided away with their order. 'Desmond,' said the Admiral, leaning a little closer, 'Ball has a proposal to make.

He knows your man, Knight, and thinks highly of him. He would like to pay for his services.'

'Agent M is on our books now, Sir, if you remember,' said Morton, 'and very glad to be.'

'Yes, yes, our man, our man,' he replied tetchily. 'An exchange of intelligence, that's all, and Ball is willing to foot the bill. It will serve our interests in parliament, and it is for the good of the country.'

Kell said, 'You know my views, Desmond. Socialism is the greatest threat this country faces to its way of life.'

Certainly, Morton knew; everyone in the room knew. A foreign creed, the Colonel told recruits to the Security Service, and those who espoused it were – wilfully or unwittingly – furthering the interests of a foreign power: the new Union of Soviet Socialist Republics.

'Socialism and communism – one and the same,' he said, emphatically.

'And so say all of us!'

'Then it's agreed,' said Sinclair.

'Ball has his own sources in the Labour Party,' said Kell. 'Mr Baldwin has just informed me that a lady with a foreign-sounding accent was admitted to, then rudely ejected from, Number Ten yesterday. There was quite a kerfuffle. Mr Baldwin's source – Ball's source, we must presume – says she spent twenty minutes alone with MacDonald before she was shown the door.'

'Intriguing, don't you think?' said Sinclair.

Morton was intrigued.

'Ah, here we are,' said Kell, gazing past them to the door. Like a burly genie, Major Ball had appeared in the room and was forging through the assembly and cigar smoke to the fire, the waiter with four brandies on a tray at his back. 'I am sure Ball will be able to enlighten us.'

He must have spoken to her! How like Mosley to keep a prime minister waiting, worrying, imagining the worst. What the devil was he thinking! Agreeing to meet her was a kindness, but to keep a friend on tenterhooks, seemingly insouciant of his feelings, well, that was intolerable – only he was obliged to tolerate it. Perhaps it had been a mistake to involve Mosley – but who else? Mosley knew the lady concerned and his reputation . . . well, he was experienced in affairs of the heart.

The switchboard had been instructed to put Mosley straight through to him in the Cabinet Room, where Miss Rosa had arranged for his work and the telephone to be placed on the table in front of his chair. His red box was gaping at him like a hungry beast, papers spilling from its jaws. For an hour or so he had tried to tackle them, but he had found it impossible to turn his mind from his own affairs to affairs of state. His failure to achieve anything and his impatience with Mosley made him feel low. He had begun campaigning for a socialist government before Mosley was born, and, oh, the sacrifices he had made on his forty-year journey from empty working men's halls to the despatch box of the Commons: Mosley had no idea. How could he? He was a good fellow – he deserved praise and thanks – but he was a political carpetbagger. Likely, no one was plotting *his* disgrace: what would be the point? 'No, it's me' – he muttered as he rose from the table – 'it's me.' Because *she* was threatening to help his enemies and thwart the will of the people – and his family, his children . . . a scandal would wound them deeply.

Ishbel brought him some tea. 'Are you feeling unwell, Father?'

'Perfectly well, my dear,' he said.

He had drawn back the curtains, opened a window, and was gazing distractedly into the garden. Beyond the pale circle of light from the room, it was possible to distinguish no more than the jagged silhouettes of last summer's roses and the high wall, like a prison. He was still at the window twenty minutes later when the telephone rang at last and dragged him from a dwam to his senses. In his haste to answer, he fumbled the phone and dislodged the receiver.

'Mosley?'

'Prime Minister? Can you hear me?'

'Yes Tom, I hear you.'

'Good. I thought I should let you know: she's leaving London at once – in the morning!' The triumph in his voice: that was very Mosley – but that was churlish. If he had persuaded her, if she was going . . .

'Prime Minister?' He sounded a little drunk.

'I hear you, Tom, there's no need to shout.' To judge from the murmur of voices he was speaking from a club or a restaurant.

'Where are you?'

'White's.'

'Your club! You *do* appreciate the need for absolute discretion, Tom, don't you?'

'Of course!' he replied. 'That's why you asked *me* to handle the matter, isn't it?'

'Yes, yes, thank you, I'm very grateful. So you think this will be the last I'll hear from her?'

'I do, Prime Minister. I left the lady concerned in no doubt what would happen if she threatened you again. Good riddance, what?'

'I can't imagine what came over her. Even after all these years in politics it is possible to be surprised and disappointed by people. No thought for our country and the people who are counting on this government to find a way out of the economic crisis. You have my thanks, Tom. Believe me, I won't forget this kindness.'

'Don't mention it, Prime Minister. I'm glad I've put your mind at rest.'

'You have, you have.'

'And you'll give my proposals for dealing with the crisis your consideration?'

'Yes, of course. Goodnight, Tom. Thank you for letting me know, and thank you again.'

He placed the telephone back on the cabinet table and the receiver in its cradle. Well, could he dare to hope? Mosley seemed certain he had settled matters with her, but Mosley was one of those expensively educated chaps who made a point of sounding certain about everything.

His gaze drifted to the photograph of his wife in their drawing room at Lincoln's Inn Fields. He had carried her into the Cabinet Room that morning. An act of penance perhaps, or in the vain hope he would feel calm in her presence. The Lord God said man should not live alone, but he had been alone for nearly twenty years. He had enjoyed deep friendships, yes, but no help-meet, no one to take her place, and it was impossible to imagine there would be while he was prime minister. But he still had the respect of his family and his good name and the power in government to change things for the better, and for that Mosley truly deserved his thanks. As for his grandiose employment scheme . . . The fellow was in too much of a hurry to become prime minister. Thankfully for Labour and the nation the position was filled.

Reaching for the silver cigar box, he took one, rolled it between his fingers and, with great care, clipped, lit and drew the rich hot tobacco smoke into his mouth. Mosley, Mosley: it was a mistake to feel beholden to anyone in politics, and never a man with as few scruples as Mosley. What an unfortunate state of affairs.

PART TWO

A weekend of clouds and blues. The world is unhappy.
The price of the war is being paid in turmoil and
unsettlement and my poor country is the greatest
sufferer.
What can I do? That question haunts me. I am worn out.
Every recondite problem comes to me.

Prime Minister Ramsay MacDonald,
Diary 10 May 1930

3

28 May 1930

T HE PRIME MINISTER was unable to expunge from his
memory the shock and pain in her white face as she gazed
up at his window from the pavement outside Number 10. The
image had wormed its way into his consciousness. Nor could
he forget the many passionate and foolish things he had written,
and that his letters were still in her possession. Waking, sleeping,
the recollection of their exchange made him shudder. At a
meeting of the cabinet, Jimmy Thomas – who knew him so well
– broke into a discussion on slum clearance to call for a doctor.

'You're looking very peaky, Chief. I think it best.'

'No, no, Jimmy, really, I'm quite well.'

But as the months passed he began to feel a little more at
ease, and, to his surprise, wistful and willing to recall some of
the happy times he had spent with her. By May he was entirely
preoccupied with the nation's troubles. Prices falling, exports
falling, output falling, and unemployment had doubled since
he had taken office and was rising still. The country was
suffering an economic slump.

To make matters worse, the Party was in revolt and the
agitator-in-chief was Sir Oswald Mosley. Impatient to get things
done, he had taken his new jobs scheme to the Labour Party
in the country, then to the press. A new executive council with
power to borrow and build; a huge programme of public works;
and Sir Oswald himself – although he was careful not to say

so – at the heart of a 'Mosley Plan' to mobilise the unemployed and direct their work, like that tinpot dictator Mussolini in Italy. The cabinet considered his plan speculative and experimental: where was the money to come from? How was the country to pay for it?

Was it too much to suppose Mosley had been emboldened by involvement in his prime minister's personal affairs? He was certainly acting in a very high-handed manner. Matters came to a head in Downing Street before a meeting of ministers to discuss the crisis.

'Prime Minister, I'm leaving the government,' he announced, coolly.

'You wish to resign? Well, Tom, I urge you not to – for your country's sake.'

'The cabinet has rejected my plan: I don't see how I can stay.'

'You know I value the work you're doing at the department. Will you reconsider, Tom?'

Mosley agreed to, but only for twenty-four hours; he tendered his resignation from the government the following day with a gracelessness and pomposity that spoke volumes about the man. To his credit he made no mention of the personal service he had done his prime minister. His departure left a bitter taste all the same.

Men like Mosley manage to acquire too much too easily in life. A man's mettle can be judged by his conduct in defeat, and some politicians fail the test spectacularly. Politics is a team game with rules; Mosley wanted to write his own. In a moment of exasperation, Lady Cynthia confided to her 'dear friend Ramsay' that her husband was a 'bit of a spoilt child' and that she blamed his doting mother for encouraging him to believe he was a man of destiny who should never feel bound by commonplace mores like loyalty and fidelity.

A few weeks before his resignation the House of Commons

had greeted his appearance at the despatch box with catcalls and laughter. A compromising photograph of the minister in a state of undress with an unidentifiable lady was doing the rounds of the opposition benches. Mosley appeared unconcerned. The prurience of members opposite was typical of the unhealthy puritan spirit of the House, he said, and with the panache of a pantomime villain he advised them not to press him for the name of the lady in question lest her husband be present in the House. Uproar! The speaker had made himself hoarse bellowing 'Order! Order!', while Sir Oswald sat on the front bench with a Cheshire-cat smile.

The newspapers were full of his 'triumph' the next morning. MacDonald had been disgusted but chose to say nothing. Mosley would have dismissed him as a puritan in any case, which seemed to be the worst thing a politician could be. They had been friends and now they were political enemies. It would have been wiser to have kept him close, used his talents, secured his silence. He was able and industrious and still a young man. The cabinet had rejected his scheme but was offering no prescription of its own for the country's ills. Britain was crying out for bold leadership, for a man like Mosley, said Mosley. He was by no means the only member of the Labour Party who thought so.

'And so my government staggers on,' the prime minister confided to his diary. Every night the shadow of the economic crisis appeared like Peter Pan to dance around the walls of his bedroom until dawn. 'What am I to do?' he asked. 'Am I equal to the task?' Reply came there none.

2

Their plan was to enter parliament one by one under the pretext of meeting an MP and, when enough of them were in the lobby, rush the police and force their way into the Commons Chamber.

Dick Stewart had the whole thing: time, target, names. Something to shake the country, they said. 'They' were the communists and their comrades in the unions, and 'they' needed to make a splash. They had marched an army of jobless workers to London only to be confronted by the very real prospect of marching them back with nothing. Their protest was fizzing like a wet firework. The prime minister was refusing to meet a delegation and the police had imposed a cordon sanitaire around Westminster and Whitehall.

The plan was to occupy parliament and a number of government ministries. Stewart's informer was present at the Communist Party's King Street headquarters when the motion was passed. 'We might start a revolution,' someone at the meeting said, 'but we should speak to Moscow first.'

Stewart met Maxwell Knight in a Soho passage to pass on the news. Drunken patrons of the pub next door were using it as a urinal and the bricks at the bottom of the walls were flaking and reeked of piss. A corner table in a well-lit saloon bar would have done perfectly well but Knight enjoyed a taste for cloak and dagger. There was something childlike in the pleasure he took in 'getting it right': right brand of cigarettes; workman's jacket worn at the elbows; tin-toe boots. Silly sod! Even in a piss-filled passage, Stewart could detect the scent of his expensive hair oil. Still, what did it matter in Soho; he was only playing.

Knight was a broad tall man, and his frame eclipsed the little light that was penetrating the passage from the street. 'Get lost,' he growled at a drunk struggling with his buttons and the menace in his voice drove the unfortunate fellow out in a state of undress. Their business together was over in two shakes of a lamb's tail: Agent Frenchie made his report on the plan to storm the Commons and was rewarded with another envelope of cash. 'We'll be waiting, don't you worry,' said Knight, 'and we'll give them something to think about, oh yes,'

'Is that so,' said Stewart. What did he care? What mattered was the money, and he could feel the weight of it in his breast pocket.

3

By common consent Mosley's resignation speech to a packed Chamber of the House of Commons was the finest anyone could remember. 'This nation has to be mobilised and rallied for a tremendous effort, and who can do that except the government of the day?' he said, throwing the gauntlet down to the prime minister. 'The Party's panicking,' he confided to his diary that night. 'Bad judgement in men was never more painfully brought home to me.' His private secretary was of the same opinion the following morning when the post room dumped a fat sack of angry letters in her office.

Miss Rosa Rosenberg was warming her stocking feet on a radiator. She had paid an eye-watering sum for green silk shoes because they complemented her coral pink dress. Fancy choosing a filthy day to wear them for the first time. What a schlub; what a waste of money. In the few minutes it had taken her to scurry from a bus stop in Whitehall to the door of Number 10 her shoes had turned from lime to forest green. They were steaming under the radiator, the post sack slumped on the Persian rug beside them like an old bulldog.

Sorting the PM's post was the first task of the day. Weapon of choice, the silver knife with the pretty yellow stone in the handle he had given to her as a gift. 'Don't upset Miss Rosenberg,' he liked to jest with visitors, 'lest she stick you wi' her dirk.' There were times when she was tempted to, and not just his enemies, but some of those who professed to be his comrades too – like that weasel, Mosley.

Lifting her feet from the radiator, she reached for the sack and slid its contents on to a table beside her desk. Letters that required an immediate response from the prime minister she would take him at eight o'clock, there would be a pile for staff and the ministries, and some of his correspondence would go no further than her spike. 'Dear Hamish' letters from Lady Londonderry were sky blue to catch the eye, like an exotic fish in a shoal of brown and white ones. Those she left for the PM to open personally.

'Ah, Mr Mac.' She was devoted to her Mr Mac. But she wasn't blind to his . . . idiosyncrasies. In particular, his appetite for grand company and the antique trappings of a 'gentleman'. But who was she to criticise? Satin and silk made her happy, they were her suit of armour. Posh folk were inclined to view you as a social climber and scorn you for spending money on things they took for granted, and posh socialists were the worst snobs of all. 'Our prime minister is the sort of fellow who has to buy all his own furniture,' she had heard one say. The great service Mr Mac was rendering the country meant nothing to M'Lord and Lady, who were always going to look down their noses at the son of a ploughboy.

She put M'Lady Londonderry's letter to one side. Turning back to the rest of the correspondence, a salmon-pink envelope caught her eye. A handsome fellow Mr Mac, women wrote to him from all over the empire. Fishing it out between her thumb and her forefinger, she was on the point of inserting her blade to fillet the flap when – *Oy gevelt!* – she noticed the French stamp and that it had been franked in Paris. Could it be? She gave a little shudder. The bitch had written *Personal for the prime minister* in dramatic loops and curls. For six months nothing and Rosa had dared to hope he was free of her. Oh, but not that woman.

'And I'm the one who must tell him.'

She slumped forward with her forehead resting on the

unopened business of government. In troubled waters the country needed a calm captain with a firm hand on the tiller, and now there was this . . .

4

At the same time, hunger marchers were gathering in their hundreds from their billets across the city, frustrated and angry that after many footsore miles the government was refusing to treat with them. They wanted work and a fair wage, they wanted to take hope back to their northern cities and towns. But the police were penning them into Hyde Park and forming a line at its perimeter. Inside the security cordon, in a palazzo overlooking the park, Lady Londonderry was discussing her plans for a ball to honour her friend the prime minister.

Outside in the park, the Communist Party had erected a platform draped in banners stitched with the face and maxims of Marx and Lenin. A stage party was waiting to make speeches the marchers had heard many times and were in no mood to hear again. Dick Stewart was among them, the assistant secretary of the transport workers' union at his side. They had caught a bus from Rotherhithe with the men from the commercial docks who were joining the protest to show solidarity with their unemployed comrades. Stewart was a familiar face and respected as 'a bit of a war hero'; people remembered his late unlamented father, they knew his 'la-di-da French' mother, and that his children went to school at St Mary's Church primary. He was thick with the King Street communists, it was said. No one knew for sure how he made a living. 'This and that,' he told anyone who troubled to ask. His neighbours in Rotherhithe took that to mean, 'something dodgy'.

A member of the platform party was calling the crowd to order. 'Comrades,' he said, addressing the meeting through a megaphone; 'Comrades, I can tell you, representatives of this hunger march are taking part in a demonstration in parliament and Whitehall as I speak. A party led by Comrade Hannington has forced its way into the lobby of the House of Commons and a second group is occupying the boardroom of the Ministry of Health.' He paused for some half-hearted applause. 'Our comrades have carried out a surprise action to highlight our demands. Prime Minister, can you hear me? The working men and women who elected you to parliament will be heard! You promised jobs and a living wage. We are calling upon you now to keep that promise.' Another ripple of applause. Stewart touched the assistant secretary's elbow. 'I'm off! See you later then?'

'Yes, comrade.'

The hurly-burly done, they would meet at the Fiddlers and pretend to be old soldiers yarning over a pint. All the greedy bastard really wanted was the price of a motorcar and he was willing to sell his union short to acquire it. Stewart despised him almost as much as he despised himself. Truly, it was impossible to fathom the depths of the human heart and what moved in that darkness. And his own paymaster, that other bugger, Knight, what was his game? He had the time of the raid on parliament and the names of the protestors, but he had done nothing to prevent it taking place. The devious cunts in the Secret Service who gave him his orders must have decided on a different course. They were such clever geezers. Lemon tart smart. All the same, it took Dick only a few yards of muddy park to grasp their intention: tomorrow's front pages! The newspaper subs were already sharpening their pencils: 'MacDonald unable to control wild men of the Left!' Or perhaps, 'Attack on Democracy!' Or the single word, 'Revolt!'

Labour's enemies in the press would raise the spectre of a revolution again. Because the secret state, the landed interest and big business, the press barons, would have their way. The people might march, strike, storm into the lobbies of parliament, but the entitled would have their way. Money would have its way. That was the lesson of the great 'country fit for heroes' lie, and it made him angry, angry, angry, and ashamed, because he took their Judas money. He had seen so much blood spilled in the name of freedom and democracy for other countries, spying on those fighting for decency and equality in his own felt like a betrayal of the men who had made the ultimate sacrifice. Ha! What difference did it make what he thought and did: none, nothing, no bloody difference at all. That was the bone-aching truth of the little man's life.

Rain was beading his jacket and the cuffs of an old khaki shirt, his chin down, touching the collar. Turning his back on the protest, he walked quickly from the park, his gaze too fixed on the gravel path in front of him to notice three men splinter from the crowd and follow. Nor did he think it strange when they boarded his bus and sat in circumspect silence together, waiting for their stop, that was going to be his stop.

5

They behaved deplorably, like a bunch of ruffians. No discipline, no leadership, chanting their slogans like a soccer crowd, and the Speaker's decision to suspend the business of the House presented them with a victory of sorts. To Mosley's mind it was a demonstration of the weakness and stupidity of his colleagues and proof the country was crying out for a leader of vigour and vision. His new friend from the Welsh valleys, Aneurin Bevan, seemed to agree. 'Tom, this will strengthen your case,' he observed. 'Think, man, fair pensions and public works today or rev-ol-ution tomorrow.' Bevan rolled it out like a line of Welsh song.

But Hannington and his communist gang fell short of the Commons Chamber. Conservatives whooped and cheered as the police wrestled and clubbed the protestors to the tiles; Labour cried, 'For shame.' The lobby was crowded with members of both parties. Cimmie was sitting on a stone bench with their friends Strachey, Oliver Baldwin and Brown. Beneath the chandelier, a few feet from them, cabinet ministers, Henderson, Chancellor Snowdon, and Mosley's old boss, feckless Jimmy Thomas, who dropped his aitches as deliberately as a beautiful woman puts on her make-up.

'What a bunch they are,' said Mosley. 'God save our country from our cabinet.'

'I stopped putting my trust in the Almighty a long time ago,' said Bevan. 'Look out! Here comes the enemy.'

Mosley followed his gaze. Enemy? Fiddlesticks! It was his friend, Boothby. The honourable member for Aberdeen was approaching with his right hand raised in greeting and with an artful smile. He was dressed in a sober Savile Row suit like his backbench colleagues, but there was something in his manner and appearance that was not quite respectable. Dark looks, handsome and charming, he was the sort of honourable member who in an earlier century would have joined and relished the antics of the Hellfire Club.

'Bob's a Conservative, yes, but a jolly fellow, you know?' said Mosley to Bevan. 'I'll introduce you.'

'All right, Tom, later perhaps,' said Bevan, touching Mosley's elbow as he turned away. Well, he was new to parliament, he would learn. Yes, Mosley had great hopes for Mr Aneurin Bevan. Just the sort of bright young working-class fellow he needed at his side.

'The colour of my bow tie?' Boothby touched it lightly.

'Your political complexion, Bob. You know what new boys are like.'

'I do, and your Mr Bevan is a very earnest fellow. Hates Tories, I hear. But I say . . .' Boothby leant closer. 'I'm glad he's gone because I want a private word. Perhaps we might . . .'

That look of Boothby's! Straight-mouth smile, the narrow gaze, and rings round his eyes like an old tart: bad Mr Hyde had a scheme he wished to impart to his friend. 'Only not here,' he said.

'All right, Bob.'

Mosley followed him from the lobby, past the postroom and the voting office, and down stone steps to a half-landing with a view over the Star Chamber Court.

'This will do,' he said, settling at a window seat. 'What do you know of Major Joseph Ball? He seems to know a lot about you.'

Mosley reached into his jacket pocket for his cigarette case and offered it to his companion. 'Go on.'

'Naturally, it's his job to,' said Boothby, refusing with a little shake of the head; 'you know he's the director of our new research department? He's close to Neville Chamberlain, which makes him a force in the Conservative Party to be reckoned with.' He leant closer. 'Here's something you won't know: Ball came to us from the Security Service.'

'And what does this have to do with me?'

'Well, Ball is a devious fellow. He wants me to speak to you on his behalf. Since you have become a thorn in your prime minister's side, he would like to propose a mutually beneficial arrangement.'

Mosley turned his head to direct a stream of cigarette smoke down the stairs. 'My dear fellow, unless your major has a contribution to make to my employment scheme—'

'No. An exchange of secrets is what he has in mind. Look, I don't know the man and from the little I have learnt I'm not sure I want to. He should have spoken to you directly. "Oh, that would never do," he said to me. The thing is, one of his spies

83

– oh yes, he has them – has told him that our family man prime minister is in trouble with a tart. Ball thinks you know all about it and wouldn't be sorry to see the details in the newspapers.'

'Does he? Does he?' Mosley took a step forward to open a window on the court. 'Well, Bob,' he said, grinding the remains of his cigarette on the stone lintel, 'I hope you disabused him. Or do you think so poorly of me?'

'Tom . . .' He held up his hands.

'The prime minister and I have our differences, certainly, but this . . . It has nothing to do with politics. I wouldn't dream . . . even supposing Ramsay had taken me into his confidence!'

Boothby flapped at him – 'My dear fellow, keep your voice down' – then sighed – 'How can you be so naive? Must I remind you, in politics it is sometimes necessary to be ruthless to get things done. It isn't enough to be clever or right, that doesn't win you friends. The Labour old guard doesn't want to be told what's good for it by the likes of you. My dear fellow, you're far too posh. You've stormed out of the government, you're rocking the boat, the prime minister looks bad – the old guard won't forgive you.'

Mosley twitched with irritation. 'I won't, Boothby, and frankly I'm surprised you've asked me. You know my views . . . I deplore puritanism and the hypocrisy of our press. Your major will have nothing from me.'

Boothby held up his hands in surrender. 'Tom, Tom, I am merely a messenger. I thought you should have an opportunity to consider Major Ball's offer. Look, I know you admire Mr Lloyd George. Well, L-G says, "To succeed in politics, you must keep your conscience under control." That's something you ought to consider. You won't become a leader if you aren't prepared to play a little dirty.'

'No. Ramsay should make way for someone more energetic, but not this way,' he said. 'I'll not allow the puritans – and this place is full of 'em – to turn a perfectly ordinary affair into a resigning matter. My God, if that were to happen where would any of us be?'

6

Midday on the Lower Road and – 'fuck it!' – Stewart missed his stop. The number 82 carried him to the infirmary, and, insult to injury, the heavens opened to promise a soaking.

From the bus he ran for the shelter of All Saints, only to curse them all roundly when he discovered their church locked and barred to him. Pulling his cap lower and his jacket tighter, he walked on briskly towards the docks. The yards were forbidden to those without a good reason to be there, but he was as familiar with the maze of ponds and warehouses as the porters who unloaded lumber and stacked it on the quays. As a boy he had gazed in wonder at their timber towers and at the barques and square-riggers from Sweden and Finland that were crewed in his imagination by Baltic pirates. 'Onkers', the porters called them, because their bilge pumps used to 'onk' like geese on the wing. On his way to school he would creep into the Greenland Dock to watch a liner manoeuvre alongside or the grain coming off a freighter; and when the rafts of timber in the settling ponds were packed together the porters would race across the water from one set of steps to another.

But the Surrey docks were not what they used to be. Fewer ships meant fewer porters and families in the neighbouring streets struggling to get by. As he crossed the swing bridge into Coates' yard, a dismal prospect of the ponds at the heart of the docks opened before him. From thriving port to nineteenth-century relic in only a few months, its grey waters disturbed by no more than the driving rain. A dozen or so men were sheltering inside the gates of Richie's vast brick warehouse. They watched him stride past without comment. At the northern edge of the ponds he walked between iron sheds to the ship channel from the Basin and the river lock. Cargo was coming off a freighter to his right, the tips of two cranes circling over the roof of a warehouse like storks in flight. The rain stopped and there was enough blue sky above the river to the north for a pair of sailor's trousers. Something of the little boy, something of the spirit of the place, made him pause for a moment at the edge of the ship channel; something of the taiga and the prairie; the smell of unseasoned timber sap, acrid pitch smoke and oil; the clanking of chains, the grinding of a steam-driven windlass, halliard ropes beating a crude rhythm on ships' masts; gulls mewing, porters shouting, and the slap-slapping of water on stone that was the dark music of the docks. That full-throttle assault on the senses that he had experienced as a boy was thinner, sadder now, like a big-band piece played by only the rhythm section.

The rain had seeped through his jacket and his shirt was clinging to his chest. He was a silly bugger lingering in the docks when his children were home from school for dinner. He would have to hurry now or he would miss them. But turning towards the Basin a shadow movement caught his eye, so slight it might have been the wing of a gull or a piece of tattered sackcloth. Instinct – a little shudder of apprehension – suggested it was something more. Eyes front he walked on as if nothing was amiss, his senses alive to every sound and movement. He had learnt not to surrender to fear. Trouble had come at him like a train in the trenches. Panic there and the wonders of no-man's-land were Tommy's for keeps. The dock-gate bridge across the Basin was a hundred yards ahead of him, wide enough for only one man. Command the bridge, play the troll and he would be able to force a pursuer into the open. It was a decent plan, only no sooner had he settled on it than he heard more than one pair of boots on the cobbles behind him. He lengthened his stride, and his pursuers did the same. He could run for the bridge, but they would run too. No, he would have to turn, tough it out, give them the eye.

'Hello, lads.'

Rough-looking buggers they were, too. He remembered the oldest from the bus queue. Short, wiry, he wasn't the brawn, he was the brains. Three working men in their late twenties or early thirties. Caps, collarless shirts, cheap suits. An acre of cloth on the big fella. He was a prizefighter or played rugby without rules. His face was a mess and he was missing the bottom of an ear.

'You want to talk to me?'

'Not really, boy,' said the brains. 'We're 'ere to give you a lesson.'

They were Welsh. 'What lesson is that, Taff?'

'A lesson in honesty; that's what we want to give you. Bit of decency. Remember me?'

'Nope.'

'Well, I's remember you. The Patriot in Dowlais? I bought you a drink. You was workin' for the union, weren't you? Leastways, pretendin' to. Hoped we'd see you again, we did.'

'Oh? It's a long way to come to collect the pint I owe you.'

'Ha bloody ha. You 'ear that boys?'

'Won't be laughin' soon,' said the big fella, clenching his right hand in a fist. There were thin white scars on his knuckles and on his brow, and something else, something to Stewart's advantage: the light had gone out in his left eye. The big fella, that big ugly fella was blind in one eye.

'We was hopin' to see you,' said the one with brains, 'didn't expect to, mind, not in London. Then there you was walkin' in the park. *Mae gan Iesu!* A chance to give you a bloody good hidin'.'

'Apart from the pint I owe you, this is about . . .?'

'Friends of Billy Owen, see. You remember Billy? He bought you a pint too.'

'Three,' said the big fella.

'And you want to punish me for that?'

'You can smile,' said Brains, 'but Megan Owen 'as four little 'uns without a Tad. And you, you is the reason. That's a sin, and in his wisdom God 'as made us his instruments.'

'You and Cyclops here?'

Brains frowned. 'Funny man, aren't you?'

'It was the war.'

The war. Was he hoping for some sympathy? Make them think twice. Anything. The dock porters, witnesses, where the hell were they? It had been so busy in the Basin before the crash. Those fucking brokers and bankers were to blame. Because of the bankers he was going to take a beating.

A look from Brains and the big man led the way. Fists raised as if he was in the ring. A heavy right hand swept past Stewart's ear, then a clumsy left laid the big man open for a counter-punch. Stewart lunged at his good eye: two fingers with force, catching the corner, driving him on to the back foot with both hands to his face. But his companions were swinging too. One of them struck Stewart's right cheek, the other a heavy blow to his gut. He tried to grapple with them, left hand gouging a throat, punching with his right, but their combined weight was pressing upon him and the big bastard was back in the fray. He felt a blow to the side of his head, then another, and he lost his footing. 'Bloody done for,' he thought, because he was falling and once he was down their boots would fly. The first kick was to his forearms, covering his face, the second to his back; the next few blows were too hard and fast to place.

7

Weir said, 'He won't see you, Mosley.'

How irksome that he had to treat with Weir for an audience. The PM's decision to appoint a lazy toad as his parliamentary gatekeeper was just one more proof of his failing powers.

'You can say what you have to say to me,' said Weir.

Mosley gazed contemptuously around the room at the secretaries scribbling at their desks, at the runner lounging in a chair, at Dalton, the junior at the Foreign Office, hovering by the door. 'Nonsense, Weir! This is a private matter.'

'Which you can share with me.'

'Of course I can't.'

'You've got a nerve, Mosley, after all the trouble you've caused the prime minister.'

'Are you going to tell him I'm here or not?'

No matter: the door to the inner sanctum he was guarding like a Scottish terrier opened before he could reply.

'Ah, Mosley.'

'Hello, Prime Minister. May I have a word with you?'

'What a surprise.' Not a pleasant one to judge from his narrow gaze.

'It concerns a private matter, Prime Minister.'

'I see,' he said. A certain softening in his demeanour suggested he understood the private matter concerned his own unfortunate affair. 'All right, Tom, come in.'

Mosley made a point of smiling at Weir on his way past.

'Well Tom, you're making my life awful difficult.' The prime minister had retreated to the end of his office and was standing beside his desk with his hands buried in his jacket pockets. There would be no back-slapping for Mosley the renegade, no handshake, not even a chair.

'You know my views on the unemployment situation, Prime

Minister. The country is facing an appalling crisis. My programme of investment in jobs—'

'Yes, yes. I understand your position perfectly.'

'. . . because if all you do is tinker, history will be very unkind to you and your government.'

'You were quite clear about that, yes: you don't have confidence in my leadership of the government or the Party. Do you really care about the unemployment situation, I wonder? No, please, don't answer that, I have other business to attend to. You wished to speak to me on a personal matter?'

'Yes, Prime Minister. A friend' – he hesitated – 'a Conservative member of the House has spoken to me. There's a rumour . . . How can I put this . . . he knows something of your relationship with Frau Forster.'

MacDonald closed his eyes for a moment. 'How, Mosley?'

'From Conservative Central Office.'

'But I only received her letter yesterday. How can Central Office have—?'

'You've heard from her again?' Mosley interjected. 'The shameless hussy!'

MacDonald studied him intently, a frown like Moses hovering on his brow.

'I came at once,' he said, awkwardly. 'I felt it was important you should know.'

'A friend of yours, you say? Why did he approach *you* with this rumour?'

'His source seemed to know I'd played some part.'

'How can that be?'

'I've no idea.'

'No idea? Aye, so you say.'

Mosley flushed. 'I resent the implication of your tone, Prime Minister.'

'Do you, Mosley?'

'Yes, I do. I came in good faith. I came because it was the right thing to do, I came because I'm a gentleman.' Oh dear. His tone was unfortunate: spoken intemperately and regretted soonest spoken. 'What I mean, Prime Minister—'

'I'm sure you've said all you mean to say. Now I'll ask you to leave. Please give my regards to Lady Cynthia.' He turned to his desk, picked up a document and pretended to give it his intention: Mosley dismissed.

Oh, to be treated in such a perfunctory manner . . . it was unforgivable. He had come with the best of intentions, he was willing to offer his assistance. Badly done! It was damned ungrateful, and, yes, not like a gentleman! Ramshackle had flirted with his wife, drunk his wine, smoked his cigars, he had introduced the old fool to his friends and taken him on holiday, and all that time and care had amounted to nothing. Well, he wasn't going to reason with him. He had shown his true colours: Labour old guard. He would fade and die with the rest. The time had come for younger men, the war generation, to step forward; the time had come for radical solutions – government and parliament were in decay – the time had come for a Party coup. 'And I'm the man to lead it.'

8

Weir had slipped back into the prime minister's office and was wearing a hole in his carpet.

'All right, Lauchlan, what is it?'

'I believe it's my duty to urge caution, Prime Minister.'

'You are referring to . . .?'

'A rapprochement with Sir Oswald Mosley, Prime Minister. The man can't be trusted!'

'Aye, right enough.' He didn't need to be told. Regrettably, Weir seemed to believe he did. On he ploughed with a rambling denunciation of Mosley the philanderer; supercilious Mosley; ill-mannered Mosley. 'He isn't one of us, Prime Minister.' Implicit in his remarks was a thinly veiled criticism of the man who had eased Mosley's passage into parliament, the man who made him a minister and his confidant. Weir at his best spoke honest Scots to power; at his worst, he was a pedlar of gossip and prejudice. His prime minister had heard more of the latter in recent months. Nevertheless, there was no denying he had been flattered and as thoroughly beguiled as one of the baronet's mistresses, and now the stability of his government, his reputation and the happiness of his family were in the hands of a ruthless narcissist and a Viennese vamp. Mosley was crushing his faith in friendship.

'God's sake, man! I ken well enough,' he snapped, 'now will you leave me alone.'

Weir stared at him coldly. 'As you wish, Prime Minister.'

'Aye, Lauchlan. I thank you for your thoughts. Rest assured, Oswald Mosley will not be returning to a government led by me.'

Free of Weir at last, he held his head in his hands and groaned. To let slip to Mosley that she was still plaguing him for money was a terrible mistake. And Conservative Central Office . . . what did the Tories know of his affair? The lobby was always a seething pit of rumour. Oh, how parliament would rejoice in a scandal – a prime minister's affair – newspapers would pay handsomely for proof and Kristina Forster had a bundle to sell. Mr Lloyd George was a liberal of low morality, and yet he had been spared exposure; Mr Ramsay MacDonald was a socialist, so he wouldn't be. To think he had treated her like a lady. The letters he wrote her – passionate words tumbled on to the page – the excitement he felt in sharing his most intimate desires; and she was so bold! What would the newspapers call her? The loving husband still mourning his long-dead wife . . . his enemies would use her to blacken his name and bring down the government. Protesting the injustice of it would count for nothing. No price would be too much to pay to prevent that from happening.

To the Westminster switchboard, he said, 'Operator? Put me through to Miss Rosenberg in Downing Street, please. What? Yes, the prime minister. Yes, I'll wait.'

He was prime minister, but who could he trust? His mother used to say, you need a long spoon to sup with the diel. The Chief of the Secret Intelligence Service, Sinclair, had conspired to bring down his first government and was probably plotting against him again, but one of his officers was a member of the Labour Party . . . Jimmy Thomas was a poor cabinet minister but a canny man and a decent judge of character, and he was impressed by the fellow. Sinclair had made a fanfare of appointing him to the Service after the election in a shameless attempt to curry favour.

'Putting you through now,' cooed the operator.

'Rosa?'

'Yes, Prime Minister.'

'Rosa, will you speak to the lord privy seal? I want to meet his contact in the Secret Intelligence Service, the one who used to be a Liberal member of parliament but is now with us.'

'Commander Fletcher?'

'You know him?'

'Mr Thomas mentioned him.'

'Ah. Well, I want to meet him tonight. Jimmy's to arrange it. Just Fletcher. No one else is to know. And not in Downing Street – the Foreign Office. And, Rosa . . .'

'Yes, Prime Minister?'

'Jimmy's not to mention my name.'

4

A MASS OF slate-grey cloud shot through with copper hung over St James's and a breeze was furling the lake, as Reginald T.H. Fletcher, Lieutenant Commander (retired), strode through the park to his meeting at the Foreign Office. Fletcher – Reggie to his friends and family – was a navy-patent no-nonsense sailor, shaped and moulded for service as a boy cadet, disciplined, wary, jealous of his personal space, awkward in female company, generally genial in male. He was in better shape at forty-five, leaner, fitter than most of his younger Secret Service colleagues. A little too quarter-deck in his manner to be popular with subordinates, but a respected and experienced officer nonetheless. Admiral Sinclair had brought him ashore to work in naval intelligence after the war, and when Labour won the election into the Secret Service. They were old mess mates and alike in many ways, only not in their politics – which is never a small thing. The government's decision to 'cosy up' to the Soviets was straining an uneasy truce. The wild men of the Secret Service talked in their cups of counter-revolution, of guns on the street, and the defeat of socialism, but not to Fletcher, never to Fletcher. And Fletcher was careful to say nothing that might betray his parliamentary ambitions and his association with a member of the Cabinet.

A direct approach from a minister was embarrassing. Jimmy Thomas had handled it badly. He had rung the Secret

Service operator at Broadway Buildings and enquired bellig-
erently, 'Do you know who I am?' He had set the switchboard
girls a-twittering.

'Reggie? I want you to meet me at the Foreign Office tonight,'
he said when the call was put through to Fletcher at last.

Tonight? Was it really that urgent? Mrs Fletcher was
expecting him at home for dinner. 'Yes, most urgent,' came the
reply; 'a matter of national importance.' Well, with a safe parliamentary seat at stake, how could he refuse.

But as he climbed the back steps into Downing Street his
grumbling stomach reminded him his evening was spoiled
and it would soon be too late to dine at his club; and, damn
it, matters of national importance were matters for Sinclair
and the Service. To his left, there were lights in the windows
of the chancellor of the exchequer's residence, but with the
exception of the entrance hall and the lamp over the step,
Number 10 was dark. Where was Ramsay Mac? Was he
working to solve the crisis? More vigour was needed, in
Fletcher's opinion. Pleading with bankers for help wasn't a
policy, nor was it enough to wring one's hands and bleat of
a world crisis beyond the influence of a single country. Oswald
Mosley had the right idea: borrow to pay for a programme
of public works to create jobs. Not that he would dream of
saying so before he secured a place in parliament.

A young woman stepped out from the carriage arch at the
entrance to the Foreign Office. 'Mr Fletcher?' She was small
and plain of face but exotically dressed in a dark-green hat and
velvet coat with a fox-fur collar.

'It's Commander Fletcher. And you are?'

'I'm to take you to your meetin',' she said, with the hint of
a cockney accent. 'Follow me, Commander.'

2

As Fletcher entered the Foreign Office, Mosley was searching for his clothes. The Education Bill would be put to a vote within the hour and Labour's whips were expecting him in the Chamber. His shirt was on the floor at his feet and as he bent to retrieve it warm air from the heater tousled his hair. The division bell he had installed at home would ring to remind Cimmie to vote, but he was in the single-room flat he had rented for adventures. The door had only just closed on his latest and a ghost of her perfume and their sex lingered in the room, and a knot of white linen cascading from the bed bore witness to a tempestuous hour.

Mosley told party colleagues that the apartment was a quiet place to work. In truth, he spent more time in the alcove bed at the back of the room than at his desk by the window at the front. As far as he was concerned, work and pleasure were inseparable, and his amorous adventures gave him vigour and confidence for his life in politics. 'My own beloved moonbeam,' he would say to his wife, 'I can't deny my nature,' and when she raged at him for abusing her trust – as she had done that evening – he accused her of being tediously bourgeois and petty.

Grasping the bed sheet, he shook it into place and then rearranged the pillows. The recollection of that termagant, Jane, her fingers with their bright pink nails wrapped round the brass bedhead, made him smile. What a battle they had fought – tooth and nail – because they had known it would be their last. Curiosity and his desire to conquer satisfied, he had been searching for an excuse to end the affair. But she had pleaded with him to meet her, and it had suited him well because there were things he had wished to whisper in her ear. When the biting and scratching were over she had rested her head on his chest and spoken to him of politics and her husband, dull old *Mr B*—. 'He's suspicious,' she said. 'Then we must finish it,' he had replied, although he knew their trysts were already the talk of the Commons tearoom.

'You're very charming, Tom, but only until you've had us,' she said; 'really, you're a devil. A handsome demon.' Dear Jane; he had smiled and kissed her forehead. She wasn't clever or even very pretty but she had the wit to recognise their match was over. His lovers never lasted longer than a few weeks.

He turned away from the bed – the maid would see to it – and stepped over to the desk to telephone for a taxi. 'Yes, Sir Oswald Mosley; 22 Ebury Street. Yes, to parliament.'

Cimmie would be preparing to set out for the Commons too. Smart but sober to avoid the sort of 'rich bitch' bile she sometimes endured from her comrades on the government side. He had left her at home in tears. 'What about Nicholas,' she had shouted, 'are you in such a hurry to see her you can't find time to say goodnight to your son?' Explaining that his tryst with Jane was policy not passion would have been futile. Jealousy was so unnecessary: wasn't it enough that she was his wife and he always returned to her?

Picking up his coat and his documents case, he made his way to the door. He would be in time for the closing speeches and some gladhanding in the lobby too. How to rouse the lumpen majority on Labour's backbenches to rebellion? What a task! Well, he had taken a step tonight.

3

Reggie Fletcher had climbed the grand marble staircase at the Foreign Office many times; he had paused to gaze at the burgundy and gold ceiling, like an Eastern potentate's palace, and the painted night sky in the dome; he had studied the first-floor murals depicting the triumph of the empire,

Andrew Williams

he'd drunk champagne with diplomats in grand reception rooms, and briefed the foreign secretary in his office over-looking the park. Tonight his guide was leading him into the heart of the building, along corridors ministers were encouraged not to visit, and the only sound was the monastic echo of their footsteps. The lateness of the hour, his nameless guide, their circuitous route . . . he was willing to bet a new ten-bob note that his meeting with Thomas had nothing to do with policy or the great affairs of state. What was it he could smell? Not even the cloud of perfume his diminutive guide was trailing along the passage could mask the whiff of a scandal. It wasn't hard to imagine Jimmy Thomas taking liberties with money and the law on his way to the top of the greasy pole – just think of the opportunities he would have for feathering his nest now he had reached it.

'Here we are, Commander.' His guide led him through a door into a dimly lit office. 'The lord privy seal will be with you in a minute.'

The curtains were drawn across two west-facing windows. There was a decent-sized mahogany desk, a silver inkstand, two burgundy leather easy chairs, an empty bookcase, an empty whisky decanter, another door – to a secretary's office, he presumed – undistinguished prints of Whitehall and a map of the world with the British Empire a lighter pink than was customary, either to intimate fading glory or to differentiate it from the new red socialist empire in the east. He was on the point of taking a chair when Thomas slipped into the room through the connecting door.

'Reggie, 'ow are you?' he said, his voice gliding from high to low in its soft Welsh way. 'Thank you for coming at short notice.'

'You said it was a matter of national importance, Minister.'

'Call me Jimmy,' he said, offering his hand, 'and so it is, so it is. Please sit.' He walked round the desk and leant forward, fat fingers splayed on its green leather top. He was ten years older than Fletcher, fifty-five or fifty-six, his features un-remarkable – grizzled moustache, a broad nose, jug ears, sleepy blue eyes, auburn hair in headlong retreat – and yet the impression was of an uncommonly good-humoured face. There was nothing to suppose childhood poverty and his years of struggle on the railway and in the union had cast a shadow on his life. It was said in the Service he was a rogue, but a generous one.

'You'll think this an odd way of going about things,' he said, 'but I've brought you 'ere to give you a message from the prime minister. I want you to promise me you won't breathe a word of what you 'ear in this room to a living soul. Not your colleagues, and not to your chief.'

'If it's a matter of national importance, Admiral Sinclair should know. He's my superior—'

'But you 'ave a 'igher duty to the prime minister, now don't you?'

'I appreciate that, Minister, but—'

'Jimmy,' he said.

'Jimmy, but I wonder whether—'

'I 'ave your word?'

'I'd like to know why I'm here and Admiral Sinclair isn't.'

'I would 'ave thought that was obvious: you're with us and he's against us. You 'ave'nt forgotten the Zinoviev letter? He was behind the forgery, wasn't he? Or he bloody well knows who was.'

That was probably true. Gut instinct and an acquaintance with those reputed to have been involved inclined Fletcher to the view that the letter was a fake and that a cabal of former and serving intelligence officers had conspired to engineer Labour's defeat in the '24 election. They were dyed-in-the-wool

Conservatives to a man. As one of his colleagues had put it recently, hoi polloi had to be saved from hoi polloi.

'Well?' said Thomas. 'Can he count on your support?'

'Yes, the prime minister can count on my support.'

'Good, good. Right. Whisky? Of course you will. Rosa, can you do the 'onours, my dear?' The door to the adjoining office was ajar and Fletcher could hear the woman called Rosa pouring the minister's whisky. 'Miss Rosenberg works at Number Ten for the prime minister,' Thomas explained. 'Wonderful girl.' A moment later she appeared with glasses and a bottle.

'Water, Commander?'

'Just a drop. Thank you.'

'Rosa's going to take a note for the prime minister,' said Thomas. 'Cheers!'

'Cheers.' He raised his glass. 'So, can you tell me why I'm here?'

'Blackmail, Reggie. Blackmail. A plot against the prime minister. An old friend is blackmailing 'im. A woman. She wants to sell 'is letters, private letters, and the prime minister wants you to get 'em back. For his sake and for the good of the country.'

'Why me?'

'A delicate negotiation, isn't it. Someone we trust to be discreet, keep things out of the public eye. And someone who can be . . . Let's say, persuasive, if necessary. Someone with your sort of experience. The woman's in Paris. Your patch, isn't it? You're responsible for the whole of Europe, I 'eard. An intermediary, that's how we sees you.'

'The letters . . . they contain state secrets?'

'Not exactly, no.'

'Then why pay anything?'

'They're very personal letters.' Thomas pretended to inspect his whisky. 'I'll be 'onest with you, Reggie. The prime minister's a passionate man. He 'as a passionate nature, and he felt deeply for this woman. Turns out she wasn't worthy of 'is affection. Speaking frankly, he wrote things he regrets. If the Tory party's friends in the press get 'old of the letters they'll use 'em against 'im. You know that! They haven't gone away, Reggie, they're still there – your lot in the Secret Service – they're waiting for another opportunity to thwart the will of the people. That isn't in the national interest now, is it?'

'They're not "*my* lot", Minister.'

'I know, I know, excuse me, Reggie. That's why you're 'ere; we know we can trust you.'

Fletcher nodded. 'This woman . . . you want me to pay her for the letters? How much?'

'Seven hundred and fifty thousand francs.'

'That's about—'

'Six thousand pounds. The prime minister's own money, you understand.'

Fletcher raised his eyebrows. 'He is desperate to get them back.'

'It's a terrible stretch for 'im. He's hoping you'll persuade her to settle for less.'

'And if she doesn't, what then? Force her to give them up?' he asked, flippantly. Thomas shifted awkwardly: he wasn't going to discourage the possibility. *Be persuasive*, he had said, only spare him the details. Well, any sensible politician would feel the same. That was the unspoken contract government had with its Secret Service.

'I'll need help, and a brief. How much you're prepared to pay, that sort of thing.'

Thomas glanced at Miss Rosenberg, who was sitting very upright, her hands cradled in her lap.

'Would you excuse me a moment, Minister?' she said.

'Of course, Rosa, and pour us a little more whisky, would you?'

Fletcher watched her rise and step into the adjoining office. This time she closed the door behind her.

Thomas was talking: '. . . you should know, this isn't the first time. She tried to do the same thing six months ago. Mosley saw to things then—'

'Mosley?'

Thomas pulled a face. 'Yes. The prime minister was desperate, see. The tramp visited Number 10 and made a scene, and the PM was on good terms with Mosley and asked 'im to 'elp.'

'I see. And Mosley dealt with it satisfactorily?'

'He's an abrasive chap, he can be downright unpleasant . . . Not that he wasn't right to be with Frau Forster. That's her name, by the way: Kristina Forster.'

The interconnecting door opened and Miss Rosenberg glided back into the room. Fletcher watched her step over to the sideboard and pick up the whisky bottle.

'Mosley threatened 'er with the police,' said Thomas. 'Told 'er she would be arrested and prosecuted for blackmail . . . Ah, thank you, Rosa.'

Miss Rosenberg turned to pour some of the spirt into Fletcher's glass, and as she leant over him he was bathed in her perfume again. For a few seconds he felt quite giddy, like a member of Odysseus' crew tempted by the lotus-eaters – and perhaps that was her intention. He was not too intoxicated to notice her sleight of hand as she slipped a square of paper to Thomas, though it was executed with the slickness of an East End pick pocket.

'Frau Forster's from Vienna,' said Thomas, fighting for his attention; 'that's a problem too. Imagine what the press would say if they knew he had been writing confidential letters to a German: It isn't impossible she *is* a spy.'

Miss Rosenberg returned to her seat beside Fletcher, her notepad on her knee. What was her game? She had brought a note back into the room and left the door of the adjoining office ajar. Perhaps it was the whisky on an empty stomach or Miss Rosa's scent, or the desperate feeling he was going out on a limb, that made him rise on an impulse and step over to the door. He heard Thomas stumble mid-sentence – 'Reggie!' – and push his chair from the desk.

'Minister?' Fletcher looked at him, then took hold of the handle.

'Sit down man, for goodness sake!'

Too late! Door open, he was staring in slack-jawed amazement at the Prime Minister. Mr Ramsay MacDonald was sitting a few feet from the door, his elbow on the corner of a desk. He looked embarrassed and irritated, but only for a moment. A politician of Ramsay Mac's experience is never lost for words for long.

'Commander, I hope you'll excuse me,' he said, his voice lilting and contrite. 'You see, I resolved after the Zinoviev affair to have nothing directly to do with members of your profession. I prefer to act through an intermediary.'

'I see.'

'You'll think me ridiculous. A politician has to deal with some pretty unsavoury foreign characters, but here at home, well, it's a matter of trust . . .'

Fletcher stiffened.

'My dear fellow . . .' The prime minister put a hand on his arm. 'It's obvious to me you understand the delicacy of the situation. I'm grateful to you. It may not seem so, but it is work of national importance. The country needs a strong and stable government. We are confronting a terrible economic crisis, but that is of no consequence to this government's enemies, they'll do anything to thwart the will of the people.'

''Ere, 'ere,' said Thomas.

'Who are those enemies, Prime Minister?' said Fletcher.

'I think you know, Commander. The entitled. The Conservatives and their friends in the press and, I'm afraid to say, some of the country's public servants . . .'

'In the civil service and the intelligence services,' said Thomas.

'Aye, I'm afraid there are some . . . Which is why we want you to deal with this matter personally, and involve no one else. Are you prepared to take on this responsibility – for your country, Commander?'

The emotional pull of the man! He had always admired Mac for fighting the good fight for the people. Mac was a moral force, enduring, like granite – and yet, and yet, even as he heard himself say, 'Yes, Prime Minister,' the part of him that was Secret Service cynic wondered if the mission he was being asked to undertake was for the good of the country or to save its leader from scandal. 'I'll do my best,' he said, weakly. 'I'll need to know as much I can about the lady—'

Jimmy Thomas grunted.

'—the blackmailer, I mean, also the licence I have to negotiate, and in the event of negotiations breaking down . . .'

'Yes,' said the prime minister, 'well, sit down, please,' and he gestured to a chair. 'You understand, it is painful to have cared for someone then . . . ah, you ken well enough, I'm sure.' His voice shook a little. 'I want you to act at once, Commander. Who knows what she may do next. When can you leave for Paris?'

4

Paris, the city of light, was in Desmond Morton's thoughts too, as he stepped into the lift at Secret Service headquarters and slid its cage door into place. Maxwell Knight was waiting for him on the other side of Broadway. A reliable fellow, Knight; he would understand the delicacy of the mission. Yes, he had been involved in some knockabout stuff with his fascist pals in the past, breaking up meetings, breaking heads, but he was quite aware that his new role in the Secret Service called for more discretion.

The lift! Morton cursed roundly. With a screech of metal it juddered to a halt a few feet from the ground floor. What rotten luck! Maintenance would have to be called to free him. Damn it, nothing at 54 Broadway Buildings worked as it was supposed to. For the second time in a week he was caught in a no-man's-land between the fourth and the ground floors. 'Billy, here man!' With his head between his knees he could see the night concierge at his desk in the lobby. 'Billy!' The gap was too narrow to crawl through for a man with a bullet lodged near his heart. My God, he would play hell with the property manager. Maintenance had to be called every few days to rescue someone.

'Bill-eeee! What *are* you doing?'

'Is that you, Major Morton?'

'Of course it is. Get me out of here.'

'In a jiffy, sir.'

'Come on, man!'

He didn't want to give Knight the excuse to cross Broadway. On the other side of the street he was deniable, and if his mission went west he would have to go with it. He was only a letter in the books: M. 'Because we can't afford to look dirty, Desmond,' the admiral said; 'this has to be as tight as Zinoviev.'

The lift groaned, then sprang to life with a scream like a demon. Morton was free and walking swiftly across the lobby to the doors.

'Well, I'll be blowed!' said Billy in his booth. 'What did you do to it, sir?'

'For God's sake, get them to look at it again!' he snapped.

On the pavement outside he lit a cigarette and cast an eye

up and down the street. The entrance to St James's Underground station was not a sensible location for a rendezvous. He had chosen it for his own convenience and to nourish M's hope that he would be welcome on the other side of Broadway one day. There were a couple of fellows on the pavement outside the Old Star pub, and an employee of the Underground Electric Railways Company was leaving its new white stone headquarters opposite. Knight would be waiting for him in the shadows beneath its colonnade.

He had given the poor fellow only a couple of hours' notice. Fate in the guise of Major Joseph Ball had rung him at seven o'clock with a first-class piece of intelligence, and he had hurried along the corridor to report the substance of it to the Chief.

'The prime minister's tart has contacted him again, sir. She's threatening to sell his letters to a foreign newspaper.'

'Does Ball know what's in them?'

'Not the sort of correspondence you would share with your mother or your wife, he says. The letters are . . . the word he used was "pornographic".'

Sinclair had spluttered. 'Preposterous! How the hell does Major Ball know?'

'My thoughts, sir. "Not Ramsay MacDonald," I said to him, but Ball insists his source is a reliable one. MacDonald is certainly desperate to get them back.'

'And who is his source? We have to know.'

'Well, here's the thing, Chief . . . He says it's Oswald Mosley – not directly, you understand – it seems he's romantically involved with Ball's informer.'

'Mosley!'

'She's the wife of a Conservative member of parliament.'

'My God. You mean he's fucking the wife of a member of the Opposition!'

'That seems to be the case, yes. Major Ball got wind of the

affair and threatened to expose her if she didn't agree to pass on their pillow talk. Ball says the lady in question was good for nothing but gossip at first, but when Mosley's ardour cooled, she began to cooperate, and it seems Mosley was ready to confide in her even in the dying days of their relationship.'

Sinclair had guffawed. 'Desmond, that fellow . . . he was expecting her to tip off someone or other.'

'Major Ball came to the same conclusion.'

'Macbeth, ready to bury his dagger in old King Duncan, what?'

Morton dropped his cigarette end in the gutter and nudged it into a drain with his foot.

'Hello, Major.'

'Ah, there you are.'

Knight's shadow loomed across the pavement: tall, imposing, beaky, softly spoken, and dressed in a dinner jacket for a jazz club stage. Jazz was one of his passions. A decent clarinettist, it said in his service file. The leader of a hot little band that performed in some of the city's most insalubrious clubs. His other passions were collecting creatures – he had turned his flat into a zoo – and spying.

'How are you, Max?' said Morton. 'How well do you know Paris?'

5

The prime minister said little and made his excuses after only a few minutes, pleading 'affairs of state'. In their short time together he had made it plain he was 'terrible weighed doon' and that fear of exposure was polluting his mind and sapping his energy when the country was relying upon him to devote both to the economic crisis.

''Ee won't forget what you're doing for 'im,' said Thomas, as he escorted Fletcher from the Foreign Office. 'There's a safe seat in this for you. Somewhere in the Midlands. Nuneaton, perhaps Smethwick, because Mosley won't last long there. Where are you from?'

'Westmorland.'

'Ah. No 'ope.'

'For the Labour Party, no.'

Taxis were turning about Nelson in Trafalgar Square and streaming down Whitehall. The curtain had fallen on a routine Thursday night in the West End: at the Theatre Royal, *The Three Musketeers*, a transfer from Broadway, and *Lilac Time* was enjoying its fourth run at the Lyric; *Heads Up* was on stage at the Palace – the critics weren't kind – and at the Gaiety a musical called *Darling I Love You*. Sweet, sweet songs and high-kicking girls: sugar for hard times.

Fletcher had stepped out of Simpson's restaurant earlier in the week and been swallowed up by members of the smart set as they bubbled from the playhouses in the Strand. Crisis? Depression? Where? The hunger marchers trickling out of London to their homes in the manufacturing towns of the North were from that other country of chimney stacks and terraces where it was commonly supposed folk wore only fustian and clogs and spoke of *thee* and *tha*. A nation apart from comfortable Hampstead and Highgate. It had been different during the war when everyone was in it together. Men from the Mersey and the Clyde and the Tyne with whom Fletcher had served in the navy were looking to Ramsay Mac to make good promises that were made to them then. Work for the working man, and if it cost a few bob more in taxes, that was a small price to pay. Labour had a responsibility to keep Hampstead and Highgate honest. But what was Labour without Mac?

Perhaps Thomas was thinking the same. 'We've got to save

'im, Reggie,' he said, as they stood on the pavement together. 'You'll keep me updated, won't you.'

'Don't ring the Service switchboard again, Minister, or people will ask questions.' Was it necessary to spell it out? Sinclair's service considered Jimmy Thomas, minister of the crown, a threat to national security. 'I'm afraid there's a good chance someone will be listening.'

Thomas opened his mouth, only to snap it shut again, like a carp.

'The Service decides who is a security threat and Sinclair *is* the Service. That's why you came to me, isn't it?' Fletcher offered his hand. 'Goodnight, Minister.' Whitehall was not the place to linger. A passing taxicab might be carrying one of his colleagues home. 54 Broadway was a sponge that sucked rumour and intelligence from every quarter of the globe – not forgetting its doorstep. Fletcher did not want to be the story of the morning: 'Rum thing. Saw Officer G/Europe outside the Foreign Office last night. You'll never guess: he was with that Labour clown, Thomas.'

His mind turning on the possibility, he walked towards Parliament Square. How was he going to slip away to Paris? What was he going to say to Sinclair? It could take days, even weeks, to arrange things with the blackmailer. He would need assistance. Then there was the question of loyalty. Fletcher admired Mac and was flattered to be drawn into his circle, but the admiral was his superior officer and it went against the grain to turn his back on the quarter deck.

'Damn it!' There wasn't a cab to be had anywhere, not even in front of parliament. He was going to have to walk back to Broadway Buildings and telephone for one. Mrs Fletcher would have gone to bed without him. She would be in a terrible mood in the morning.

6

Dick Stewart lay in his old iron bed and watched the fire flickering in the glass of the photographs on the wall opposite. 'I can't, Dick. No!' Connie used to jest when she shared the bed with him: 'your grandparents are watching us!' Connie, his wife, who would be young in his imagination for ever, like his soldier comrades who left their skins in France.

Lifting his right arm free of the covers, he reached over to the bedside table for his cigarettes. The simple act of extending it sent a searing pain washing through his body. Rolling on to his side would be worse, but he was going to all the same. He needed a cigarette and he needed to embrace the pain as a penance, like the saint ascetics his mother honoured on her knees in church every day. Because in his feverish mind pain was a way to make amends: for putting those poor Welsh lads, Owen and Eyre, in jail; for not dying at the Front, for being a complete cunt. One. Two. Three. Roll! And, oh, the pain! He couldn't lock it behind his teeth. For seconds it seemed to suck the light from the room, and the next thing he was conscious of was his mother's face and her hand upon his brow. 'I need a fag,' he muttered.

'Rest,' she said in French, 'and when you're ready I'll roll you on to your back again.' The cracked mirror on the chest of drawers was opposite him now, and – Christ! – what a mess he looked with rat's tails of hair plastered to his forehead and evil rings around his eyes. He looked like his father. 'Aaagh! Mother!' She had whisked him on to his back. 'I wasn't ready!'

'This is what you want, isn't it?' she said, holding a cigarette to his lips. 'A policeman came to see you, Richard. He wants you to describe the men who attacked you. And Father Mark—'

'No!'

'Just to wish you well.'

'No.'

She looked at him reproachfully. 'And the policeman?'

'I don't remember their faces,' he said, which was a lie. Spies remember faces: 'Brains' with the thick toothbrush moustache; Brawn with cauliflower ears and fists like the piston of a mine shaft pump. Thankfully half a dozen timber porters had arrived in time to break up the party and save him from serious injury. The Taffy miners had legged it before they could put their case, otherwise he might have been bumping timber in the dock. The porters had carried their wounded 'war hero' home and a doctor had been summoned to prescribe rest and some pills.

He had woken to the heartache of crying children. 'What's wrong with Daddy, Grandmère?' That was an hour ago. They were still awake, pottering below, too frightened and upset to go to their beds.

'Do you want to know why they attacked me?' he asked his mother, as she smoothed creases from his quilt. Small, dark, restless as a wren, her thick brown hair streaked with grey and pinned in a bun, she was a vital and an indomitable woman, a fine-featured attractive woman, the more so for the care lines of the last ten years and the air of sadness that never left her.

'I won't ask you why,' she said, 'I can't be sure you'll tell me the truth.'

He didn't protest, only drew deeply on his cigarette.

'There's a letter for you, Richard. The landlord of the Ark sent a boy. But it can wait.'

She was trying not to catch his eye, because nothing good could come from the Ark, nothing honest, nothing decent. In the past she had asked him for the truth and he had refused to speak to her, and that was worse. Was her beloved son a criminal? A job you couldn't talk to your family about was surely a shameful one. But perhaps it was secret police work. That was what she wanted to hear him say, and it would have been an easy lie to tell. Only making her miserable was another part of his mad cruel penance, for how could he be happy when his mother was tormented and fearful for his soul?

'Do you have the letter? I better look at the letter,' he said. 'Will you fetch it for me?'

He listened to her make her way carefully down the stairs and the children clamouring, *comment va Papa*? Papa was tired, Papa would see them in the morning, she said. Now to bed and they weren't to forget their prayers: 'Pray for Papa, my dears.'

'I always pray for Papa,' said Florence.

The note was from 'M', as he knew it would be. Knight wanted to meet him at the Jesuit church in Farm Street the following day.

The Farm at Six. There would be an evening Mass at six but with no more than a dozen elderly folk in the congregation. Knight would be waiting on his knees in front of candles in the chapel dedicated to the English Martyrs. He wasn't 'a Roman', he said, but he loved the spectacle, and he made a point of blessing himself ostentatiously before and after their meetings. Stewart had dumped the Father, the Son and the Holy Spirit and his first communion beads in the valley of the Somme, and yet fourteen years after turning his back on them he was still uncomfortable talking to a fraud like Knight in front of an altar.

The paper trembled in his hands as if charged with excitement by the man who wrote it. The meeting was 'imperative' and Stewart was enjoined to 'arrange things at home'. That meant Knight was planning to send him out of London. Just as long as it wasn't to Wales.

'Are you going to stare at that piece of paper all night?' His mother was gazing at him disapprovingly. 'You must sleep.'

In reply he reached a hand to her and she stepped forward to take it.

'Tell them I love them,' he said. 'No. I would like to tell them myself.'

She smiled and bent to kiss his hand. 'I'll call them.'

Call to Florence, daughter with the flaxen hair and summer-sky eyes, generous and as bright as a button; call Pierre, his son, six, and small for his age, dark hair and sallow skin, quiet and intense.

Here they come rushing into the room with their arms open to embrace their father.

7

At half past ten the following morning Commander Reginald Fletcher stepped out of his office on the fourth floor with a thick folder of papers and walked purposefully along the senior officers' corridor into Production at the rear of the building. Prod – as it was known in the Service – was responsible for intelligence on Soviet activities. The officer in charge of Prod was Major Desmond Morton.

'Is he alone?' Fletcher enquired of the Major's secretary. 'Will he see me?'

Morton was alone with the crossword. He looked immaculate in a dark-grey waistcoat, powder-blue shirt, and a red and navy artillery tie.

'Hello, Reggie,' he said, half rising to offer his hand. 'To what do I owe the pleasure?'

The frost with which he had greeted Fletcher in his first months had thawed of late. 'Do you have something for me?'

'These?' Fletcher lifted the folder he was carrying as a prop. 'No, no. Look, Desmond, can we talk somewhere private?'

Morton pursed his lips and his sleek, perfectly trimmed moustache rose as if it was poised to jump off his face. 'This isn't private enough for you?'

'I thought St James's Park. We might take a turn about the lake. It's a . . . delicate matter. I would appreciate your advice.'

'Of course, but what about here and now? I will make sure we aren't disturbed.'

'Well, yes, I suppose so.' Fletcher flushed. Delicate? What a foolish thing to say when every piece of business transacted inside 54 Broadway Buildings was 'delicate' in one way or another.

Morton stepped out from behind his desk. 'Let me speak to my secretary. Would you like a cup of coffee?'

'No, thank you.'

Fletcher took one of the polished wooden chairs in front of Morton's desk and dumped his papers at its edge. Nine months in the Service and this was the first time he had set foot in the head of Prod's office. There was very little in its decor that could offer a clue to Morton the private man. It was as bare and impersonal as the cabin Fletcher had shared with the other midshipmen on his first voyage across the Atlantic. Was it wise to trust Morton when he barely knew the man? He was going out of his way to be friendly but his smile was as precise as a good Swiss timepiece. There was no suggestion of good humour in his eyes. Approaching Morton for help was a desperate thing to do but that was the course he was set upon. There was no one outside the Service he could turn to and he needed to act swiftly.

He could hear the major telling his secretary that on no account were they to be disturbed, not even by God Almighty. A moment later he was back and sliding behind his desk, bolt upright, hands clasped on his ink blotter.

'It's like this, Desmond,' said Fletcher, 'I need someone I can rely on in Paris. Someone resourceful who knows the city; someone outside the Service.'

Morton pursed his lips and his moustache twitched like a fat mouse again. 'Outside the Service? A bit of freelancing? You want to keep the Chief in the dark, I suppose. Well, Reggie, I really think you—'

'It's official, Desmond, sanctioned at the highest level. But, if you feel uncomfortable . . . It's unfair to ask,' he said, reaching for the papers he had placed on Morton's desk. 'Presumptuous of me.'

'Not at all, not at all. Look, tell me more. Official, you say? Civil service or government?'

'Government.'

'The foreign secretary?'

'I wish I could say. You'll have to take this on trust. I've been charged with a mission of national importance, but I can't use our people in Paris.'

'Why ever not?'

'Because it's official but at the same time unofficial.'

'Political, you mean?'

'If you like,' said Fletcher, defensively, 'but in the national interest.' He gathered his papers and was poised to rise. 'To say "political" is to say nothing, Desmond, because everything government does is political in one way or another. No, don't protest, you're sceptical, I can hear it, and no doubt your scepticism is an expression of *your political* opinion. In my judgement, the thing I have been asked to do is in the national interest because stable government in a crisis is in the national interest. But I'm sorry—'

'Reggie, don't be so prickly. Sit down. You're asking me to take this on trust and keep my mouth shut, too. You'll grant, anyone in my position would have questions.'

'Of course, only I can't give you answers. I *am* asking you to trust me: it has been sanctioned at the top of government.' He paused. 'The very top.'

'I see. The prime minister?'

'I'm not at liberty to say.'

'And why you, why not do this the usual way? Why not the Chief?'

'I think you know the answer to that!' Fletcher was losing patience.

'All right, old boy, keep your hair on. What do you want?'

Fletcher took a deep breath and exhaled slowly. Should he stay or go? He had said more than was wise already. Better stay and recruit Morton to the cause now. 'I need one of your casual agents,' he said. 'He would report to me and no one else.'

Morton lifted his hands and touched his thumbs to his lips. 'There is someone. He isn't on our books but we use him from time to time.'

'French?'

'Perfect French. Discreet. One of the best. He was decorated in the war.'

'I'd like to meet him. Can you . . .? As soon as possible.'

'Of course.' Morton smiled broadly again. 'Leave it with me, Reggie, and mum's the word, of course.'

8

A tricky situation, but a good one! What a turn-up for the books! Morton waited until he was sure his visitor had closed the door of his outer office, then he gave a short laugh of relief and pleasure. New rules. The game was changing. The Chief would have to be informed at once. Lifting the telephone, he dialled Sinclair's secretary.

'Can I have a word with him, Miss Pettigrew?' . . . 'I'm sorry, it has to be the telephone' . . . 'I know I'm just along the corridor' . . . 'Yes, the telephone. Really, Miss Pettigrew, do I have to explain to you?' . . . 'I do? Well, isn't it obvious? I can't be seen in his office!' . . . 'Well, I'm sorry you find my tone offensive but it's urgent.' . . . 'Yes, of course I'll wait for him to ring me back. Thank you.'

Morton slammed the receiver back on the telephone: the bloody impertinence of the woman. Monstrous. Reaching into a desk drawer, he took out a small sheet of blue paper and wrote:

Plans changing. Request meeting, usual place. 20.00.

On the envelope he wrote Maxwell Knight's name and the address of his flat in Knightsbridge.

'Miss Vickers.' He could hear her bustling about his outer office. 'Miss Vickers . . . Ah, there you are. Have despatch deliver this at once, please.'

It was hard to believe their luck: an agent inside and a key player in the prime minister's affair. Sinclair would be delighted, Ball, too – and Morton . . . he couldn't stop smiling.

9

It wasn't until the following day – the Saturday – that Stewart was able to rise and catch a bus to Hyde Park Corner for his meeting with Knight. The hunger marchers had left the park with no more than a promise from their communist comrades that the fight for jobs and a decent dole would go on to victory. 'Heroes of the class struggle,' the new *Daily Worker* paper called them in its Saturday editorial; 'trouble,' a government source in *The Times*. And in the park where the revolution was to have begun, prosperous London was strolling in the spring sunshine again: mothers and nannies pushing their prams, smart little boys in plum velvet shorts running after a kite; and trotting past the giant bronze figure of Achilles, a troop of Horse Guards in scarlet and white uniforms, swords and silver helmets. How strange that after all the khaki killing of the new century they should have returned to the antique empire uniforms of the last. Hanging from the railings close to the park gates were twisted canvas banners the park-keepers were still to clear away. The first read, 'Down with the starvation Labour government,' and the second, 'Down with caning in schools.' Stewart hobbled across Park Lane.

The trees on either side of the entrance to the Farm Street church were dressed in bridal white as if they had been decorated by one of the many society couples who chose to marry in the church for its Gothic Revival splendour. There must have been a wedding that morning because a young lad was sweeping rice and petals from the steps. If you could afford to dress Mayfair smart, Farm Street was an acceptable place for a Saturday rendezvous, but Stewart didn't have that sort of wardrobe. Without the cover of the Mass he was going to stand out like a beggar at a bishop's banquet.

There were six elderly women on their knees in the nave, their heads bent over their beads, and he counted another six in the church's side chapels. Light was pouring through high clerestory windows as if to remind them of the warmth of spring, of park life and the bustle of West End shopping streets a short walk away. That anyone would choose to spend hours in the perpetual twilight of the church on such a day truly was a mystery of faith. The women would probably be on their knees until the priest bid them rise for the evening service. Knight was kneeling too. When he heard Stewart's slow footsteps he rose and slipped his rosary beads into his jacket pocket. What a fraud! How long would it take to choke him with a rosary? With a firm grip and strong beads, no more time than it would take to say ten Hail Marys.

Knight turned to greet him with a benign smile, like one of the saints in the chapel altar.

'I've got something good for you, Frenchie,' he said in a low voice. 'You're going to Paris.'

'Is this the best place to talk, Mr Knight?'

'Call me M. Oh, I think it's fine, if we whisper. We don't have much time.'

Knight settled on the bench again and patted the space to his left, as if he were inviting a child to listen to a story. 'Have you done something to your leg, Frenchie?'

'Nothin' serious, Mr Knight.'

'Call me M,' he said. 'I'm glad because this is the perfect job for you. Challenging but you will be well paid, and it's your chance to impress some very important people. Do it well and they may reward you with a permanent position. How would you like that?'

Stewart nodded slowly.

'Good,' said Knight. 'Good. So there's someone you must meet, his name is Fletcher. Commander Reginald Fletcher. He used to be a Liberal MP but he has turned to Labour. You'll have to use all your rough charm to convince him you're trustworthy. He knows something of your history; he won't know you're my agent. Do you understand? He knows nothing about me and that's how we must keep it.'

'I'm your spy.'

'Yes. Commander Fletcher will tell you he's working for the prime minister. That's true. But I've been asked to keep an eye on things . . . on him.'

'Asked by who, Mr Knight? '

'By whom, Frenchie, and I've told you; call me M. All you need to know is that it's for our country and it's official, but like all our work, it's deniable. Here, telephone this number . . .' He dipped into his jacket and pulled out his rosary. A slip of paper was caught in its ebony trail. 'Ring him between six and seven o'clock this evening to arrange a meeting.'

'And this Fletcher, what's he doin' for the prime minister?'

'You should hear it from Commander Fletcher's lips, that would be best.' Knight glanced over Stewart's shoulder. A young woman was climbing the side chapel steps with a candle. 'I think we better leave. I'll go first and you can stay and say a prayer for the success of your mission.' He smiled broadly, relishing his own wit.

Stewart caught his arm as he began to rise. 'One more thing, Mr Knight – the money.'

'You can discuss that with Commander Fletcher.'

'Not if I'm workin' for you. Twelve pounds. That's twelve a week. And my expenses, of course.'

'Twelve pounds! Don't be ridiculous.'

'Perfect job for me, you said. Short notice, too . . .'

'Don't you want work?' he said, a little too loudly. He was inviting the curiosity of their nearest neighbours in the nave. 'I suppose you'll be asking Fletcher for money, too!'

'He would think it strange if I didn't ask, wouldn't he? Is that agreed then? Same pick-up arrangement and this week in advance.'

'You're a thief, Frenchie!'

'It's the market, Mr Knight. Capitalism: isn't that what you're defending?'

10

At about the time Stewart was arranging to meet Commander Fletcher, the prime minister was dressing for the ball at Londonderry House: full fig evening dress, white tie, gentleman's tailcoat, a new piqué waistcoat from Stovel's on Savile Row. His court shoes needed more polish and his man had carried them away to work up a shine. Dear Lady Edith would be at his side and the eyes of the other guests would be upon them both all evening. In the last few years he had begun to enjoy dressing for grand occasions. Edith said he looked distinguished and more handsome than a sixty-three-year-old man had a right to be. He was fortunate in that regard, and he took great care in his choice of clothes, his coiffure, in the way he carried himself and his gestures, because thoughts and speeches were not enough, a politician had to cut a convincing figure if he was going to be remembered as a statesman. Some in Labour ridiculed him, accused him of being a peacock, a sell-out, seduced by privilege and the trappings of high office. Because privilege is forever vigilant on its own behalf and canny enough to know that one way to frustrate its enemies is to furl them in a warm embrace.

But the working people he had grown up with, his family, friends, comrades, expected him to look his best, and not just on a Sunday. They wanted a champion as easy in the company of a king as a miner, in touch with his roots but not constrained by them. His critics in the Party had no more understanding of working people than the High Tories he would be rubbing shoulders with at the Londonderrys' Ball.

Lady Edith was a collector and all the people of the day would be invited to Londonderry House. Her husband, Charley, the marquis, was a great Conservative. Churchill would be there – 'Winston the Warlock', Edith called him – his party leader, Stanley Baldwin, too. To her many admirers she was 'Circe', the enchantress, who cast a spell on artists and politicians of very different hues.

'Father? Are you ready?' Ishbel was at the door. 'The driver's waiting.'

'Aye, only my shoes.'

'Yes. They're here,' she said, placing them on the floor in front of his easy chair.

A band of well-wishers was waiting outside Number 10 and he paused on the step to wave. From Whitehall they drove into the Mall along the route he took for his audiences at the palace. The king seemed easier in his company of late. Only the other day he had felt able to frankly confess he was hoping Labour would change its tune. 'Really, Prime Minister, can't you prevent your people singing "The Red Flag"?'

'They've got into the way of singing the song, Your Majesty,' he had said, 'but I hope to break down the habit.'

As the motorcar turned on to Park Lane he tried to collect his thoughts for the address he was going to offer to Lady Edith. He had written a few lines to her a week ago and said more than was wise. One had to be so careful in dealing with a sorceress. In a weak moment he had let his imagination and passion suppressed get the better of him. He had gushed with the force of a Highland burn, words that made him flinch with embarrassment but with excitement too. He had warned her that his *bold spirit* had wrestled with his *shy spirit* and his bold had won, so he was bound to declare, *you are very beautiful* and, *I love you*. In sober moments of regret since he had cursed that bold spirit, and his only excuse was that she had encouraged him in a letter of her own with, *all my love is yours, Hamish*, and, *you are a great man*.

Was she playing the sort of game spirited marchionesses play with *great men*? He was twelve years her senior, which was no great difference in age. Only how could he forget that it was his *bold spirit* that had tempted him into an affair with a woman who was threatening to ruin him? Just a few column inches would be enough to shatter his reputation irredeemably. That a man who had grown up in honest poverty and spent forty years in politics should have been so deceived by her veneer of sophistication. He had learnt during his first election campaigns that there was no such thing as a private life in politics. After the death of his wife he had found happiness for a time with another Margaret. She was a society lady, he was the socialist leader, and their affair had been a very secret affair. His comrades in parliament and the country would have accused him of 'betraying' his roots and the people, and what sport the newspapers would have had with the bastard son of the ploughboy and the grand aristocratic lady. But after his first term as prime minister he had let his guard slip. He had been bewitched by Kristina Forster. She had nurtured and rewarded his bold spirit and, oh, the things that bold spirit had dared to write. As the motorcar drew up to the pavement in front of Londonderry House, he shut his eyes tightly and groaned. He had placed his premiership and his government in the hands of a Viennese socialite.

'Can I help, sir?' His police bodyguard was holding the car door.

'No, I'm fine, thank you.'

The press and members of the public shouted, 'Here, Prime Minister' and 'A photograph, Prime Minister,' and as he walked from the car he took a fat cigar from his coat pocket and turned to flourish it at the cameras. Cameo over, he climbed the steps to the house and walked into the vestibule where a footman was waiting to take his hat and coat. A snake of guests was edging out of the vestibule and up into the staircase hall. Neville Chamberlain, the Tory Party chairman, greeted him stiffly and introduced his wife, Anne, and the dramatist Sean O'Casey stepped forward to shake his hand.

'You see the painting above the chimneypiece, Mr O'Casey? Seaham Harbour in my constituency in the north-east of England.'

'Very fine, to be sure,' said O'Casey with barely more than a glance.

That was a pity because the painting was pregnant with history and meaning. The house – the Londonderrys' palace – and every fine piece in it, and there were many, were only one part of a vast canvas of rolling hills and country estates, blast furnaces and quarries, a dock, a harbour, pit villages with grimy clifftop terraces that seemed on the point of slipping into the sea, along with the grey slag mountains on their doorsteps;

and the collieries themselves, where thousands of men laboured underground for the black stuff that was the price of Mr O'Casey's champagne.

Even as he was shaking hands with another of the well-to-do guests he could see in his mind's eye the Londonderry family in their golden carriage in the centre of the painting, colliers in leather helmets standing below them at the bottom of the frame. Was it merely coincidence that Lady Edith should choose to hold her ball on the anniversary of his election to parliament? A year ago to the day, the grandsons and granddaughters of the miners in the painting had gathered at Seaham Harbour to celebrate the return of Labour to power. What hope they had invested in his government!

Birkenhead was at his shoulder now. 'Prime Minister.' Legs planted wide apart and yet swaying like a full-leaf tree in a gale, and so early in the evening. His face was swollen and mottled yellow, the shade of good dry sherry wine. Behold the former lord chancellor and head of the judiciary in his almost natural state of inebriation.

'Lord Birkenhead.' MacDonald accepted his hand, because it was necessary to be civil to the most uncivil of men on occasion. For years Birkenhead had used his influence with the newspapers to publish lies about Labour and its leader. A pacifist and a communist, he whispered to his friends on the *Spectator* and *The Times*, when he knew perfectly well it was untrue. Ah, but that's the game, he would say, that's politics. And here they were together in starched white shirts, privy councillors both, and lifelong players of that game.

'Our hostess!' said Birkenhead. 'A fine woman! But a bit of a handful, what?'

They were standing in the staircase hall and rising above them were magnificent returned flights of stairs supported by pairs of columns and a coffered ceiling and clerestory, like the dome of a baroque cathedral. Their hostess was at the first-floor gallery rail, resplendent in a dark-green ball gown and the famous Londonderry tiara. With a graceful flourish of her right hand she beckoned to him, bidding him climb to her.

'You are summoned, Prime Minister,' said Birkenhead with an impertinent smile.

'Then I must obey.'

Glancing up as he did so, he wondered if his first words to her should be, 'Forgive me for writing so boldly.' What a tiresome romantic old fool she must think him: Caliban to her glittering Miranda. Her face was full of fascination and life: he had nothing to fear. She took his arm at once.

'How are you, Hamish?' she whispered as she led him round the gallery towards the ballroom. 'You are as handsome as ever, but a little tired: the cares of the country. And yet you found time to write such a beautiful letter to me. You are the most human and understanding of men. Let's hurry to the Western Isles and live there in peace and happiness together.'

'Ha. My dear lady, your encouragement means so much to me. The dark clouds lift and always reveal your shining face. You look so beautiful this evening. Your dress . . . dazzling in colour and line. My dear, you *are* the dress.'

'Oh, Hamish.' She reached across her body to squeeze his forearm. 'But first you must say hello to Charley,' she said in a voice that all might hear.

The marquis was with their guests in the ballroom. They spoke only a few words. He pretended to be interested in his host's rambling views on the Coal Mines Bill. There were two hundred people at the ball and every one of them with an opinion on what should be done to save the country from the economic crisis. None of them were for Labour. Baldwin, Birkenhead, Churchill and the other Chamberlain were civilised company at a ball and he listened politely to their policy pronouncements without learning anything new. The worst of it was the shadow in his mind that smiles would turn to laughter the moment he turned his back upon them. If Conservative Central Office was investigating his affair then the party's most prominent figures may have heard a rumour of it too. Worse still, the marquis would tell dear Lady Edith: what regard would she have for him then?

The circle about him was constantly changing. 'Prime Minister, may I have a word about your plans for housing?' said someone he was expected to recognise. 'Really, gentlemen,' said Edith, 'the prime minister is here to enjoy himself. He deserves a little peace. I'm taking him from you.'

Dear Edith. *She can never know.* Until the letters his too-bold spirit had penned to the Austrian were back in his hands he would have no peace. He was of an age to care for his good name and his place in history. The ballroom was hung with portraits of great men that the family had been associated with in the last century. Kings and tsars and famous statesmen gazed upon the guests from their gilt frames. Would they make room on the wall for the country's first socialist prime minister one day? There would be no place in this or any house if he were to be forced from office by the Viennese. 'A tart,' they would say, 'and the things he wrote to her!' After the years of toil, after all he had achieved in rising to the first rank in the land, he deserved better.

'You look vexed, Hamish,' Edith whispered to him in a quieter place.

'Aye. As you say, my dear, the cares of the nation.'

'Oh, Hamish, we live in horrible times. That awful man Mosley. What a beast! Charley wanted to invite him; I wouldn't hear of it. The way he's treated you – after all you've done for him – and the way he treats poor dear Cimmie.' She patted his hand gently. 'But the country can't get on without you. You do realise that, don't you? You have all our prayers and thoughts, you dear brave creature.'

PART THREE

Sunday reflection: the debts of folly are the heaviest to
* pay . . .*
There are candle-men for moths,
who will fly and make messes on the candle by their remains
* if the candle does not blow blasts in self-defence.*

Prime Minister Ramsay MacDonald,
Diary 27–28 July 1930

5

1 June 1930

THE WOMAN IN black hurrying across the Pont au Double seemed to be out of step with everyone. Beneath the bridge well-to-do Parisians in light bright summer clothes strolled along the left bank of the Seine; a young man in a white coat and straw hat was selling ice cream to children from the box at the front of his bicycle; and a party of students at the edge of the quay laughed, drank wine from a bottle and gazed across the sparkling river at the stone heart of their city as it turned to burnished gold in the evening sunshine. Paris had the languid summer-slow air of a provincial town on that first Sunday in June. The Pont au Double was a favourite place for promenaders to linger and admire the view of Notre-Dame Cathedral and the woman in black was forced to weave her way from pavement to gutter and back, like a drunk. A casual observer might have taken her for an elderly widow hurrying to the cathedral for the last Mass of the day, but Kristina Forster was neither a religious woman nor at fifty-two a very old one. Sober and serious was how she chose to dress for her teaching engagements. From her lodgings in the Marais district it was an hour's walk to the Aubry family apartment near the church of Les Invalides, and after an hour of dismal German conversation with girls who had no wish to learn the language she was obliged to walk the entire way back. To walk any great distance across the city would have been unthinkable a year ago but the collapse of her late husband's investments had left her with no choice. No choice but to teach; no choice but cheap lodgings; no choice but to risk an appeal for help to a man she had loved and who once claimed to love her. No money; no choice.

The soles of her button boots were wearing thin and as she hurried across the square in front of the cathedral she tripped and almost fell. On another day she might have sought refuge from the heat in a side chapel or by a pillar in the nave. She did not believe in God but she believed in the cathedral of Notre-Dame, in its soaring arches, in the piety of its stone saints, in the wit of its devils, in the miracle of its rose windows, the sunset reds and twilight blues of its medieval glass, in the pomp of its organ and the purity of its choir: she believed in the best of human endeavour that it represented, and sharing its beauty in her troubles sometimes brought her peace. Oh, for peace! She was sure she would know no peace until she received some kind word from the British prime minister. Ten days after her letter to Downing Street, she was still waiting for a reply. Would he have a change of heart? That was to hope for too much perhaps. No, he would be afraid and because he was the prime minister she was afraid.

'You'll disappear, madam,' Oswald Mosley had said, and he had clicked his fingers; 'poof.' Was she naive to imagine the man she had loved and who had made such passionate love to her would prevent Mosley carrying out his threat to do her harm? Champion of the people: what did it mean if he was not prepared to champion her? A quiver of rage shot through her. Yes, she was naive. He had used and discarded her, thrown her from his door like a pair of old shoes. Well, she wasn't going to stand for it.

Her pace quickened over the next bridge and then across the busy riverside thoroughfare to the Hôtel de Ville. Behind the city hall she turned into a street of tall houses and shops with boards advertising their wares in more than one language. Wet washing dripped from balconies on to the cobbles, and at the entrance to a courtyard barefoot children were spinning a hoop with a stick. This was the Marais, where the poor were crowded into decaying mansions the rich had deserted for greener pleasanter places. Their occupants were new to the city and a visitor was as likely to hear Polish, Russian and German spoken as French. The foreign character of the district was even more marked in the rue des Écouffes where the signs were in Yiddish and the butchers were selling cuts of kosher meat. The men she passed were wearing the kippah; the women, scarves and unfashionably long dresses. They were Jews, all of them Jews. The old broom-seller who greeted her every morning, a refugee from Poland; the baker where she bought her bread, Romanian; and her landlord was from a shtetl in the old Russian Pale. They were the new Jewish residents of the old Paris ghetto, a district within a district known in Yiddish as the *Pletzel* – the place. A place for immigrants, for the stateless, for the persecuted, the poor and the criminal. A place where a woman who wished to hide from those who might do her harm could afford to live on very little. Bern without money was out of the question, Berlin was changing for the worse, and she would never return to her childhood home in Vienna. Paris was home for now, but not the grand hotels on the Avenue des Champs Élysées where the staff used to know her by name, or her old apartment near the Bois de Boulogne; nor could she dine at Fouquet's or Larue or the Ritz in the Place Vendôme as she used to. She was returning to a cheap room in a run-down lodging house in a dead-end alley in a district les Parisiens viewed with suspicion, even hostility. Oh, how devoutly she longed to escape the heat of the street and lock her door on a world that seemed to care nothing for her. Only before she could kick off her boots and rest she had one more call to make.

Eli Weiss's little bookshop was on the corner of the rue des Écouffes and the rue des Rosiers. On Sundays and every day excepting the Sabbath he was open until six, and on Tuesday evenings he opened again for his comrades and they would discuss the education of the proletariat and the socialist revolution to come. Weiss would brew bitter coffee on a little coke stove and when there was a disagreement on policy that could only be resolved by Marx or Lenin he would search his shelves for the answer.

From the shade in front of a tailor's on the opposite side of the street Kristina Forster watched her friend return books from a table in front of his shop to the shelves inside. Not only books but pots, pans, a kettle, a coffee grinder and candles too. On the window of his shop in Hebrew and Yiddish was a list of his services. The one he performed free of charge for his friend Kristina Forster was confidant and confidential postman.

She had warned him to 'look out for Englishmen.'

'My dear, I know nothing,' he had joked in German. 'In Russia, I know nothing. In Austria, I know nothing. Here in France – nothing.'

A couple of small boys caught up in their small-boy world ambled towards her, and on the opposite side of the street there were three men in close conversation, the oldest in a bloodstained butcher's apron, his companions – his sons perhaps – dressed in cheap wool working clothes. They had beards and the distinctive twisted sidelocks called *payot* favoured by some Orthodox from the east. Satisfied no one was watching the bookseller's, she crossed the street and tapped lightly on the window.

Weiss had drawn the blinds and was locking the door. 'Come, come,' he said in German, and she could tell from the excitement in his voice that he had something for her. 'Kristina, my dear, come.'

She followed him to the back of the bookshop and from the drawer of a small unvarnished oak desk he produced an envelope that was addressed in a fine cultivated hand to *Frau Kristina Forster, c/o Monsieur E. Weiss, 201 rue des Rosiers, Paris.*

'The letter you've been waiting for, yes?' he said, plucking at his impressive white beard. 'Delivered by hand but I didn't see by whose. Do you want a paperknife?'

No, she wanted to open the letter alone. She had told him she was expecting a letter from someone she 'loved' with 'enemies in the British Secret Service.' He knew nothing of the British prime minister. Was that fair? He was an old socialist, an immigrant, a Jew: reason enough to fear secret policemen and spies. They had chased him from the east to the west, to France and no further: 'Please God, no trouble here.' She had assured him there would be none. The less he knew of her affairs the safer he would be. Wasn't being a Jew hard enough?

'Wait, my dear,' he said, 'let me check there's no one there.'

She watched him peer through the window at the street. 'All right, all right, you can go. Hurry!'

'Thank you, Eli, my friend, thank you.'

Her landlord had chosen to call his boarding house L'Hôtel du Printemps in an attempt to attract a better class of customer. The name was peeling from a wooden board above the entrance. Painted on the wall below it was the price of the rooms in Yiddish and in Polish. The lady of the house, Madame Finder, was sitting on the front step in a nest of skirts, and the two youngest of her five children were playing at her feet. She ignored Kristina Forster, which was the kindest thing she could do; Madame was on good terms with nobody. Monsieur appeared as Kristina was crossing the hall but turned as soon as he saw her and retreated into his office. The stairs were an ordeal. She was exhausted – the walk from Les Invalides – and the instant her room was open she collapsed in a chair, tears of frustration and fatigue welling inside her. 'No, Kristina!' she muttered. She had shed so many tears over the years to no purpose. She needed help and if it was not given freely then she had a right to insist upon it.

Please God the letter signalled a change of heart. With a shiver of apprehension she tore the flap of the envelope and drew out a single sheet of paper. Her former lover had written three short sentences.

I am sending Mr Reginald Fletcher to you. He has authority to act on my behalf. Please do nothing until you have spoken to him.

With eyes closed, she leant back in the armchair. Was she foolish to have hoped for more? Perhaps his note did signal a change of heart but not the one she had so dearly hoped for. No words of affection or regret, no hope of reconciliation, only a willingness to parley with her through this Fletcher. He was treating her like a whore.

He had spoken only a year ago of a lifelong friendship. They had driven down to Cornwall with the Mosleys. A beautiful early-spring evening, the balcony of her room at the hotel in Fowey: 'My love, I'll never forget these few days together,' he had said. 'You look so beautiful. If I were free . . . I weary so of politics. Have I not done enough? Is it time to walk away?'

She had taken his hands and said, 'No, James; your country needs a Labour prime minister, needs you.' He had smiled, swept a lock of hair from her forehead, then kissed her passionately. Ah, the memory of that kiss and the many that followed that night . . . Two months later he was back in Downing Street; and from that day in May, not a kind word. He had simply ignored her love letters and her appeal for financial assistance, and then to be humiliated by him in Downing Street . . . *Zut!* The recollection of their last exchange made her *so* angry. If he was intent on treating her like a whore, *ai-yi-yi,* she was going to behave like one.

6

2 June 1930

FLETCHER AND STEWART caught the train to Paris the following morning, the officer and aspirant Labour politician at its head in first class and the ex-sergeant son of a seaman at the rear in third. They had met and spoken once. Stewart's terms, fifteen pounds a week plus expenses; Fletcher's terms, complete discretion. 'In the national interest,' he said. Four words the spy and the politician use to cloak their choices with a semblance of respectability. Sacrifice on the Somme? 'In the national interest.' A conspiracy to bring down a Labour government? 'In the national interest.' A favour for a prime minister? 'In the national interest.'

'You report to me and no one else,' said Fletcher. That was agreed too. A professional liar will agree to anything. Trust, they say, arrives on foot. Fletcher could count on one hand the friends and colleagues he trusted completely. But in this matter of the prime minister's affair what choice did he have? There was only one candidate for the job. He was catching the train with Morton's spy, leaving trust to follow on foot.

As far as his service colleagues were concerned he was meeting the French secret police. He had arranged to visit his opposite number the following morning – couldn't be helped – it was the expedient thing to do. But he would have to assume the Bureau would make a point of monitoring his movements. Thankfully, it would know nothing of the man who had limped along the platform after him and was gazing upon the grimy yellow-brick streets of London south from his seat at the rear of the train.

'Do you speak German, Stewart?' Fletcher had enquired.

Stewart said he could get by.

'Well, German's her first language. I'm told her English is good and her French perfect.'

He had given Stewart a photograph of Frau Forster in a party of five or six men and women in smart summer clothes, standing on the balcony of a hotel or villa. Mosley was grinning like a donkey at the camera, he recognised Lady Cynthia, and someone had gone to great lengths to cut another member of the group from the picture and only his arm remained, gently squeezing Frau Forster's waist. Fletcher was in no doubt that the arm had once been attached to the broad frame of Mr J. Ramsay MacDonald, and it was easy to imagine a smile lifting his celebrated moustache.

'She's 'andsome,' Stewart had opined, 'but with sad eyes.'

'A poet, are you?' Fletcher replied. 'Don't be soft, man. She's a thief. She's stolen the prime minister's letters and if she lived in Britain he would put the police on her. But in Paris . . . The prime minister wants to keep it from the newspapers. Complete discretion, Stewart. Complete discretion.'

That the letters belonged to Frau Forster was neither here nor there. Stewart's task was to help Fletcher recover them.

'That's any old how, is it?' he had asked.

'We're to negotiate a price.'

'With a thief?'

'That's right. No fuss. Nothing to raise suspicion or cause a scandal.'

'I see.'

'I'm sure you do, Stewart.'

2

A nursery rhyme was turning in Stewart's head to the clickety-clack rhythm of the track. The words had popped into his head without thought. *Old MacDonald had an Affair, ee i ee i oh,* sang the worm in his brain, *And on his knees he had a Frau* . . . There were more verses, barrack-room verses as filthy and as memorable as the ones his comrades composed to hymn tunes in the trenches. In his own bastard ditty he took no pride, rather the opposite. Ramsay Mac was a widower, his wife had died when the children were only young, and he had been on his own for years. Knight and his Secret Service paymaster were trying to engineer a scandal, but what on God's earth was wrong with him taking another woman?

He reached into the pocket of his old wool jacket for the photograph Fletcher had given him and held it on his knee. She didn't look like a woman who expected to be paid for sex, and Mac was not the sort of man to pay. Impossible to be certain of course. It was say one thing and do another with politicians. Who would have thought a liberal like Lloyd George would have consented to the waste of so many lives at Passchendaele. Mac had been against the war; Stewart respected him for that, and for more besides.

The train pulled into Dover Marine at a little before eleven. Stewart caught a glimpse of Fletcher's cream trilby and jacket on the platform and again at the shelter deck rail of the ship. Press-ganged during the war, the Channel packet, *Victoria,* had made a triumphant return to Civvy Street in a dazzling coat of white and blue. Twice she had brought Stewart home from France, once flat on his back, gazing at her smoke and the soaring falling gulls that trailed in her wake. From her stern as she steamed out of Dover he could see the hospital at the top of the cliff that they had taken him to. He had babbled like a madman for days, the rumble of battle trapped inside the bone wall of his fevered brain.

The approach to Calais brought back more memories. He rattled down the gangway behind a small party of posh Americans who were on an express tour of Europe. The lady in front of him was twittering about art and food and a fashionable boutique she was going to patronise in Paris. She had made instant 'friends' with a well-to-do honeymoon couple from London. 'Oh, my dear, the fun you'll have in Nice. It's marvellous at this time of the year.' The newly-weds were catching *le train bleu* to the south, where they were to rendezvous with 'Bertie's father's yacht' for three gay weeks cruising. 'Then we're going to stay with the Mosleys in Antibes. It will be heavenly. Britain's such a grey place these days,' the new bride explained.

Stewart shook out a cigarette, lit it and smoked it hard, until his head swam with nicotine and memories. Always there was the first fag off the boat, smoked in haste before the order was given to fall into line, shoulder rifle, shoulder pack, the Front train waiting in the Gare Maritime. Bertie's bride was giggling like a prepubescent girl, and the bloody old Americans were honking about their holiday. Shut up, he wanted to shout. Forget your fucking Old Master paintings, listen, will you! Can't you hear them? Picking up his rucksack, he limped into the station, like the lame boy trailing behind the rest in the tale of the magical piper of Hamelin. He was only thirty-seven, and yet he was a member of the last generation, the war generation, a living member of the lost generation, something akin to a ghost – the station ghosts. The smart people boarding at the head of the train were oblivious to their presence. Only those who had marched to the same tunes could hear them.

The couplings clanked and the engine took the strain. A stationmaster was blowing a whistle. *We're off boys!* Never in the time left to him would he be able to hear a whistle without flinching. First stop, St Omer, then on through the battlefield towns, Armentières, Béthune and Arras, where in the early hours of the morning those who were left behind like him would be forever haunted by soldiers marching, like the steady rhythm of a threshing machine winnowing chaff from the wheat.

A young mother in the seat opposite caught his eye then bent shyly to kiss her baby.

'Girl or boy?' he asked her in French.

'Florence,' she said.

'Ah, like my daughter.'

'You're going to Paris, Monsieur? Your daughter is in Paris?'

'No, but I hope to see her soon.'

'It's so difficult to be away from family.' She smiled sympathetically, then blushed and looked away. Her eyes were *charmante*. They reminded him of a whore he had slept with in Arras. The prostitute's face was lost to him now, but her eyes had been hazel-brown too. He turned to gaze out of the grimy window at the gentle chalk hills of Picardy, a little ashamed of the association. Not of the sex – a desperate drunken moment of forgetting – the sex was nothing: the killing was the sin.

The stations they were passing . . . what were they to Fletcher? History, that's all. He was not going to break into a cold sweat at the sound of a stationmaster's whistle. But the communist boyo, Owen, that the police had arrested at the barracks in Brecon was an old trench soldier. Stewart had stabbed him in the back all the same. Wasn't right, bloody hell, no. But the way he saw it, there were two ways to go in life now. The first was to campaign to honour the wartime pledge of a land fit for heroes. Owen had chosen that way, his four children conscripted to fight for the cause. Result: front line to breadline. Then there was the other way, the dog-eat-dog way. Not noble but getting by. Fletcher had introduced himself as a land-fit-for-heroes crusader too. Recovery of the PM's letters was in the interests of the working class, he said. How much he knew about the working classes wasn't clear. He was a politician so he could sound sincere. Not that it mattered really. It was fifteen pounds in the pocket that mattered.

3

Beneath its monumental glass canopy the Gare du Nord was its own season. Gazing from platform to concourse, the silhouettes of travellers waiting for their trains appeared to skip in and out of an autumn fog like actors in a poorly cranked piece of film. Here and there a shaft of sunshine forced its way through a broken pane to pierce the soot and steam with dancing light, the promise of summer, and freedom from the madhouse of the Paris evening rush hour.

On platform four Thomas Cook agents were waiting to transfer passengers to their hotels. A porter barged past Stewart, followed by three more. They reappeared a few minutes later with the American party's luggage on a cart and, with reckless determination, jostled and hectored their way towards the platform barrier. A peasant woman asked Stewart to lift her coffin-sized trunk from the carriage.

'My husband's meeting me,' she said.

'He isn't inside it then?' he replied, tapping the lid of the trunk.

Heads the length of the platform turned in alarm as she whooped and cackled with mirth. 'That's where the old fool deserves to be,' she gasped, dabbing her eyes with a tiny lace handkerchief.

Stewart joined the passengers shuffling to the barrier and presented his passport and ticket for inspection. The purpose of his visit? 'To see an old comrade.' The length of his stay? 'A few days only.'

There was no sign of a cream-coloured trilby on the concourse or in the queue for a taxicab outside the station. Fletcher was already on his way to a posh hotel in the Elysée district. Stewart was expected to find something more lowly near the bookshop the Austrian was using as a post box. The boyos down at the docks had done a proper number on him, and his right thigh was aching. In a kiosk opposite the station he bought a book of tickets and joined a queue for the tram.

The second-class car was crowded with hot and irritable people. A young woman watched him limp up the steps and, taking him for a disabled veteran, rose to offer her seat. He turned her down graciously and stood between the broad shoulders of brothers who worked in a wholesale market near the station. From the tram stop at the bottom of Boulevard de Sébastopol he limped into the Marais, where the shopkeepers were selling end-of-the-day produce at knock-down prices and packing the remainder of their goods away. There was a tailor's on the opposite side of the street from the bookshop and he pretended to be interested in the only suit on display in its window. Rabbi-black and cut in an old-fashioned way, it was not to his liking at all, but swaying to the right a reflection of the little *librairie* and the man he took for its proprietor appeared in the glass as if by magic. Monsieur Eli Weiss was clearing an eccentric assortment of goods from the tables in front of his shop. To judge by his name, his beard, the cut of his coat and his skullcap as he bent to pick up a kettle, he was a Jew, and so were most of his neighbours. Stewart was conscious that one of them – the tailor – was gazing at him suspiciously from the other side of the glass. He had spent war leave in bars and a boarding house of ill repute beneath the monstrous wedding-cake basilica of Sacré-Coeur that religious fanatics had built above Paris as an act of propitiation for its sins. Sober time had been spent visiting the sites but there had not been much of it, and none at all to spare for the Marais. The character of the district was a surprise and a challenge. Jews were pretty tight together. He had been on good terms with a few in the army and he knew his way around their streets in London. Why people got so worked up about them was a mystery. His old man had been a Jew-baiter – the hateful bastard – and Knight's fascist comrades . . . they were a bad lot too.

'Hey!' The tailor was standing at the door of his shop, a pocket watch in the palm of his hand. 'Are you coming inside or aren't you?' he asked.

'I'm new to the area,' he replied, 'I'm looking for a room. Can you help me?'

'Gey avek!' exclaimed the tailor. With a great jangling of bells he shut the door firmly and, taking up a position in the window, flapped his hands, shooing Stewart away from his shop. His performance caught the eye of passers-by – and of one of his neighbours. 'Hey you!' The bookseller had ventured from the pavement into the street and was beckoning to Stewart. 'Don't mind Rosen, he's always angry. Come. Come,' and he turned back to the table in front of his shop to gather another pile of books.

'Can I help you?' said Stewart.

'If you knew Madame Rosen . . .' said Weiss, with a shake of his head. 'You're looking for somewhere to stay, comrade? Where are you from?'

'Liège.'

'Liège? I know nothing about Liège. Here.' He thrust the books into Stewart's arms. 'And what brings you to Paris?'

'Work. That's what brings me here, Monsieur. I need a job.'

The bookseller nodded and the frizz of hair at the sides of his head rose and fell like an old spaniel's ears.

'Carry these inside for me, would you? As you can see, I'm closing.' He held the door open. 'So, you're looking for somewhere to stay?'

'Yes.'

'Put them anywhere. Over there', he said, pointing to a table in front of the window. 'On top, please. Doesn't matter how.' Stewart was struggling to balance his pile on an alp of books without precipitating an avalanche.

'Your name, Monsieur?' said Weiss.

'Dumont. Richard Dumont. And you must be Monsieur Weiss.'

The bookseller inclined his head in the affirmative. 'What do you do for a living, Monsieur Dumont?'

'Painter and decorator mostly, but I can turn my hand to anything in the building line.'

'And why do you want to live in the *Pletzel*?'

'The *Pletzel*? Is that what you call it? Someone told me I could rent a cheap room – I don't have much money – and perhaps find some work. But you ask a lot of questions, comrade. If you can help me, all well and good; if you can't I shall take my leave. I need to find somewhere to stay tonight.'

The old man smiled and held out his hand. 'Habit. I'm careful, you understand.'

Not careful enough. The bookseller had slipped up outside the shop with just one careless word: 'Comrade.' The character of the district, Weiss's skullcap and the knotted fringe that hung below his waistcoat suggested he was a religious Jew, not a socialist or a communist. But who knew more about exploitation, estrangement and persecution than the Jews? The word 'Comrade' was Stewart's entrée.

'It's best not to advertise, even in Paris.' Weiss pulled a face. 'I was a member in Vienna for a time, but that is another story: and you? Are you a member of the Party?'

'Since the war.'

Weiss nodded. 'Well, comrade, you need a room. Wait here will you.' He set off between his shelves for the back of the shop. Stewart picked up a novel from the table: *Germinal*. It was about a miners' strike and the poor. It didn't take him long to decide it was too bloody miserable for his children.

'You like Zola?' said Weiss, puffing towards him. 'A genius, a genius. But you look worried, comrade, don't be.' He held a scrap of paper between two tobacco-stained fingers. 'I have this for you'. His nails were like talons. If there had ever been a Madame Weiss she was surely in the Hebrews' heaven. 'Here, here. Take!'

'What is it, Comrade?'

'Didn't I say?' He thrust the paper at Stewart. 'This place has a cheap room. Thirty-five francs a week. One meal a day. Here, here. You have a map? Good.' He had written the address in a spidery hand:

Madame Bilbaut, 34 rue Vieille du Temple.

'Look for the courtyard between Rosenberg the baker's and . . . I forget. But you have a map, you say.'

'Thank you, Monsieur.'

'Comrade, please.'

'Thank you, comrade.'

'You will come to our meeting, won't you? Not an official meeting you understand, just friends. Comrades. Tomorrow at half past seven.' With that the old man ushered him out to the street. 'Don't forget: half past seven.'

4

Madame Bilbaut had left many years ago. Her *pension* at 34 rue Vieille du Temple was run by a Polish Jew and his family. Monsieur Frenk was overweight and slovenly and so were his wife and three children. Affable enough, but not one of the socialist comrades.

'No, no. Monsieur . . .?'

'Dumont.'

'Weiss . . . Weiss is a *luftmensch* . . .'

'I don't understand.'

Frenk squinted at him suspiciously. 'A dreamer. *Luftmensch* is dreamer. Don't get me wrong. A good Jew, but his politics . . . You're either a communist or a Jew. One or the other.'

'A socialist?'

Frenk shook his head impatiently. 'No. No.' What did this goy know? 'He's a dreamer. A romantic. Communists hate Jews. They're no better than the tsars. *Paskudnik!*'

He spat the last word with venom and for a few seconds was too overwrought to speak. When he did, it was to present Stewart with the register and to ask for his *carte d'identité* granting permission to work.

'I only arrived today, Monsieur.'

Room 16 was on the second floor with a window overlooking the courtyard. The wallpaper was bubbling with damp, the floorboards grey with dust, and the curtain was drooping from a piece of string. There was a single bed with a horsehair mattress and thin grey sheets, a table, a chair, a wardrobe. The bathroom was at the end of the corridor and he was to share it with the other three rooms on his floor. No cooking; no parties; no politics; no prostitutes: Madame Bilbaut's was a respectable house, apparently. Run-down but respectable.

One of Frenk's daughters brought him a trench meal of dumplings in a thin meat sauce, and he polished it off without tasting, then he lay on the bed, smoked a cigarette and watched the sun work its way down the wall. How fortunate to have made a connection with Eli Weiss so quickly. What was it Frenk had called him? A *luftmensch*. Maybe, maybe, but a decent human being too. To have lived for sixty-five years or more, an exile, a Jew, to have lived with the prejudice of others, the old blood libel trope, the world conspiracy lie, and still be prepared to welcome a stranger, a gentile, find him a roof, invite him to return to his shop, well . . . that old man was surely at peace with himself. Ha! Stewart closed his eyes and shook his head like a drunk struggling to see clearly. He was going soft. 'Bugger it,' he muttered, and a few seconds later, 'bugger it' again. Because when he opened his eyes the world was still blurred at the edges. Old man Weiss was troublingly decent . . . he was a menace.

7

3 June 1930

Fletcher's room at the Métropole was quiet and comfortable; he enjoyed a fine dinner of filet mignon, accompanied by a bottle of Chateau Pavie – the 1921 was spectacular – and tumbled into bed confident he would sleep like a baby. But come the dawn he was still turning, his top sheet twisted about his chest and through his legs, cascading from the bed to the floor, a fiendish knot only a sailor of his experience could tie. Shaved, bathed and soberly dressed, he made his way down to breakfast in a filthy temper. Really, what was this affair of the prime minister's?

He had taken a ship around the Horn in a storm, her deck shuddering as she reached for the peak of one wave, only to slide into a seething trough before the next. He had fought the enemy in the Channel when all was smoke and confusion: these things he had done and more. To allow the PM's letters to eat at him was maddening. Recover the damned things and be done with it, and if he was lucky Admiral Sinclair would be none the wiser.

Only first he had to shore up his cover story, and to that end he had arranged to meet his contact at the Bureau to talk of communism, cooperation, fascism and the rise of an upstart corporal in Germany called Hitler. To talk, in fact, about anyone and anything that might paint a gloss on his visit.

Captain Toussaint was a genial fellow, but with the cunning

of a fox. His grand office on the boulevard des Invalides smelt of good coffee and strong tobacco, and from its tall windows there was an impressive view of the veterans' hospital and church where Napoleon Bonaparte lay in his red porphyry sarcophagus. Fletcher felt a pang of envy; intelligence-gathering was a hole-in-the-wall sort of business, but was it necessary for those in London who conducted it to occupy one?

'You've seen his tomb?' said Toussaint, as they gazed from a window at Les Invalides. 'Very fine, no? His funeral was quite an occasion.'

'Napoleon?'

Toussaint laughed. 'Do I look that old, Commander? Foch! Marshal Foch. He died last year.'

'Of course, Marshal Foch.' Supreme Allied Commander in the final months of the Great War: what a fool. He had seen it in the papers. Foch had been buried alongside Bony. 'I was in the navy,' he said, weakly.

Toussaint smirked. 'Ah.'

They shared a glass of wine – '*pourquoi pas?*' – and Fletcher asked him to dinner at Maxim's. Then they discussed a new security arrangement, a coded exchange, communists in the colonies and '*une époque difficile.*' They agreed that sharing was in the interests of both their countries. It was all very amicable. But it was the fox's smile rather than the warmth of his words that made an impression on Fletcher.

'You are staying a few days in Paris, Commander?' enquired the Frenchman, when Fletcher rose to leave. 'At the Metropole, *n'est-ce pas?*' The Bureau kept an eye on its friends as well as its enemies.

Fletcher gazed at its elegant white stone front from a taxicab and wondered whether it would have been wiser not to have set foot inside. Coffee, cigarettes, a chat about communist spies, 'really, *mon ami*'? In attempting to allay suspicion in London he was arousing it in Paris.

The Pont de Passy was closed, the traffic on the embankment at a standstill, and by the time Fletcher's driver had found his way across the river it was almost midday. Mr Jimmy Thomas, lord privy seal, had telephoned the hotel and left a message: 'ring me back soonest.' Well, Mr Thomas could go hang. Of more immediate concern to him was a blue telegram card – a *petit bleu* – sent from a post office in the city and delivered by its pneumatic tube network. Stewart had written a time and a place in pencil and nothing else:

1600 Eglise St Roch.

Fletcher had visited the church on his honeymoon: modest baroque exterior, marble and gold interior. The new Mrs Fletcher had dragged him to a piano recital by a Polish chap called Hofmann. A sensation, the newspapers and Elspeth Fletcher said, but it had not been her husband's idea of a honeymoon evening at all. He would take lunch, then walk to the church through the Tuileries Garden and lose any unwelcome company he might collect on the way between its parterres.

2

From beneath the canopy of a kiosk, Stewart watched Fletcher climb the steps of the church, consult his guidebook, and then disappear inside. Satisfied no one was dogging his steps, Stewart put the newspaper he had been hiding behind back on the stand and bought some cigarettes. Two francs, fifty! Prices were rising in Paris. Bloody Wall Street was to blame for that too.

The church was, as always, a place of last resort, convenient, cool and empty. There was the customary collection of suffering saints, the customary smell of dampness and incense piety. Fletcher's guidebook would certainly have something to say

Andrew Williams

about the impressive painting of the Virgin in triumph in the dome. Stewart could hear the stop, start, shuffle and start of his footsteps as he drifted from chapel to chapel. He sounded a little flat-footed, as if the years of struggling across wet and heaving decks in the navy had left their mark on his gait. Stewart caught up with him at the crossing. He was standing in a puddle of red light like a Montmartre streetwalker, a frown hovering between his thick eyebrows.

'Ah, so you *are* here,' he said, coolly. 'Where shall we go?'

'Why not 'ere?' Stewart nodded towards a side chapel. 'Pretend you want to confess.'

'To you, Stewart!'

They settled on a bench before the altar of Saint Clotilde. The saint appeared in the altarpiece as a plain full-figured young woman, borne aloft on a cloud by golden-haired cherubim.

'Have you seen her?' said Fletcher.

Stewart snorted. 'No, I haven't.'

'What about the bookshop?'

'Old man Weiss, yes. I'm invited to a meeting at the shop this evening. He's a socialist . . . like you, comrade.'

Fletcher ignored his sardonic smile. 'Frau Forster may be there.'

'Do you know the Marais, Commander? Asking questions isn't easy. There are lots of Jews from the East. Short of running into her . . . But she visits the shop to pick up letters, so you should send one. Offer to meet her. And send someone to deliver your letter to the bookshop between six thirty and seven this evening.'

'She wants money, it should be a simple exchange.'

'If it *is* about the money. It's a pity you know so little about her.'

'Yes, I'll see what I can do about that.' Fletcher got to his feet. 'How do I contact you?'

Stewart took a slip of paper from his pocket. 'My name and address. I'm Dumont. Call yourself LeClerc. Monsieur Dumont is looking for work, so . . .'

'A job for Dumont.' Fletcher offered his hand. 'Well, Monsieur Dumont, I imagine you'll want to stay and say a prayer for success.'

3

The British Embassy was a spectacularly plush affair, a few doors down from the president of the Republic's own palace. An impecunious member of the Bonaparte family had relinquished her home to the British and a long line of titled diplomats had lived and entertained in imperial splendour there ever since.

'But we can avoid the ambassador, if we don't go through the garden,' said Drysdale. 'He's hosting a drinks party for deputies from the National Assembly.'

Station chief in Paris was a cushy posting, perfect for an older man, a family man with connections, someone who enjoyed the cocktail party set: Sidney Drysdale was not that man. He was young, ambitious, and eager for somewhere 'livelier', like Moscow or Berlin. Fletcher liked Drysdale but his host at the Embassy did not, it seemed. The ambassador had exiled him to rooms beneath the roof and, like the Embassy pigeons, he was tolerated as long as he avoided making a mess. The station office windows overlooked the gardens where the French deputies were twittering about politics and sipping *entente cordiale* champagne.

'Sorry it's untidy', he said, sweeping papers from his desk into a drawer. 'Do sit down, Commander.'

'Can you find someone to deliver a letter?'

'Of course, of course.'

Fletcher waited for him to leave to make the necessary arrangements, then drawing his chair to the desk he took paper and wrote:

Dear Madame Forster

I am charged with responsibility for settling this matter of the correspondence in your possession. I feel sure we can reach an amicable arrangement. A swift resolution would, I hope you agree, be in the interests of both parties. I suggest we meet tomorrow afternoon in a discreet location of your choice, perhaps a park or a gallery or a church. A message can be left for me at the Métropole Hotel, rue de Chaillot. I believe I will be able to . . .

He smiled and lifted his pen from the paper: 'satisfy' wouldn't do.

. . . compensate you for the loss of the letters.
   Yours etc. etc.

He hoped his note was imprecise enough to be defensible if it came into the possession of a newspaper or the Bureau, or – God forbid – Admiral Sinclair. Disconcertingly, he heard a peal of laughter in the garden below.

4

'Monsieur Dupont! You're early,' grumbled Weiss, 'I said come at seven!'

Stewart had dragged the old man from the rear of his shop and his supper of fish and fried potatoes. 'It's *Dumont*, comrade. Richard *Dumont*. Please, finish your meal. I'll look at some of your books.'

'The politics section is half way along,' he said, gesturing to the third row. 'Have you read Fourier?'

No, Stewart had no knowledge of Fourier, nor did he wish to have. French fiction interested him more because it was at the front of the shop where he could keep an eye on the living breathing world of the street. Full of life during the day, of mothers shopping with children, a cheesemaker with tethered goats, an old Hungarian flower seller who pressed him to buy a bouquet, and a one-legged veteran festooned with broom heads at two francs apiece. Quiet now though, with only a trickle of working men hurrying to whatever small piece of the *Pletzel* they could afford to call home. Yes, he had spent the day exploring the district in the faint hope of running across her. Coffee at Kohn's cafe, lunch near the rue Pavée synagogue, and his landlord, Frenk, had found a man who was willing to give him a job: 'even though you're a goy.' Work was his story, a route into any business or lodging house, but it wasn't easy to ask questions without arousing suspicion. The bookseller was still his best hope.

A middle-aged man with a walrus moustache appeared in front of his shop and stooped low to slide Fletcher's letter through the flap in the door. Task complete, postman genie was gone in a jiffy, sucked by some strange magic perhaps into one of the lamps or copper kettles on display in the window. 18.45. Bang on time. There on the mat, Fletcher's letter, waiting for some kind soul to pick it up and carry it to the back of the shop.

Weiss was balancing a plate of grey fish patties on his knees, a fork in his right hand and a book in his left.

'Delivered in person.' Stewart lifted the letter to show him. 'Madame Forster, care of your shop: is it a mistake?'

'Not your business.' He almost lost his plate in his haste to rise. '*Verdammt*! Let me have it, will you.'

'Don't get excited, comrade!'

Weiss pinched it from him with greasy fingers, glanced at the name and the address and slipped it into his jacket pocket. 'You saw who left it?' Their eyes met, Weiss's rheumy and narrow with suspicion.

'As it happens, I did, but only out of the corner of my eye. A big bloke with a big moustache.' He painted it on his face with a forefinger. 'About forty-five. Smartly dressed.' He shrugged. 'That's all. It was over in a flash.'

Weiss considered this with his chin on his chest, and then raised it with an embarrassed smile. 'Sorry, Dupont.'

'Don't give it a thought, comrade, everyone has the right to a private life.'

He looked puzzled – 'You mean . . .?' – then he chuckled – '. . . me? With Frau Forster? Ha!' – and for a few seconds he couldn't speak for laughing. 'Comrade, thank you.' From somewhere about his person he produced a large handkerchief and dabbed his eyes. 'Ah, the thought! She is a lady, you know. Kind. Generous. I'm proud to be her friend.' He took the letter from his waistcoat. 'No, this is a small favour, that's all.'

'A forwarding address for Madame . . .?'

'Forster.'

'Madame Forster picks up her post here?'

'Sometimes,' he said, slipping the envelope back in his pocket.

'She will be at the meeting tonight?'

'No.'

'Oh well. I don't suppose the letter's urgent.'

'Perhaps not,' he said, glancing wistfully at the remains of his gefilte fish, 'but perhaps yes. There is something I must do before the others arrive. It will take me no more than a few minutes. You must excuse me.'

'If you're happy to let me browse, my friend . . .' Stewart turned towards the front of the shop. 'Or is it something I can do for you? It's your meeting, perhaps you should stay here.'

'No, no,' the old man said as he followed Stewart to the door. 'It's nothing. I must speak with Rosen the tailor, but I'll be back in two minutes.' He sounded flustered.

'All right, comrade.' Stewart held the door open and watched him scuttle across the street.

Was Forster living above the tailor's? No. The tailor was another intermediary. Stewart took a step from the window to avoid arousing suspicion and drew another book from a shelf. The tailor's hands were pressed to his cheeks. He was one of those little men who live their lives close to boiling point. Weiss was trying to reason with him and fumbling in his waistcoat – ah! – for money – a pecuniary inducement – and they must have agreed upon a price because the tailor's hands dropped to his sides. A boy of about eight – his son, to judge by his sallow features – appeared on the doorstep with his boots. He tied his laces, Weiss gave him the letter, and off he went, stumbling, almost falling, in his haste to carry out his charge.

The bookseller hurried back to his shop. 'Done,' he gasped, bending forward to catch his breath. 'That's that. Now, I see you've found something you like.'

'Oh, just *The Hunchback of Notre Dame*.'

'There is no "just" about it my friend. No, no,' he said with feeling, 'What can't that story teach us about human nature? The persecution of the hunchback . . . The thought of it . . .' He seemed close to tears. 'Victor Hugo was a remarkable human being!'

'Yes,' said Stewart, who had read nothing by him.

'Ah, look,' said Weiss, 'Comrade Martinez.' A young man in a light brown suit and collarless shirt had appeared at the door. 'Come in, come in, let me introduce you. This is Comrade Dupont—'

'It's *Dumont*. Richard Dumont.'

'. . . Comrade Dumont, from Liège.'

'Comrade.' Martinez offered his hand.

'Let's sit,' said Weiss, 'the others will be here soon. We might have some wine.'

'After you,' said Stewart. 'I'll return the hunchback to his shelf.' Good old Victor Hugo. A classic, no doubt, but it was the messenger boy that concerned him, because he was back in the street already. Stewart watched him trail across the bookshop window, in and out of view, hiding in the Hebrew and Latin letters pasted to the glass. The little beggar had been away no more than five minutes. He would have run to Forster's as fast as his legs could carry him, but he was taking his time to walk home. One thing was for certain, Madame was living close by, something like two or three minutes' fast walk from the bookshop – no more than three. That was progress!

The comrades assembled in a little circle at the back of the shop. Martinez and two student friends who were hot for the barricades, Goldenberg, an elderly refugee from 'the corrupt Soviet system,' and Kogan, another Russian émigré, who said nothing all evening except 'another glass of wine please, comrade.' They talked about the education of the proletariat and the threat to working people posed by a false consciousness. No one invited the only proletarian in the circle to speak. Like Marx, like Lenin, they knew best. Stewart let them ramble on, nodding from time to time and interjecting *voilà!* and *en effet* to demonstrate he was still breathing. Madame Forster was mentioned only once.

'Where's Kristina tonight?'

'Busy,' said Weiss, pulling anxiously at the tip of his beard. 'This is the second week . . .'

'She's teaching.'

That their friend, Madame Forster, was making a living that way was common knowledge.

'I'm sure next week . . .' said Weiss.

Kogan was the first to leave them, perhaps to search for more wine. The students and Martinez left together, the fire still burning in their bellies. 'Shush, comrades, the neighbours!' whispered Weiss. 'You'll wake their children.'

Stewart was the last to say goodbye, 'and thank you for making a stranger welcome, comrade.'

'You'll come again, Monsieur Dupont?' Was the old man lonely? He was certainly no revolutionary. He had spoken on three or four occasions only, to urge consideration, moderation, respect. No Robespierre, no Lenin, Eli Weiss; he still loved his old God.

'Of course I'll come again, Eli,' said Stewart, with a hand to the door. 'You've been very kind. First the lodging house, then tonight.' He paused. 'I wonder is it too much to ask another favour . . . Am I presuming too much on your generosity?'

'Monsieur Dupont, speak!' he said. 'Ask!'

'Can I give your bookshop as a correspondence address, too? You know I'm looking for work?'

Weiss frowned. 'What about Frenk's *pension*?'

'It's good enough, thank you, but I may have to move, and now we're comrades . . . A more reliable correspondence address would be helpful for a week or so. If I could . . . But it's an imposition. Pardon me, Monsieur.'

'No, no. It's all right. Just a week?'

'Until I find a job, yes. Of course I'll pay to have letters delivered to me. Perhaps the boy across the way . . .?'

'Ezra.'

'Is that his name? Yes, Ezra. Well, I can't thank you enough, Monsieur, really I can't,' he said – and he meant it too.

It was slickly done. He was leaving the bookshop with a certain sense of pride. How peculiar that he should still feel that way after so many years of professional duplicity. He watched Weiss bolt the bookshop door, wave to him and move away from the window. The poor bugger was worn out by the confidence and callousness of his young comrades and their earnest talk of revolution – and me, he thought. Patting myself on the back for deceiving a generous old soul. Really? What a triumph!

At the corner of rue des Rosiers he turned to look back at the little *librairie*. There was a dim light upstairs in what he took to be Weiss's bedroom. A moment later he appeared at the open window and wrestled with the curtains. They shivered in the draught and the chink of light he left in them flickered like a candle. Funny, but it put Stewart in mind of a hymn he used to sing as a boy: *Lead kindly light amid the encircling gloom*. Perhaps the old Jew was a kindly light. You could view the world like Eli Weiss or you could view it like . . . like Dumont. Christ! He turned from the bookshop and into the next street. He was going to walk or drink and, with luck, by the time he was ready for bed he would be either too tired or too drunk to waste any more time on such thoughts.

8

4 June 1930

LOITERING LIKE A thief in a smart street in Kensington was not an easy thing to do at any time of day. Morton was a very private man and he would be furious in his quiet way if he knew one of his agents was watching his home. But on fine mornings he was in the habit of walking to the office and it was Knight's intention to follow him and engineer an accidental meeting. If the major turned right at the top of Beaufort Gardens his route would take him to Hyde Park and Buckingham Palace; left, through Belgravia.

'Major? Is that you?' – Knight rehearsed his opening lines in his head – 'yes, quite a coincidence . . . that's right, not far. I live on Sloane Street.' In a modest apartment compared to Morton's six-storey house, with its fancy white stucco portico and window mouldings, its thick silk curtains and crystal chandeliers. Private means, of course.

Eight o'clock sharp, there he was at the door in his customary dark suit and artillery tie, a light mac in the crook of his arm, pausing on the steps to adjust his trilby. Would he turn left or to the right? He turned to the left, and for a man with a bullet only an inch from his heart he was setting a cracking pace.

Knight overhauled him in Eaton Square. 'Major? Is that you?'
'Knight.' He turned with a tight smile. 'Where did you spring from?'

'Sloane Street. My flat—'

'Ah. So this is a coincidence?'

'Not entirely. Can we talk?'

'What do you mean by "not entirely"?'

'I've spoken to my . . . *our* man in Paris.'

'I see. And it can't wait? This is highly irregular. It wouldn't do for us to be seen together.'

'No, I'm afraid it can't wait: Agent Frenchie telephoned me this morning. Shall we walk?'

'We better! Can't stand here: Neville Chamberlain lives at number thirty-seven.'

Morton led the way, Knight a few steps behind like a concubine or cup-bearer: my God, the arrogance of the man! They walked south towards the river, until they crossed a bridge over train track from Victoria. 'Eccleston Square,' said Morton, 'this will do.' There was a communal garden in the centre of the square with a thick screen of mature trees and shrubs. The path through it was hidden from all but the topmost windows of the elegant white terraces. 'So,' said Morton, 'what is this about Frenchie?'

'He says Fletcher's meeting MacDonald's *Frau*. He's hoping to secure the letters today.'

'Then Frenchie must make contact with her first. I hope you told him that.'

'Of course. And he's trying.'

'You *do* trust him, don't you?'

Knight hesitated. 'As much as I trust any of them. He's the right man for this job.'

Morton touched his elbow. 'Wait a minute.' An elderly lady was sitting on a bench a few yards ahead of them, a tiny arthritic dog at her feet. They passed her with smiles and a 'good morning.' 'But to state the obvious,' said Morton when they were out of earshot, 'we don't want Fletcher to acquire the letters.'

'We'll need to send Frenchie the money.'

'Of course, and our friends are willing to pay. He must find her and make an offer.'

'He may have to steal them from Fletcher.'

'If Fletcher secures them first, yes, of course, he must do whatever he needs to do. Is that clear?'

'Perfectly.'

'Good.' Morton stopped and turned so sharply he sent a shower of loose gravel pattering into a border at the edge of the path. 'Then there's something else I want to say' – his eyes almost disappeared in a frown – 'don't come to my house again unless I invite you. Do you understand?'

Knight flushed with embarrassment. 'If I had your home telephone number . . .'

Morton didn't reply. The meeting was over. Terminated. It was bloody high-handed of him, bloody insulting, turning his back, striding along the path to the gate. Knight was sure he had no reason to apologise. All the same, he had the uneasy feeling his credibility with Morton and the Service was resting on the shoulders of his agent in Paris.

2

At about the same time, Stewart was gazing into the courtyard below his room at Bilbaut's to where the lady of the house was berating her daughters in a stentorian voice, legs apart like the Colossus, hands on her broad hips – *Oy vey* – what a bitch. He picked up his ashtray and carried it from the window ledge to the bed with half a thought to bury his thumping head in the pillow. He had risen with a hangover and walked to a post office a decent distance from the *Pletzel* to send a telegram card to Dumont care of the bookshop. An imaginary Madame le Brun was willing to pay him to paint her cafe. Would the bookseller be suspicious? The old man had only agreed to accept his post the evening before.

He had slipped the *carte bleue* across the counter with a franc fifty, then telephoned Knight from a booth in the post office. 'You've got to prevent her meeting Fletcher!' Knight had said. 'If she gives him the letters, everything becomes complicated.' He had sounded uncharacteristically anxious. 'I have it in hand,' Stewart assured him, 'trust me' on the tip of his tongue. Ha! No one with any sense would trust a man who made his living as a spy. But Knight was right, he had to gamble. Eli Weiss would have the *carte bleue* by now: would he send the tailor's son?

'Monsieur Dumont? Are you there?' The master of the house was at the door. 'I have a letter for you. Ah, Monsieur . . .' He was leaning against the wall. 'The stairs . . . it's a long way up.'

'Where's the boy?' said Stewart.

'You mean the tailor's son? No, no, it came in the ordinary way.'

'I see. Well, thank you, Monsieur Frenk.' The card was speckled with his sweat. 'Remember, when the boy comes, I need to speak to him.'

'Ezra.'

'Yes, Ezra. Send him up. That will save you climbing the stairs.'

The telegram card was from Fletcher. The meeting with Mac's tart was confirmed: *Church of Saint-Paul-Saint-Louis.* Stewart was to *observe and follow.* Settling at the table, he opened his copy of Baedeker and leafed through to the pink maps at the back of the guide. On the map of the Marais he had drawn a circle. The tailor's shop was at the bottom of the circle and its circumference was his estimate of how far a small boy in big boots could run in three minutes. Forster was living somewhere inside that circle, and the church she had chosen for her meeting with Fletcher was no more than two minutes' walk beyond its perimeter. She was living close enough to the church to be woken by its bells on Sunday. Arranging to meet a secret agent on the doorstep was a reckless thing to do. She must have been thinking of the money. Three quarters of a million francs was a very tidy sum and she would be anxious to carry it to a safe place as soon as possible.

'Well, let's see how anxious,' he muttered, reaching into his knapsack for a pen and paper. He needed only two minutes to compose two lines, which he sealed in a coffee-stained envelope. Mac would have written his *billets-doux* on something finer, no doubt. Job done, he folded the map of the Marais back in the guide and slipped the envelope between its pages. Frenk was clumping up the old oak stair again, this time with someone lighter of foot in tow. Stewart had the door open before he could knock. 'You must be Ezra,' he said to the boy. 'Come in, come in. No, not you, Monsieur.'

Frenk placed his fat hands on the boy's shoulders. 'I'm looking after him.'

'This is confidential.' Stewart leant forward and grabbed the sleeve of his jacket. 'Monsieur Weiss sent you with a letter for me? I'm going to pay you to deliver another.' The boy was staring at Stewart with rabbit eyes. 'Don't worry, I don't bite; not you, at least,' he said, 'but you, Monsieur, perhaps.' Frenk opened his mouth as if to protest, but – 'No!' – Stewart held up his hand – 'goodbye, Monsieur' – and he shut the door in his landlord's face.

'Now my young friend, the letter,' he said, 'where is it?'

Ezra fished the *petit bleu* out of his shorts. 'Excellent. How much do I owe you? Sit down. Sit at the table.'

'A franc,' said the boy. His brown eyes flitted round the room, window to rickety table, cupboard, bed, and to Stewart's feet. He was all knees and elbows like a badly strung puppet, and his shorts, shirt and jacket were too big for him. They were probably a brother's cast-offs.

'A franc, you say. Is that what Madame Forster pays you?'
Ezra nodded.

'A franc. All right, and another for your trouble: two francs.
You'll be able to keep one for yourself now. Here!' He slapped
them on the table, then sank to the edge of the bed. 'Take them
and leave the letter there.'

'Thank you, Monsieur.' The boy shuffled towards the table.

'Can you read, Ezra?'

'Yes, of course!' he said, indignantly. 'I read Yiddish, Hebrew
and a little French.'

'Good, good, clever boy. Well, you see there's another letter
in this book. It's addressed to my friend, Madame Forster. Will
you take it to her for me, for say, another two francs? And
if you don't tell your papa, you'll be able to keep them both.
It's not far, is it? Rue . . . I've forgotten. Is it rue Pavée?'

'No.'

'Ah. Remind me, will you.'

Ezra looked doubtful. He needed coaxing, some honey, and
Stewart was about to pour some more when the little beggar
blurted out, 'five!'

'Five? Five francs to deliver a letter!' Little boy? Little
monster more like. Tongue-tied reticent Ezra . . . what had
happened to him? Gone! His place was taken by Ezra the
capitalist and businessman-to-be.

'All right,' said Stewart, taking a five-franc note from his
pocket; 'but it's our secret.' He placed the note on the envelope
and slid them both across the table. 'Do you understand?'

Ezra nodded.

'Good. Where does she live?'

'Hôtel du Printemps. Rue Ferdinand Duval.'

The boy's fingers crept across the table and were closing
round the money when Stewart caught him by the wrist. 'Please,
don't hurt me,' he squealed, 'please!'

'Our secret, Ezra. Remember? Don't tell Monsieur Weiss; don't tell your father.'

'No,' he jabbered. 'I promise.'

'Good.' Stewart patted his cheek. 'Thank you. Do this well and I may have more work for you. All right, go.'

The boy needed no encouragement.

3

Fat raindrops burst on the steps and speckled Fletcher's linen jacket as he hurried to the door of Saint-Paul-Saint-Louis. A minute later and he would have been soaked to the skin. Shoppers in busy rue Saint Antoine were racing up the steps behind him or scurrying for the shelter of street awnings. In a cafe opposite the church, Dick Stewart at a window, with cigarettes and a coffee. When Madame Forster left the church with her money he was to follow her to her lodgings. Well, they couldn't trust her, could they? There was no way of telling what they were buying. A woman like that, with the morals of a polecat . . . what was to prevent her keeping some of the prime minister's letters and coming back for more? A profitable business blackmail; three quarters of a million francs profitable.

The fancy baroque clock above the ceremonial door struck three. Was Madame inside on her knees? She should be! Three o'clock was the time she had stipulated in her note. But there were so many refugees from the rain streaming into the church, shaking umbrellas, genuflecting, sliding on to benches, it was going to be difficult to find her. Fletcher loitered at the door for a few minutes, then ambled round the church, gazing like a pervert at women with their heads bowed in prayer. Her choice the church; where was she hiding?

The front rolled past, the sun streamed through clerestory windows into the nave, and the foul-weather faithful gathered their shopping and made their way out, leaving the church in the custody of its widows and priests once again. Fletcher found a chair in a side chapel with a view of the door, the briefcase with the money between his knees. A sleek young sacristan in a black cassock rustled the length of the nave to wrestle with the lock of a donations box. Straining over the lid, he reminded Fletcher of a crow picking at a carcass. The baroque clock chimed the half-hour and then another quarter. My God, thought Fletcher, the bitch has left me in the lurch.

He was on the point of rising when Stewart entered the church cap in hand, dipped his fingers in the holy water and crossed himself with a convincing air of devotion. Spying Fletcher he made his way into the side chapel, lit a candle from one of the many that were flickering at the feet of a saint and pressed it on to a spike.

'If that's for luck,' said Fletcher, 'it's too late, she isn't coming now.'

'For my wife,' said Stewart, staring at the candle.

'Your wife? Is she a Roman?'

'She's dead.'

'Oh. I didn't know.'

'Well, you wouldn't.' He glanced sideways at Fletcher. 'Didn't you light one?'

'Mumbo-jumbo. We're wasting time here.'

'Then let's go somewhere less public.'

They settled on the south transept, and found chairs in front of a white marble altar with a statue of the suffering Christ. A pigeon was loose in the dome and the tortured beat of its wings rippled through the body of the church like a stone in still water.

'Do you know where she's living?'

Stewart pulled a face. 'Not yet.'

'We need to know more. Friends in Paris, contacts . . . Is she talking to a newspaper? What about the bookseller? I should speak to him.'

'He'll tell you nothing.'

'*You* ask him where she lives then.'

'Send Forster another letter.'

'You don't understand, Stewart, we need to resolve this quickly. I *must* speak to her.'

'I know! I'm doing my best, Commander.'

Fletcher half-turned to stare at him.

'What?' said Stewart. 'Look, it's Wednesday; we only arrived on Monday.'

He seemed genuinely aggrieved, which only proved he was good at his job. He was a spy and, no doubt, a consummate liar, and on fifteen pounds a week plus expenses, what possible incentive did he have to wrap things up quickly. 'Look, if we can bring this to a satisfactory conclusion before the weekend, Stewart, I'll pay you a bonus.'

'How much?'

'Twenty. That's thirty-five for the week.'

Stewart nodded. 'Well, thank you. I'll do my best.' He got to his feet and began to edge his way out between chairs. 'Better get on with it then.'

'Hey, wait,' said Fletcher, 'when can I expect to hear from you?'

4

They were waiting at the Spey Bay course to photograph the Prime Minister dressed in tweed plus fours and persecuting a ball. The trick was to swing with confidence and style, then the caption in the one or two newspapers Labour could count on might be 'Man of Vigour.' The rest were bound to print something snide, perhaps 'PM on Holiday in Scotland as Crisis Deepens.' Malcolm and Ishbel were there to compete, and to pose for a family picture. They watched him struggling with a stiff onshore breeze. God knows where his ball came to earth. 'Oh, rotten luck, Father,' said Ishbel, for the benefit of the hacks. When they left he took the shot again.

Matches with Malcolm and Ishbel were keenly fought. Yes, they talked of the Labour Party and government policy but only as far as the sixth hole, which he managed with a magnificent putt for par. He handed his club to the caddy with 'I say' and 'Good shot, Pa' ringing in his ears; and as he walked towards the next tee he felt the web of anxieties that had ensnared him in London loosen a little, drawn and borne away on the breeze.

Malcolm drove him home by the churchyard where his Margaret was buried and where he would be laid to rest in time too. They held hands at the foot of her grave and he spoke to her silently, asking for understanding, for forgiveness, for love, even though he knew she was lost to him for ever. The last few miles to Lossiemouth he spent in contemplative silence, happy and thankful for the day.

The London newspapers had nothing good to say about 'Lossie'. 'Remote and insular,' 'gaunt and grey,' was how they presented the town to the world. Aye, well, maybe to an outsider, but the prospect of the harbour from his home and the sweep of the Moray coast was cut into his heart. Neighbours were waiting outside his house to greet him with gentle applause. He smiled, waved, shouted, 'Good day to you all.' The same people had painted 'traitor' on his wall during the war, and they would probably turn against him again if the newspapers managed to acquire his letters to Kristina Forster. Pulling the bastard son of a ploughboy from his pedestal would be great sport even in Lossiemouth. But not today, not after a glorious few hours on the golf course, with *the hills of home before us and the purple o' the heather.*

His housekeeper was whistling in the parlour. 'We're home, Mhairi,' he shouted. 'My, what a spread! How kind you are.'

'Sit yersel doun, sir, and I'll fetch ye a cup o' tea.'

In the modest parlour of his modest house, his favourite chair was set to the right of the range. 'Join me, Mhairi, my dear.'

'Naw, a will nae, sir.' She lifted a kettle from the range to hot the teapot, and then she cut him a slice of fruit cake.

'Aw, thank you, thank you,' he said, taking the plate from her. 'Is that *The Times*?'

'It came wi' the government despatch box frae Lunnon, sir.'

The lead story was a report on Conservative Party leader Stanley Baldwin's address to a large public meeting. He had plenty to say about the economic plight of the country under Labour but offered no policy of his own, which was hardly surprising since he had none. Elsewhere on the front page there was a report on the reshuffle, with Jimmy Thomas moving to dominion affairs, and a new committee for 'solving the unemployment problem'. Solving the problem!

'Father!' Ishbel was standing at the parlour door.

'I beg your pardon, my dear.'

'Jimmy Thomas is on the telephone.'

'Oh?' he said, closing the paper.

'He says it's urgent. Shall I take your tea through to the study?'

'It's always urgent, my dear.'

The stack of papers on his desk appeared to have grown six inches while he was on the golf course. The 'Hillocks' was a retreat, a holiday home, his study only a boxroom, a place of last resort. A despatch box was open on a chair where he could reach it, and there was space at a corner table for a secretary with a typewriter. When he was obliged to speak to London he sat in front of the fireplace with the telephone on top of the mantelpiece.

'Your tea.' Ishbel cleared a space for his cup. 'Is there anything else I can fetch you?'

He shook his head and smiled at her fondly.

'Prime Minister?' London sounded every mile of six hundred away. 'Prime Minister, I've spoken to Reggie Fletcher.'

He closed his eyes and stifled a groan.

'Did you 'ear me, Prime Minister?'

'Yes, Jimmy, yes I heard you.'

'He's made contact with 'er. She agreed to meet him, and then she didn't show up. He's worried. He wants to know what sort of woman he's dealing with.'

'I would have thought that was obvious; she's extorting money from me, Jimmy.'

'I mean he needs something concrete,' said Thomas irritably. 'Family. Friends. As much of 'er history as you can remember. He wants to be sure she's workin' alone. He wants to be sure she isn't a spy.'

'Och away. No, Jimmy. Look, do you think Fletcher is up to it?'

'Yes, I think so.'

'You don't sound sure.'

''Ee says foreigners use women for this sort of thing all the time. Pardon me, Chief, but for the sake of the country—'

'If he really thinks it's a possibility . . .'

'He's trying to find her, and 'ee will, but if you can help . . .'

'All right, Jimmy. All right.'

They had met at a gathering of socialists in Paris in the autumn of 1926. In those days Kristina Forster had lived in great comfort. He was a guest at her house in Bern and at a hotel in Paris. She understood the delicacy of his position and had agreed to keep their relationship a secret. She was charming, cultivated, musical, and like many old empire people she spoke four languages.

What nationality was she? He was sure she was Austrian. She was about fifty. Her husband was dead, of course. No, he didn't know her maiden name. He had written to her three or four times a week and arranged for her to join him on his driving tour of Europe with Mosley, and then again in Cornwall. Was she a socialist? In a 'let's build a kinder world' sort of way. She was drawn to him by his stand against the war.

'That's all?' said Thomas.

'How can any of this help?'

He could almost hear Jimmy Thomas shrug. 'To be sure we know who we're dealing with, Chief.'

'All right. If I think of anything else I'll let you know.'

There were other memories; ones he didn't want to share. They came crowding back the instant he finished speaking to Thomas. Happy memories of a passionate, thrilling woman. There was gypsy fire in her veins. Yes, he *had* told her he loved her. Oh, she was bold. Life was to be lived to the full and to the end. She had scorned hypocrisy and convention and what she called religious cant. He had spoken to her of his troubled war years, of his time in the political wilderness, and of the need to have a regard for public opinion, and she had assured him that she would be careful. Oh, she understood her advantage! The strong friend and spirited lover he thought he knew had turned on him and was preparing to feed him to the public for money.

'Your tea's gone cold.' Ishbel was at the door again. 'Come back to the parlour and I'll make you a fresh cup.'

'Thank you, my dear.' He took off his glasses and pinched the bridge of his nose. 'I'll be through in a minute.'

'Promise?'

'I promise.' He paused. 'Ishbel, I'm sorry but I will have to return to London.'

'Oh! So soon?'

'I'm afraid so, my dear. Things I must do . . . the Channel Tunnel commission report, the new ministerial appointments. Will you ask Malcolm to speak to the air force and make the arrangements? We should leave first thing tomorrow.' He sighed. 'Let's enjoy this evening. I'll be through presently.'

My, the debts of folly were always the heaviest to pay. To think for an hour or two he had felt quite free of his past. An illusion, an illusion, how could one ever be?

5

Stewart dawdled up and down rue Ferdinand Duval with a shopping bag, hoping no one would notice or care. When the shops shut he squatted in the shadow beneath a carriage arch. Was Madame in her room or working in the city? The Hôtel du Printemps was not a salubrious-looking establishment. Green slime had leaked from a broken pipe on to the honey-stone face of the building. At one time the house of a minor noble or merchant, it was home now to Monsieur the landlord's family and his scrape-a-living tenants. According to the tailor's son, Madame was on the second floor of four. Her room was at the front of the *pension*, overlooking the yard and a building opposite, which was occupied by Jewish families from the old Russian Pale.

By eight o'clock the street was empty. Through the open windows of crowded tenements Stewart could hear children crying, a couple arguing and a neighbour urging them in German to pipe down. Someone was playing a violin badly, someone else a plaintive air on a flute. The ordinariness brought a lump to his throat because in Rotherhithe it was his children's story time. Tomorrow he would send them a postcard of the Eiffel Tower. A woman turned into the street, her face hidden by the brim of her hat. She was wearing a black skirt and a white blouse, and she was carrying a cumbersome embroidered bag. She glanced up and with a shiver of anticipation he realised it was Frau Forster at last. He waited for her to turn into the courtyard in front of the Printemps and then hurried after her.

'Madame? Madame Forster?'

She gasped and raised an arm as if to parry a blow.

'No, no, you've nothing to fear,' he said in French. 'I'm Dumont. I sent the message with the boy, Ezra.'

'Get away from me!'

She lifted her bag into the light that was shining through the frosted panel in the *pension's* door. The shadow of the iron tracery protecting the glass cut harsh lines on her face.

'I won't hurt you,' he said.

She was rummaging in the bag for something. He assumed it was for her key: it was for a pocket gun. 'Step away!'

'Please, Madame, put that back before someone calls the police.'

'I'll shoot!'

'That would be very unfortunate for both of us. I'm here with a message from Monsieur Fletcher. Don't you want to hear it?'

'Not at my lodgings,' she said, indignantly; 'not here.'

'I can explain, but for your own safety, put the gun away.'

'Are you threatening me?'

'I'm here to help you. Monsieur Fletcher is ready to pay. Ah. Look!' He glanced pointedly over her shoulder. 'You see, we have company.' An elderly man with white hair spilling from beneath his homburg hat was shuffling towards them with the aid of a stick.

'Can we go inside?' He inclined his head towards the door. 'Believe me, it's in your interests to hear me out.'

She looked him up and down, at his cheap working-men's clothes, his scuffed working-men's boots. 'How do I know you won't hurt me?' She was expecting someone better, the ambassador in velvet and braid perhaps, or Commander Fletcher, or

Sir Oswald bloody Mosley. He wanted to smile, because m'lady wasn't so fine, not in those boots, not in that hat, the mink of her jacket approaching the end of its second life.

'I'm not going to touch you. Mr MacDonald wouldn't permit it.'

'He said so?' That the prime minister wanted to protect her seemed to appeal to her vanity.

'Those are my orders, Madame.'

She considered a moment, then slipped the little popgun in her pocket and opened the door. There was no one in the hall, but the landlord could be heard giving his wife a piece of his mind in Yiddish. Madame led Stewart up to the second floor, pausing twice on the stairs to catch her breath. 'This isn't my home, you understand.'

Did she have one now she was penniless? He watched her key hover over the lock, still in two minds whether she should permit him inside. Then they heard footfalls echoing on the stairs and that seemed to settle the matter. Perhaps she was afraid a neighbour would see her with a younger man and draw the wrong conclusion.

Her apartment was no more than a large bedroom and a bathroom. Along one wall, the unmade bed; to the left of it, a monumental wardrobe – open; next to that a tallboy, its top drawer disgorging clothes; also a vanity table with silver boxes and perfume bottles beneath the mirror. In the body of the room, a tired-looking sofa and two chairs and a threadbare rug. None of the furniture would have looked out of place in a dock worker's home, excepting the wardrobe, which was large enough to shelter a family and too large to manoeuvre through the front door of a terraced house in Rotherhithe.

'Well?' she said, drawing a pin from her hat. 'What is it you have to say? Why did you send a message? You say you work for Monsieur Fletcher, but you warned me not to go to the church.'

'Yes. Commander Fletcher decided it wasn't safe.'

'Why?'

'There are some other people.'

'Who?'

'I don't know.'

She was only a few feet from him, but she met his gaze defiantly, unwilling to step away. He could try to force her to surrender the letters. Threats wouldn't be enough, he would have to hurt her, because only a determined woman would embark on such a hazardous enterprise. But he had never struck a woman and the memory of what his mother had endured at the hands of his father, the scars . . . he wasn't going to start now. Not for the Prime Minister; not for anyone. No, he needed to win her confidence.

'Your Monsieur Fletcher, he is ready to pay?'

'The prime minister's friends will pay you three thousand pounds in exchange for all of them.'

'His friends! Sir Oswald Mosley perhaps. Three thousand? I said six thousand.' She turned to place her hat carefully on one of the armchairs. 'What is your name, Monsieur?'

'Dumont. Richard Dumont.'

'La, la . . . No, your *real* name.'

'Richard Dumont.'

'And you are English? You don't sound English. Well, Monsieur Dumont, you are here, you can see my predicament for yourself . . . Tell Sir Oswald Mosley, tell him I need more. The price has gone up.'

'Mosley has nothing to do with this any more.'

She wasn't listening. 'He threatened me,' she said, her right hand balled in a fist. 'I was hoping for kindness. To be turned away by someone you have helped, someone who said he loved you, turned into the street like a common prostitute. Was that just, Monsieur Dumont? Was it fair?'

Fair? What was fair? What if he told her that to be common and a prostitute was not so terrible a thing, and that many young men had paid for sex during the war. Like cheap wine, it helped them forget that their next day might be their last. To die a virgin was unthinkable. The war work done by those French tarts . . . they should have received recognition, the *Légion d'honneur;* and in his experience there wasn't a type, unless desperate and hungry was a type. Madame claimed to be both. She was hoping for sympathy and perhaps she deserved some. Mac must have enjoyed a good deal of credit, and yet he wanted to change the terms of their arrangement. Maybe Madame was right to call in the debt; good men settled their debts.

'The things your prime minister wrote to me,' she said.

'How much more do you want?'

'The words of love. The poems he wrote—'

'Madame. How much?'

'Eight thousand pounds.'

Stewart started. 'Eight thousand! That's a lot of money.'

'Not for a prime minister.'

'I don't know . . . Are the letters here? I need to see them.'

'You think I'm a fool?' she said in English.

'You have them safe?' He replied in the same.

'Of course.'

'The prime minister wrote to you in confidence. You should give them back to him for a fair price.'

'A fair price! He has used me, is that fair? Is it? Answer me. You have seen something of the world, no?'

'People fall in and out of love.'

'You have been in love?'

'Yes.'

'Then you should understand how I feel. He has used me very badly. I will return his lies for eight thousand pounds.'

'You've offered them to no one else?'

'No.' She paused. 'Not yet.'

'I advise you not to, Madame.'

'Now you *are* threatening me. You said James would not permit it.'

How could she be so naive? Stewart stared at her. She spoke with intelligence, and she was tough enough to blackmail a prime minister. She was attractive too, like the film star, Pola Negri in *A Woman of the World*, only thirty years older and not so glamorous. But, really, this . . .

She was gazing at him with battle in her eye: Madame, they will break you.

'I'm just the messenger,' he said, 'a foot soldier.'

'Then go. Speak to your Fletcher, or whoever sent you.' She dismissed him with a petulant flourish, trying to rescue some dignity perhaps. Stewart nodded curtly and turned to the door, but with its handle in his grasp he looked back. 'You don't know me,' he said in English, 'you don't know if you can trust me. I'm going to say this anyway: blackmailin' a prime minister . . . you're either very brave or very foolish.'

'Very desperate, Monsieur.'

He nodded. 'Some say he's a decent man. You can judge . . . But there are men who are paid to protect him, to do what is necessary. He has enemies too, and they will take if they can't buy. Madame, watch out!'

'Watch whom? Who are they?' she said, pulling her tired mink tighter.

'Goodnight, Madame.'

'Dumont!' she shouted after him; but he shut the door firmly, satisfied he had said enough to unsettle her.

5 June 1930

'EIGHT THOUSAND!' SAID Fletcher, the next morning. 'Outrageous. That's more than he earns in a year.'

Stewart was smoking on the bench beside him, drawing deeply and often. He needed a shave; he needed a bath; he needed a change of clothes. Fletcher had received his *carte bleue* at breakfast proposing a rendezvous on the right bank of the Seine near the Pont des Invalides. A fine blue June day, and on the left bank opposite, the Quai d'Orsay and picture-postcard Paris before them, the Ministry of Foreign Affairs, the National Assembly, the Eiffel Tower.

'Why didn't she come to the church?' We should see her, see her *now*, this instant,' he said, slapping his hand on the bench.

'Not without the money. She'll make a fuss.'

A fuss would be a very bad thing, upon that they could agree. 'You must break into her flat.'

'The letters aren't there. She's not stupid.'

'Try. Only don't get caught.'

'And if they aren't there?'

Then the choice was the same and very simple: pay her price or force her to hand them over. 'The PM will have to decide,' said Fletcher. The author of the letters was the only person who knew their true worth. He may have said more than was wise about his colleagues, his political enemies, affairs of state. Newspapers on the continent were bolder than they used to be and if one of them chose to publish, journalists in Britain would stampede through the open gate. With no more deference due, they would feel quite within their rights to serve a sensational lip-smacking helping of hypocrisy to their readers at breakfast.

'I'm returning to London for instructions. If necessary, telephone me on this number,' he said, handing Stewart a square of hotel notepaper. 'Pinch the bloody things, please, and if you can't, well, keep an eye on her, in case it enters her head to speak to one of the correspondents at the ministry of foreign affairs.'

Stewart nodded.

'You'll be vigilant?'

Stewart sucked on his cigarette and gazed at him like a Parisian waiter obliged to listen to *l'anglais stupide* complain about the service.

They parted without a handshake, Fletcher walking along the Seine in search of a taxi to take him to the Embassy. Trusted to negotiate for the letters, he was returning to London with an even more preposterous demand for money. It was damned unjust but the bearer of bad tidings always ended up shouldering the blame. Honestly, the greedy bitch was making the whole thing unnecessarily complicated – MacDonald too.

As if to prove the point, there was a letter from Jimmy Thomas waiting for him at the Embassy. He made no mention of Mac by name, only of 'our friend'; and either 'our friend' was reluctant to talk about his former paramour or there was nothing much he could say. An address, some dates, very little for Fletcher to go on, which was a great mistake, because if the papers got hold of the story they would be certain to do a proper job on her.

'I say, Drysdale, would you go to Bern for me?' A decent

fellow, head of station, and anxious to get on in the Service. 'Any chance you can go today?'

'Today!' Drysdale pushed his chair away from his desk. 'It's just that—'

'The Service needs a check on a person of interest.'

'Goodness. Who is he?'

'*She* is a Frau Kristina Forster.'

'A woman! And who is this Mata Hari?'

'Well, that's what I want you to find out, old chap. We think she's Viennese. A socialite *and* a socialist.'

'Is it possible to be both?'

'Of course.'

'Can you tell me why we're interested in her?'

''Fraid not, old boy. This is very sensitive. Absolute discretion. Whatever you find out, contact me and no one else. Do you understand?'

He was taking quite a chance involving a Secret Service agent, but as he made his way down to the taxi at the Embassy gates he felt better for taking matters into his own hands. The eleven o'clock from the Gare du Nord would arrive in London in time for him to defend his decision – not to Jimmy Thomas, that wouldn't do, no, it had to be the prime minister. If Mac cared for his reputation he would see Fletcher no matter the hour.

2

Stewart had sent messages to both his paymasters that morning. The second was to Agent M: were his associates willing to pay more? Walking from the river to his lodgings in the Marais he considered the possibilities, because Knight's tune was changing. He had implied at first that they were working for the same people. Not a bit of it: he was desperate to thwart Fletcher. 'Don't let him acquire the letters, Dick, whatever you do!' he said. And how was Dick to prevent that? 'Pinch them from her, of course!' And Fletcher . . . Fletcher wanted him to do the same. One of them was trying to save Mac, the other trying to screw him. Stewart was Knight's spy, so perhaps a little loyalty was due: twelve pounds a week's worth of loyalty. But if he followed the logic of the marketplace it would be Fletcher, because Fletcher was paying fifteen. Only, Knight was not a forgiving man, and what about the next time he needed a job? The daft thing, the very daft thing, the mad thing . . . it seemed like a decision that could affect the future of the country for years to come.

Frenk heard Stewart in the hall of his *pension* and stepped out of his office. 'Monsieur Dumont; a lovely day.'

One would hardly know in the perpetual twilight of the half-shuttered hall.

'Indeed it is, Monsieur.'

'Please wait, I have a message for you.' He shuffled into his office and returned a moment later with a *carte bleue*, which he waved above his head like a child with a flag on Bastille Day. 'A job perhaps?'

'Perhaps. Thank you, Monsieur.' Stewart carried the card out to the steps of the *pension*. It was from a bloke called 'Seed'.

M has sent me to assist. Request meeting soonest.
Resident at the Cosmos, Place de la Contrescarpe.

Stewart lit a cigarette and drew deeply. Seed. Seedy. Mr Seedy. He had an uneasy feeling that Mr Seed represented just the sort of trouble that had been playing on his mind since his meeting with Fletcher by the Seine.

3

Heavy rain and poor visibility forced the prime minister's plane down at Catterick and an early lunch was taken. Malcolm tried to draw his father into conversation but to no avail. For once he was too absorbed in his thoughts to be gracious to their hosts, and when the pilot declared it safe to resume their journey the relief in the air force mess was almost palpable. Finally, at a little after half past four in the afternoon the de Havilland Moth touched down at Hendon Aerodrome and a motorcar came splashing along the runway to meet them at the bottom of the steps. They were shaken and nauseous and nothing passed between them on the drive into the city.

Barnes, the Number 10 porter, was ready with an umbrella to shepherd the prime minister from the car into the hall and help him from his coat. His parliamentary private secretary Weir was hovering by the fireplace, Miss Rosenberg at his side, a despatch box at her feet. They followed him to his study, Weir with a tale of by-election woe. The left of the party was making hay in Glasgow, where the Shettleston seat was up for grabs. One in four men were out of work in the constituency and all the candidates were busy blaming the government. 'Have you seen today's *Times*, Prime Minister?' Weir shook the paper at him. '"The *prime minister has nothing concrete to offer the unemployed.*" That's our man, the Labour candidate. You'll have to speak to him!'

'Aye, well, we'll see,' he said, settling at his desk. 'Anything else?'

'Mosley's speaking in Shettleston.'

'That's to be expected.'

'Supported by Maxton and Lee.'

'That's to be expected too.' He paused. 'I've the women's conference to prepare for, Lauchlan, and these . . .' He gestured to the papers on his desk. 'I'm afraid you'll have to excuse me.'

A peremptory knock and Rosa entered with a silver teapot and china cups on a tray. Jimmy Thomas was at her back. 'Prime Minister.'

'I'll write to our candidate, Lauchlan,' he said. 'McGovern, isn't it? I'll explain what we're doing to speed up our employment programme.'

Weir pursed his lips. *Dour and din*, as the bard would say. He nodded to Jimmy Thomas – no love lost there – then turned and made for the door.

'Shettleston?' said Thomas.

'It'll be close,' MacDonald replied.

'Will you speak there?'

'Perhaps. You wanted to see me, Jimmy?'

'I've heard from Fletcher.'

'Then you better sit down. Rosa, the speech for tomorrow?'

'Mr Jones has the figures you asked for, Prime Minister.' She placed a cup of tea on the desk in front of him and turned to the papers on his desk. 'Here,' she said, handing him Jones' note.

'Thank you, my dear.'

'Miss Rosa of Number Ten,' said Jimmy, cheerily. 'What would you do without her, Prime Minister?'

'What indeed.' He made an effort to smile, and it was quite an effort. He was exhausted and apprehensive because Thomas was avoiding his gaze.

'Well, tell me,' he said, as soon as they were alone.

'Fletcher says she wants eight thousand pounds.'

'Eight thousand!' He closed his eyes. 'It's not the money but ma ruin she's after.'

'Call 'er bluff, Chief.'

'Does Fletcher think that will work?'

Thomas shifted uncomfortably. 'You can ask 'im yourself, he's coming back to London.'

'What use is he here?'

'For instructions.'

'Tell him not to. Go to Paris, Jimmy, take charge.'

'Of course, I'm willin',' he said cautiously, 'but I think we should 'ear what he has to say first.'

MacDonald sighed. 'What a mess, Jimmy, what a mess. When?'

'He'll be 'ere tonight.'

4

Mr Seed's hotel was on the left bank in the Latin Quarter, a district of fine buildings and grand institutions that was home, nevertheless, to poor immigrants and students, struggling artists, crooked tradesmen, rag-pickers and prostitutes. Mr Seed had thrown his lot in with Italians. The Cosmòs was tucked away in a corner of the Place de la Contrescarpe. There was a cafe-bistro at the front, with a red-and-black-striped awning that shivered in the breeze like the sail of a pirate ship. A waiter was serving bread and wine to working men at a pavement table. To judge by their complexions and excitable gestures, the workmen were Italian too. Rising from a bench in the square, Stewart ground his cigarette into the gravel. It was time he got the measure of the man called Seed.

The interior of the cafe-bistro was drab and gloomy. There was a photograph of Benito Mussolini behind the counter and on the wall to his left, a colourful poster of a square-jawed Italian soldier. In a bay near the window Julius Caesar was shaking hands with an Italian fascist in a black shirt, urging him to fight, fight, fight for Rome. A fat man of about forty in a bloodstained apron stepped out from behind a curtain. 'Can I help you, Monsieur? Maybe you like something to eat?' His voice was Italian-tenor mellifluous. Stewart explained he was there to see Monsieur Seed.

'Ah, Monsieur Seed,' he said, warmly; 'but you are late!' And turning to the curtain, he shouted, 'Giovanni!'

A waiter appeared from behind it at once. He was dressed in a black shirt, as waiters often are, only in the Cosmos it seemed to be a statement of the politics of the house.

Giovanni led Stewart up a short flight of stairs to a first-floor landing. In pride of place at the head of the stairs there was another photograph of Mussolini, right hand extended, left on his hip, head back and mouth wide open like the opera singer Caruso reaching for a top note. Giovanni knocked and coo-ed at the door to the right of Mussolini: 'Monsieur Seeeed.'

Monsieur Seed opened the door at once. 'All right, Giovanni,' he said in Italian, 'I've been expecting this gentleman,' and he stepped back so Stewart could enter. The room was mid-price unremarkable, with a decent-sized bed, wardrobe, chest of drawers, table and window overlooking the square, and Mr Seed had his own bath and lavatory.

'How are you, Dick?' he said, offering his hand. 'It's been a while.'

'Seed? Your choice or Knight's?'

He gave a little laugh. 'Sit down, why don't you? Whisky?'

'That would be nice.'

Stewart watched him take a bottle of the Irish and two murky-looking glasses from the top of the chest of drawers. 'When was the last time, Dick? Do you remember?'

'Can't say I do.' That was a lie; he remembered perfectly. It was a summer evening in south London. A communist, an Indian fella, was to address a public meeting. Knight and his cronies were there to give him a hot reception. Only after the bloodletting did Stewart realise that they were returning to an old battleground to seek vengeance for the cutting of one of their number.

The feud had begun at the general election in 1924. An influential group of concerned conservative gentlemen needed foot soldiers to persuade voters to see things their way – the Right way – young men capable of a muscular style of campaigning, like the blackshirts in Italy. They called their new group K Squad, and in a tribute to Signor Mussolini its members were '*Fascisti*'. They knew how to handle themselves. Only at a meeting in south London the Reds fought back and cut one of their number with a razor, cut him from his mouth to his ear. The victim was a precocious and excitable young fascist called Joyce. It was cruel, it was ugly, and William Joyce would have a lopsided smile to the grave.

Gazing at his livid scar as he turned to the table with their whisky glasses, Stewart couldn't help feeling some sympathy for him. For almost anyone else he would have felt a lot more. To be sure, Mr Seed, or Mr Joyce to give him his proper name, was clever, witty, entertaining company. He had seen a good deal more of life at twenty-four than most men ever do: teenage tout in civil-war Ireland; top of the class student; fascist-razor martyr; thug and rabble-rouser. He could talk for old Ireland, only nothing good, nothing complimentary. You could fill a dictionary or medical journal with the people and things William Joyce hated: communists, socialists, Irish Republicans, Catholics, Jews, jazz and blacks, to name a few. But communists and Jews held a special place in his heart because it was a 'commie Jew' he blamed for carving his face.

The low-level war with the Reds became vicious after the cutting of Joyce. The K Squad needed recruits and had money to pay for them. Didn't matter much to Knight what you believed if you could hold your own in a brawl. That was how Stewart had come to be at the return match in south London.

'Three years ago, wasn't it?' said Joyce, taking the seat opposite. '*Salute!*'

Stewart took a sip of whisky.

'Battersea. 1927. You were very cool and professional,' said Joyce, with a disconcerting grin. 'A good night. Come on Dick, you remember: we gave them a hell of a beating.'

Stewart remembered that Joyce had fought like a demon. He was stocky and broad across the shoulders, handsome in a way. Dark hair and dark wide-set eyes, thin lips, high forehead, cleft in his chin. Handsome if you ignored the scar, and a lot of ladies seemed able to. He could be the charming soft-spoken Irishman when he had a mind to be.

'What are you doing here, William?'

'I'm here to help *you*, old boy.'

Old boy was the sort of thing he liked to say, as if he was twenty years older and a public-school Englishman. 'Max wants us to wrap this up quickly.'

'Then his Secret Service mates will have to cough up eight thousand.'

'Oh, come on Dick, you know there's another way.' Joyce leant forward to pick up his glass, a smirk on his face. 'Max says you know where she's living. Let's break in and take them.'

'Waste of time. They aren't there.'

'You can't be sure.'

'Bugger off' was on the tip of Stewart's tongue.

'We make her hand them over then,' said Joyce. 'Where is she?'

'What about Fletcher? I was to keep an eye on him, not bugger up his mission.'

'Yes, it *is* complicated . . .'

'Don't fucking patronise me.'

'. . . but the mission's changed. M takes instructions from people who see things the right way and they want us to secure the letters. You want to be paid, don't you?'

'Fletcher pays me.'

'I'm sure M – Max – will pay you more. You make contact with her at a bookshop?'

Stewart knocked back the rest of his whisky, then got to his feet.

'Come on Dick, let's settle things. You know Fletcher is on his way to London? Of course you do. We can arrange things before he gets back. Let's see her today . . . Who would have thought it, eh? Ramshackle Mac! Let's see her and . . . and we can negotiate.'

'Fuck off, Joyce. You can tell Knight I'll do this the way I want to.'

Joyce began to rise, his glass clasped in a fist, but if he was considering using it he was too slow, because Dick was at the door. He knew what trouble in Paris looked like now. Chain-smoking, grubby-raincoat trouble, ugly, unblinking, unsparing trouble: yes, he could remember that public meeting in south London three years ago. Joyce had gone berserk. He was a bad 'un, all right. Stewart knew the sort. At the Front they would boast of taking no prisoners. Joyce was a cunt. What was Knight thinking sending him to Paris?

5

Fletcher spent most of the journey to London rehearsing the conversation to come with the prime minister. Like most naval officers, he considered plain speaking a virtue. Mrs Fletcher called him 'bluff', irredeemably so. But the word 'bluff' has contradictory meanings, and for once her husband was set on charting a course between the two. The straightforward no-nonsense seaman was intent on a career in politics, perhaps in government, where truth is often opaque and in any case not greatly esteemed, and where those who demonstrate a particular talent for varnishing it are most likely to win favour with their party and the electorate. Fletcher wanted to save Mac – he respected and admired the man – but not at the expense of either his political hopes or his career in the Secret Service. The Liberals were a spent force; he had thrown in his lot with Labour, and if he was able to manage the return of the letters he would be rewarded with that safe seat. Fail and the patronage of a disgraced party leader would count for nothing. Worse than that, it would ruin his prospects of returning to parliament for ever and earn him the enmity of Admiral Sinclair. That would be a terrible mistake. He was forty-five years old; he didn't have time for mistakes. He desperately wanted that safe seat, and so did Mrs Fletcher.

On another day he would have taken pleasure in gazing from the carriage at the quiet summer orchards and timber-framed villages of Kent, the sun blinking yellow through the window. But he gave no thought to countryside or city or the passengers in his carriage until the train crossed the Thames on the approach to Victoria station. Success or failure, the next few hours could determine the course of the rest of his life.

Travel case in hand, trench coat in the crook of his arm, he weaved his way along the crowded platform, intent on staking his place in the queue for a taxicab. But a well-built man in a bowler was standing at the barrier with his name on a card – 'Commander' spelt with one 'm'. The new secretary of state for dominion affairs had sent his driver to meet the train.

And Thomas was in the entrance hall at Number 10 to greet him. ''Ow are you, Reggie? Good journey?' He spoke softly and solemnly, like a Welsh undertaker preparing to show the grieving the body of a loved one. He was dressed like one too, in a winter black wool suit and navy tie. 'The Chief is ready to see you.'

'He knows about the eight thousand pounds?'

'Yes.'

'Good.'

Thomas led him along the corridor to the anteroom where the young woman who had acted as his guide at the Foreign Office was waiting with an armful of files.

'You remember Rosa?'

'Please go straight in, Commander,' she said.

The prime minister was standing with his back to the white marble chimneypiece, the last of a fat cigar between his fingers and the room thick with smoke. Grubbing the stub in an ashtray, he advanced around the Cabinet table to shake Fletcher's hand. 'You've come straight from the station? Good of you, good of you. Sit down, won't you? Something to drink? Fetch the whisky, would you Rosa? Take that chair, and Jimmy, you'll stay. Excuse me but I have a speech to make tomorrow morning, so I'll get straight to the point: eight thousand pounds . . .'

'Yes.'

'Is there another way? You've met her; what do you propose?'

Fletcher took out his cigarette case. 'Do you mind, sir?'

'Of course not,' he said, nudging an ashtray across the table.

''Ee can't pay and shouldn't,' said Thomas, taking the chair next to Fletcher.

'Jimmy, let's hear what Commander Fletcher has to say. Do I have a choice?'

'Yes. The same choice, Prime Minister. We pay her or we force her to hand over the letters.' He took a deep breath. 'Either way, sir, I believe it is time to seek assistance from the Secret Intelligence Service.'

Thomas snorted. 'Aren't you Secret Service?'

Fletcher ignored him. 'I appreciate that you've reason to doubt Admiral Sinclair's loyalty sir, but this woman, Forster, is attempting to blackmail a prime minister. She is a threat to national security – you said so yourself – and with respect, we know very little about her. She's asking for money now but if she decides to use the letters to influence you . . . We can't rule out the possibility she's working for a foreign power.'

'That's a bit John Buchan, Reggie,' said Thomas.

MacDonald shook his head impatiently. 'Aye, well I think I know my duty, Commander.'

'I don't doubt it, Prime Minister, but she may not be interested in the money—'

'She wants eight thousand pounds!'

'But I wonder, is it revenge? Will she go to a French or German newspaper with the story of how much the British prime minister was ready to pay her to prevent the publication of his letters? That might make even better copy.'

MacDonald closed his eyes momentarily. 'You think that's a possibility?'

'I do.'

'What can Admiral Sinclair do that you can't?'

'Well . . . In theory, anything. Everything, in the national interest. The Service could make the problem . . . disappear.'

'You must understand, I don't wish her harm.'

Fletcher was at a loss to find a way to say so, but Mac was making a mistake. Let the Service handle the matter. There was no need for him to know how. Just look the other way.

'Well, gentlemen . . .' MacDonald got to his feet. Rosa Rosenberg appeared between the Cabinet room pillars with whisky and glasses on a tray. 'Too late, I'm afraid. Commander, you'll have to excuse me. I'll think about what you've said and let you know my decision tomorrow morning. I am sure you are in a hurry to see Mrs Fletcher.'

'Thank you, Prime Minister.' Mrs Fletcher had no idea he was in London.

'I wish you both a good evening.' MacDonald settled back in his chair and picked up his pen. Thomas was making for the door, Rosa had left the room already, but Fletcher lingered, conscious suddenly that he was standing where great men had made history. The Elder Pitt had laid the foundations of the empire; the Younger Pitt, made war on Napoleon; old Disraeli had wrestled with the Turkish question; Gladstone with Home Rule for Ireland; and the Asquith government had taken the country into the Great War with Germany. And now Lieutenant Commander Reggie Fletcher had fulfilled a life ambition and taken a seat at the Cabinet table. Saving the current incumbent of Number 10 from public disgrace was not a heroic role, but politics was often a low business.

'Commander, is there something else?' MacDonald was watching him.

'No, no, Prime Minister. Goodnight.'

'Goodnight.' He smiled, then bent again to his papers.

Fletcher didn't know whether to feel sorry or angry with him for showing poor judgement. But at a time of national crisis a woman who cared nothing for the country and its people, an Austrian, was making his burden heavier. To hold a prime minister to ransom was an act of war. Preposterous. Unforgivable.

Thomas was waiting in the anteroom. 'It'll never do, Reggie. Never mind your foreign powers, it's bloody Sinclair we 'ave to worry about. If he gets his 'ands on those letters Mac's done for.'

'I don't agree. If we don't secure the letters soon a foreign newspaper will, then you, he – we will all be done for. Now, if you'll excuse me, Minister.'

'All right, keep your 'air on. 'Ee's speaking at the Kingsway Hall tomorrow morning, I'll 'ave a decision for you by then.'

Fletcher nodded curtly and turned to follow Miss Rosa along the corridor. On the whole he was pleased, even proud, of the way the interview had gone. True, he hadn't been entirely frank with the prime minister. He may have given the impression he had spoken to Frau Forster in person . . . but it was a small deception, nothing really, the sort of diplomatic omission that was routine in politics, and a politician was what he wanted to be. In the entrance hall the porter danced around the floor helping him into his coat. Glancing down at the chequerboard white and black tiles, he wondered at the foreign kings and bishops and knights who had crossed the floor seeking advice, advantage, preferment from a prime minister. Well, it was Mac's move now, his decision to make, and his position to lose.

6

Light summer rain was falling in Paris. From the shelter of the carriage arch, Stewart watched the lights in the rue Ferdinand Duval go out one by one. Madame must have paid him no heed: eleven o'clock and she was still out in the city. The threat was real now, it had a face and a name – William Joyce.

Was it too late to insist Knight call the bugger off? 'My way or no way,' he could say, and string both his paymasters along until he was finally forced to choose. With Joyce in Paris the choice seemed simpler. That stocky fucker seemed to embody everything that was rotten and ugly about the people they were working for. He was their creature, their number one bully boy. Fletcher was not the sort of man to beat a woman; Joyce would have no qualms. That was why Knight had sent him to Paris. Agent M! What was a code name if not a licence to think the unthinkable and then make it happen, and for whom? A small circle of privileged and powerful men who were sure they knew what was best for the country. Their country, the one with the rich man in his castle, the poor man at his gate; the country where a million men was a sacrifice worth making; the country where those who threatened the old order could be brought low by exposing a man's private life to public ridicule. He knew their works; he was their servant. But if he turned his back on them he would lose his living. Fletcher would pay him until the job was done, and then what? Pride and what was left of his principles would butter no bread at home.

At last he heard the click of heels in the street and, peering round the arch, he saw Madame, head bent, right hand around the pistol in her pocket. It was plain to him from her demeanour that she was afraid of Dumont or someone like him, and she was right to be. He felt a pang of guilt and sympathy. She had made an impression on him. Call it extortion, call it what you like, she was refusing to go quietly. A powerful man had used her and she was fighting back. Was that fair to the prime minister? He could not tell, only it was how he was inclined to see things since the war.

He watched her hurry into the courtyard and reappear seconds later on the steps of the Hôtel du Printemps. She was safe, and until Fletcher returned he would endeavour to keep her so. Eight thousand pounds would settle it. Mac would have his letters and the shits trying to engineer his disgrace would have nothing. Fairy tale. Except for me, he thought; what's in it for me?

10

6 June 1930

AFTER A NIGHT of doubts and imagining, he felt in control, as a prime minister should always be. Between breakfast and the women's conference at the Kingsway he spoke to his private secretary and the secretary to the cabinet, to the secretary of state for war, and the chancellor came through the connecting door from Number 11 to discuss the new Finance Bill.

But on the stage at the Kingsway his anxieties came storming back, like noisy protestors intent on breaking into the hall to heckle his speech. Gazing over the heads of the women in the auditorium below, he spied Fletcher lurking at one of the doors. The Commander was pressing him to involve that snake Sinclair. Well, he might as well urge his prime minister to confess to the newspapers and be done with it!

'Conference, it is with great pleasure that I invite our prime minister, Mr Ramsay MacDonald, to speak to you today.'

Four hundred comrades were gazing up at him, a hundred more in the gallery, their cheers ringing around the Kingsway. He rose slowly, straightened his back and swept a lock of hair from his forehead. He would say nothing until there was complete silence. The trick was always to begin quietly.

'We must speak of unemployment,' he said, 'because I know it is on your minds, in your hearts too. It is *always* in mine.' The government was doing what it could to encourage foreign trade but the home market would have to come first, he said, and the only way to develop that market was to ensure the children of the working classes, their mothers and their fathers, were able to live in decent conditions. 'Our people don't want charity handouts; they want to take pride in their work. We will find them work, but this will take time. It's a campaign, not a battle. Those who look back on our first year in office and say, "Labour has failed us" and talk of finding something new are setting up a golden calf to worship. They aren't rebels, they aren't left-wingers, they are faint hearts. Faint hearts!' He shook a forefinger at his audience. 'I say to the faint hearts in our party that in families there are always disagreements, but now in this great emergency we must bind ourselves together and march on in mutual confidence and trust. Comrades, I ask you to join me in this great national endeavour. Let us march on together.'

Jimmy Thomas rose and the hall followed his example, clapping, cheering, and there was a chorus of 'He's a jolly good fellow'. He smiled, waved, clasped his hands and shook them like a conductor at a concert podium. Some of the delegates in the hall were bound to read his speech in the papers the following day and wonder why they had made such a fuss of him – but that was for tomorrow. The secret of politics was to promise as little as possible but with great passion. Not for the first time a line or two of Lewis Carroll came to him as he acknowledged their applause.

> 'You are old, Father William,' the young man said,
> 'And your hair has become very white;
> And yet you incessantly stand on your head—
> Do you think, at your age, it is right?'

Fine words were not going to solve the country's problems. The truth was he had no more idea than the next man where new jobs would come from in a world economic crisis.

'Will you ask Mr Thomas to join me?' he said, as the members of the podium party led him from stage. To the women in the gallery it must have looked like a papal procession, with delegates crowding round him, hoping for a smile, a handshake, a socialist blessing. Thomas had to use his elbows. 'Prime Minister?'

'Do you know any poems by Lewis Carroll, Jimmy?'

'Reggie Fletcher's 'ere.'

'You know, he wants me to stand on my head? I don't know, but . . .' He paused to smile and shake hands with a delegate from Dundee. 'Jimmy, you better ask Commander Fletcher to arrange a meeting with Admiral Sinclair for this evening.'

'Are you sure, Chief?'

'No, but Commander Fletcher seems to be. I want it to be over, I want some peace. I don't think I have a choice.'

2

Dick Stewart rose early, bought coffee and bread and returned to his post beneath the carriage arch in the rue Ferdinand Duval. In stained overalls and with paint pots and brushes purchased from a yard in the *Pletzel* he looked like an ordinary working bloke on his way to a job in the street – honest and ordinary enough to convince his market-day neighbour. She had come in from the country and was sitting beneath the arch, a stool lost in the folds of her skirt, flowers in buckets at her feet. From time to time she remembered she was there to sell them – 'Help an old lady!' she shouted – but her new acquaintance seemed to interest her more.

'Painting a shop,' he said in answer to her questions, and 'waiting for my mate.'

'Well, you have the patience of a saint, Monsieur,' she was moved to remark after an hour.

By then rue Ferdinand Duval was bustling with pious-looking Jewish women shopping at the market stalls for bread and vegetables. Mid-morning, Stewart observed the proprietor of the Printemps slouching along the street, followed a short time later by his dear lady wife. Another twenty minutes passed and the old flower seller stopped asking questions and began to eye him suspiciously. He was on the point of moving when Madame Forster appeared at last. She was wearing winter black on what was already a very warm day, and her face was almost lost beneath the broad-brim of her hat. The large embroidered bag from which she had produced her pocket gun was in the crook of her left arm. Stewart watched her scurry out of the courtyard and weave her way between market stalls in the direction of rue des Rosiers.

'How much for your flowers?' he said, pointing to a bunch in one of the old lady's buckets.

'What do you want with 'em?'

'Do you want to sell them or not?'

'Five francs,' snapped the old bird.

'Three, and another franc if you keep an eye on my paintbrushes.'

Her face broke into thin lines like cracked varnish on an Old Master painting. She lifted the bunch from the bucket, shook the stems dry and wrapped them in newspaper. *'Voilà,* Monsieur!'

There were daisies, cornflowers, meadowsweet blossom, toadflax and some flowers he could not put a name to. Flowers a common man might gather from woods and hedgerows outside the city. Carrying the bouquet in front of his face like a flag, he marched into the courtyard and up the steps of the *pension*. A bell tinkled as the door swung to behind him and a girl of about fourteen stepped out of an office behind the counter.

'Monsieur?' She had a round face like her mother the landlady and a sour expression like her father.

'Flowers for Madame Forster,' he shouted breezily.

'I'll take them.'

'No, I'm to deliver them in person.'

'You can't,' she said. 'She's not here!'

He paid her no heed, only made for the staircase, shaking a trail of small petals on to the steps as he climbed them two at a time. Would she be away for long? And Frenk, the proprietor . . . perhaps he was only a street away. Stewart laid the bouquet on the old oak boards beside her door, and from his overalls he removed a wallet of picks and wrenches. The lock was just the simple sort he expected to encounter in a five-francs-a-night place like the Printemps. The room was dark, the curtains closed, and switching on the light, he noticed another bulb had gone in the chandelier.

There were clothes on the unmade bed and the couch, and yet more spilling from the chest of drawers. Tidying was plainly something she expected a maid to do. That she was too smart to hide the letters in her room, he was in no doubt, but a key, a note, an address might offer a clue to their whereabouts. He searched the vanity table and Madame's silver jewellery boxes first. Bills and correspondence in the top drawer; envelopes franked in Bern, Berlin, Vienna and Paris; letters written in French and German. Some of them were polite rejections of appeals for assistance – *Madame, I regret* . . . etcetera, etcetera – and some were downright rude. And the bills . . . No wonder her price for the return of Mac's letters had risen so steeply. Next the wardrobe, the top and the bottom, coat and jacket pockets; and then the bedside table, reaching under and around the back. In the drawer he found a photograph of a family group at a picnic and a studio portrait of a young couple. The man in the portrait was in his late twenties, handsome, with a waxed cavalry moustache; the woman was Kristina Forster. My, what a beauty she had been in her salad days.

Bed, couch, cushions and chairs – he checked them all – the bathroom too: nothing. Trunk and travel cases: nothing. The small bookcase to the right of the bed: nothing. Finally, the chest of drawers, and in the bottom drawer of three, he found a mahogany jewel box with a silver key. Perching on the arm of a chair, he lifted a bundle of letters from the box by a red silk ribbon and another photograph of a couple. This time Madame was making moon-eyes and smiling at old MacDonald, and with her hand resting on his arm he looked like the cat that got the cream. On the back of the photograph there was a dedication: *To Pussy. With love from JRM. Paris, December 1928.*

For a spine-tingling second Stewart dared to hope he was wrong and she had been a naive fool. But the first letter he opened was addressed to *Mein leiblichste Heinrich*. There was no date and no address, and Stewart could only speak a little German, but it was enough to know that *Mein leiblichste Heinrich* was more to her than a friend – *Du bist mein ein und alles* – he was her all! They were love letters, only not the ones *Pussy* was trying to flog back to JRM. The second letter to her Heinrich she had signed with *passionate kisses*. Stewart was on the point of opening a third when he heard a faint scratching noise. For a few seconds he sat motionless, straining to hear more. The claws of a mouse beneath the boards perhaps, or the scuff of a boot on the stair. In any case it was time to slide the box of dear Heinrich letters back into his lover's bottom drawer and leave.

Stepping lightly to the door, he stood and listened for a noise on the landing. He could sense the presence of someone. It was a feeling, for sure, but his instinct for danger had carried him safely through the war. A door banged in the room above; a small child was bleating in the courtyard below; and with his ear pressed to the keyhole he thought he could hear something else – heavy breathing – and only the width of a piece of oak away. Then a man with a big voice put the matter beyond doubt: 'your flower man has gone!' he said. 'Look, he's left them at her door.'

'He may be inside, Monsieur,' said the landlord's daughter. 'Perhaps we should check.'

'He's gone. You missed him!'

'Please,' she said, plaintively. 'Father would want me to.'

'Do you have a key?'

'I'll fetch it.'

'Why would he leave the flowers outside?'

'I'll fetch the key.'

'Look, I've things to do,' said the man with the big voice, 'and your father will be back very soon.'

And that was how things rested. Stewart heard him clump along the landing and down the stairs, followed by the landlord's daughter. Right. Move. It had been damn stupid of him to lose track of time.

Letting himself out quietly, he locked the door and followed them down the stairs. The flowers he left to wilt in the summer heat. On the last half-landing he paused to listen to chatter in the entrance hall. The girl was speaking Yiddish; to whom he couldn't tell. The bloke with the big voice? To be avoided if humanly possible. Eyes to the front he ambled down the last flight of stairs into the hall. 'That's him!' she cried at once, and another man – her father perhaps – shouted, 'Hey, you, wait!' But he didn't wait, he didn't turn to look at them, only carried on walking through the door, down the steps and across the courtyard into the street.

The old flower seller was sitting in her skirts where he had left her. 'Did she like them?' she said.

'She loved them,' he replied, bending to pick up his brushes.

'Then why are you here? Why are you back?'

'I wasn't invited to stay.' He shook his head wistfully. 'I'm not her only admirer, you see.'

She laughed. 'So, she has another lover.'

Her *leiblichste Heinrich*, yes. Was Heinrich the man with a moustache like the Kaiser's? The portrait photograph in her bedside table must have been taken before the war when men with extravagant moustaches were expected to charge machine guns on horseback. But perhaps dear Heinrich was her new lover and the custodian of the Prime Minister's letters. He may have encouraged her to blackmail her former lover. There was no way of knowing – not yet anyway.

'What are you doing?' The flower seller nudged his leg with her foot. 'You're in my way! Are you going to stand there lovelorn for the rest of the day?'

3

Fletcher had been in Broadway Buildings only twenty minutes when Miss Pettigrew rang to summon him into the presence. Standing in the Chief's outer office waiting for the light above his door felt like queuing to jump with a parachute, and he could think of nothing worse.

The light turned green, he entered, and walked the length of the admiral's office to stand in front of his desk like a naughty schoolboy.

'The meeting at Number Ten . . .' said Sinclair; 'your doing?'

No 'How are you Reggie,' no 'Take a seat, won't you.' No. Sinclair was in a dark mood.

'I think the prime minister wishes to discuss the matter with you in person, Chief', he replied.

'Did he tell you so?'

'No, but I—'

Sinclair gestured impatiently with his cigarette. 'You have that from his Welsh monkey, Thomas, I suppose.'

'Well, yes.'

'You work for me, for the Service, not that boyo.'

Fletcher felt the heat rising in his face. 'I counselled the prime minister to . . . I *insisted* he speak to you, sir.'

Sinclair leant forward with his arms crossed on the desk. 'You have political ambitions, don't you, Reggie.'

'I—'

'Please don't interrupt. I expect you to remember where you work and for whom. Is that clear?'

Perfectly. As clear as clear ice. As he walked back along the senior officers' corridor to his office he wondered at his own naivety. Madame Forster, the letters, his involvement in the prime minister's affair: Sinclair knew everything. That snake Morton must have told him. It was beginning to smell a little like Zinoviev. Well, Officer G (Europe) would have to be more robust in his own defence. The question of loyalty was bound to surface again, and – damn it! – he deserved some credit for championing the Service. After all, the meeting at Number 10 was only taking place at his insistence.

He lit a cigarette and reached for the paper on top of the large pile on his desk. In the circumstances it would be politic to concentrate on other duties for a while. He was paid to protect the realm from its enemies abroad, not its politicians from scandal at home, no matter how august they might be. The title of the paper in front of him was *The German Fascist Threat*, which sounded menacing but straightforward, comfortingly so. Berlin head of station was drawing his attention to the 'extraordinary rise' in the popularity of the National Socialist Party.

He noted in his report:

Its leader, Herr Hitler, has turned the worsening economic situation to his advantage.

He can count on support from *Freikorps* veterans and the Kaiser's fourth son, Prince August Wilhelm of Prussia, has joined the

National Socialist Party too, lending it an air of greater respect-ability. But one should be in no doubt; the Nazis are not only anti-communist, they are anti-democratic and anti-Semitic and if they do as well in September's federal election as many predict, they will constitute a threat to European peace.

A threat to European peace? That was quite a claim, and one Fletcher was inclined to take with a pinch of salt. Picking up his pen, he initialled a cover sheet and set the paper to one side.

'Ahem.' His secretary was at the door. 'There's a Mr Drysdale on the telephone, Commander. He says it's urgent.'

'Drysdale? Yes, yes, put him through please.'

Alcock gave him a sour look. Why? The Service recruited nice gels as secretaries because Sinclair seemed to regard trust as a matter of breeding, which was ridiculous. She would have to go. He had no time for airs and graces.

'Is that you, Commander?'

'Yes, yes, I hear you Drysdale.' The telephone line was whistling like a ship in a storm. 'Where are you?'

'I'm in Bern. I've spoken to our contact in the local police. The lady concerned has a German passport, I thought you should know.'

'German?'

'Yes.'

'Is that all?'

'She lived in a large villa outside the city. I spoke to her chauffeur, who said she was a good employer. "Generous," he said. He would pick up her friends from the station – Germans mostly, some French, some Russians. He couldn't remember their names.' He paused. 'There was one man . . .'

'Go on.'

'The driver said he was a famous British politician. Tall, distin-guished-looking, grey hair, a grey moustache, two gold rings on his left hand. You know, I think he was describing our prime minister!' He paused. 'Is that what this is about?'

'None of your business.'

'Do you want to hear more?' he said, truculently.

'If you have more . . .'

'The driver thinks they were lovers.'

'Ah.'

'I tried to have a word with the maid but she sent me packing. She was quite emotional about "Her Madame". Very loyal. But the impression I got was that "Her Madame" was very secretive. Just an impression, but . . . anyway, that's all, I'm afraid.'

'Well, thank you,' he said, 'and remember, not a word to anyone.'

Secretive; German; some of her associates were Russians: was Frau Forster working for a foreign power? The evidence was circumstantial; the risk too great to ignore. He was going to have to mention the possibility. Sinclair was sure to blame the Soviets, because he considered the country under Labour to be low-hanging fruit. 'Flatter the old man, Kristina, make him want you!' A classic espionage seduction, was that it? Oh, come on Fletcher . . . he was letting his imagination run away with him. Leaning back in his chair, he lit another cigarette. He would have to say something, yes, but not to the prime minister. That would be very unwise; it might threaten his political future.

4

In the bookshop on rue des Rosiers, Eli Weiss was working his way along the religious texts with a duster. He was closing early for the Sabbath and when the dusting was done he would buy candles and wine to take to his friend Cohen's apartment. He used to watch his father perform the same pre-Sabbath ritual in his bookshop in Pinsk. Papa would hum a little tune and flick a rag, like a conductor rehearsing an orchestra; and when on Fridays Eli tied his apron and picked up his duster he would say a little prayer for Papa and Mama and imagine with a heavy heart the knee-high grass around their graves in the old Jewish cemetery. Papa had been one of the leaders of the Jewish community massacred by the Polish army of occupation. Not long after that dreadful day in 1919, Eli had moved to Vienna and opened his own bookshop, and for a time he had done well. But he had lent money to a goy who refused to return it and threatened him with violence. He had been obliged to sell the shop and move to Paris. Never again, he would say to neighbours in the *Pletzel*: 'this old Jew is here to stay.'

His three years in Paris were the most peaceful he had known, and while he enjoyed discussing socialism and another French revolution, he was more than content making the money he needed to get by and with keeping the Sabbath as his father and mother had taught him to do. He was an optimist and a dreamer, yes, but he had learnt at a very young age that there were people with neither empathy nor decency in the world and he would have to be forever on his guard against them.

So when at five o'clock two aggressive-looking young men in black shirts entered his shop, a frisson of fear coursed through him. Bibliophiles? No! Slipping the book he had been dusting back, he took half a step toward them. 'I'm sorry gentlemen, I'm closing.'

No reply. One of them turned the notice on the door to CLOSED and dropped the catch on the lock.

'If you come back on Sunday . . .' said Eli. 'Are you looking for anything in particular?' How ridiculous. These bullies in their black shirts . . . they weren't interested in a book. If they refused to leave in the next few minutes he would make as much noise as possible to alert his neighbours.

One of them spoke at last. 'Is there anyone else here?' he said in bastard Italian-French.

'I'm expecting friends.'

They ignored him, only exchanged glances. The beefier of the two walked towards Eli, forcing him against the bookshelves as he made his way through to the back of the shop. They were young men in their twenties, olive skin, short hair, clean shaven, and they were dressed in shiny black, like volcanic glass. Eli was a dreamer, yes, but sometimes his dreams made him tremble. He had dreamt of and dreaded an occasion like this one, and yet he felt quite calm. Reaching behind his back, he untied his apron.

'You know why we're here?' said the slighter man.

'No.'

'Don't lie, Jew, where does she live?'

'I *am* a Jew, that's correct.' Beefy had finished searching the shop and was standing only a metre away from him.

'Madame Forster, where is she?'

'I've told you I—' was all he could manage to say as the big man sprang, seized him in a chokehold, and dragged him backwards to the rear of the shop.

'Tell us where to find her and we'll leave you alone.'

'I don't know what you—'

'An address!'

What could he say? Damn them, damn the *paskudnyaks*.

'Well?' The slighter man slipped on a knuckleduster and held his fist in front of Eli's face. 'This is *my* duster, Jew. Where is she?'

'Rue Aubriot,' he replied.

'Number?'

'Thirty-two.'

The *paskudnyak* considered this a moment, nodded and turned away, only to swing back with the full weight of his body. Beefy must have released his neck-hold because Eli came to on the floor. Faint with pain, the room and his tormentors a blur, he knew he was going to die – 'like Papa' – as he gasped for breath like a fish out of water.

They hauled him to his feet and dumped him in his desk chair, and the big *paskudnyak* tied his hands and dragged his chin from his chest by his hair.

'The truth this time. Where is she?'

'Rue Aubriot. Rue Aubriot.' Eli chanted, like a biblical verse.

'Liar!' Knuckleduster punched him in the face. He punched Eli until he could see nothing, hear nothing, only the thump thump of his head driven from side to side. He must have passed out again because the next thing he was aware of was water splashing his face and a glass held to his lips. One eye was closed but with the other he saw his interrogator's dark eyes a ruler's length from his face. He could hear someone whimpering: *you fool, it's you!*

'Save yourself,' said Knuckleduster.

What did he mean? The beefy *paskudnyak* was fiddling with the rope binding his hands. His right hand was free, but only for a moment. The *paskudnyak* caught his wrist and wrestled it flat to the arm of the chair. Eli's interrogator had removed his duster and was fishing in his pocket for something else: a shaving razor! With a twinkling smile, he bent over the chair with the blade vertical in front of Eli's face. 'This is going to hurt you.'

The razor, the malicious smile . . . it was too much for Eli to bear. 'Not far,' he croaked, 'Very close.'

'Where?'

'Rue Ferdinand Duval.'

The *paskudnyak* with the razor nodded slowly and exchanged a glance with his associate. Eli felt his grip tighten. 'Please, no, it's the truth. Rue Ferdinand Duval.'

*

They knew it was the truth; they took a finger anyway. The first thing he saw when he returned to consciousness was his little finger in a pool of blood between his feet. His white shirt and black waistcoat were covered in blood, the fringe of his tallit too. Lifting his gaze to his right hand, he saw four fingers and a bleeding stump. The big man had let go of his wrist.

'You can keep the rest for now,' said razor man, leaning forward to wipe his blade on Eli's waistcoat. 'I believe you. I better be right. Number?'

Eli closed his eyes in an effort to suppress his tears. 'Hôtel du Printemps.'

5

Jimmy Thomas proposed whisky and a fireside chat in the drawing room. MacDonald said, 'We're discussing a security matter, not the regatta at Cowes.' He wished Sinclair to understand that the recovery of his letters was in the national interest and not a personal favour. They would meet in the Cabinet Room. Better still, they wouldn't meet at all!

'Take him to Jones's office,' he said, 'and you can act as a go-between, Jimmy.'

Thomas remonstrated with him – 'it's discourteous, Chief' – but to no avail. He despised men like Sinclair. No one elected them, they were accountable to nobody, they served only the interests of their class, and if they didn't like the political shade of a government they thought they were within their rights to conspire against it. A single forged letter had sealed the fate of his first government; what hope for his second if his correspondence with a foreign lady, a blackmailer, made it into the press? Poor, poor judgement not to have sacked the admiral on his first day back in Number 10, for now he was obliged to seek assistance from a man who devoutly wanted him gone.

Rising from his place at the Cabinet table, he walked over to a window with a view of the garden. Ishbel and a friend were enjoying the evening sunshine. He watched the two women trying the scent of a rose, and with a stab of memory he pictured his Margaret doing the same in her father's garden. They were courting and she had been about the same age. Dear Margaret, who had given him the strength of purpose to go forth into the world and smite his enemies.

'Prime Minister.' Miss Rosa was standing between the pillars, hands clasped demurely at her waist. 'Admiral Sinclair and Commander Fletcher are here.'

'Thank you, Rosa. Show them into Mr Jones's office will you, and tell Jimmy.' He walked back to his seat and for appearances' sake opened a despatch box and spread some papers on the table. He would place special emphasis on admirable words like 'duty', 'security' and 'national interest', although on their meaning and relevance they were certain to disagree. Jimmy would be his mouthpiece.

Either Rosa or Jimmy must have communicated his wishes because he could hear raised voices. A great stooshie was taking place in the anteroom. Poor old Jimmy. For the first time he was struck by the absurdity of what he was proposing. If he was unwilling to treat with Sinclair face to face, why was he treating with him at all? He was on the point of calling Rosa to communicate his change of heart when Thomas appeared between the pillars with Sinclair at his back. 'Prime Minister, I must protest,' said the admiral, forging into the room. 'I understood I was invited here to speak to you on a matter of national security. If that's the case, I must speak to you in person.'

He took up a position on the opposite side of the table, arms folded and legs apart, as if he was addressing a junior on the bridge of his old battleship. My God, the arrogance of the man!

'I can assure you, Admiral, Mr Thomas knows my mind and enjoys my complete confidence.'

'And it's a matter of great regret that I don't, Prime Minister. You'll forgive me if I ask, but what was the point of summoning me to Downing Street only to refuse to speak to me? Commander Fletcher is the very soul of discretion but from the little he's told me this is a matter that concerns you personally. If that's the case and you wish the Secret Service to assist you then you must speak to me or . . . sack me.'

Oh what satisfaction it would give him to say 'go!' Prime Minister, make your choice. But what choice? He had no choice. Not now, not at this delicate stage.

'Sit down, Admiral, please.'

'Thank you, Prime Minister.'

'Commander, Jimmy . . . Feel free, gentlemen,' he said, gesturing to the cigarette box. His own cigar was smouldering in an ashtray, its smoke curling, swirling over the table. Through it he contemplated his enemy. 'First let me thank you for coming at this hour, Admiral.'

'Think nothing of it.'

'I *do* consider this a question of national security. How much has Commander Fletcher told you?'

'Very little, Prime Minister,' said Fletcher, a little too quickly. 'I thought it would be best if the admiral heard the details from you in person.'

'Well, Admiral, put simply, I'm being blackmailed by a lady I was once very close to. Her name is Kristina Forster. She's Austrian, from—'

'I'm sorry, Prime Minister,' interrupted Fletcher, 'May I? It's just that I've made enquiries and Frau Forster may in fact be German. I thought I should mention it.'

'Commander,' he said, spreading his hands on the ink blotter in front of him, 'let me assure you . . .' Assure him? Assure him of what? *We were lovers; she loved me; of course she's Austrian*, was what he wanted to say, because anything less would be humiliating. But how could he? Perhaps she *was* German. Nothing else she had said to him was true. How could it be?

Thomas came to his rescue. 'I don't know about you, Prime Minister, but I could do with a drink.'

He flushed. 'Yes, Jimmy. Will you see to it?'

'Back in a jiffy,' he said, pushing his chair from the table.

'I think you should tell us what you know, Prime Minister,' said Sinclair, 'or *think* you know.'

'Yes,' he said, weakly. 'Of course.' Fletcher's interjection . . . Austrian or German? It had left him quite dumbfounded. My God, he barely knew her! He had clung to the belief that his passionate letters were a genuine expression of his love for her. How could they be? He may only have been in love with his own fine feelings – not flesh and blood, not with Kristina Forster.

Sinclair prompted him – 'Prime Minister . . .' and from somewhere he found his voice.

He spoke of their first meeting in Paris, of visits to her house in Bern and of his motor tour of Europe with Mosley, when he had arranged to meet her 'by accident'. Then of their week together in Cornwall, a few months before the general election. She was cultivated, she spoke many languages, she could make him laugh out loud, and she was a socialist.

'How much of a socialist?' Sinclair enquired. 'Is she a communist?'

'No!' he said, sharply. 'She is – *was* – a wealthy woman. A generous woman . . . with everybody.'

'Generous?'

'With her money.'

'Did she give you money, Prime Minister?'

He hesitated. 'I was her guest. She would sometimes pay.'

'And her friends? Did you meet her Russian friends?'

'A couple, yes. I can't remember their names.'

Russians, Germans, Austrians had wanted to shake his hand, some of them great bores.

'Anything else?' said Sinclair.

'I don't believe Frau Forster is working for a foreign power. She is a desperate woman.'

Sinclair inspected his whisky. 'Prime Minister, you've said nothing that would lead me to discount the possibility. This woman – German, Austrian, we don't know? Socialist, communist, we can't be sure? – this woman seems to have sidled her way into your circle, can I say, your affections, without disclosing anything of importance about her past, her family or her contacts. Doesn't that strike you as suspicious? Forgive me, but I know how enemy agents operate, and she may well be one. She wants money now, but next time it may be intelligence, because there's always a next time. She may even ask you to do something to bring about a revolution—'

'Oh, really, that's nonsense!'

'You're trapped!' Sinclair snapped. 'You're trapped! She has trapped a British prime minister. Do you think that's nonsense? The letters you speak of, is there anything of—'

'They're personal.'

'But damaging nonetheless.'

MacDonald felt the heat rise to his face.

'We can't allow a foreigner, a communist agent perhaps, to compromise a British prime minister,' said Sinclair. 'You've done the right thing bringing this to my attention. I only wish you had done it sooner.'

Fletcher was staring at his hands, Thomas shifting uncomfortably.

'Aye, well, that's as may be, Admiral,' he said, coldly. 'Now you know, what, pray, do you intend to do?'

'Simply, recover your letters. Commander Fletcher will return to Paris tomorrow. The sooner we can secure them the better. You're anxious to keep them from the press, I'm sure, but *my* principal concern is to secure them before they can be used by those who wish to undermine this country and its government.'

'I see.' He leant forward on his elbows to stare at Sinclair. Undermine the government? *Listen to yourself, man,* he wanted to say. *How dare you?* But disarmed, defeated, he said nothing.

Jimmy came to his rescue again. 'And 'ow, Admiral, do you propose to go about it? She wants eight thousand.'

'You can leave that to us, Minister,' said Sinclair.

MacDonald turned to Fletcher. 'But no violence.'

'Well, I . . .'

'The less you know the better, Prime Minister,' said Sinclair. 'Now if you'll excuse us, we must see to things.' He touched Fletcher's elbow. 'You'll have many affairs of state to deal with, I'm sure.'

6

That Sinclair was leaving Number 10 with a spring in his step was plain to see, but nothing passed between them until its famous door closed with a thud and they were in Downing Street.

'Café Royal?' said Sinclair, cramming a bowler hat on his head.

'Home to Mrs Fletcher.'

'Oh, you poor bugger. Hop in then, and I'll drop you at Victoria station.'

His antique open-top Lancia was parked in front of the Foreign Office. It was a strange choice for the chief of a secret service because it was one of the most conspicuous cars in London. 'He'll hear that in the Cabinet Room,' shouted Sinclair, over the roar of the engine.

They turned right on to Whitehall, paused for traffic in Parliament Square, then Sinclair opened up the throttle. 'Miss Pettigrew has you on the eight thirty from Croydon Airport,' he shouted. 'Collect the money from Drysdale in Paris. Make sure you pay her the full eight thousand pounds.'

'Pay whom?'

Sinclair glanced across at him. 'God's sake, Reggie, the prime minister's tart, who else?'

'Of course. Sorry.'

'Let's see if she's the poor madam she claims to be. Oh bloody hurry up!' He stepped hard on the brake to avoid a drunk dawdling across Victoria Street. 'Make sure she gives you all the letters. Convince her it would be a grave mistake not to.' He gave a wry smile. 'You can place special emphasis on "grave".'

'She may accept less.'

'No negotiations, Reggie, do you hear? Secure the letters.'

Fletcher stared at him in amazement. The Chief despised Labour and its works – why, at the Cabinet table he had been close to accusing Mac of sleeping with a communist – and yet he was willing to find the money from the Service's meagre funds and pay her without question. 'And if she refuses to return all the letters?'

'Here we are.' They were approaching the entrance to Victoria station. 'Well, *you've* met her, Reggie, haven't you? You must have some idea of what she wants.'

Did the admiral know he was yet to meet her? He really had no idea.

'Don't worry,' said Sinclair, 'she'll accept the money.' The motorcar cruised to a halt in front of the station. 'Here we are.'

'Do you think she's working for a foreign power, sir?'

'She might be. Watch out for the French. We don't want them to get wind of this.'

'No.'

'And Reggie,' said Sinclair, resting his large hand lightly on Fletcher's arm. 'You will keep me informed won't you.' He smiled, but without warmth. 'My regards to Mrs Fletcher. Elspeth, isn't it?'

What was in that devious man's mind? Fletcher was waiting for a stationmaster to confirm the platform number of his train when it came to him: Sinclair had probably known of Mac's liaison with Frau Forster for weeks, from the first week perhaps, even their first meeting.

'Your train will leave from platform three, sir.' The station-master pointed to his right.

'Thank you.'

Files on MacDonald and other leading members of the Labour Party would have been removed from the intelligence registry when Labour won the election. That they existed somewhere, he was in no doubt. Mac may have been under surveillance. If so, his liaison with a German socialite socialist would have excited great concern.

His train was making steam, doors were slamming, the stationmaster blew his whistle, but Fletcher was standing stock-still, a few feet short of the carriage.

''Ere,' the guard bawled at him, 'are you catching this train?'

Yes, he was, with only seconds to spare. The couplings clanged, the train jolted, and he stumbled across the compartment, brushing the knee of an elderly gentleman, a countryman to judge by his clothes. No matter. His mind was racing back over his days in Paris, madam's refusal to meet him – naive to have accepted Frenchie's word for that! – and now the admiral, urging him to pay her in full: what was going on?

'She'll accept the money,' Sinclair had declared with a star-tling degree of confidence. How did he know? Would she be instructed to? Sinclair suspected her of being a spy – he had

216

told the prime minister so – well perhaps she *was* a spy. Not for a foreign power, but an agent of the British Secret Service. A fading foreign beauty, a socialite, a socialist, a sophisticate was perhaps the perfect spy to catch the eye of a lonely old man weighed down by his country's cares.

'Has he made a fool of me?'

'What's that?' said the elderly gentleman in the seat opposite.

'Nothing,' said Fletcher. Nothing? After Zinoviev? No! The Secret Service conspiring to bring down another government . . . The notion was almost too twisted to contemplate.

7

On an ordinary evening Kristina Forster would have crossed rue des Rosiers to speak to her friend, Eli, but it was the Sabbath and he would have company and she was too tired for polite conversation.

Her last lesson on a Friday was with the daughter of an arms manufacturer, a spoilt pudding of a girl. To save money she was walking back to the boarding house that was her home, for now at least. There was no joy in her heart, only the prospect of ease for her aching body and a supper of sorts from the Printemps' kitchen. She would take some wine too, not to drink with a fine dinner and in good company as she used to, but as an offering to Morpheus, the only god she felt able to turn to. In crowded tenement rooms above the street, families were breaking bread together, and as she walked beneath their windows she tried to close her ears to their laugher, snatches of conversation, the clatter of cheap crockery, lest the ordinariness and the conviviality excite feelings she could not hold in check. A young Jewish man in a black hat and frock coat stepped from the pavement to let her pass by, and her gaze slipped beyond him to the opposite side of the

Andrew Williams

street where someone in secular clothes was gazing in the window of Goldenberg's *Charcuterie Orientale*. But for these stray males rue des Rosiers was deserted, with only rotten fruit and litter and the summer stink of drains to remind her of the colour and noise of the working day. On the corner with Ferdinand Duval she paused for breath and to rummage in her bag. Oh dear, how foolish! She had left the pistol in her room – and, oh, it was so important because it helped keep her calm.

A large motorcar was approaching at a stately pace, its lamps sweeping shop windows, creeping into doorways and under carriage arches. The rumble of its engine filled the narrow street like a river in a canyon, and like a force of nature the noise and light exerted a mesmerising effect upon her. It was not until its lamps were lapping the pavement in front of her that she started at the sound of footsteps. She was turning to look back when a man grabbed her by the shoulders, his arm sliding down across her chest. Dumont! She cried out, wriggled, fought to break free of him, and when he lifted the crook of his arm to her neck and clamped a hand over her mouth she bit him and heard him grunt with pain. For a second she thought she had broken loose, but he caught the sleeve of her jacket and his arms tightened around her chest again, squeezing the breath from her. Faint, dazzled by the car lights, she was only able to gasp, 'Stop, please.'

The motorcar had come to a halt and the driver was standing at his door. She tried to call out to him but the words died in her throat. This was what Mosley had threatened to do! The British Secret Service was going to kidnap her. Her attacker was bundling her towards the car. She tried to cry out but she didn't have the strength. The will to fight was draining from her. Hopeless, hopeless: a third man had suddenly appeared from the darkness of the street.

'*Attento! Attento!*' her attacker was shouting in alarm. 'Fabrizio!'

She saw the driver turn – but too late! The man from the shadows punched him in the face and he staggered back against his car. There were more punches, to his face, his body, his face, and his assailant grabbed him by the hair and swung his head against the door. With a sickening clunk, the driver called Fabrizio dropped like a stone. His associate released his grip on her at once, and she sank first to her knees and then on to her side. The motorcar was close enough to touch, her senses polluted by the throb and fumes of its engine. Her saviour was blinking in and out of the beam of the headlamps, and his face . . . only how could it be? It was Dumont! And her attacker – Fabrizio's comrade – was circling him like a crab, thrusting at him with a knife. She groaned, 'Please, God,' because she had been wrong, oh so mistaken. Monsieur Dumont was trying to free her!

Her attacker lunged at him with the knife again. Too slow! Dumont caught his arm, snapped it back at the elbow, pirouetted closer and aimed a kick between his legs. He sprawled backwards on the pavement and Dumont kicked him again, once in the head, twice in the head, thrice for good measure. The dancing done, her attacker lay quite still.

'Can you get up?' said Dumont, stumbling towards the car.

She stared at him blankly.

'Let me.'

She brushed his hand aside. 'No!'

'The police may come and these two . . .' – he glanced over his shoulder – '. . . we should go before they find their feet. Madame, let me help you.'

'Where?' Her voice cracked. 'Go where?'

'You'll be safe in your room tonight.'

She gazed beyond him to where her attacker lay curled in a ball on the pavement.

'Madame, please, if you can walk . . .?'

'Yes.' But she was shaking so badly she needed his arm.

Someone shouted down to them from a window on the other side of the street. 'An accident,' replied Dumont; 'no trouble here.' From another window, a complaint: 'Turn off that engine!'

The driver had risen to an elbow. He was hovering at the edge of consciousness. Blood was seeping from a gash on his forehead into his eyes and he was blinking furiously, with neither the wit nor the strength to wipe it away with a finger. He looked very young and pitiful. Why was he there? Who had sent him?

'I can't go any further, Monsieur Dumont,' she said.

'You can, it isn't far. Look, here's the courtyard.' He glanced back at the motorcar. 'I'll carry you.'

'No, no, I'll manage.' She was not going to let him sling her over his shoulder like a sack of coal, that was beneath her dignity.

Monsieur le propriétaire, Finder, had heard the commotion in the street and was waiting anxiously in the hall. 'Who is this man, Madame? What's going on?'

'We're going to carry Madame,' said Dumont, pointing to an old rout chair by the door. His voice . . . he was in command and would brook no refusal – 'and I have money. So you'll bring food – bread, cheese, whatever you have in your kitchen – and wine. Do you have anything stronger?'

Finder said he had brandy.

'Then bring the brandy too.'

8

She lay on the couch with her eyes closed and tried to breathe deeply. Finder was close to collapse, too. 'This is the Sabbath!' he gasped. She heard the tap running in the bathroom, she heard footsteps and Dumont say, 'Madame, drink this.' She lifted her head a little, clasped his hand and drew the glass to her lips. She was still trembling: how silly and weak he would think her.

'Enough?'

She nodded.

'Then rest.'

She closed her eyes again and tried to be calm but she was haunted by images of the attack, then the shocking thought that it had been nothing more than a pantomime and the young men who had tried to kidnap her were working for Dumont. But she remembered the knife and Dumont's vicious kick to the body of her assailant. No, he had come to her rescue; he had saved her.

'Monsieur . . .' He was sitting on her left, head back, his fingers spread on the broad arms of the chair. He was trying to recover his equilibrium too. 'Monsieur . . . thank you.'

He smiled. 'Your landlord has gone for food and wine.'

'Thank you for saving me.'

She stared at him longer than was polite. What did it matter? He had seen her at her lowest. Was Richard Dumont his real name? He was tall, handsome, in his thirties, with dark-brown hair and eyes and fine Gallic features. He dressed like a workman but spoke French like an educated Parisian. 'You told me to watch out and that something like this would happen,' she said, 'well, you were watching out for me.'

He smiled again.

'Who were those men?'

'I don't know.' He hesitated. 'I know who sent them.'

She swung her legs from the couch and sat up straight, to look him in the eye. 'Was it Commander Fletcher?'

'No, it was a man called William Joyce. He's here in Paris and he wants the prime minister's letters.'

'How do you know?'

'Calm yourself.'

'Tell me!'

'I will, but you're shaking. Let me fetch you a blanket.'

'I . . .' She leant back again and took a deep breath. 'Yes.'

The room was untidy, the bed unmade: what would Dumont think of her? And Monsieur Finder, what would he think of a widow with a younger man in her room? But that didn't matter because she would have to leave the Printemps in any case. Dumont had stripped the counterpane from her bed. Their hands touched as he placed it round her.

'I will tell you,' he said, settling back in the chair. 'William Joyce is a British fascist – actually, Irish. He hates communists, he hates socialists, he hates Jews; in fact, there aren't many people he doesn't hate, and he will use your letters to embarrass the prime minister and bring down the Labour government if he can. Well, the people who give him his orders will.'

'They're fascists? How do they know about my letters?'

'Because they have friends in the British Secret Service.'

'Fletcher?'

'Not Fletcher.'

'And these men in the British Secret Service, they wish to hurt Mr MacDonald?'

'Yes.'

'How do you know this William Joyce?'

He looked down momentarily and swept a hand through his hair, and she noticed his knuckles were grazed and bloody. 'It's complicated.'

'Is your name Dumont?'

'Does it matter?'

'Yes.'

'My name is Stewart. Richard Stewart.'

'That is your real name?'

He reached into his jacket for cigarettes. 'Do you mind?'

'Richard Stewart? You are English.'

'Richard Stewart, yes.'

'And this man Joyce? I have a right to know.'

'Do you?' He raised his eyebrows. 'I suppose you do. We work for the same man . . . or we used to.'

'You work for Fletcher.'

'And a man called Maxwell Knight. They're both employed by the British Secret Service, only Fletcher is working for the prime minister, and Knight is working for his enemies.'

'This is true?'

'Yes.' He lit his cigarette and inhaled deeply. 'Yes, it's the truth. The men who give Knight his orders will use the letters to try to bring down the Labour government and replace it with the Conservatives.'

'And this Knight is a fascist? *You're* a fascist?'

'No.'

'But you work for this Knight. Why? Do you want to hurt James?'

He frowned. 'Well, I . . . I have two children. I need to make a living.'

'You work for fascists for a living!' She folded her arms across her chest protectively. 'Like those two men?'

'They *are* fascists, true believers, and I'm not.'

'But you've hurt people too?'

He didn't reply and he didn't meet her gaze, only drew on his cigarette.

'You say you aren't a fascist but you do these things for money!'

'Madame! *You* are blackmailing your former lover, threatening to sell his letters to a newspaper even though you know it will ruin him and damage his party.'

Her turn to look away. 'I don't want to,' she said, quietly.

'You need the money, well, so do I.'

'Does Fletcher have the money?'

Andrew Williams

'I don't know. Perhaps tomorrow.'

'And he will return the letters to Mr MacDonald?'

'I think so.'

They sat for a while in silence, the Englishman called Stewart smoking his cigarette. She knew she should be grateful to him but she was disgusted. He should know how she felt about those people. He had to understand that what she was doing wasn't the same thing, not at all, because it wasn't only for the money. She loved James and he had returned that love – their letters were proof – only now he wanted to turn his back on her completely, and she wasn't going to let that happen.

'Your landlord,' said Stewart, leaning forward to extinguish his cigarette in the dregs of a coffee cup, 'where is he?'

'I have an ashtray,' she said, icily.

'Ah. Look, if you're feeling stronger . . .' He leant forward as if to rise. 'Let me see what happened to the food.'

'Monsieur Stewart—'

'Dick.'

'I *do* want to hurt him. I want revenge. You must understand, I supported him. I loved him, and on his terms. The Labour Party wouldn't approve, he said, his colleagues wouldn't approve, his family and the public wouldn't approve of me. "But Kristina, I love you," he said, and I accepted his terms because I loved him and I believed him to be a good and sincere man. I believed in his cause. I'm a socialist, Mr Stewart—'

'Dick.'

'You smile. You think only workers can be socialists?'

'I don't know many people with money who like paying more taxes.'

'You must understand, Dick, I didn't expect or want to fall in love again. I'm a widow . . .' She paused. 'It's difficult to explain. I loved my husband very much and I was sure I wouldn't fall in love with anyone else. Then I met James.' She

224

paused again. 'The things he wrote, if you read his letters you would understand. But the instant he became prime minister he turned his back on me. He wouldn't answer my letters. He refused to help me. He's ashamed of me; he treats me like a prostitute! So, yes,' she shifted excitedly, 'yes, I want revenge. Don't you think I deserve it?'

'Perhaps you do. I don't—'

'You think I should leave it to God? Where is God? No. We must make our own moral choices. There are men I would kill just like that,' she said, with a click of her fingers, 'and I would be sure I was doing the right thing, that it was the moral thing to do.'

'You think Ramsay MacDonald deserves to die?'

'No!' She leant forward with her elbows on her knees. 'He is weak and vain. He lied. He deserves to be punished and the only court I can turn to is the court of public opinion.'

He was staring at her intently. 'If it's revenge you want you must have made up your mind to sell the letters to a newspaper or to his enemies, like William Joyce.'

'Is he ashamed of me, Mr Stewart? Is that why he wants the letters – to destroy them? Because he poured out his love and his passion . . . He's a passionate man.'

'You want the world to know about your relationship, to read his letters: why? To prove to everyone he loved you? What do you think the newspapers will do with them? What will they say about you? You will have revenge, yes, but will the price be worth paying?'

She opened her mouth to speak but her chest and her throat were tight with emotion and she knew she would choke on her words, so she turned her head away and rested her cheek against the back of the couch. She wanted to end their conversation; she wanted her old life back; she wanted Stewart to leave her alone, but she was afraid to be alone. She tried to swallow her tears but was unable to school her body and they rose like a great wave until she was gasping, drowning in them, lost.

'You're in shock,' he said, quietly. He placed a hand on her shoulder. 'Drink a little water.' Impossible; she couldn't; not until the storm had passed.

9

Monsieur le propriétaire enquired after the health of his tenant but there was nothing in his voice or demeanour that suggested it mattered to him. To the contrary, he was sharp to the point of rudeness. With time to reflect as he prepared their supper tray he must have made the connection between Madame's 'friend' and the workman with the wild flowers who had disappeared in his lodging house for a suspiciously long time.

'You can go now, Monsieur,' he said, 'I will see to Madame.'

Stewart stood in the doorway. 'I'll take that,' he said, reaching for the tray. Monsieur must have noticed the cuts on his knuckles because he relinquished it without protest and stepped away. 'I don't want any trouble,' he said, pathetically.

There would be no trouble, no cause for complaint, because Stewart was willing to pay twice what their meagre supper of bread, cheese and cold old chicken was worth. He balanced the tray on a chair.

'A glass of brandy?'

'A glass of wine will be sufficient,' she said, dabbing the corner of her eyes with a handkerchief. 'That was *peinlich* . . . embarrassing. What must you think of me. And Monsieur Finder . . . A widow with a younger man in her room so late at night.'

Stewart smiled with amusement, and Madame too. He watched her press the handkerchief to her face. She was shaking and she began to cry again – only this time they were tears of nervous, convulsive, tempestuous, infectious laughter.

'I'm sorry,' she spluttered.

Stewart raised his glass of wine to her. 'Don't be. Are you hungry? You should eat something.'

'Perhaps a little.'

She took some bread and cheese and they ate and drank in silence, carefully avoiding each other's gaze. When she had finished, she said, 'I'm feeling better, you don't have to stay with me.'

'Then I'll wait downstairs.'

'Is it necessary?'

'Joyce may try to reach you again. He'll be expecting you to leave this place, and you should, first thing. I'll help you.'

She raised a perfectly defined eyebrow. 'Please understand, I'm grateful, I want to trust you but if you know where I live . . .' She paused. 'My friend, Eli Weiss – he has been so kind, but he's old, and these men, these fascists . . . I don't want to place him in danger. There's no one else in Paris I can turn to since . . . my misfortune. Well, you can see.' She opened her arms and gazed pointedly about the room. 'But you . . . You were a soldier?'

He nodded.

'I thought so. It's just, if you know where I live . . .'

'I'm not asking you to trust me.' He took another cigarette. 'In fact it would be a mistake to. But it's my job to keep you and your letters safe. Commander Fletcher will be back in Paris soon, perhaps tomorrow. I only ask that you meet him before you arrange to sell the letters to anyone else.'

She raised her glass to her lips, and then lowered it again. Her long fingers and her many rings reminded him of a gypsy fortune teller who had read his palm during the war. The gypsy had predicted he would 'live a very long life.' She had been astute enough to say the same thing to all her soldier clients. No one had ever returned to her tent to ask for their money back.

'Are you married, Richard? You have children, yes?'

'My wife died.'

'I'm sorry. Did you love her?'

'Yes.'

'You know what it is to love and to lose love then. Tell me about your wife?'

He sighed, picked up the bottle and poured her more wine. 'I . . . why?'

'Is it too painful?' She was gazing at him intently. 'Men find it so difficult to be honest about their feelings and Englishmen are the worst. Not Mr MacDonald. Well, at first, yes, he was reserved, even a little cold, but he has a passionate nature.'

'You said.'

'Yes.' She smiled weakly. 'Yes, I did. But we were talking of your wife . . . I ask because I want to trust you.'

'I see. Well, her name was Connie. Constance. We were neighbours in Rotherhithe – that's in London. I don't expect you've been there. Connie was a good person. Good to put up with me, you know, what with the war . . . some of us weren't quite right in the head – most of us.' He inspected his wine. 'Mac was right about that, wasn't he? Right about the war.'

Her face was twitching with suppressed emotion again. 'Yes, he was right about the war. Right about many things. You were in France?'

'And Belgium,' he said.

'My husband, too, and' – her bottom lip trembled – 'well, nothing was the same after, or will be again. Nothing.'

'But soldier on we must.'

'Yes.'

'More of this talk, Madame, and I will have to open the brandy.'

She gave him a warm smile. 'Thank you for rescuing me. Thank you for being kind to me.'

'You've thanked me enough.'

'Well . . .'

For a while neither of them wished to speak. Stewart watched her sip her wine and tidy some loose strands of hair, a small frown hovering at her brow. She looked tired and older in the dim flat light of the room, and yet she had presence. She was a very striking woman.

'You know I'm German?' she said at last.

'I wondered.'

'Do you hate Germans?'

'Kaisers and kings perhaps. German soldiers did some terrible things – my mother is from Belgium – but the men at the Front? No.'

'My husband said the same.'

'He died in the war?'

She looked down at her hands, cupped in her lap. 'No, after the war. Would you like to see a photograph?' Without waiting for an answer, she rose a little stiffly and walked across the room to her bedside table. 'Here. Do you recognise me?'

It was the portrait of the handsome young couple he had discovered only that morning.

'I was so young. It was taken to mark our engagement. He looks very dashing, don't you think?' She hummed and fumbled in her sleeve for her handkerchief again. 'He was very proud of his moustache.'

'What was his name?'

'Heinrich. Heinrich Forster. He looks aristocratic but his father was a businessman.'

Stewart felt the heat rising to his face. The letters he had found in her chest of drawers weren't written by a rival to Mac, or by an agent, a controller, a co-conspirator; there was no hidden meaning in them, no code; they were an expression of the deep love a husband and a wife had felt for each other.

'My Heinrich,' she said, taking the photograph from him. 'My poor, poor Heinrich. His father didn't approve of me.'

'Why?'

'Oh, because' – she dismissed the question with a wave – 'Heinrich refused to listen: We were in love.' She resumed her place on the couch and tucked the counterpane over and under her knees. 'Heinrich was a good man. He cared for his soldiers after the war, and his politics . . . in this he was very like James. The war turned him into a social democrat. He introduced workers' committees to his factories, he was full of ideas . . . he might have saved Germany.'

'From the war?'

'From the next war.'

'The war to end all wars: isn't that what we were promised?'

'Do you believe them?'

'No.'

'What *do* you believe?'

He drew deeply on his cigarette. 'What does it matter what a man like me believes? Sergeant Stewart reporting for duty.'

'The war has scarred you.'

'The war; the broken promises of the peace; the lies told by our politicians; the death of my wife . . . God,' he said, and tossed back the last of his wine. 'I'm having a glass of brandy. You?'

10

How peculiar that the only confidential conversation she should have enjoyed in months was with an English spy and working man. He was dressed like a market stallholder or bricklayer, even a road sweeper, and if he had been any of those things she would have assumed he had nothing intelligent to say, or nothing she cared to hear. As she watched him uncork the brandy and pour a large measure she felt embarrassed and a little ashamed of the privilege she had taken for granted all her life and was yearning to recover. Heinrich had invited his political colleagues to their villa in Berlin, and she had met many socialists. An economics professor had lectured her on proletarian revolution in Maxim's restaurant; while at Taverne Olympia she had danced with a Spanish count who was turning his estate into a workers' collective; she had drifted through fine art galleries with James and listened to his plans for the nationalisation of the coal mines. Lady Mosley had spoken of her campaign to enter parliament for Labour and Sir Oswald had outlined his programme for public works over a cocktail in the Adlon. They knew what was best for the 'masses' – a word they would often use in a slighting and patronising way – the singularity and importance of their own thoughts and feelings they took for granted, naturally. James knew and cared for people he called 'ordinary', but he had confided to her more than once that he wearied of the fight, and he felt at times like the chapel minister who delivers his 'love thy neighbour' sermon on a Sunday, but has no time for his congregation the rest of the week. In the years before the financial crash she had listened to many sermons from men unfit to make them. Here and now in the intimacy of her cheap boarding house room – unmade bed, clothes spilling from her drawers – she was breaking stale bread and drinking cheap brandy with one of the masses, and she knew at last what it was to be poor, and it was not a poverty of feeling or thought.

'Richard . . .?'

He raised his gaze.

'Do you think about the men you knew who didn't return from the war?'

'Sometimes.'

'What would they want us to do?'

He snorted derisively.

'What does that mean?' she said, angrily. 'You think because I've lived a privileged life I don't have scars, that I haven't known loss and pain?'

'I didn't mean to suggest—'

'I lost both my brothers, and, and . . . others I loved deeply. My husband you know, he—'

'Madame, I'm sorry. It's just . . . it's hard to talk about. What would my comrades want? Something better. And like them I used to believe we were fighting for a fairer country. Now my only concern is my family.'

'How old are your children?'

'Florence is eight and Pierre is six.'

'Don't you care what sort of world they'll grow up in?'

'We'll get by. What can I do?'

'Well, if I may . . .' She spread her hands on the counterpane, smoothing some of the creases. 'You could stop working for this man Knight, stop helping fascists. You don't know what these people are like, Richard. I've seen them in Germany; they are full of hate.'

'I'm not a fascist, didn't I say so? I make a living. If you want me to consider more than that, hand over the letters.'

'I don't—'

'Give them to me!' he said, forcefully. 'Give them to me and I'll give them to Commander Fletcher. You look shocked. Why? You want money, you want revenge, you want to hurt him and you don't mind if you bring down Labour in the process.'

'How dare you,' she said, her voice shaking with fury. 'There's no comparison. You should leave!'

'I meant no offence. You are doing what you need to do to get by. I do the same.'

'You should go.'

He placed his glass on the tray. 'I'll be in the hall. We should leave here first thing in the morning.'

'I don't need your help.'

'Please, Madame, for your sake and mine. These people, you say you know their kind . . .'

She stared at him defiantly, her hands balled in fists. She was angry, very angry, mainly with her little outburst. She may as well have admitted he was right to reprove her for preaching.

'Look, if it helps,' he said, 'my arrangement with Knight and his friends came to an end on the street out there' – he reached into his waistcoat pocket for a badly scratched watch – 'three hours ago.'

'You want me to say I'm sorry?'

'It's late.' He got to his feet. 'You should rest, and I'll knock on your door at half past seven.'

'No, stay!' she said. 'You can't sleep in the hall. Sleep on the couch.'

'What will *Monsieur le propriétaire* say?'

'He'll say, "can't that young man find someone better to sleep with than that old tart?"' She gave a short laugh. 'Honestly, it doesn't matter what he says.'

He smiled. 'Madame, thank you.'

11

Stewart waited on the landing until she called him inside. The room was dark but for a candle on her bedside table. He removed his boots and socks, his jacket and waistcoat, and hung them on the back of a chair. The couch was too tight for his shoulders, but it didn't matter because he wasn't going to sleep.

'Richard?'

'Yes.'

'I'll leave the candle.'

'Goodnight, Madame.' He turned on his side to face the back of the couch.

'Richard?

'Yes.'

'Please call me Kristina.'

He smiled. 'Goodnight then Kristina.'

Madame Kristina Forster. He lay there listening to Kristina shifting in bed. He expected her to lie awake but her breathing changed after only a few minutes. What a strange evening it had turned out to be. Madame the blackmailer, the woman Knight referred to as 'Mac's tart' and 'the bitch', was Kristina, the lover, the widow, the socialist socialite, vivacious, thoughtful, determined, suffering. He had a sense of her now and to his mind she was a decent, straightforward woman, trying to keep her head above water. Where was her family? Did she have a friend she could turn to? He should have enquired. She talked of selling her story and bringing MacDonald low but he didn't believe her. She wanted Mac to acknowledge the pain he had caused – was causing her. She wanted him to *want* to help her. That's what he was going to tell Fletcher: 'She'll take the money.' She deserved her money; 'and I deserve my money'; Mac deserved his letters, and fucking Knight and whoever was paying him deserved nothing and would receive nothing. Oh, how she hated fascists! It was visceral: she shuddered at the name. His own mercenary arrangement with them she was prepared to overlook because she was desperate to trust someone. Trust nurtured the giving of trust. The wine, the breaking of bread, the intimacy of the evening; he felt she had bound him to act in good faith. He didn't regret that – on the contrary, he felt happier. Goodness, it might even be the right thing to do. As he lay on her musty old couch staring into the shadows of the room, the scent of her perfume in the air, he was suddenly conscious that he was smiling.

11

7 June 1930

M AJOR MORTON WAS waiting at the foot of the bandstand steps in his customary uniform of city suit and artillery tie. At a more civilised Saturday hour he would have stood out like a sore thumb in the weekend crowd of mothers and fathers with their children and dogs, but at half past six in the morning Hyde Park was deserted. The sun was yet to dissipate the mist lying low over the lake and there were fine pearls of moisture on Knight's cricket sweater. He was a few minutes late, and punctilious, fastidious Morton made a point of consulting his watch to demonstrate his displeasure. What matter that decent folk were still in their beds or buttering their toast.

'I'm sorry to ask you here at short notice, Max,' he said, slipping his umbrella into his left hand to offer his right; 'but the plan has changed. Can you contact your chaps *tout suite*? Reggie Fletcher is back in the fold.'

Knight frowned. 'I thought he was freelancing for Mac?'

'He was, and now he isn't. The Service is seeing to things.'

'Then what do you want my fellows to do?'

"Fletcher is still relying on Frenchie. As for your other man . . . I forget his name?'

'William Joyce.'

'Joyce, yes. He may still be of use. Let's see how Fletcher gets on.' He paused. 'Shall we walk?'

They turned towards the lake, Morton pushing forward at a good marching pace. 'Joyce still has the money?'

'Yes.'

'Major Ball will want it returned to the Conservative Party's fighting fund, naturally. I don't imagine the Party Chairman knows about this little enterprise. Ball will have thought it best to spare him the details. He was hoping your chaps would be able to acquire the letters without paying.'

'Is Fletcher paying?'

'Those are his instructions.'

'Eight thousand pounds! Why? Surely it would be—'

'Why?' Morton swung the tip of his umbrella at a piece of litter. 'Why? Because the prime minister has approached the Service and the Chief, in his wisdom, has decided it is in our interests to make him feel beholden to us.'

With a grinding of gravel he turned smartly, as if answering an order to perform an about-face. 'Well, Max, you better get on and contact your people. I hope it isn't a great inconvenience.'

They shook hands again and Knight watched him march away to breakfast. Smoked haddock perhaps, or eggs and bacon, and thick marmalade on lightly buttered toast. Knight sighed. One day they might be able to conduct their business over a breakfast table instead of meeting in a park like sexual deviants. With Mac in disgrace and Labour on the slide, Morton would have felt obliged to bring him inside the Service lest he be tempted by a sudden remunerative attack of conscience to speak to a newspaper. But the plan was unravelling, his own role diminishing. The Service was still relying on one of his agents to acquire the letters, only it was unclear now what use it intended to make of them. There was a problem with the agent too: Frenchie was behaving very strangely. 'Is it my fault?' In all conscience, no. Morton would hold him responsible all the same. He was going to have to clean up the mess and quickly.

It wasn't going to be easy with his wife at home. She would be up and about and the second he crossed the threshold she would start haranguing him about his pets. How could he bear the smell? Why was it necessary to have so many? The monkey should be in a cage! Thankfully she spent most of her time in the country. She had come to London for a meeting of their fascist comrades and she was expecting him to accompany her. But he was going to have to square things with Joyce in Paris first. She would be angry about that too. Everyone was angry. Joyce had telephoned him in the early hours: 'I'm going to kill that cunt Stewart.'

'Come on, William, I don't expect he realised they were working for you,' he had replied.

Joyce had refused to listen. 'I'll get that bitch Forster next time, don't you worry, Max.'

Well, there would be no next time. Order from the top: leave her alone, watching brief only, oh, and bring back the money, won't you. Joyce was going to spit blood, and damn it, he had a right to. Frenchie had gone too far. Was it part of a devious scheme to win Frau Forster's confidence? If so, he had not thought to communicate it to his comrades. But that was the trouble with mercenaries: you couldn't be sure they acknowledged having any comrades.

'You're up early, Mr Knight.' The newsagent at Sloane Square Underground station was arranging papers on the stand outside his kiosk. 'There you go,' he said, folding copies of *The Times* and the *Express*. 'Regards to Mrs Knight.'

Gwladys would be bossing their maid about, like an opera diva exercising her voice for the big scene to come with her husband. His marriage had been a terrible mistake. She would be waiting with her hands on her hips in the hall and if she was in a mood to she would try to humiliate him. From the pavement outside their mansion block he gazed up at his windows. The curtains were drawn: she was ready for battle.

'All right, my darling,' he muttered. He wasn't going to put up with her tantrums, any more than he would permit Frenchie to undermine his standing with the Service. He sighed – 'that's decided' – and he reached into his trouser pocket for his keys. If Stewart couldn't do the job, Joyce would have to relieve him of his duties and secure the letters in whatever way he saw fit.

2

As Knight was mounting the stairs to his apartment with the leaden tread of the condemned, Stewart was rattling out of Paris on a train with his charge.

They had carried what they could from her lodgings, bought a second-class Metro ticket to Gare St Lazare and another from the station for the suburbs. Madame Forster had protested, 'I have pupils to teach. I can't live without money.'

'You're selling the letters, aren't you?' he had replied.

Were they in the embroidered bag on the seat beside her? He tried to put the thought from his mind.

She chose to leave the train at pretty Marly-le-Roi because she had visited the town on her honeymoon and had fond memories of strolling arm in arm with her husband in its royal park. Her honeymoon hotel was out of the question. Stewart found her a room in a modest *pension* on the cobbled main street. 'You'll be safe here.' He carried her luggage to her room, then made to leave.

'You'll speak to your Commander Fletcher?' she said.

That was his intention, yes.

'Thank you, Richard.' She held out a hand, her green eyes shining with weary tears.

The *pension* was close to the station and he was able to board a train for Paris almost at once. He caught another to the Boulevard de Sébastopol, where he found a cafe for coffee, a pastry and a cigarette. There was a lazy summer Sabbath feel to the streets of the *Pletzel*. The kosher butchers and bakers were shut, the tailor's, and Weiss's bookshop too. Visitors to the district strolled from window to window in the sunshine, intrigued by its exotic reputation, hoping to observe shtetl Jews in their broad hats and frock coats and to hear the locals speaking in a foreign tongue. Stewart was on the *qui vive* for anyone showing the same sort of interest in him. Thankfully, there was no one. That it was just a matter of time, he did not doubt. A bugger like Joyce would neither forgive nor forget him. He was going to have to leave Bilbaut's that day, that morning, at once.

In the entrance hall *Monsieur le propriétaire* was watching his son slop filthy water on the floor with a mop.

'Ah, Monsieur Dumont, I have two messages for you.' He produced them from his jacket pocket. 'You are popular, no?'

'So it seems.'

'But Monsieur, you will not have heard! Eli Weiss has been attacked.' Frenk clutched his head with both hands. 'They beat him in his own shop. An old man . . . Who would do such a thing?'

'When?'

'Yesterday afternoon.' Frenk's voice shook with emotion. 'Terrible. They called him a stinking Jew!'

'Is he badly hurt?'

'They found him this morning. It's a wonder he didn't die in the night. The pigs: they cut off a finger. That old man has endured so much. He's from Pinsk, you know, where they massacre Jews.'

'I didn't know. I'm sorry. Sorry for all that has happened

to him.' *Sorry*? To be sorry wasn't enough. Turning to the stairs, he raced up to his room; leant against the door to catch his breath; tried to make sense of his feelings. Careless, careless, careless not to recognise that his refusal to treat with Joyce had put the old man in danger. Knight must have given that vicious cunt the address of the bookshop. Mother Superior wasn't safe in his hands, let alone a socialist and a Jew. His blackshirt thugs had clearly tortured him for the name of Madame Forster's *pension*. Of course, code name Frenchie was paid not to care – only this time . . . this time he did care.

He lit a cigarette and considered what was to be done. There were the messages, the first a telegram from Fletcher: *Returning with fresh instructions. Arrive Paris 11.30. Report at once.*

The second – a *carte bleue* – was from the man at the front of his thoughts: *Orders from M*, Joyce had written, *request meeting at Cosmos as soon as able.* Accepting his invitation would be a mad and dangerous thing to do, and something to ponder calmly for at least the length of a cigarette.

When he had drawn all the inspiration he could from it, he packed his things into his knapsack, glanced around the room and made for the door. Kind decent old Eli had directed him to Madame Bilbaut's, Eli, the *luftmensch* – the dreamer – who was incapable of hurting a fly. In a bookcase at home in Rotherhithe there was a translation of the collected fascist ramblings of the leader of the blackshirts, Benito Mussolini. It was a gift from Knight, who wanted his casuals to become true believers. He should have saved his money and his breath: it was rotten stuff. But there was a line Stewart remembered and it seemed appropriate now: 'Better to live one day as a lion than a hundred years as a sheep.' He would hold that thought at the front of his mind on his way to the Cosmos.

3

Fletcher was booked on the early flight from Croydon Airport.
The passengers were late boarding, the pilot perilously close
to the end of the runway, and the plane bucked and reared like
a wild stallion, only running out of cloud into the blue on its
descent into Paris. After so many years at sea it was a blow to
his pride to lose his breakfast over the Channel. And the turbu-
lence seemed to follow him into the terminal at Le Bourget.
Drysdale was there to meet him.

'See the fellow with the thick moustache and the newspaper
at the tabac? He's from the Bureau.'

'You're sure?' said Fletcher.

'Oh yes. Captain Toussaint telephoned me yesterday. His
chaps in Bern have spoken to the people I spoke to. "We're
allies, Monsieur Drysdale," he said, "so if there's anything we
can do to help you find Madame Forster. She is a close friend
of your prime minister, no?"'

Fletcher groaned. 'If she has a work permit it won't take
them long to find her.'

An embassy car was waiting outside the terminal. The driver
took his case and he slid on to the red leather bench seat, the
station chief at his side. As they turned from the airport on to
the road to the city, Drysdale leant closer. 'I have the money,
by the way. I imagine that's what this is about.'

Fletcher glared at him – 'don't imagine' – then turned back
to the window. The flight from London, the Bureau agent – he
was in a filthy mood. Worse still was his growing sense of
unease about the role the service was now playing in the affair.
He felt out of control, as if he was still bumping along the
runway. Just the thought made him feel queasy. He had
invested too much in another man's agent. Madame could have

her money, but he would insist on handing it to her in person, and he would impress upon her the consequences of double-dealing the British Secret Service. Only, who was double-dealing whom? Sinclair seemed so certain she would accept it. Admirals sound certain about everything, but Fletcher was haunted by an image of this one at the wheel of his ridiculous motorcar, his bowler hat pulled low, a smug smile twitching the corners of his mouth.

They were driving through La Chapelle and glinting in the sun to his right was the dome of Sacré-Coeur. Drysdale was humming a tune under his breath.

'Will you ask your secretary to make a reservation for me?' said Fletcher. 'I want to catch a train back to London tonight.'

Drysdale raised an eyebrow. 'That soon?'

'Yes. And I need a couple of good men for some street work. They'll have to be top-notch because the man they will be following is one of the best.'

4

The red and black pirate awning was stretched taut across the pavement as before, and there were families sitting at tables in its shade. The Cosmos was a popular bistro with a reputation for reasonably priced food and friendly waiters – if they weren't serving you their politics. Stewart watched them from a bench by the fountain in the centre of the square. There were three waiters working the tables, cooks and a proprietor inside, and if they were preparing a reception for him that would be where it would take place. But there was nothing he could learn of their plans from the square. Rising from the bench, he walked towards the entrance.

The fat forty-something proprietor of the bistro was behind his counter. His easy expression changed at once. 'You!'

'And at the invitation of Monsieur Seed. No need to show me the way.'

Up came his counter all the same. By Christ, he was a big fellow, and he was disconcertingly dressed like a butcher in a bloodstained apron. The curtain parted behind him and a waiter emerged with a tray of clean glasses. His right eye was purple and closed, his bottom lip swollen and split. Stewart thought 'the driver,' because the face of his companion had made intimate contact with his boot and would be worse. Waiter-driver-kidnapper recognised him at once. The glasses tinkled as he placed them clumsily on the counter. A champagne flute toppled and rolled off the edge and with surprising dexterity *Monsieur le propriétaire* caught it in flight. He rose with the glass clutched in a fist like a weapon. Oh, he was itching to use it, but how much of a scene was he prepared to tolerate in his bistro at lunchtime?

'Get on with it or get out of my way,' Stewart snarled at him. The table to his right was laid with silver cutlery if he made the wrong choice.

But the proprietor nodded to his waiter and they took a step away. Perhaps they were hoping their friend Seed would manage things. That he knew a thing or two about knives was carved in a ragged line across his face. Dick climbed the stairs quickly to the well-lit landing and knocked firmly at room 4. To the right of the door, Mussolini was still straining for his top C.

'Well, Dick, you do know how to make friends,' said Joyce.

He was wearing a striped shirt and flannel trousers, and if he was carrying a knife it was hidden in a very discreet place. 'Come in. My room is the only safe place for you to be,' he said, taking half a step back to let him pass.

'After you, William.'

'Ah, Dick. Have it your own way now.'

A small suitcase was open on the bed and his wardrobe was draped around the room. 'Packing, as you see,' he said, flinging a corner of the bedspread over the case. 'Not much for me to do now they've decided to pay the tart what she wants. Sit down. Whisky?' There was a bottle of the Irish on the vanity table. 'I spoke to Max –that's Agent M to you – this morning: it's Secret Service now. Here.' He handed Dick a glass. 'I don't suppose Fletcher's had a chance to tell you. Cheers.' He took a sip, then flourished his glass at the chair. 'Sit. Sit. I'll take the bed. Yes. Fletcher; he's counting on you, of course. We all are . . . after last night.' He smiled again, ruefully. 'I don't know how you managed to do it.'

'What?'

'Well, she seems to trust you. Her landlord at the Printemps told Giovanni she left with a younger man. Dark-brown hair and eyes, thin face, cheap suit, your height . . . *you*, in fact. He seemed to think you were having an affair? That *would* be a turn-up for the books . . . you and the prime minister's old tart. It isn't true though, is it? The grubby Jew has a dirty mind. Anyway, as I say, Max wants you to do as you're told. Arrange a meeting, then your job's done. Let Fletcher sort it out.'

Stewart raised his glass to his lips. He associated whisky with the war. At seven and sixpence a bottle it was an officer's tipple, but he had managed to take a drop from time to time. He had emptied a dead officer's hipflask on the first day of the Somme.

'M isn't happy with you,' said Joyce.

'Oh, dear,' he replied with faux concern. 'Why the change? I thought he wanted the letters for his own contacts.'

'You're not privileged to know.'

'And you are?'

'A different tactic, that's all,' said Joyce. Clearly he didn't have a clue. 'Pity. If you hadn't interfered we would have them by now and there would be no need to involve Fletcher. You must have forgotten where your loyalties lie.'

'I haven't forgotten.' Dick reached into his jacket pocket for his cigarettes.

'What did you think you were doing then?'

'I told you not to touch her. We agreed I'd do it my way,' he said. 'Ashtray?'

Joyce snorted sceptically. 'We agreed no such thing. Are you hoping to make more money? You won't, you know.' He picked up a thick cut-glass ashtray from the chest of drawers – 'Here' – and slid it across the low table.

'Thanks.' Stewart cradled it in his left hand, then tapped the ash from his cigarette. 'What about another drink?'

'You've got a bloody nerve. Where is she, Stewart?'

'Montmartre. A *pension* called le Petit Oiseau.'

Joyce squinted at him. 'Expect you're lying. Can I tell Max you're going to follow his orders?'

'That drink . . .?'

'All right, a wee one.' Joyce rose and reached for Stewart's empty glass, which was perfect: he struck the bugger on the temple, and like a tree torn up by its roots in a storm he toppled against the foot of the bed. Stewart fell upon him, grabbing his hair, jerking his head forward then crashing it back against the bed end. 'Were you there? Did torturing an old man make you feel good?'

'I wasn't,' Joyce groaned.

Stewart hit him with the ashtray again and the bridge of his nose gave way. 'Did you tell them to take a finger?'

He raised a feeble hand to his face, but Stewart brushed it aside. 'You're going to pay. How much did Knight give you?' Blood from a gash in his forehead was trickling into his eyes. He was in no fit state to answer. Stewart placed the ashtray back on the table, stepped over Joyce's legs and swept the bedspread back from the case. There were six brown-paper bricks of money inside. He felt the weight of one, then tore the wrapping: a thousand in twenties and fifties. Six thousand pounds altogether. It was the price the men who gave Knight his orders were willing to pay before Joyce and his blackshirts decided there was no need to pay anything.

The Irishman was stirring, struggling to his knees. Stewart picked up the ashtray with half a mind to lay him flat again. 'Stay down.' A shove with a foot was sufficient to topple the bugger. He would be no more trouble. His blackshirt comrades, however . . . they would be waiting with a bag for Stewart's head and a knife for his ribs. They were Italian fascists, they had been whipped and humiliated: the only dish they would want to serve him would be the one they always served cold. He needed something, a distraction, a diversion – he needed a wooden chair. Lifting it by the back, he heaved it out of the window and watched it land on the bistro's awning then bounce on to the pavement. A woman screamed, men were shouting, children wailing. Perfect. He was counting on a kerfuffle. Joyce was stirring again and as a precaution he took the room key from the dressing table and locked the door.

The waiter with the bruises was lurking beyond the curtain at the foot of the stairs, but distracted by the commotion outside he turned too late. Stewart shoved him across a table, snatched a jug from the counter and crowned him with it. On the pavement at the front of the bistro, *le patron* was wringing his hands apologetically and gesturing as only Italians know how to. He caught Stewart's eye for a moment with a look of ineffable hatred. Sooner or later there would be a reckoning, only not now. No, Stewart was walking away from him with a light step, the weight of six thousand pounds bumping his hips and his chest.

5

With nothing to do but bide his time Fletcher chose to lunch at the Métropole. He ordered sea bass with a lemon and herb dressing on a bed of spinach, washed down with a crisp white wine from the Loire. But the cork was barely out of the bottle when the waiter returned to his table with a note:

St Roch, rue Saint-Honoré 15.00.

He was going to have to leave his fish spitting in the kitchen. A taste of the wine and he dumped his napkin on the table. At the door he paused to sign a chit and observe the dining room in one of its many mirrors. A thin middle-aged man with a dark pointy beard and tortoiseshell spectacles was gesturing frantically to a waiter. No doubt, he was cursing under his breath too.

Fletcher was waiting for a cab when pointy-beard from the Bureau walked out of the hotel and joined him on the pavement. 'Taxi, Monsieur?' said the doorman.

Yes, Bureau man wanted a taxi. He stood a few feet from Fletcher, a cigarette drooping from the corner of his mouth, his gaze fixed on the other side of the street. From his easy manner Fletcher took him for an agent of some experience. A taxicab drew up in front of the hotel and the doorman beckoned: 'Where to, *monsieur*?'

'Bois de Boulogne,' replied Fletcher.

But as soon as the cab was clear of the hotel he tapped the driver on the shoulder and instructed him to turn in the opposite direction: 'Place de la Concorde, *s'il vous plaît.*'

Stewart was waiting in the chapel of the queen saint with the pigtails where they had met on their last visit to the church. A note on the wrought-iron screen described her as the patron saint of good wives with bad husbands.

'There's blood on your shirt,' said Fletcher, settling beside him.

Stewart was leaning forward, with his forearms across his knees and his hands clasped in reflection or prayer. 'Nicked myself shaving,' he replied, which was plainly a lie.

'There's been some trouble?'

'It's not my blood.'

'Then who's—'

Stewart cut across him. 'I've spoken to her. She's ready to sell.'

'Then arrange a meeting today. We're going to pay her what she wants.'

'Who's paying? The prime minister?'

Fletcher frowned. 'What does it matter? It's not your concern.'

'Secret Service money then.'

'Just arrange the meeting.'

'Madame Forster will ask me.'

'Nonsense. She's a blackmailer. She asked for eight thousand pounds and that's what she's getting, *with* the authority of the man who wrote the letters.'

'She's frightened.'

'Not of you, it seems.'

'Oh, of me too.' Stewart paused. 'Her postman, old man Weiss, was badly beaten yesterday.'

Fletcher turned to face him. 'By whom?'

'Someone else wants the letters, it seems.'

'Do you have any idea who?'

Stewart shrugged. 'Someone workin' for a newspaper? Mac's enemies, I suppose.'

'Bloody hell, man, why don't you know? Is she safe? Where is she? The sooner we exchange the better.'

'That would be best, but I think it would be safer if I do it.'

Fletcher snorted. 'Safer?' Heads turned in the nave. An

elderly woman who had been engrossed in saying decades of her rosary tut-tutted and wagged a finger. Fletcher was in the mood to raise two in return. 'Safer? With a toerag like you, Stewart? Just arrange the bloody meeting. That's what I'm paying you to do.'

Stewart shrugged again. 'I'll try.'

'Do you have an address?'

'I have a telephone number.'

'Then arrange the handover, you hear?'

'Madame will insist on choosin' the location.'

'Fine, fine, just do it today. In time for me to catch the last train home.'

6

Stewart left the church with an uneasy feeling that something had been decided that he was not privy to. Perhaps for once in his miserable life William Joyce was telling the truth. Fletcher had been tetchy, belligerent, reluctant to answer questions and look Stewart in the eye. He seemed out of sorts with the world. His stomach had rumbled through their meeting like a distant earthquake. Perhaps it didn't matter. Payment in full, *with* the authority of the man who wrote the letters, was what mattered. There was nothing to be gained by delay; on that they were in complete accord. Joyce would be after his blood. His black-shirt friends would consider spilling it a matter of honour, which was their word for pride. The sooner Stewart said *au revoir, Paris* the better.

The taxi driver was unimpressed by his appearance and insisted on payment in advance. That made him smile. Why, with Joyce's money in his knapsack and jacket he was almost a French-franc millionaire. The cab drew up in rue Ferdinand Duval where the blackshirts' big Daimler had parked the evening before. The kerb and pavement were speckled brown with dried blood, like the breast of a thrush.

'*Oy gevalt!*' The Printemps' proprietor greeted him with a look of horror. 'You!'

'Please be calm, Monsieur. I'm to collect Madame Forster's trunk, that's all.'

'The police were here!' he said. "Monsieur Finder, tell us where she is or you'll be in trouble!" "Look, how do I know?," I said, "how do I know?"'

'The local police?'

'Criminal. The *Sûreté*. They were polite, they were decent but the other two. . .' He said something rude in Yiddish. 'They said they were police too, but they weren't. No, no.'

'Describe them. Were they Italian?'

'*Feh!* Is it my business?' Finder threw up his hands theatrically. 'I need to be sure you're not stealing Madame's trunk. She has a new address?'

'Is that your business? Did they tell you to ask?'

He was avoiding Stewart's gaze. 'I don't know what they promised, but you should be careful, Monsieur. Do you know Eli Weiss, the bookseller?'

The taxi driver was smoking a cigarette. He had no intention of helping Stewart with Madame's luggage. As the cab pulled away from the *pension* Stewart caught a glimpse of a stout male figure beneath the arch he had shared with the flower lady the day before. Police informer or fascist? It didn't matter; the pack was in pursuit.

At the Gare St Lazare he bought tickets for three different destinations and caught the train to Marly with seconds to spare. To be sure no one was following him he left the train at Bougival and sat on Madame's trunk to wait for the next. By the time he had hauled it up the stairs to her room at the *pension* in Marly it was half past five. She had left him a note:

would her *'protecteur'* join her in the royal park? She would wait for him on a bench above the formal garden, at the edge of the gravel ride known as the Allée Royale.

7

The sun was shining through the leaves of a lime tree and casting heart-shaped shadows upon her skirt. The joy Kristina Forster felt was indescribable. To find the same bench after so many years! The view to the Sun King's mirror pool, cone-shaped conifers on guard at the edge . . . it was just how she remembered it on her honeymoon. *Le jardin à la française.* Peace and a promise of order in a perfectly symmetrical arrangement of parterres, topiaries, manicured lawns, white stone statues and reflecting pools. Everything as it ought to be; *le meilleur des mondes possibles.* That was how it had seemed to her thirty years ago when she was certain of the world and her place and full of hope for years that were now past. Eyes closed, she could hear in the whispering limes an echo of that time, of their laughter and the soft words Heinrich had spoken to her. What plans they had made!

From the bench at the edge of the ride she watched gardeners at work below. They were clipping away new growth that threatened the old shape and order. There was a gentle rhythm to the snapping of their shears as they worked their way round the conifers. Through changing seasons they mowed and trimmed and raked to capture a moment in time and hold it there. The happy consequence of their dedication to preserving the past was an hour of memories she thought she might have lost for ever in the pain and grief of the last few years.

But when the sun slipped behind a cloud there was a chill in the air, and she remembered that the sense of timelessness was an illusion as insubstantial as the sun-gold that had glittered in the water of the reflecting pool below her and in her memories of her husband in the garden. There had been a palace here once, courtyards, pavilions, a famous statue called the Globes, water jets and waterfalls. Their son, Lorentz, was born a year after their honeymoon. Eighteen years later he had died fighting in France. Millions died, and, when it was all over, Heinrich had died too. She had lived most of her life in the years since her honeymoon and the journey they had set out on together she was going to complete alone. The world had changed for ever and was still changing for the worse. There was peace in the garden and she wanted peace, but she wanted to laugh and sing too – laugh and sing to the end. But with whom?

She recognised Dick in silhouette as he crested the rise of the long gravel ride. He was still half a kilometre away but approaching quickly, knapsack slung on his left shoulder, right arm swinging straight like a marching soldier. For all the kindness he had shown to her, she found it hard not to think of him as a menacing presence. By his own admission he was not a good man; he *was* a clever man, although he tried to disguise it with his rough manners. Those who have suffered grief and pain are quick to recognise its shadow in others. He spoke as one who viewed the world from a great distance. He was one of the hollow men. She had been acquainted with many after the war. What was left, what the war had spared, was difficult to know.

She rose self-consciously to greet him with a smile. For the first time in many months she was gaily dressed in a pink silk blouse and a light blue skirt rather than the sober workaday blue or black that she wore for her teaching life in the *Pletzel*.

'You're well, Madame?' He took her hand lightly.

'I thought we agreed it was to be Kristina. Yes, thank you. This park . . . But I'm sorry you've had to walk so far to find me. Please sit.'

He took off his jacket and his cap and his hair was wet with perspiration.

'The Palace of Versailles is only a few kilometres away,' she said, 'this was where King Louis came to escape his court. You look tired. Have you eaten?'

'No.'

'Here.' She opened the bag at her feet. 'I have some bread and sausage and an apple.'

He took them from her with a small smile of gratitude and placed them on the bench. 'Thank you.' He smiled at her again, then looked away. Should she let him enjoy the peace of the garden? Only, she was anxious to know: 'You've spoken to Commander Fletcher?'

'Yes,' he said, turning back to address her; 'and he's willing to pay eight thousand pounds. He wants to conclude everything today.'

'I see.'

'You don't look very pleased. Isn't that what you want? Or were you going to ask for more?'

'No. No more.'

Picking up the bread, he tore it in half and folded it around the sausage.

'Commander Fletcher will give my letters to James?' she said.

The sandwich was hovering at his lips – 'Hum. Now that's a question' – he lowered it to his lap. 'He has good intentions, but the Secret Service are in charge now.'

'He was always working for the Secret Service, no?'

'He was working for the prime minister.' He placed his sandwich on the bench and dusted flour from his hands. 'There's something I have to tell you. I'm sorry but it's bad news. The men who attacked you visited Monsieur Weiss's bookshop first . . .'

'Oh, no.' She raised her hands to her mouth.

'That's how they found you.'

'Please God.'

'He's alive. He'll recover.'

'That poor dear man.'

'He's all right, he'll survive.'

'You've seen him?'

He hesitated. 'My landlord, Frenk—'

'Tell me what he said. Was it that man, Joyce?'

'The men who attacked you. They beat Eli and cut off his little finger—'

She cried out and covered her face.

'He's a tough old bird. Finder says he'll recover.'

'Because he's a Jew. They hurt him because he's a Jew.'

'They wanted to know where to find you.'

'You don't know these people like I do!' she said, her voice shaking with fury. 'But of course you do! You do! They're your friends, you help them! How did they know to go to Eli's bookshop?'

He looked down at his hands. 'You gave Downing Street his address. We were to leave messages for you there, remember?'

'I didn't give it to those beasts!'

'No,' he said quietly, 'that was me.'

She stiffened. 'Are you saying you're—'

'Listen! No, I'm not. You saw what happened last night. But I *was* working for those people – not Joyce, the Secret Service, at least that part of it that wants to bring down the Labour government . . .'

She opened her mouth to speak but he raised his right hand to prevent her.

'Let me explain. I told you, there are men in the Secret Service that see no difference between Labour socialists and the communists. I told you, Knight is one of them and I do . . . *used* to do jobs for him. Joyce works for him too. Knight and whoever in the Secret Service pays him want the letters. I don't know, to leak them to a newspaper in Paris or at home – they've done that sort of thing before. That's why the prime minister approached Fletcher. He's Secret Service but he's Labour too. He was working for the prime minister and no one in the Secret Service was to know, only somehow they found out . . .'

She opened her mouth to speak, but he was too quick again.

'A spy perhaps or Mosley. Knight asked me to work with Fletcher, and I was the one who told him about the bookshop. I'm sorry. I didn't expect him to send Joyce, but I should have done. Yes, I know these people, I know what they're like.'

She glared at him, and wanted to lash out: 'You!' He was to blame. 'But I'm responsible too – and after all I've been through, I should have known.'

'You couldn't know. Important men, accountable to no one, see your letters as a way to subvert a government they hate. They don't care if an old Jew gets hurt, or you, if it's in the national interest, by which they mean their own interest. Yes, they use fascists like Knight and Joyce, they use ruthless men – they used me.'

No, she knew she was responsible. Tears of frustration and regret filled her eyes. Her judgement had been clouded by her anger and her desperation. She had placed Eli in danger in pursuit of something unworthy.

'I'm sorry,' he said again.

'I've been very foolish.'

'I don't know if . . .' He took a handkerchief from his jacket pocket. 'It's not very clean.'

She brushed away a tear with her finger, then laughed. 'Thank you, but I have one,' she said, fishing a cotton square from her sleeve. 'You see'; and she made a show of dabbing her eyes.

He smiled. 'Wise choice.'

They sat in silence for a while. She was embarrassed and perhaps he felt the same. It was so hard to judge from his face. He was gazing down the ride to the garden pool. A change in the weather was reflected in its waters, dark with cloud and the threat of rain. The breeze was stiffening from the west and the heart-shaped limes behind her were whispering and swaying like conscience-stricken penitents. She wasn't sure why, but she suddenly felt the need to tell him the truth. Tell him everything. Because once she had told him, he would know her, and she would know what to do.

'You're shivering,' he said, 'here, take my jacket.'

'I . . . thank you.'

He rose and stepped round the bench to drape it about her shoulders. It felt heavy and smelt fusty and smoky.

'You haven't eaten,' she said.

He smiled. 'No.'

'Richard . . .'

'Yes.'

'I would like to tell you something. It's . . .' She swallowed hard. Oh dear, did she have the courage? 'You will have to be patient with me . . .'

'Then don't make yourself—'

'Why?' Her turn to hold up a hand. 'Are you afraid? I want you to know. But first . . . Do you hate Jews?'

8

Why 'hate Jews'? He wasn't sure he hated anyone. No, that wasn't true, not at all. He hated Joyce and all he stood for; he hated Knight too. He hated the 'big push' army commanders with their big moustaches and their big motorcars who had wasted the lives of thousands in pursuit of their 'big breakthrough'. He hated the doctor who had helped Connie into an early grave. Most of all, he hated a shit he knew called Stewart.

'Is it something I've said?' That sounded defensive. 'Hate the Jews? Why would I? No, of course I don't.'

'Why "of course",' she said, 'do you think the world is full of people who love the Jews? You work for these nationalists and fascists, this man, Knight—'

'I don't hate the Jews,' he said, firmly. What else could he say to convince her? Why did he have to? 'You will have to take my word for it.'

She smiled. 'I suppose I must.' She closed her eyes and took a deep breath. '*I* am a Jew,' she said. 'There! You know. Four words that I never uttered to James Ramsay MacDonald. What do you say?'

He shrugged. 'What is there to say?'

'I'm not religious but it is who I am. It's my story.' She sighed. 'I want to tell you, and then you can help me decide what to do. You're impatient to wash your hands of me . . .'

'No.'

'I'm causing trouble.' She smiled, ruefully. 'You want me to give you the letters. Please be patient and when I've finished my story I'll tell you where to find them.'

He nodded.

'Are you warm enough?' The breeze was plucking at his shirtsleeves. 'We can walk?'

'No, I'm all right,' he said.

'Then I should . . .' She took a deep breath. 'I've told you, my family's Jewish but not religious, not at all. Prosperous bourgeois Viennese. Good subjects of the old emperor. My father went to the synagogue a few times a year, we celebrated Pesach – Passover – and my brother's Bar Mitzvah, but in all other respects we were typical Viennese. Our family name was Strauss, and that's as . . . as Viennese as apple strudel!' She gave a short laugh. 'My father was a businessman, an educated man, and he wanted his son and his daughters to be well educated too. I speak four languages, even a little Hungarian. We all did. It's a pity . . . I have a photograph of the family, I wish I could show you.'

Dick reached into his trouser pocket for his cigarettes. He knew the one: the picnicking family group he had found among the pills and lotions in her bedside table. 'Do you mind if I smoke?'

Kristina waved a hand in assent. 'There are many thousands of Jews in Vienna, good, successful people, musicians, writers – you've heard of Sigmund Freud? No? He's a famous psycho-analyst, and he visited our house once. I met a famous composer, too: he became a Catholic. I don't know why because the Catholics seem to hate us. The more successful Jews become the more they hate us – it's always been like that. Harvest fails, prices go up: blame the Jews. Rents go up in the city; blame Jewish immigrants. Politicians stir up anti-Jewish feelings to win elections. But I don't suppose you want to hear about that. What matters is that we were a bourgeois family like any other, at least, I grew up believing so. Then, when I was eighteen, I met Heinrich.

'By happy chance I was placed beside him at dinner. He was spending three days in Vienna on business for his father, who owned a company in Berlin making fertilisers. What must he have thought of me! I had so little conversation. But we met again a few days later. He had extended his visit especially to see me. Well, you don't need to know how but we fell in love. You think it's ridiculous for a woman in her fifties to speak of falling in love? There! Now you know my age.'

Dick turned his head sideways to blow a thread of smoke away. 'I don't think it's ridiculous, no.'

'We were in love, so in love, and only three weeks after

dinner at the Frankls' he asked my father for my hand in marriage. You know what my father said? "He isn't Jewish. He's a gentile." Madness! I don't think many of my father's business associates had any idea he was a Jew. The things he used to say about the new Jewish families arriving in the city from the East! Not like us, he said, with their ridiculous beards and hats and traditions. Heinrich was like us, only he wasn't Jewish.'

She closed her eyes. What could she see? Was it the handsome man with the cavalry moustache and languid expression in the photograph?

'I was the headstrong opinionated girl my parents brought me up to be,' she said; 'I married him anyway. No one from my family was at the wedding; no one from his family. His father didn't approve of me. My father-in-law couldn't see beyond the label: Jew. How could he tell I was a Jew? I was no different from his daughter and his neighbours' daughters. So we were on our own, but happy all the same because we were in love. We lived a comfortable life in a fashionable district of Berlin and that was where our son Lorentz was born.' She sighed and leant forward as if to touch his arm. 'May I have one of your cigarettes?'

Stewart placed his own in the corner of his mouth and fumbled for the packet.

'I don't smoke very often.'

'They're strong.'

Delicately pinching one from the pack, she drew it slowly to her lips.

'Here,' he said, cupping his hands round a match. As she bent over the flame a lock of her white-blond hair broke loose and brushed against his thumb.

'Thank you.' With a graceful sweep of her right hand she tidied it behind her ear. 'Well, as I was saying, Heinrich's father couldn't come to terms with his choice of wife. But the years before the war were good, prosperous years, happy years, all the same.' She inhaled deeply. 'Then . . . well, then the war. Heinrich was wounded in Belgium almost at once. Later, he was on the Staff.' She paused, her lips drawn to a thread, straining to control her feelings. 'Everyone suffered, of course,' she said at last. 'On and on it went to no purpose, and Lorentz, my son, was old enough to serve at the end. He was killed near Ypres. British artillery fire, they said. My only child, just eighteen years old, consigned to oblivion.'

Her face was trembling with emotion and she turned her head away.

'I'm sorry,' he said.

'You *know*,' she said, reaching out to him. He took her hand and squeezed it gently. 'You know what it is to lose someone,' she said again. She brushed away a tear, then turned to look at him with a pained, a crooked smile. 'We don't have time for grief, do we? There is never enough time.'

She let go of his hand – 'so, a family of two again' – and lifting the cigarette she drew on it again. 'Heinrich came home, and he was determined to make Germany a better place for ordinary people. The business had done well during the war – making explosives, of course – but he didn't care about the money. He threw himself into politics. Germany was in turmoil after the war. Perhaps you read about it? There was the revolution, the abdication, the armistice, nationalists fighting socialists, and people were starving. We lived near Walther Rathenau. I don't suppose you've heard of him, but was a great German. Like my Heinrich, a successful businessman, a rich man, who believed it was his duty to help save his country. They became friends and political allies. Walther was minister for reconstruction, then foreign minister, and my Heinrich represented him on committees and was one of his chief advisors. I'm sorry, you don't understand why I'm telling you this – you'll see.

'Germany was falling apart. There were no jobs, shortages, no law and order, and old soldiers were riding around in motorcars with guns, shooting communists and social democrats. *Freikorps*, they called themselves. They were nationalists, militarists, monarchists: anti-communist, anti-socialist – anti-Semite. Germany lost and it was our fault, of course. Not the soldiers, not the generals; no, they were betrayed by communist spies and Jewish profiteers on the Home Front.

'They hated Walter Rathenau. He was a Jew, you see. His service in the war and his dedication in the peace to paying people a decent wage and creating jobs . . . none of that was important to these people because he was a Jew. Their blind hate . . . You know, Walter used to say, "I'm a German of Jewish origin. My people are the German people, my home is Germany, my faith is German faith, which stands above all denominations." His enemies saw only the Jew.

'Militant *Freikorps* nationalists tried to seize power, but they were defeated because workers went on strike to save the new republic. That should have been the end of it, but of course it wasn't. The nationalists couldn't convince the people, so they murdered their representatives. That's how these people are! The worst of them were in a terror unit called Organisation Consul. Members of Organisation Consul shot Erzberger, the finance minister, while he was walking in the Black Forest; Gareis, the Bavarian deputy, on his doorstep; Scheidemann, the former chancellor, had acid thrown in his face: can you imagine such a thing in your country? There were hundreds of murders, and not just prominent men, ordinary law-abiding citizens who came forward with evidence against them, too. There were many such cases: a soldier brutally butchered with knives because he was believed to be in communication with communists; another found in the lavatory of a cafe with his head battered in because he was suspected of doing the same. The perpetrators were never brought to justice. They were protected by their anti-republican friends in the police and army and the ministry of the interior. *Ja,*' she said, grinding the butt of her cigarette into the gravel; 'it was only a matter of time. You understand, Richard, this Organisation Consul was only the largest and the worst of many. They were all the same: breaking up political meetings, torturing, murdering their enemies – and Jews were their enemies. Their mission was to wage *warfare against Jewry, social democracy and leftist-radicalism* – those were their aims – dictatorship and the overthrow of the new constitution.

'I won't bore you with the threats and the abuse that we put up with. They hated Rathenau because he was a Jew and the foreign minister of Germany and they hated my Heinrich because he was one of Walter's most prominent supporters and because he was married to me – a Jew. Walter Rathenau was murdered on the twenty-fourth of June 1922. It was a Saturday morning. He was driving from his home to the Foreign Office when he was passed by assassins in a touring car. They opened fire with a machine gun, then threw a hand grenade into his car to make sure. It was news around the world, I discovered later. There was a state funeral service; Walter's coffin was taken to parliament; there were rallies in sympathy all over the country. But his advisor and closest friend, my Heinrich, wasn't among the mourners.'

She looked away momentarily, trying to compose herself again. 'You see members of the same gang visited us the night before. Friday the twenty-third of June. It will be the anniversary in a few days' time. Friday the twenty-third. We were getting ready for bed. We had been to a concert together – Mahler at the

Bernburger Strasse concert hall – he was the composer I met in Vienna when I was a girl. I mentioned him . . .'

'Yes. The composer. Sorry, but I've never heard of him.'

'It isn't important.' She sighed again. 'This is so difficult . . .'

'Then don't . . .'

'You see, you *are* afraid. You have your own pain, why share mine?'

'No. I . . . Go on.'

'All the servants had gone home but my father-in-law's old butler. We had kept him on to do small tasks around the house, and it was Frederick, the butler, who opened the door to them. Oh, we'd told him to be careful, to check, but he was old and half asleep and they managed to convince him there was an urgent communication from the Foreign Ministry. He could see only one man, but as soon as the door was open three more appeared with guns. Frederick tried to close the door but it was too late. They knocked him unconscious. I heard a noise but nothing remarkable – Heinrich was in the bathroom – and it was only when a bedroom door banged along the landing that I knew something terrible was going to happen. You know, don't you? You can't say how but you feel the moment pregnant with menace and you are helpless.'

'Yes.'

'I shouted to Heinrich. His name was all I had time to shout. Perhaps it was a mistake because there were four doors on the landing and they were able to reach ours before I could lock it, before Heinrich could fetch his army pistol. Three of them burst in, armed with revolvers and a butcher's knife. The fourth was downstairs and there was a driver in a motorcar outside. Young men; my Lorentz would have been the same age if he had been spared. I was in a dressing gown and nightdress and Heinrich was in his nightshirt. I screamed, Heinrich tried to speak, to reason with them, but that was impossible. They had come to our house for one purpose only. Their leader – a naval officer called Müller – shouted that he was going to execute sentence. These terrible people in Organisation Consul had held a pantomime trial. When Heinrich tried to intervene again one of them struck him across the temple with the butt of a gun. There was going to be no mercy. He held me tightly while they shouted "traitor" and "communist" – which was ridiculous – and "Jew-lover", which wasn't, because he did love me . . .' She gasped. 'They waved their guns and tried to tear him from me. They hit him again. They hit me. And when they . . . when they . . . when they succeeded they slashed him with the butcher's knife, again and again . . . and again, and . . . and there was nothing . . . nothing I could do to stop them.'

Dick watched her bury her head in her hands. That was enough. Enough. What purpose was served in dredging up this pain and savagery from the past? What purpose? Fat tears were falling through her fingers. He wanted to comfort her but he couldn't. He felt impotent, angry, and some of his anger was directed at her for insisting he listen to her story. What about the meeting? What about the money?

'They butchered him, Richard. They butchered the Jew-lover.' She began fumbling in her sleeve for her hanky and when she found it she moaned, 'Oooh, that won't do. Not now. May I have yours?'

He fished his grubby handkerchief from his pocket. 'Here.'

She took it and blew her nose loudly. Then she laughed. 'You see, I was saving it,' she said, and laughed again.

He laughed too. 'You better keep it.'

'Thank you.' She gave another heavy sigh. 'I feel a little better. I think I've done well. There isn't much more.' She paused. 'They found the Jewish bitch covered in his blood. No one cared about Heinrich Forster, soldier, businessman, politician, patriot, husband, because the terrorists murdered his friend, Rathenau, the following day. I was able to identify two of them but there were no arrests. I should have done more, but I wasn't . . . I wasn't well. And I was alone. No family to help me. My parents never met their grandson, you know. They're dead now. I have two sisters in Vienna. Heinrich had a sister. But . . . And I couldn't bear to live in our home because Heinrich's killers had defiled it. Germany . . . I had to leave Germany. I sold the company and moved to Bern the week that man Adolf Hitler tried to seize power in another *putsch*.'

Dick shifted impatiently. 'I haven't heard of him, I'm afraid.'

'Oh, you will. His Brownshirts – he calls them his storm detachment – are the worst sort of thugs. Ah, these bloody people with their brown and black shirts, marching and drilling . . . they can't wait to fight another war. Hitler is like your Joyce; he hates communists, socialists and Jews . . . especially Jews. Hebrew corrupters of the nation, he calls them. Eli has his book. He says Hitler blames us for everything. He wants to make us suffer. "Pray he never has the opportunity, Kristina," Eli said to me, but he knows I don't pray. Perhaps I should because he has become important, and the man responsible for my Heinrich's murder has joined his party. Not the butchers but the man who sent them: Manfred von Killinger. The murderers and thugs and anti-Semites of Organisation Consul have found a new home in the Nazi Party.'

She looked down at the fingers of her right hand splayed on the bench between them. 'I'm not a clever person, Richard. Heinrich and Rathenau were clever, and old Eli is clever . . . As far as I can see the world is really divided into good people and bad people. The people who murdered my husband were bad people, criminals, and so are the men you work . . . worked for.' She raised her gaze to his face. 'But you know, I believe you are a good person.'

He laughed – 'I'm afraid . . .' – and to hide his embarrassment he fumbled in his jacket for another cigarette.

'But Richard,' she said, 'when you talk about fascists and the British Secret Service and their conspiracies, men like Knight and this man Joyce who tortured poor Eli, and you admit to taking their money, well then I see my poor husband butchered in front of my eyes.' She gave a little shudder.

'I . . .' He didn't know what to say.

'You don't want to hear a lesson from a . . . what did you say? A blackmailer.'

'Thank you for telling me.' He looked down at his hands, turning his brass lighter, round, round with his fingertips. 'I . . . I want to say . . .' What? That he despised himself for taking their money: the words stuck in his throat. 'Sorry.'

She smiled. 'You were right: I shouldn't preach. But you understand Kristina Forster a little better now. Ha! Look at me! I hate being poor. I'm still trying to come to terms with being poor.'

'Not for much longer.'

'Well, we'll see. This time in Paris has taught me a few things. I'm going to be a Jew. I'm going to embrace who I am. I don't mean I'm going to stop eating oysters if there's an opportunity, only I won't hide, there are no apologies to make, and when the letters have gone back to Mr MacDonald there will be no one to run away from – and whatever happens I'm going to make myself useful.'

Rising from the bench, she ran her hands lightly over her skirt to smooth out the creases. 'There, you've heard enough about me, my friend, and it must be nearly six o'clock. You're impatient for the letters, no? You shall have them. I shall tell you.'

9

They were waiting on the concourse at Gare St Lazare, squinting into the sun pouring upon the passengers filing along platform five. A stroke of luck that it had burst blinding through the grimy glass roof as the Marly train was pulling into the station. Flat cap and his pal with the curly moustache were struggling to see more than a few metres. They were evidently searching for someone, and not to kiss and carry the luggage: Stewart thought it wise to assume the someone was him. Who they were he couldn't tell. As he approached the barrier the man in the flat cap drifted towards his companion on the concourse and exchanged a few words. They were taking an interest, but keeping their distance. Just as well, because Joyce's money was still in his knapsack and the pockets of his jacket. Damn silly, but that woman . . . the promises he had made her. He smiled as he remembered her lips brushing his cheek in the park when they parted and the tears sparkling in her green eyes. Ramsay Mac was a good man, Ramsay Mac was also a fool – or was she making a fool of them both?

He rang Fletcher from a post office near the station. The Hôtel Métropole took its time to find him and by the time he came on the line the postmaster was outside the booth with his watch.

'Dumont, is that you? What's going on?' Fletcher sounded in a bit of a state.

'I have new friends. They met me at the station.'

'Who?'

'Not sure. I thought you might know?'

'Get rid of them. There's an apartment . . . top floor 6 rue Louis le Grand, take her there.'

'No, the Tour St Jacques in . . .' – Stewart leant forward to peer at the postmaster's watch – '. . . forty minutes.' The money ran out before Fletcher could protest.

The young man with the curly moustache was gazing in a shop window at one end of the street, his partner pretending to do the same at the other. They followed Dick to the Metro and watched him buy a ticket and then they followed him down to the platform. They didn't look like fascists, they looked like policemen, but not clumpy-booted unshaven coppers of the ordinary sort. They were smartly dressed in summer jackets and ties.

The train carriage hop was known to every petty criminal and copper in Paris, and these two would certainly be on the *qui vive* for something of the sort. Stewart was going to have to attempt it all the same or they would be breathing down his neck all the way to the Tour St Jacques.

The rails were singing; a train approaching; and curly moustache edged closer. He would have to board and lose the pair of them at a busier station, or perhaps . . . but that would be foolhardy. The train burst from the tunnel and rumbled along the platform and he turned to follow a carriage, passing the young copper without a glance. If he walked six or seven metres or so he would become flat cap's responsibility, and flat cap was older, larger, slower. Sure enough, it was flat cap who followed him into the last of the second-class carriages. Stewart stood at the centre set of doors and watched the guard drop the lock. The copper was to his left, the other passengers settling on the benches. As the train pulled away he caught the policeman peering at him furtively. He resisted the temptation to smile: what was there to smile about? The train was gathering speed quicker than he imagined possible. He had seconds only – if he could summon the courage. But he must! Forcing the catch, he tugged the carriage doors open and with his eyes half closed leapt towards the platform. The next thing he knew he was on his side, his cheek against concrete, smooth and hard as black ice. The dirty white tiles round the gaping mouth of the tunnel were close enough for him to touch – too close. Nothing was broken but his hip was very sore. What an idiot! What was he thinking! What about Florence and Pierre!

Fletcher chose a bench in the shade of a horse chestnut tree, a few metres from the base of the Tour St Jacques. Gazing up at its statues and arches, he remembered Elspeth describing it on their honeymoon as *gothique flamboyant*. 'Like our union,' he had joked. Oh, the black looks! To be fair to Mrs Fletcher it was a remarkable tower, and with a rope dangling from one of the dog's-head gargoyles at the top it would make an impressive gallows too. The higher the better for an insubordinate toerag like Stewart.

The park was unusually quiet for a Saturday evening in June. Couples strolled past in search of a dark place to spoon; half a dozen drunks were seated on steps at the foot of the tower. They passed bottles and talked nonsense loudly, too inebriated, too scabrous to be agents of the Bureau in disguise. No, the only foot-sloggers in the vicinity of the park were from the embassy and they were working for him. They were stationed at observation points beyond the wrought-iron railings with orders to follow Frau Forster when she left with the money – if she put in an appearance.

He ventured another glance towards the park gates. Stewart was walking towards him – and he was alone. My God, he would have to have a cast-iron excuse this time, or Fletcher would . . . well . . . it was too bad! It was Morton's fault. Morton had recommended the bugger. And what a tramp he looked, his clothes grey with dust, a hole in a knee of his trousers. Fletcher shifted impatiently, resisting the urge to rise. 'Where is she?'

Sinking on to the bench with a sigh, Stewart bent forward to inspect the hole in his trousers.

'Well?'

'She isn't here.'

'That's bloody obvious!'

'After the attack on the bookseller—'

'That was nothing to do with us.'

'Doesn't matter. She *will* give me the letters' – Stewart stared pointedly at the briefcase he was pressing to his side – '*if* you give me the money.'

'We've been over this.'

'That's what she wants.' Stewart gave a wry smile. 'Don't you trust me?'

'Of course not. Where is she?'

'I don't know.'

He snorted. 'You think I was born yesterday? What have you told her?'

Stewart considered a moment then said, 'I told her about Agent M.'

'Who?'

'A fascist called Maxwell Knight who works for your Secret Service. I used to do jobs for him.'

'What are you talking about?'

'Spyin' on communists, on socialists, breakin' up meetings, stealing documents from the Labour Party, that sort of thing.'

'What?'

'I was to buy or steal the prime minister's letters for Knight . . . from you if necessary. I suppose whoever he works for was going to give them to the press – or was it blackmail? I don't know.'

'Don't be soft, man.'

'Come on! Who put you in touch with me?'

'None of your bloody business.'

Stewart shrugged.

'Don't shrug your shoulders at me!' – my God, his blood was up now – 'your job, my job, is to return those letters to the man who wrote them.'

'Then give me the money and I'll do my job.'

Fletcher opened his mouth to speak, then closed it again. He needed time to think and he needed to remain calm. He watched Stewart take a crushed packet of cigarettes from his jacket pocket. 'Bugger it. Do you have one for me, Commander?' he said, dropping the remains of the packet between his feet. 'She'll give me the letters. You can trust her.'

'What were you supposed to do for this man, Knight?'

'I told you. I was to take the letters from her *or* from you, if necessary.'

'But you were working for me!'

'I *am* workin' for you.'

Fletcher glared at him.

'What about that cigarette?' said Stewart, impatiently. 'Look, there was nothin' to stop her comin' to an arrangement with the prime minister's enemies.'

'You would have arranged that for her?'

'Yes. No. I don't know. It doesn't matter. What matters is that you have the money, she has the letters: we can make the exchange tonight.'

'Tonight? Where?'

'What was the address? Louis le Grand?'

'Number six, top-floor apartment. Tonight?'

'Tonight.'

'All right.' He lifted the leather briefcase on to the bench between them. 'Don't think . . . don't dare imagine . . .' Words failed him.

11

Stewart had money, lots and lots of money in his jacket and his knapsack, but no fags. As for the letters . . . he knew where to find them and they were close, only a short walk from the Tour St Jacques. But first he would have to deal with the three foot-sloggers who were trailing along rue de Rivoli after him.

Andrew Williams

Blackshirts or Bureau, or were they working for Fletcher: what did it matter? He could run but they would run faster. He needed people, hustle and bustle, and the only place he was sure to find it on a Saturday in summer was along the banks of the Seine. From rue de Rivoli he turned right intent on making his way there, and walked into a *fête* crowd almost at once. On a stage in front of a district town hall a dance band was playing popular ragtime tunes, while beneath it couples, families, the young and the old shuffled round a temporary wooden floor. Stewart queued at a kiosk to buy cigarettes and get his bearings. The short sides of the Place Baudoyer were open to the street, the long sides occupied by the town hall and an austere white stone barracks building. There were no lanes, no alleys, and very little possibility of giving the three men dogging his footsteps the slip. One of his pursuers was loitering beneath the awning of a food stall only a few metres away; his comrades patrolling the fringes of the *fête*. Dick bought his cigarettes and turned to the stage, where a *chanteuse* with a smoky voice was singing the new city favourite, 'Ça c'est Paris'.

'Dance, dance,' she cried, and young couples began to rise from tables where a simple meal was being served and weave their way through spectators to the dance floor. Without much thought Stewart did the same. Yes, he looked like a tramp in his dusty clothes, but a good-natured tramp, a happy, dance-with-a-bottle tramp, arms raised, shimmying towards the floor. Too late, the foot-slogger at the stall made to do the same. Happy tramp was in a hurry now, shouldering his way between dancing couples until he reached the foot of the stage.

Behind it local officials and their wives were eating canapés and drinking champagne. They looked at him in astonishment. Thief? Thug? 'Monsieur, what are you doing? Where are you going?'

He was going to retrace his steps. One of the foot-sloggers watching the edge of the *fête* was bound to turn back towards rue de Rivoli, but half a problem he could manage – with his fists if necessary. The last of the light was dying in the sky above the barracks opposite; beneath the trees at the edge of the square it was dead already. Couples were kissing and fumbling in the darkness, a drunk swigging from a bottle, and as he approached the street a prostitute crossed his path and asked him to light her cigarette. Her two companions were standing by the wall of the town hall, waiting for another likely-looking customer. Stewart was on the point of pushing past when it came to him in a flash that there *was* a service a tart might render him, if she had a mind to. 'Hide me,' he said in a low voice. 'Kiss me over there' – and he nodded towards the wall – 'I'll pay.'

'How much?'

'Ten.'

'Twenty.'

'Twenty!'

'You might want more.'

'I won't.'

'That's the price.'

'Come on then . . .'

'In advance.'

'There isn't time.'

'You better pay,' she said, grabbing his sleeve. *Ouille!* She was no beauty. She had a hard-lines twilight face. But just in time she embraced him, covering his body with hers. Someone in hobnails of the sort the *Poilu* had worn in the war was approaching. A few seconds later a proper Frenchman shouted in proper French, 'Anyone walk by?'

'Hundreds,' replied one of the women.

'Clever. I mean in the last few seconds.'

'A few. How much?'

'*Putain!*' He wasn't going to pay her.

The exchange was over before Stewart needed to draw breath. His pursuer would have seen no more than a man's hands clutching a tart's arse.

'You're safe, he's gone,' whispered her friend.

He wasn't going to remember a passionate encounter or even a convincing performance, but a few seconds of kissing had bought him some time.

'And which way did he turn?'

Kissing companion held out her hand. 'Ten for my friend.'

He paid her the money.

'Left on to rue de Rivoli,' she said, slipping the notes down the front of her dress. 'Any time, dearie. Ask for Claudette at the Bar du Commerce.'

Claudette, who tasted of fish.

The sun that was still to set on the Jewish Sabbath had set in rue des Écouffes more than an hour ago. The street was dark and deserted but for an old man with *payot* and a beard like a patriarch who was sitting on a step smoking a cigarette, and a mangy-looking dog tugging at a bag of food waste in the gutter. Lamps and candles were lit in tenement apartments above the shopfronts and through open windows Stewart could hear the rhythm of everyday life. Madame had told him of a back entrance to the bookseller's in a courtyard opposite a pawn shop. Picking the lock at the front of the shop was too risky. If they caught him they would clean him out, and that was bloody unthinkable. Fag-packet reckoning, he was carrying one and three quarters of a million francs – and he had plans for every centime. Turning into the courtyard, he paused in the shadow of a doorway to be sure no one was watching him. Eli was in hospital – poor old bugger – his house was dark, his curtains open, his rescuers had not thought to close a bedroom window, and even at twenty paces in twilight Stewart could see his back door was secured by nothing more than a simple warded lock. Well, who was going to break in and steal a book?

A final check on the neighbours then he drew from his jacket his wallet of picks. It took him only a matter of seconds to open the door. In the thin blue he could distinguish kitchen cupboards, a range, a table – cooking things – and on the sickly yellow floor tiles the shattered remains of a china bowl in a pool of milk. Slowly, delicately he opened the door into the bookshop and listened: he could hear nothing but his own shallow breathing. Someone had tried to clean up the mess with a rag, and then dumped the bloody thing in the wastepaper. He switched on the desk lamp. The old man's blood was smeared in an arc over the boards like a rainbow, under his chair and on top of his desk. There was more blood on the wall and upon some of his papers, an inkwell, some books, on a photograph of an elderly Jewish couple and a small brass torch. Stewart picked up the torch and wiped it clean with the lining of his jacket.

Shielding its beam with his left hand, he made his way down the centre aisle to the politics section and authors beginning with M. Packed tightly at the end of a row of books by Marx were two thin volumes by Mr J. Ramsay MacDonald. Kneeling in front of the shelves, he ran a finger down the spines until he reached the bottom. No, he was going to have to go lower. He shrugged off his knapsack and switched off the torch. If the police or that cunt Joyce saw a light in the shop they would be through the door and on him straight away, and he was risking more than a finger. They would find him prostrate on the floor, his face a target for a flying boot. Groping left and right under the shelf, he touched what felt like wooden battens. He switched on the torch to check and, yes, the battens were securing a rough square of timber cut in the old elm floorboards.

He fished from a side pocket of his knap the clasp knife he

275

had carried through the war, blade and marlinspike. Opening the spike, he reached under the shelf and was on the point of driving it under a batten when he heard rustling – Christ! – like fabric brushing against a bookshelf. There it was again, and closer! Slowly, heart pounding, he withdrew the spike and rolled on to his side. Someone was creeping towards him, and, oh, they were good, bloody good at it too. The board beneath him creaked as he shifted from his side to his knees. He was on the point of springing to his feet when, fuck, fuck, fuck! Two green eyes were staring at him from the darkness at the end of the row: green eyes with vertical black pupils. It was a fucking cat. The cat that spilled the milk. My God, pussy better keep away from him or he would end its days.

The batons were tacked in place with beading pins that took only seconds to raise. He lifted the cut boards out and felt between the floor joists. There were two bundles of letters sitting in the sawdust, each one six inches high, wrapped in soft leather, tied with a piece of string. He loosened the knot and switched on the torch again. The envelopes were addressed to Madame Forster at a house in Bern. To be sure, he drew out a letter:

My Dearest Kristina,

The night is far gone and I will rise at six tomorrow morning to catch a train, and yet I must just tell my sweet Pussy that I am thinking, dreaming of her. It is too ridiculous to think of this heart of mine being in love. But it is. To hold you in my arms you little white angel . . .

He turned the page to check the signature.

Ever your own Sweetheart
R
XX XX

How much would a newspaper or foreign power be prepared to pay him for the prime minister's very personal correspondence? Ha! Was he holding the fate of a government in his hands? But he needed to spirit letters and money out of the *Pletzel* before some other shit could steal them from him. First there was the matter of his account at the bookshop to settle. From his knapsack, he took a brick of Joyce's money, clambered back on to his belly and dropped it in the cavity between the joists. Some small compensation for the finger old Eli had sacrificed for Madame Forster. The *sweet Pussy* was still giving Stewart the eye. Did the cat approve? He felt warmer towards her, actually, quite euphoric. The life he would give his children; the things he would be able to buy. He ditched his shirts and socks in the wastepaper and stowed the letters with the money in his knapsack. It was time to leave, and quickly. Someone was making a noise somewhere. *Shabbat* was over.

12

Fletcher knew it was a balls-up and he knew he was to blame. Sinclair and Morton were to blame, yes, and Stewart would be made to pay, but Lieutenant Commander R.T.H. Fletcher was most to blame for being unforgivably trusting and naive. Contemptibly so. He was sitting at an open window in the elegant empty drawing room of number 6 rue Louis le Grand, smoking and glancing too frequently at his watch. The room boasted a chandelier fit for a palace but he was intent on sitting in the dark for as long as he could – until midnight. My God, who would have credited it? A solid fellow, ex-navy, married to a clergyman's daughter, and he had been foolish enough to bet the house on a bad 'un. Yes, it was a bloody balls-up, but not one he was going to admit to anyone before the city's clocks struck twelve.

There were voices in the street below, a woman, a man, and for a fleeting moment he dared to hope it was Stewart. He leant over the sill to catch a snatch of what was being said. God save him from the excruciating embarrassment of admitting his mistake. But it was the wrong man, the wrong woman. To judge from the huskiness of their voices they were drunk and amorous. He sat back and lit another cigarette.

Drysdale was talking to someone on the landing. The door opened and his slight frame appeared in silhouette. 'They've returned, Commander,' he said, switching on the room lights.

'What?' said Fletcher, irritably, his hands shielding his eyes.

'My men . . . They've been to Bilbaut's *pension*; Dumont left this morning. They searched the streets but there's—'

'The bookshop on rue des Rosiers?'

'No sign. I think they've done all they can for one night.'

'Bloody hell. He'll be gone by tomorrow!'

'Frau Forster may have skipped the rendezvous. He may be in trouble,' said Drysdale; 'he may have been detained by the Bureau.'

They were possibilities, true, and there were more, but Fletcher had an old salt's nose for foul weather and he knew he had made the mistake of sailing into it. 'He's buggered off with the money. Perhaps he's agreed to share it with her.'

'We can search again in the morning. I can—'

'Wait!' Fletcher held up a hand. 'Hear that?' A church clock was striking the hour, and it was joined a moment later by another. 'That's that then.' The time for feeling sorry for himself was over. 'Will you accompany me to the embassy?' he said, getting to his feet. 'I must send a message to the Chief.'

8 June 1930

S HE WAS CURLED in an anxious ball on the bed when she
heard him at the door of the *pension* at last. Half past three
in the morning, nine hours since they parted in the park, seven
since his meeting with Fletcher, and in the last five she had
felt increasingly desperate.

At first she had drawn on memories of her husband and
son and her family in Vienna. She thought of what she had
learnt in the *Pletzel* and of what she might do with the rest
of her life, because there could be no return to the old
Kristina Forster, no more champagne receptions, no first-
night performances, no dresses from Lanvin or shoes from
Ferragamo, but a new way of living. Gay times still – without
laughter how was it possible to see life through to its end?
– but she owed it to poor dead Heinrich to do more, be
more. To start afresh she would have to bury the hurt and
resentment she had felt since James's rejection: she must
return his letters.

Only as the hours slipped by she wondered what had
possessed her to put her faith in a man she barely knew and
who still frightened her a little. She had begun to imagine the
mischief Stewart could do her. She shrank from recollection of
the pain she had shared with him, seduced by what she had
taken for quiet decency. Fear of another betrayal had driven
her from the only chair in the room to the bed, where she lay

curled in a ball, her knees, hands and handkerchief tucked under chin.

But how weak and foolish of her to have worked herself into such a state. Stewart was rapping at the door of the *pension*, as a man buried alive might beat on the lid of his coffin. She rose with a glad heart and stepped over to the wall mirror to tidy her hair. The shouting and banging stopped and, opening her bedroom door a fraction, she could hear him in the hall with the lady of the house.

'Wake Madame Forster, Monsieur? Everyone's awake!' complained *Madame la propriétaire*. 'The street, the town's awake!'

'It's an emergency,' she heard him say; 'accept my apologies, Madame, and this.' He must have offered her a penance payment, and enough to satisfy, because *Madame la propriétaire* was suddenly full of concern. Was it a death in Madame Forster's family? What could she do? She would show him to Madame's room at once.

'Madame?' she cooed. 'Madame Forster, are you awake? There's someone here to see you.'

The someone's clothes were dirty and torn, there was blood on his sleeve, and his face was drawn and unshaven. There was a graze on the palm of his left hand, cuts on the knuckles of his right. He looked like a convict.

'Sit, sit.' She gestured to the chair. 'Where have you been? I was so worried.'

'You thought you'd seen the last of me?' he said with a wry smile.

'You were away such a long time!'

He dropped his pack and turned the chair from the window to face her.

'I have your letters.'

'Thank you, Richard. Thank you.' She had told him her story

and he had done this thing for her. 'Was it difficult?' She found it hard to speak. 'Oh, and you've hurt your knee. Are you all right? I can fetch you a glass of water?'

'I'm fine. Fletcher was expecting me to hand over the letters. He'll be panicking. Do you know what you're going to do with them?'

She took a deep breath. 'Yes. I want them to go back to James.'

'Then I'll contact Fletcher again. Cook up a story. Tell him I missed the exchange because I was being followed by the police.'

'Do they know?'

'Something. I don't know. Joyce and his friends in black shirts are the ones I worry about. They'll be searching for me . . . for you.' He paused. 'That old man—'

'Eli?'

'He must have known your letters were in his shop.'

'He offered to hide them for me. Oh, it was unforgivable of me.'

'He gave them your address, yes, but he said nothing about the letters.'

'Oh, I shouldn't have,' she said, covering her face with her hands, 'the poor dear man.'

'He did a very brave thing.' Stewart's voice cracked with emotion. 'The right thing.'

'Yes.' She lowered her hands a little and peered at him over her fingertips. 'I'll never forgive myself.'

He bent down to fiddle with the straps of his knapsack. 'I'm very tired. Perhaps I'll have that glass of water.'

'Yes,' she said, glad of an excuse to leave the room.

The bathroom was along the corridor. She shared it with the other guests, which was a trial. She hated sharing with anyone – then, she hated being poor. Getting used to it would take the rest of her lifetime, but she would endure – if she could find a reason to. Heinrich used to say, he who has a reason to live will put up with almost any how. She filled a glass and walked back to her bedroom. Richard had taken her letters from his sack and placed them on the little dressing table. She noticed one of the bundles had been opened and clumsily retied.

'Thank you,' he said, taking the glass from her.

'You've read my letters?'

'Only an address and a signature, to be sure.'

She picked up the bundle he had opened and carried it to the bed, where she sat with her left hand resting on it lightly. Only the address? The signature? Or had curiosity got the better of him? A widow and a widower, two lonely people, who had fallen in love. Their passion for each other had been exhilarating, revivifying. *I feel so young; you make me feel so young*, James had written more than once. Because he was a passionate man who had enjoyed pouring his passion on to the page, and she had done her best to satisfy him by doing the same. But British politicians, especially socialist politicians, were not permitted to have such feelings, it seemed.

'He *did* love me, you know. Here,' – she patted the letters – 'in these. Only, he didn't love me enough to acknowledge me publicly. He didn't love me enough to help me. *I'm* ashamed of nothing we said and did. *He's* ashamed of me.'

Stewart shook his head sympathetically. 'All I know is, Labour's enemies are ready to use you to undermine him.'

'I put him under no obligation. I understood that his private life would have to stand up to scrutiny. If only he had been prepared to respect me by being honest with me. To drop me without explanation . . . That was so cold. But politicians almost never tell the truth because they know the public doesn't have enough patience for it. The public would like everything to be straightforward, when it almost never is.' She looked down at her hands, twisting in her lap. 'I try to remember he's a good man, and that the people judge him by a higher standard because he's their prime minister, and that to do the best he can for them he must make sacrifices. I am one of those sacrifices.'

'He was against the war. He was right about the war.'

'And he must have the letters for his peace of mind. He must,' she said, gazing at the bundle under her hand. 'I'm sorry I threatened to sell them. Will you return them for me?'

'Later this morning, yes. He's paid for them. Here . . .' Reaching down to the pack at his feet, he produced a neat brick of money. 'Your money,' he said, 'about a million francs'; and he tossed the brick on the bed behind her. 'See!'

'No, Richard!' She groaned and pressed a hand to her brow. 'I can't take it! Not now.'

Steward closed his eyes and took a deep breath.

'Take it back now, Richard. Please, please, take it back. I don't want him to think of me in that way.'

'Bloody 'ell.' He shook his head impatiently. 'Kristina . . . It isn't his money, and he won't think any the better of you for changing your mind. Madame, that ship has sailed.'

She stood up, touching her necklace, rolling one of its ebony beads between her thumb and her forefinger. 'I—'

'Be sensible. How will you manage without it?'

I know, she thought. I know. I know, he's right. She had asked for the money; she wanted the money. 'But I can't accept it.'

'You can,' he said, his tone softer; 'you should.' He seemed to sense the battle inside her and that she was weakening.

'Would you take it back if I asked you to?'

'Yes.'

She hesitated. 'I want to do something worthwhile. I want a purpose, a reason to go on.'

'This will help.' He gestured to the cash on the bed.

'We used to support a school for poor children in Berlin. Jewish children.'

'Then give the money to your charity, if you must.'

'I shouldn't accept it.'

'Spend it on the school.'

'Is it wrong?'

'Wrong? Ha! Compared with what? No.' He was on his feet now too, and picking up the pack he emptied the rest of the money on the bed beside her. 'A million francs. And half a million more from Joyce too.'

'You stole it?' She was shocked.

'Confiscated.'

'And it was to buy the letters?'

'To buy the letters, yes . . . until the price went up. I can't be sure where it came from. Businessmen or a newspaper editor. People willing to pay to bring down Mac. I reckon I can spend the money on a better cause too.'

'You're keeping it?'

He shrugged. 'I may be one of the causes but not the only one. Your friend, Eli. Don't you think Joyce should pay for his finger?'

'Yes, of course,' she said, sitting back on the edge of the bed; 'and I'll send him some money.'

'See! And you don't need to worry about the bookseller. That's taken care of.'

'You've given Eli money?'

'I left him some, yes.' He took a packet of cigarettes from his pocket. 'Do you mind?'

She shook her head.

'Look, I'm no saint,' – he paused to light one – 'you know that, of course, but the money's come from some entitled buggers – excuse me – who think they've a right to undermine an elected government. You know I know these people, well, the men they use as their tools anyway. They were content to let soldiers who weren't even permitted to vote die for the country, young men like me, and when those that survived could vote and voted socialist they conspired to bring down their choice and are ready to do the same again. So . . .' He drew deeply on his cigarette. 'Yeah, I think I can spend the money better.'

'Then *I'll* have to hand it back myself!'

'What are you talking about?'

'James will think I've taken that money too!'

He snorted. 'Don't be daft. They aren't going to tell him, are they? Take your money. Spend it well. That's what you want to do, isn't it?'

She didn't reply.

'I know you'll spend it well.'

'Do you?'

'Yes.'

She was touched. 'If I take it, will you explain? Tell him I want to do something worthwhile. Will you tell him that?'

'Who?' He lifted his right hand to his forehead, the cigarette burning between his fingers. 'Sorry, I'm tired. Who? Ramsay Mac?'

'Yes.'

He laughed – 'Madame!' – then turned from her to flick his smouldering cigarette out of the open window into the street. 'How on earth—'

'Well, *I managed*,' she said. 'I walked up to his door.'

'You were his lover.'

'You would be representing her, *and* you would have my letters . . . his letters.'

'It's asking for trouble – trouble for me!'

'You're paying yourself!'

'Not for this!'

'Then I'll find another way,' she said, hotly. 'I want him to know I'm sorry for the anxiety I caused him, that I mean him no harm, and that I still respect him. He should know that . . . that it wasn't for money. He must know how I feel . . . felt . . . How much he hurt me, but that I forgive him. And someone must tell him about the Secret Service, about your Mr Knight and Mr Joyce.'

'Give a letter to Fletcher.'

'How can I trust Fletcher? He's working for the Secret Service – you said so yourself.'

Stewart didn't reply.

'See!' she said, seizing on his silence.

'Who can be sure of anything in this life?'

'You can tell James about the spies in the Labour Party and the fascists.' Her voice dropped. 'You can tell him about me.'

'Madame—'

'Don't call me that!'

'Look, Kristina . . .' He let out a long sigh. 'They'll be searching for me. It's madness.'

2

Les Marlychois were still abed, the streets deserted but for an elderly couple hobbling arm in arm to early-morning Mass and a baker preparing to open his shop on the Grande Rue. The station ticket office was shut and would be for another hour, but Stewart found a side gate and a bench on the platform where they could sit in the sunshine and wait for the first city-bound service. They had talked about their plans until they were too tired to talk and then at her insistence they had slept side by side on the bed for an hour. There would be no more heroics, no leaping from a Metro train with Madame and her luggage. They would leave the city service at a station in the suburbs and pay for a cab to drive them to the Gare du Nord, where Stewart would catch the boat train to Boulogne, and Madame a train to the city of Lille.

Her eyes were closed, her face turned to the sun. She looked serene. Her expression brought to mind an altarpiece painting of a nun saint in the church his mother used to take him to as a boy. She was dressed like a German widow in black and purple, but there was a worldliness in her bearing that suggested someone more interesting than the sober bourgeois respectability of her attire.

'I don't know why, but I feel strangely light-hearted,' she said.

'You have a million francs in your luggage.'

'It isn't the money, Richard.' She turned from the sun to gaze at him. 'There will be police at the Gare du Nord?'

'I don't know.'

Perhaps Joyce, perhaps Fletcher, perhaps the agents from the Bureau.

'You're worried. That frown . . .' She raised a hand and touched his forehead lightly with a finger. 'I ask too much of you.'

He smiled. 'Don't worry.'

'What will you tell Commander Fletcher?'

He shrugged. 'Perhaps, "I've done what you wanted me to do."'

'Ha! They'll say I bewitched the prime minister and then—'

'Then me.'

She laughed. 'You're flattering me.'

He smiled again.

'You have a lighter heart?'

'Perhaps. I feel somehow . . . freer.'

'And you're returning to your children. You are very fortunate to have the children.'

'Yes, I am lucky. But . . .' He hesitated. 'Madame, I worry . . . I mean, about what kind of father I am to them. You don't know, how could you . . . I want to be better than my own father. And that means more than food on the family table, more than . . . yes, as you say, more than money.'

'Yes.'

'I forgot. My head has been in the wrong place too long. I need to be with them, at home.' He took out his cigarettes – 'Bloody 'ell, listen to me!' – lit one and drew deeply.

She touched his hand. 'Men are uncomfortable speaking of these things.'

He grunted.

'And it will be safe for you to go home?'

'Yes, I'm sure it will be,' he said, though he was sure of no such thing.

A plume of smoke and steam was rising above a red pantile roof, against the azure sky. The train would be with them in minutes and their time together was almost over. He had known her for four days. Lives can change in four days. Lives change in the blink of an eye; that much war teaches a soldier. Perhaps his life was changing. *Oh you daft bugger.* He was going soft. 'Ready?' he said, getting to his feet.

She lifted her handbag on to her knees. 'You will be glad to see the back of me.'

'Fishing for a compliment?'

She laughed. 'Of course! At my age . . . You *will* write and tell me you're safe? Write and tell me about him. About James. Send a letter here . . .' She took a scrap of paper from her bag. 'This is the address of the Jewish school in Berlin. Write to me there.'

'Madame, will you—'

'Kristina!'

'Will *you* be safe? Goodness sake, they murdered your husband.'

She smiled. 'A frumpy old Jewish widow . . . Who's going to bother about me?'

3

Footman-butler, James, tapped on Morton's bedroom door. Would sir care to speak to Admiral Sinclair? Sir would prefer not to, but what sir wanted counted for nothing in this case. A telephone call from a night bird and *bon viveur* like the Chief so early on a Sunday could only mean more than the usual degree of trouble. Morton padded down the stairs to meet it in his silk dressing gown and slippers.

The admiral wasted no time on an apology or pleasantries. 'It's Paris, Desmond. Fletcher's making a pig's ear of everything.'

Damn fool Fletcher. Fool to trust Frenchie with a farthing. Well-to-do socialists were so sentimental about the working classes.

'That toerag Frenchie has taken our money,' said Sinclair, 'and where are the letters?'

He had to have the letters, he had to return them in person: that was the plan. Only, it seemed some other bugger had another plan. 'It isn't you is it, Desmond? Is it something you've cooked up with Major Ball and Conservative Central Office?' Who was giving Agent Frenchie his orders? Was it Agent M?

'We need to find Frenchie, Desmond. *You* need to find him!'

Cook served coffee; James brought round the car; Mother fussed over his tie. A quarter past seven in the morning: Knight would be up and feeding his menagerie. Throwing caution to the wind, Morton was going to ring his bell and look him in the eye.

'Oh, Desmond, it can't be so urgent you don't have time for breakfast,' said his mother. Mother didn't know; Mother wouldn't understand; Mother thought his job was something diplomatic dull.

It took James only ten minutes to whisk him round to Sloane Street. He announced his arrival to Knight on the mansion block phone.

'Major Morton? Is that you?' Knight sounded flustered. 'My wife's at home.'

'Is that unusual, Knight?' he said, tartly. 'You have a room where we can speak in confidence, I suppose.'

Knight was waiting at his open door. He was dressed in a bright pink smoking jacket and matching slippers, like the Pope. 'Gwladys is still in bed,' he said.

'And who can blame her.'

'I would like to introduce you . . .'

'Another time.'

Morton heard a squeak and a pop, as if someone in the apartment was opening a bottle of wine. Was it Gwladys? Knight didn't appear to notice.

'We'll talk in here,' he said, his hand on a door knob. 'I hope you don't mind my creatures, Major.'

The room was full of them, the walls lined with cages, a small dog fussing at their feet, a green parrot gurgling on a perch by a window. It was the bird that was responsible for the squeak and pop Morton had heard in the hall. 'Glass of wine,' it croaked, 'glass of wine.'

'A little early for wine, I think,' said Knight, 'but perhaps some tea?'

The room smelt like a pet shop with bowls of dog biscuits, fruit and seed on the floor. Knight pulled a chair from a table covered in newspaper and invited him to sit. Coiled tightly in a glass tank in the centre of the table, a brightly coloured snake was tasting the air.

'I don't want a cup of tea,' said Morton, 'and I don't want a chair.'

'Is this about Paris?'

Paris, yes, and Morton explained why. No sugaring, no civility, no attempt to share the blame. No. Your agent, Knight, your responsibility, and have you come to a separate arrangement with a newspaper or the Conservative Central Office?

Calm and grave, he replied; 'Major, you know me better.'

'Then why has Frenchie done it?'

'With men like Frenchie it comes down to money,' said Knight. 'But his children are in London, so he'll be back and I think he'll bring the letters with him. We should watch the ports and Victoria station, and obviously his house.'

'For your sake, for all our sakes, I hope you're right,' said Morton, turning to the door.

'Please, Major, mind your step!' Knight bent to scoop a tortoise from the carpet.

'Silly boy, silly boy,' said the bird, and then it screeched like a madman.

4

'Prime Minister, thank you for coming.'

'Thank *you*, Lady Chamberlain,' he said, taking her hand. 'A cultural triumph!'

To have assembled nine hundred Italian Old Master paintings and sculptures by Leonardo, Michelangelo, Titian, Bernini, Raphael and many more was a truly remarkable feat. 'Your diplomacy, your persistence,' he said, 'The country owes you and Sir Austen a great debt of gratitude.'

In Gallery 3, Botticelli's *Birth of Venus;* Donatello's *David* in the Central Hall; Mantegna's *Crucifixion* in Gallery 4: its like had never been seen at an Academy exhibition before. To mark the occasion, a private view for a select gathering of politicians, peers and their wives, newspaper proprietors, diplomats, bankers and established churchmen. Champagne glass in hand at the top of the stairs, Conservative Party leader, Baldwin, with Austen Chamberlain and his half-brother Neville. From the House of Lords, Rothermere, the proprietor of the *Daily Mail*, the maker and breaker of reputations – oh, what he would give to bring down Labour a second time. At the centre of an admiring circle, Edith, Lady Londonderry, and outside her orbit that preening peacock, Mosley, with Lady Long Suffering, his wife.

'You should know, Prime Minister,' said Lady Chamberlain, 'the exhibition was only possible because we were able to count upon the enthusiastic support of His Excellency.'

He did know. 'I'm sure we're all grateful to Signor Mussolini.'

Not grateful enough to satisfy, it seemed. His Excellency was a great lover of art, she said, *molto simpatico*, and so anxious to promote understanding between Italy and Great Britain. Why, that very day Mr Churchill had spoken of his admiration for *Il Duce*, of his simple bearing, his calm and gentle nature and of his triumphant struggle against the bestial appetites and passions of communism. And Lord Rothermere, well, Lady Chamberlain had heard him describe Signor Mussolini as 'the greatest man of the age'.

'Really?'

'Yes, really, Prime Minister.'

'Signor Mussolini can have no finer champion than you, Lady Chamberlain.'

'Sir Austin and I consider His Excellency to be a close friend, yes, Prime Minister.'

'We have good reason to be grateful for your friendship, Lady Chamberlain.' He turned to gesture at the paintings, the nearest of which was a large oil of the crucifixion. Never mind 'His Excellency' was responsible for turning his country into a fascist dictatorship and for inciting his blackshirt followers to murder political opponents. Mention of murder and fascist politics would be considered in very poor taste, and taste was everything at a Royal Academy exhibition.

Lily Chamberlain and her committee had taken the unusual step of holding the preview party on a Sunday for his convenience. A national event worthy of a Prime Minister's presence, she had said. She had praised his judgement, flattered him, because she knew he spent a good deal of money on art.

'May I introduce you to Mr Kenneth Clark, Prime Minister. Mr Clark is an expert on Botticelli and will be saying a few words about *The Birth of Venus*.'

'I look forward to that, Mr Clark.'

The Labour backbenches wouldn't approve. Prime minister, Leader of the Opposition, a hundred and fifty members of London society toasting a dictator so anxious to burnish his reputation he was prepared to empty his country's treasure houses and ship their contents to London. Mussolini's spirit hovered in the Central Hall of the Academy like a shade at the feast.

'And this is Count Cippico, Prime Minister,' said Lady Chamberlain. 'The Count is to conduct a public lecture on Venetian painters. He is a friend of His Excellency.'

'Whose generosity we applaud, Count.'

Yes, the exhibition was a triumph. To complaints about his presence he would offer the customary defence, namely that his position obliged him to deal with unsavoury characters and countries, and it was generally best to conduct diplomacy discreetly at a party or exhibition rather than in a glare of publicity at Number 10.

'I believe you have met the Italian ambassador, Prime Minister,' said Lady Chamberlain.

'Signor Bordonaro. A pleasure.'

Andrew Williams

'His Excellency wishes me to convey his greetings, Prime Minister, and deliver a personal message.'

'Ah. Of course. Rosa?' he said, turning to Rosa Rosenberg. 'Can you find a time?'

When he had praised everyone he was expected to praise, shaken every hand he needed to shake and made his speech, the young art historian called Clark conducted him through the galleries, pointing out some of the most interesting pieces.

Lady Londonderry found him with the Venetians in Gallery 6. Clark wanted to show him Mantegna's *Christ on the Mount of Olives*. A panel from an altarpiece painted for the Basilica of Saint Zeno's in Verona, he said. Christ was kneeling, the disciples were sleeping, and on the left of the painting soldiers led by Judas approached them from Jerusalem. Guests who were there only to be seen drifted through the gallery, and he was careful not to catch their eye. He thought he had managed very well, only to discover when he turned from the painting that Oswald and Cynthia Mosley were hovering close by. Presuming on parliament and party, they had followed him with the express intention of engineering a meeting.

'Prime Minister.' Mosley greeted him with a grin like an ape. Really, there was no one in the world he was more anxious to avoid speaking to than the honourable Labour member for Smethwick.

'Hello, Mosley.'

'*Such* a long time since we saw you at Savehay, Prime Minister,' said Cynthia.

'You know Lady Londonderry; this is Mr Kenneth Clark, our guide to the exhibition.'

Mosley barely gave him a glance. 'I've just returned from Scotland, Prime Minister. Shettleston will be close. We may lose the seat.'

'Aye, well not now Mosley, if you please.'

'Our man, McGovern, asked me to have a word, Prime Minister. One in four men in the constituency are out of work, you see. McGovern would like you to do or say something this week. He thinks it would make a difference.'

'I'm sure our people in Scotland are very capable of explaining the energetic steps we are taking to guide the country through this difficult time, and they need no advice from you, Mosley. Now, if you will excuse me.'

Mosley held his ground. 'I must say, Prime Minister, I don't think you are in touch with the mood of the party there, or in the rest of the country for that matter.'

'No, Mosley . . .' – the bloody man – 'it's *you* who has lost touch with the mood of the party. I hear talk of you establishing your *own*. Well, why not, man? Why not? You've tried all the others. You know nothing of our party or our people, man. Nothing. Now stand aside.'

Mosley was twitching with anger. 'That's enough, Tom' – his wife had him by the sleeve – 'I'm sorry, Ramsay.'

Mosley turned to her with a look of utter contempt. Poor woman.

'Mr Clark, lead on,' he said. 'What do you wish to show us now?'

'*The Banishment of St Mamas*, Prime Minister. From an early Venetian altarpiece.'

'Good, good. Politics, Mr Clark, politics. You were wise to choose another way to make a living.' And to Edith Londonderry, he said, 'I'm sorry you witnessed that, my dear.'

His confrontation with Mosley had left a sour taste. He was shaken by his own anger. To think he had nurtured the snake at his own bosom. The insufferable pride of the man! But it was undignified of him to lose his temper in public, and in this case very foolish, because Mosley knew enough of his personal affairs to make his life a misery.

'My dear, will you excuse me?' he said.

But Lady Edith wouldn't let him leave without a private word. 'You're out of sorts, Hamish. That creature, Mosley! You are the most human and understanding of men – he has betrayed your trust.' She let her hand rest lightly on his arm. 'You will visit us soon, won't you? We can't get on without you, you know. The country can't get on without you.'

Dear Edith.

5

Customs at Boulogne was a breeze. Stewart's knapsack was inspected by a veteran of the Somme and the Chemin des Dames. Travellers were forbidden to take more than five thousand francs from the country; Stewart was carrying three quarters of a million. Unshaven, unkempt, he looked like a working man and the *douanier* showed no interest in searching either his sack or his person. He told a story touching enough to melt even the heart of an old *poilu*: Monsieur Stewart was looking for his lost love, carrying her letters with him everywhere.

The ferry crossing was straightforward too. He spent it in the company of two stonemasons who were returning from a month of cutting and tidying in the war cemeteries. 'Beautiful,' they said, 'have you been there?' They were amiable and content chatting to each other as he gazed over the stern rail at the dazzling wake of the ship streaming back to France.

He boarded the boat train at Folkestone Harbour Station at half past two in the afternoon. Passports and luggage were to be inspected on arrival in London, eight hours after leaving Paris, twenty after his no show at rue Louis le Grand. Time aplenty for Fletcher to have notified his Secret Service colleagues and to have arranged a watch at London stations. The boat train into Victoria would run in on number two because the customs office was at the end of the platform, and that would be where the police and Secret Service would be waiting. He was going to have to skip the train or find a way to switch platforms at the station. It wouldn't be easy, he needed to think clearly, only the sun was pouring through the carriage window and he was struggling to stay awake. Opposite him an elderly bloke, buttoned tight, smart like a bank clerk, tried to engage him in conversation: 'You were in Paris?' Stewart was curt with him and they lapsed into an awkward silence after only a few minutes. Well, he couldn't tell the truth and he was too tired to lie. He was hungry too. No bread, no beer, he had nothing to eat but five-pound notes and a prime minister's prose.

The letters intrigued him: what was the fuss about? Bank clerk was buried in the newspaper and his next nearest neighbour was a bench away. It seemed safe to reach down, unbuckle his knapsack, untie a ribbon and slip a letter from one of the bundles. It was written in a small neat hand, like his mother's.

> . . . oh to lie upon your beautiful breast, kiss your noble neck, run my hands up your soft thighs, to touch you in your hairy bower, feel you tremble, and those little kitten whimpers as you climb to paradise . . .

Well! Further down the page, Mac had written of his *porcupine pressing hard, climbing to meet you . . . oh, that night of bliss in Geneva . . .*

Porcupine was code for Mac's prick, Dick supposed. He couldn't imagine his Mother welcoming a letter like that, though she was a spirited woman and ten years younger than the Prime

Minister. Marguerite had married a brute who cared nothing for her and would have made no effort to help her 'climb' further than the top shelf in the larder. Mac was plainly a passionate and more considerate man. Fine. Good. Hats off to Mac. He folded the letter and slipped it back in his sack, 'and shame on me for prying.' God, it was like peeping through curtains in the hope of catching the girl across the road at a lighted window. The boy Richard had done that twenty years ago. But he knew the woman at Mac's lighted window and had sworn to put things right for her. Reading their correspondence was a small betrayal.

Bank clerk neighbour was snoring beneath his paper now. Wheat and barley fields were shimmering in the heat – the glass was close to 90 degrees – and as they rattled over a level crossing, he saw a charabanc waiting at the gates, a dozen or more women in broad-brimmed hats on its benches. A church outing perhaps, a visit to a produce show or tea with Vicar at the vicarage. On a sultry June Sunday were their thoughts only of climbing to heavenly paradise or were they permitting them to wander, perhaps to the handsome lad with red hair on the bench next to the driver? T'would only be human. As they flashed past, how could he tell?

6

Hum. Could the conductor be induced to mislay his jacket? Dick watched him make his way through the carriage punching passenger tickets. Forties, heavy, with a high colour and cheery-looking disposition, he had an honest face someone less cynical might say – that someone was not Dick Stewart. Not since Kitchener's flinty 'do your duty' poster face. What trust could you put in a face? The conductor was probably corruptible, if they could agree on a price.

The train stopped once on its way into London and too briefly for Dick to escape from it. Heralding its arrival with a blast on the whistle, it trundled under the tangle of steel and glass that had grown like a briar over the years to cover the platforms at Victoria station. The occupants of Dick's carriage were on their feet and reaching for their cases a long time before it came to a halt with a hiss. Quarter to four on a Sunday and everyone wanted home. By the time Dick stepped down to the platform the queue for customs stretched almost the length of the train. Through the pall of smoke and steam he could see First Class at the front of it and peaked-cap porters pushing luggage on trolleys. Above and beyond the customs barrier, there were baggage and booking halls, waiting rooms, adverts for Wright's soap, Buchanan's Black & White, Foster Clark's Soups, and WHSmith, the newsagent, with a billboard that made him smile: 'PM to hold meeting.' Yes, a day short of a week he was home, and if he could give police the slip, home in time to hug the children before bedtime.

Only, there they were, three men in trilbies, lit by a shaft of smoky sunshine like characters in a Keystone cops and robbers movie. They were a decent distance away – he couldn't see their faces, but they were dressed like plainclothes policemen, they walked like policemen, they were big, they were thorough, and they were plainly intent on sweeping the entire length of the train.

Along one side of platform 2, the old wall built to bisect the station when it was owned by two companies; along the other, the Folkestone express and the track. Beyond that, running parallel to platform 2, a carriageway for luggage and post vans and the suburban service platforms. That was plainly the route to take, only if he was going to attempt to pick his way across the track he would have to look the part. A peaked cap perhaps, a torch, a flag – the conductor's jacket – anything that would make the coppers think twice.

The boat train's brake van was close-planked and painted Southern Railway green with two sets of double baggage doors facing the platform. The first set was open, and a trunk, suitcases, sacks of post were stacked within reach, waiting for a station porter with a trolley to collect. He hauled himself up without pausing to peer inside. Thankfully, there was no one. A light was on above the guard's pulldown desk. His fountain pen was open and the luggage receipts he must have been marking were on top. Above the desk there was a periscope to check the sides and roof of the train in motion. The brake pillar was in the centre of the van, around the sides a letter rack, steam gauges, dials, lockers, a coke stove, a dog ring, and at the far end to the right of the gangway door a coat rack. The guard's uniform jacket and peaked cap were hanging from a peg, and on the bed of the van beneath them was one of the cast-iron box lanterns that he hung at the rear of the train at night, white light forward, red light back. Jacket; cap; lantern; no need for negotiations, no need for intimidation, no need to pay a penny. Taking no trouble to tread lightly, Stewart hurried to the coat rack and was shrugging the knapsack from his back when someone called out: 'Pete? Is that you, mate?'

The voice came from the other side of a dunny door, a couple of feet from him. In his eagerness to half-inch the guard's jacket he had missed the fucking lavatory. The guard was taking a shit – and in a station too! The dirty bastard.

'Pete?'

'It's Frank,' said Dick, 'I'm 'ere for the trunk.'

'Who? 'ang on a mo!' Stewart heard a frantic rustling of paper, and then the tinkle of a belt buckle. That wouldn't do! Stepping across the van, he lifted the folding chair from the desk and wedged its back under the handle of the dunny door.

'With you in a tick,' said the guard.

'No hurry, mate.'

The jacket fitted him well.

''Ere! What's goin' on?' The guard was wrestling with the handle of the lavatory door.

'Jammed? I'll see what I can do.'

'Hey, wait! Where'd you think you're going?'

Perhaps he heard the lantern glass rattle. In any case, he clearly believed Stewart had done enough for him already because he started to kick up a stink. Stewart dropped down to the platform and pulled the goods van doors shut and the guard's protests were drowned out by the hubbub of the station. But a couple of porters were pushing a trolley towards the van, and the coppers had finished checking the passengers and were only two carriages away. He needed to be quick.

''Ere! Where are you goin'?' One of the porters shouted after him.

Half-turning, he shouted back, 'Wait there, back in a mo,' then he jumped down on to the track. The porters would hear the guard in the van bawling for his freedom in about a minute. They would take another minute to release him and listen to his story, and maybe a third to raise the alarm. Stewart reckoned he had three minutes before the coppers came haring after him. The goods carriageway was just across the track in front of him and that would be the next place they would look for him. His best bet was to cross to one of the suburban platforms – but, my God, he felt conspicuous.

'What the hell are you doin'?' A member of the station staff had appeared at the edge of the carriageway and was gazing down at him.

'Passenger lost a wedding ring,' he said.

'Not your job.'

'A favour—'

'Completely against regulations. Get off the track at once.'

'Oh, fuck off!'

'Bloody idiot. You'll get yourself killed,' he said, gesturing frantically to an inbound train. 'It's coming in on five.'

The rails were squealing, the engine hissing like a mechanical serpent as it approached the first of the suburban platforms. It was going to pass very close to him and if he moved quickly . . . He felt a shudder of apprehension pass from the nape of his neck to his toes. Its brakes were screeching, his mind was numb, but on he stumbled from sleeper to sleeper. The draught from the engine plucked at his jacket and cap as he cleared the track with no more than a couple of seconds to spare.

Conscious that all sorts of people were now raising all kinds of hell behind him, he ran up the ramp of platform number five, checked his pace, and began to walk towards the concourse. His three minutes were up; it was time to ditch the uniform. Ahead of him the train he had avoided by the skin of his teeth was disgorging its passengers. The cap, jacket and lantern he dropped in the first empty carriage he came to. He was an ordinary bloke again, an unshaven face in the crowd. With shoulders and elbows, he barged his way through the passengers queueing to show their tickets at the gate. 'Out of my way!'

A la-di-da lady protested and her gentleman grabbed him by the arm. Interfering shit, 'Let go!' he said with all the menace he was able to muster. Then he shouted to the ticket collector, 'Hey, you! I need help! It's an emergency!'

Ticket collector shouted back, 'What's the matter? Let him through, let him through.'

'An old bloke in the last carriage,' said Stewart, 'I think he's dying.'

'Brighton train?'

'This platform.'

'Show me.'

'What? No! 'Ee needs help now! Didn't you hear? 'Ee's dying. There must be someone . . .'

The ticket collector was tortured by indecision. Poor sod. He was only young, bum fluff still on his chin. 'Go on!' Stewart gave him a shove. 'Fetch someone, move, why don't you?'

'Yes, yes, I will,' he said, closing the gate – 'back in a second' – and then again to the queue – 'Just a second!' Poor bum fluff wasn't a commanding presence. A pack of platform 5 passengers surged on to the concourse. Stewart glanced left towards the customs office on 2: the assistant stationmaster he had abused on the carriageway was in earnest conversation with half a dozen policemen. Turning out of the pack, he weaved his way through the crowd around the departures board and a posse of porters leaning on their trolleys, on past the booking office and left luggage, into the gloom of the east passage exit, the hum of traffic in the street rising to meet him.

Sunny city street in the Pimlico district, a luggage repository opposite, the Warwick Arms public house to his right. A nun walked past with a poodle: he had to smile. Oh, yes, he had given the buggers the slip. They would carry on searching but he was away. Free to arrange things properly.

He caught a bus to Borough, changed on to another, and stepped off it in Rotherhithe. Low tide on the Thames and children were playing on the muddy beach in front of the Angel pub. As a boy he had scoured the strand for river-frosted glass, rusty pennies and shards of blue and white china. Grandma was refusing to let little Pierre do the same. 'Too young,' she said. Their neighbours accused her of being hoity-toity, and perhaps she was: Marguerite was Marguerite. She was strong, she was a survivor, like Madame Forster. Too often he took her love and care for granted – shame on him! He was going to depend upon it even more in the months to come.

Marguerite would be preparing to take the children to Mass

at the yellow-brick mission church in Paradise Street. They would walk through the old village, past the tunnel engine house, the Spread Eagle, the saltpetre wharf and St Mary's, where the bell ringers were waiting by a door in the tower for their captain. Stewart found a tabletop tomb with a view through the railings to the street, and with the knapsack between his knees he rested his back against the crumbling stone and lit a cigarette. Thankfully, the vagrants who swigged spirits, argued and pissed in the churchyard from dawn until dusk were preoccupied with begging for pennies from members of the congregation arriving for the evening service. The church bells began to weave their patterns, loud and so insistent he was unable to concentrate on anything else. But it was only for a few minutes. They stopped as suddenly as they had started, and even as the hum of the heaviest was dying away he heard a small boy in the street exclaim, '*Enfin!*' And, yes, it was his *petit Pierre*. He was almost overcome with emotion. Ha! He had given his hanky to Madame Forster!

'*Pierre. Attends, mon chéri,*' he heard his mother say.

They were crossing the street to the pavement in front of the church, Pierre in a red shirt and blue shorts, Florence in sunflower-yellow. *Mes chéris!* He shifted impatiently, resisting the urge to call out to them. They walked past the church gates and his tomb and disappeared in the cut between Tunnel Mill and the old sugar warehouse. He was on the point of rising when a sly movement caught his eye and he shrank back behind the stone. Through the branches of a churchyard yew he could see a wiry-looking man of about thirty with a ferrety sort of face walking slowly towards the cut. The bastard! Ferret face was one of Knight's casuals. Oh, how satisfying it would be to punch his face. But, no, he would have to forgo the pleasure. He waited instead for the bugger to slink into the cut like a stray, then he rose from the tomb and crossed to the gate on the other side of St Mary's. 'Fuck off,' he growled at a tramp who asked him for money, but he regretted it at once. 'No, here you are,' he said, tossing the man two shillings. Why not?

The Norwegian seamen's mission on Albion Street competed with the local pubs and prostitutes for the attention of its nationals serving on ships of the timber trade. Stewart had visited the old mission church – the Ebenezer – many times as a boy. Marguerite had sent him there to escape from his father. The Norwegians were plain prayerbook Protestant, but she had trusted them not to fill his head with heretical notions. Their new church was a much grander affair. For a small fee seamen were able to leave luggage and arrange for post to be forwarded to their next port of call.

The young woman in the mission office greeted him with a warm smile and listened patiently as he explained his business. He wished to send money to two families in Wales that were in need of some assistance, he said, and in return for the mission's help he was willing to make a handsome donation. That Owen and Eyre were serving sentences for sedition and it was their anonymous benefactor who had put them in prison he chose not to share with her. Knight had paid him eight pounds for the Brecon barracks job; eight hundred was the sum he was sending to their families. Why? Because he needed to rub the slate clean – or cleaner – and what better way than to hand over some of the money he had pinched from Joyce. Four hundred to each family would see them straight. A gift from newspaper, Secret Service, business and fascist conspirators who paid men like him to undermine the government: guilty of sedition and yet never brought to justice.

From what was left of their money, he set aside a donation to the church and enough for his mother to get by, and the rest he emptied from his knapsack into a safe deposit box. Three thousand eight hundred pounds, he reckoned.

'How long will I need the deposit box for? Six months, maybe a year.'

She made a note. 'You've been very generous.'

'*Ja*,' he said with a weary smile. 'What is it you say in Norway? "I'm in the middle of the butter eye."'

Money stowed, money paid, he picked up the sack of letters and made his way into the mission dining hall. He needed to eat, he needed to wash, he needed a clean shirt, he needed a shit, and then he needed to catch a bus to Downing Street.

7

Sinful to labour for anyone but the Lord on the Sabbath his Wee Free grandmother used to say. She might have made some allowance for a prime minister. That she would have offered an opinion in any case he was in no doubt: the Ramsay women were never short of opinions.

He was not a religious man, a religious prime minister. Bible-soaked in speech, yes, and he was sure he knew right from wrong and what it meant to be a good Christian, and when on public occasions it was necessary to pray, he could do so with a convincing air of sincerity. He cared nothing for doctrine and drew no spiritual strength from organised worship, and yet, with or without God, Sunday was a sacred day for family.

At eight o'clock he closed his red box and rose stiffly from his desk. 'I'm awfa sairy I've kept you so late on a Sunday, Miss Rosenberg.'

She smiled and clicked the top on her fountain pen.

'A taxicab home,' he said, 'you'll speak to the porters?'

'But it's a lovely evening and some fresh air will do me good, Prime Minister,' she replied.

'The family are here. Sheila's come down from Oxford. I think we'll go out to the rose garden.'

His children were waiting in the small drawing room, and Malcom had already popped his head around the study door to chide him for working late on a Sunday. 'You're sure about the taxicab now, Rosa? Catch the bus home and you'll barely have time to set foot in the door before you're back here again.'

He would have an early breakfast on Monday with the Hungarian prime minister, then meet a delegation from the trade unions. The new employment committee was to hold a session in the afternoon, and the chancellor of the exchequer was in the diary too. In the evening, he was to receive the freedom of the borough of West Ham in recognition of his 'service to the nation and the cause of peace'. He would speak of 'duty', 'decency' and 'service': three words the newspapers would make him choke on if Frau Forster was permitted to sell them his letters.

'Goodbye Rosa, my dear,' he said, holding the door open for her.

'Will you give Miss Sheila my regards, Prime Minister, and the others too, of course.'

He watched her retreating along the corridor, a little in awe of her youth and vigour. His brain was fagged by business and the meeting in the gallery with Mosley, his spirits a little low. That was too often the case these days. He needed a few minutes alone to compose a smile. A father should admit to no weakness that might cause worry to his children, although most of what troubled him they might read in the newspapers.

Head bent, hauling on the banister, he began to climb the stairs. Malcolm would be sharing party and parliamentary gossip with his sisters. They knew their father would hear none of it on a Sunday evening. He had read them Bible stories when they were little. The memory of their faces in the firelight made him smile, and now, as he approached the drawing room, the sound of their laughter gladdened his heart too. So much so, he tiptoed the last few steps to listen at the open door. Yes, they were talking politics, but student politics, with Sheila in full flow: '. . . and then, and then . . .' – she was choking with laughter – '. . . a man in a red dress and high heels fell through the door and . . . and shouted, "I'm the Prince of Prussia and I second the motion." Then he was sick. He was sick everywhere!'

'And was he?' said his daughter, Joan.

'Was he what?'

'The Prince of Prussia, Sheila?'

'I think he was, yes.'

Well! Sheila! He disapproved, naturally. There were young men at the old universities who thought too well of themselves. They seemed to labour under the misapprehension that privilege was a licence to behave badly. He was on the point of bursting into the room and saying so when he was distracted by a ladylike cough behind him on the stairs.

'Why, Rosa . . .'

His private secretary was climbing towards him in her hat and coat, and it was plain from her expression that she was the bearer of troubling news. 'I'm sorry to disturb you again, Prime Minister, but . . .'

'Father?' Malcom had opened the drawing room door.

'I was about to join you all,' he said, 'only, it seems Miss Rosenberg has other plans for me.'

'Oh, no, Father!' Sheila was at her brother's side, Joan and Ishbel two steps behind.

'A delegation. You'll not be popular, Rosa. Can it wait?'

'I don't think it can, Prime Minister.'

'You can't tell me . . .' No, it was foolish of him to ask her in front of the family. 'That's all right. I won't be long, my dears. I promise.'

Malcolm looked sceptical, they all looked sceptical, and they had a right to be: it was a promise he had broken a thousand times.

'Admiral Sinclair?' he said, as he followed her down the stairs. He was sure it was something to do with the letters. 'Is he on the telephone?'

'No,' she said, 'not the admiral.'

'Then who?'

Either she didn't hear or she was pretending not to.

'Who is it, my dear?' he said, raising his voice a little.

She stopped and turned reluctantly. 'A messenger, Prime Minister. I was waiting to tell you somewhere more private.'

'Yes, of course, that would be best. My study.'

Rosa was so reticent, it had to be a messenger from *her*. Could it be from anyone else?

He switched on the study light, then the lamps, and stirred the embers of the fire. He would take his time, behave with some dignity. He was still ashamed of his outburst on the evening *she* visited him in Downing Street. What an exhibition! To think Rosa had witnessed him that way. He had acted in an unseemly manner, unworthy of a prime minister. So, yes, some dignity, no matter what *she, they* were preparing to throw at him.

'Well Rosa?' he said, his back to the stuttering fire, 'a message from whom?'

'From Frau Forster, Prime Minister.'

'A letter? Give it to me.'

'The messenger says he must deliver it to you in person.'

'Oh? Who is he? He might be a reporter.'

'No, I don't—'

'Any Tom, Dick or Harry could walk up to the door with a message. Where did you meet him?'

'Outside the Foreign Office.'

'Where on earth was the policeman?'

'He came to speak to me . . . to *us*. He was concerned. Mr Stewart – that's his name – looks quite . . . rough. But he told me he worked for Commander Fletcher and that he was with Frau Forster in Paris this morning.'

'Is he here on behalf of Commander Fletcher?'

She hesitated. 'He said the message was from Frau Forster.'

'You've asked the police to search . . .' – of course, of course, it was insulting of him to ask her – 'then you better show him in.'

This man, this messenger, who was he? How dearly he wanted to leave everything to the Secret Service. Where was Commander Fletcher? Fletcher he could trust; Fletcher wanted a seat. Sinclair wanted nothing – yet. Was she selling her story? Was that the message? Because he would have to warn the party and his children, draft a statement, consider his position. He lit a cigar and sat at his desk. Glasses; pen; red box; government papers: his props were in place. The messenger must see his prime minister toiling for the nation.

The man who followed Rosa into the study was in his late thirties, fine-featured, dark, unshaven and poorly dressed in a collarless shirt, dirty trousers and tackety workman's boots. A soldier's knapsack was slung over his right shoulder.

'Prime Minister, this is Mr Stewart,' she said.

'Mr Stewart, please come in,' he said, rising to offer his hand. 'Thank you, Miss Rosenberg. I don't expect we'll be very long. You understand, Mr Stewart . . .' – he gestured to his open despatch box – 'matters I must attend to this evening.'

Stewart nodded.

'I understand from my secretary you are an associate of Commander Fletcher's, Mr Stewart, and that you are bearer of a message.'

'That's what I told her, yes.' There was a hint of London in his voice, and more than a hint of belligerence.

'Did you know that Miss Rosenberg was my private secretary?'

'No. A lucky shot. She was first out of the door. But I would have knocked if it was necessary. I was sure you'd see me.'

'Oh, were you?' He bristled. 'And why was that?'

Stewart made no answer. Swinging the knapsack from his shoulder to the rug, he unfastened the buckles and removed two bundles neatly tied with a ribbon. Then he reached forward and stacked them on the desk between the ink stand and the photograph of Margaret with the children. 'You know what those are.'

Of course! He recognised his own hand. Thank God! How could he explain . . . the broken nights, wild imaginings, the day-to-day distraction from his duty – over. The fear of family disgrace and of disgracing his family – over. 'My letters,' was all he was able to say.

'They are now,' said Stewart.

'Thank you for returning them, Mr Stewart. Please, sit will you. I intend to smoke . . .' His cigar had gone out. 'May I offer you one of these?' He rolled the brown stub between his fingers. 'Or would you prefer a cigarette?'

'A cigarette, thank you.'

'Please . . .' He lifted the lid on the cigarette box and turned it to Stewart. 'I'm sure you know . . . these letters are very personal. There was some confusion . . . Miss Rosenberg said you were here on behalf of their recipient, but you have come from Commander Fletcher, have you not? Why didn't he deliver them in person?'

'Because Madame Forster asked *me* to return them to you. She doesn't trust the Secret Service.'

'But she was prepared to trust *you*, and you say you work for Commander Fletcher.'

'Yes, she trusted me. She hasn't met Fletcher. Who knows if he can be trusted. I thought so at first, but something has changed. You know that agents in the Secret Service are workin' against you?'

'You don't think Commander Fletcher can be trusted?'

'I don't know. Doesn't matter now, does it? You've got the letters.'

'How do you know British agents are working against me?'

'Because I worked for one of them.'

He frowned and leant forward, his elbows on the desk. 'You better explain, Mr Stewart.'

8

He tried to. First, his own part in the affair. He was serving two masters, one trying to save a prime minister, the other to ruin him. A parallel Secret Service operation to recover the letters until they had become one operation.

'I was being paid by both,' he said.

There was an agent called Knight working for rogue elements in the service, and another called Joyce: fascists dedicated to fighting communists and any shade of the same. Labour was an enemy; Mr Ramsay MacDonald was an enemy. A battle for the soul of the nation, they said, and they were prepared to undermine the government of the day to win it. Bribes, break-ins, breaking up meetings; spies on the inside to protect the people from the people's party – well, to protect *some* people. How did he know this? Because he took their shilling. Simple as . . . That was his explanation. Succinct. Forceful. Just one swear word once: he noticed the prime minister flinch. Mac was gazing at him intently now, the smoking stub of a cigar between his fingers, an Old Testament frown on his brow.

'Well, Mr Stewart . . .' – he leant forward to squeeze the stub into an ashtray – 'that's quite a story. You know, you're alleging a conspiracy against the government, against me.'

Yes, of course he knew.

'Apart from this fellow, Knight, do you have any other names?'

He didn't. 'I'm just a foot soldier.'

'*You* are the man who brought back my letters,' said the prime minister with feeling. He reached across the desk to the top of the stack. 'You think that's all of them?'

'Madame Forster said so.'

'She took the money, of course.'

'I insisted.'

'You *insisted*?' That was sharp. 'I don't understand. Mr Stewart, why would you *insist*?'

'Because she needed the money, Prime Minister.'

'And you think that a good reason for stealing from the state?'

'The Secret Service was ready to pay for them, Commander Fletcher was prepared to – so, I paid.'

'You said *you* insisted. Mr Stewart; on who's authority? She was attempting to blackmail me. You were rewarding a blackmailer. If she was sorry, truly sorry – as you say – well, Mr Stewart . . .' – his right hand was clenched in a fist on the blotter – '. . . you should have encouraged her *not* to take the money.'

'Seemed to me, Mr MacDonald, that she was alone. 'Er friends had deserted her. It was a contract, Mr MacDonald: You was buyin' and that was the deal.'

What was Mac fussing about? Look at him! Eyes closed and fingertips to his forehead: it was bloody mean of him. Not very Labour. The woman was destitute. Why begrudge her the money? Bloody hell, it wasn't as if it was his money.

Mac opened his eyes. 'I suppose it was always her intention to take it.'

'Excuse me for sayin' so, Mr MacDonald, but she has a better opinion of you.'

'Aye, well, a woman who attempts to blackmail her friends . . .'

'She was hurt, wasn't she, because she . . .' – did he dare say it? – 'she loved you and trusted you. Seems to me that was no small thing after what she had been through.'

'I don't know what she told you Mr Stewart . . .' – Mac pushed his chair from the desk to rise – 'I don't want to know. I think you've said all you need to say. I thank you for returning my letters, and now I'll thank you to leave.'

'I mean, you know her husband was murdered in front of her eyes, don't you? And her son was killed at the Front.'

Mac said nothing, but his expression . . . he didn't know. He didn't have a clue. That was as a plain as a pikestaff. 'Her husband was a politician like you, Mr Mac. Butchered by *Freikorps* fascists in her house, her bedroom, the "Jew bitch" forced to watch: that's what they called her, because that's the sort of rubbish they were . . . they *are*. They hated her for being a Jew. 'Course, she left Germany, after that, and meetin' you restored her to the land of the living, she says. She admires you for what you've done 'ere, what you represent: you are hope. That's it, that's what you represent.'

The prime minister was still on his feet, his right hand toying with a pen. 'I don't know what to believe,' he said at last, 'or what to say.'

'Speaking for myself – I mean, Madame Forster doesn't live 'ere, does she? – hope is a chance in life. Hope is a decent job, a decent hospital – I lost my wife, when, well . . . Hope is a proper education for our children, and that's what we were promised after the war.'

He nodded. 'Yes, and this government will do all in its power to give that to our people, Mr Stewart, I promise. These things take time, you understand, and there is only so much a prime minister can do without a working majority in parliament. My hands are tied' – he made a big fist of them – 'and this country of ours, it is buffeted by strong winds, thrown off course by a world financial crash. Anyway . . .' – he shuffled clear of his desk – 'you will have to excuse me.'

Stewart rose from his chair. 'You won't 'ear from her again; she told me to tell you that.'

'She's living in Paris?'

'She's returning to Germany. Says she wants to teach in her husband's school, which is brave, considering. There's a new fascist party there . . .'

'Herr Hitler's party.'

'She says they're Jew-haters who strut around in brown shirts.'

'Very troubling, yes,' he said, impatiently. Did he care? She said he should if he cared for peace. 'And you, Mr Stewart, what are you going to do?'

He shrugged. 'See my children and keep my head down.'

'This Mr Knight, do you think he will pursue you?'

'Oh, yes, and your enemies in the Secret Service, Prime Minister, them too.'

'Rest assured, I'll do what I can to help you.'

'Will you? That should be enough then, shouldn't it? You're the prime minister.'

Was he listening? Was Mac concentrating? Was he picking it up?

'Ah, Miss Rosenberg,' he said, standing back from the open door, 'would you show Mr Stewart out. Thank you again, Mr Stewart, I'm in your debt, I'm sure.'

9

From the door he turned to gaze across his study at the letters. A strong gust through the open window and they would topple.

They were two rulers high, the size of a pauper's stone. How many? Fifty? Sixty perhaps. How many words? Thousands. A monument in paper to vanity and wasted passion.

Oh, my dearest, Kristina, I long to hold you close; Dearest, the peace I feel in your arms, truly, it is a peace that passeth all understanding; My love, when I am inside you I feel an overwhelming sense of joy and peace etcetera, etcetera, etcetera.

He had poured a torrent of feeling and wild imagining on to the page in his bedroom at the end of every evening for months. Impossible to understand how he could have written and spoken so fervidly of his love when he barely knew her. He had held a Jewess, grieving mother, political widow and blackmailer in his arms, and entered her in ignorance. Better judge him for that ignorance than his bold imagination. Judge him too for writing and saying more than he meant. So eager to escape the straitjacket of politics, and yet so schooled in its ways, its soapbox passion and easy promises, its half-truths and insincerities. He hadn't weighed the import of his words on a passionate woman who must have seen in him a saviour. Judge him for that. Judge him for giving it no consideration until it was too late. She sent Mr Stewart to make him see – he did now, at least a little. That she claimed to have faith in him still was touching in a small way, but not enough to make him think of her any more warmly.

Lifting the top of the pile from the desk, he carried it to the hearth, untied the ribbons and dropped the first letter in the fire. The flames ate slowly into the envelope – too slowly – and the next letter he tore into pieces. He watched *My dearest darling Kristina* scorch, shrivel, catch and burn with a hint of blue. Fragments were floating up the chimney – to fall where, he wondered? Marylebone might wake to find a charred scrap of his love stuck to a window or step or the roof of a motorcar.

He needed more heat, more coal, lest he choke the fire with ash and sow the city with misplaced sentiment.

She would be shocked that he was ready to burn them without even a second glance, but she would never know. He would have nothing more to do with her. Sad to think that he would remember her as a blackmailer and not as a giving lover and agreeable companion. Yes, he was at fault, but so was she. Politics for her was a simple matter of principles. Full employment? Perfectly possible. Wealth redistribution? Why not tomorrow? Faith and principles were nothing without power.

Stewart said she had faith in his judgement. Well, in his judgement their affair had posed a threat to his premiership, his government, his fragile parliamentary majority, a chance for some change, and the promises he had made his wife before she died. As a young man he had scorned Otto von Bismarck's famous maxim: politics is the art of the possible, the art of the next best thing. Not now, not after forty years of church hall meetings, conferences and committees, policy forums and parliamentary caucuses; forty years of learning to accept that something was better than nothing. That was the nitty-gritty of politics. Why, it was even the case in revolutionary Russia, where the people were a great disappointment to the Party.

As much as he could do he would do. His premiership was the culmination of his life in politics and, yes, he should have been honest with her and handled things better, but their relationship was over on polling day when he won the election. It was sad, even cruel, but necessary.

'Prime Minister?' Rosa Rosenberg was standing at the door. Lost in thought and the bonfire of his letters, he hadn't heard her enter. 'Mr Malcolm was enquiring . . .'

'Yes, yes, I won't be long.'

He saw her glance at the pile of letters spilling on to the hearth.

'It must be late,' he said, fumbling for his pocket watch.

'Nearly half past.'

'Then you must go home. Only, before you do, will you do one thing more for me? I would like to speak to Admiral Sinclair. Please contact whoever you need to.'

She hesitated. 'This evening?'

'As soon as possible.'

'Yes, Prime Minister.'

Lifting a poker from the fire tree, he raked the letter ash through the grate into the pan. Number 10 staff would wonder at a fire on a warm summer evening. It was quite stifling in the study and the acrid paper-smoke was irritating his throat. He took off his jacket and laid it on the chair. His eyes were stinging.

Mr Stewart claimed it was never her intention to sell the letters to a newspaper. What did it matter? The threat of public disgrace had driven him into the arms of his enemies in the Secret Service. They must have enjoyed and wondered at his desperation, and irony of ironies: it was Fletcher who had persuaded *him* to involve the Secret Service, and Stewart who had persuaded *her* to take the money, and both of them claimed to be Labour. They clearly had no idea what they had done. Yes, the letters were in the fire, but he was never going to be free of the smoke from them – not now.

The telephone was ringing. That would be Sinclair. He stepped away from the heat of the fire and back to his desk. 'Yes? Thank you. I'll speak to him now.'

'Prime Minister?'

'Yes, Admiral.' He could hear voices. 'You're at your club?'

'Yes.'

'Perhaps you should come here.'

'It's perfectly all right, Prime Minister. No one can hear us.'

Should he insist? No. Keep his powder dry. 'I've had a visitor. One of your people. A Mr Stewart.'

No reply.

'He brought me a package of letters.'

'*Did* he now?'

'You sound surprised.'

'Not at all, not at all.'

'He told me quite a tale. He claims your officers, he mentioned a fellow called Knight, were paying him to acquire the letters with the intention of undermining the government – of undermining me.'

'Well, that's nonsense, Prime Minister. Nonsense. Knight works for Special Branch from time to time, but he's not one of ours. No, no, he has never worked for us. Really, Prime Minister, Stewart has his uses, but . . . Did he tell you he was working with Commander Fletcher?'

'He did.'

'There! A messenger—'

'With a most disturbing message, Admiral!'

'He's one of our casuals, that's all.' He paused. 'He gave the Forster woman the money?'

'He said so.'

'Well, there you have it, Prime Minister, what more proof do you need of the service's good faith. Fletcher gave Stewart the money to exchange for the letters and that's what he's done. In search of glory he has decided to play Downing Street postman. Fishing for a reward, I'm sure: he's a mercenary fellow. The important thing is, we've recovered your letters.'

'Yes. Thank you, Admiral,' he said, coolly. 'But am I to assume your agent, Stewart—'

'He isn't *our* agent, Prime Minister—'

'Let me speak, please. Am I to assume Commander Fletcher has lost control of him?'

That took the wind from the admiral's sails.

'Well, Prime Minister, the thing is . . . The thing is, Stewart is a rogue. The right man for the job, but a rogue. I'm afraid we come across them in our line of work quite often.'

My God, yes, you do, he thought. 'And this . . . "rogue", you say – this rogue was in possession of my letters long enough to read them, copy them, sell them. I can't even be sure he's returned them all.'

'Oh, I think so, Prime Minister. He knows not to tangle with the Service.'

'You're sure?'

'We'll find him and ask. We have . . .' He paused. 'Let's say, a bone to pick with Mr Stewart. Did he—'

'Home, Admiral.'

'That's where he said he was—'

'Yes.'

'Good, good. That's helpful, yes.'

Sinclair was smiling; he knew it! When the admiral spoke again, he could hear it too. 'So pleased we have been of service to you personally, Prime Minister.' No doubt! 'We understand each other better, I think.' Indubitably! 'It's important the Secret Service is in step with Downing Street, I've always said so.' Sinclair paused. 'Is that all, Prime Minister?'

At least the awful man had the grace not to mention the money. Yes, that was all for now – until he came knocking for repayment in kind, as one day he surely would.

10

Ten to midnight at the bus stop outside the Baths, and, praise the Lord, not a soul to be seen. Not a drunken sailor, not a dockyard doxy, not a late-shift stevedore, cabbie or bobby – and none of Knight's old fascist crew. Just as well, because Dick was stumble-weary with the strain of being on the *qui vive*. Special vigilance was needed at such times; any trench veteran would tell you so. Forget to duck in a fog of fatigue and your brains would be painted on the parados. So, he wouldn't take his usual way home. Collar up and cap down low, he would approach from the river.

From the dock office entrance he walked around the Albion to the gasworks, scrambled a sooty wall, and peered into his street. One side was in coal-hole shadow, the other dimly lit by the sickly yellow glow of the dockyard arcs. The only municipal light in the street was an old gas wall mount above the shop on the corner of Clarence and Brunel. The Bristow family's marmalade cat was washing her paws on the step of number 9. There was a chink of light in the bedroom curtains at the Browns', another light two doors down; and in the parlour of the only double front, the flicker of a candle flame. Number 17: his mother was still up and doing. Was the candle a warning not to come home? Perhaps the police or one of Knight's bully boys had spoken to her about her troublesome son. They wanted their money back. The prime minister would have informed the Secret Service that the letters were in his possession by now – and 'lay off Mr Stewart.' He said he would, and, 'goodness, he owes me that much.' He owed the Bristows, Browns and O'Briens, too, and Billy Mason who lost a leg on the Somme and was good for nothing now; and the widow Brewer and her five children in Swan Street, whose husband, Charlie, was killed by falling timber on the Canada Dock; and McCully in Canon Beck Road who was dying of cancer; and the Johnsons, Jacksons and Proctors trying to get by on the dole. Jobs, fair pay, a chance for everyone: that was the Labour Party, right? Madame Forster said she still had faith in Mac; well, he wanted to have faith in Mac too. Not for his own sake but for the two-up, two-down families in the street below – for his own family. Madame had put her faith in him – he hadn't let her down – and returning the letters . . . well, that was a demonstration of their faith in Mac and his government. That was how he saw it, anyway.

Dropping back down the wall, he walked on past the gas-works and the river entrance to the dock, crossed the bascule bridge and turned left on to the road round the peninsula. Low-tide slack water the Thames, silver-tipped by a sliver of moon. A coastal freighter was moored at a dolphin in the coil of the river. On the north shore the mud beneath the wharves was a slick yellow, and above the wharves, the white stone spire of the sea captain's church piercing the night sky. He was almost home.

Mrs Bristow's cat came slinking towards him, brushing his leg as he hurried past. Would an order from Downing Street have trickled down to coppers and casuals on the street? Maybe. His mother had tied back her Belgian lace curtains and balanced the candle on the window frame. He slipped his key in the lock and let himself in quietly. Marguerite appeared from the kitchen before he had time to close the door.

'Richard?' she said, a tremor in her voice.

'Yes.' He switched on the hall light and she stepped forward, her face white, wide-eyed, her hair down over her shoulders and her blue nightgown.

'What is it?' he asked in French.

'You can't stay!'

He took a step towards her, then checked: she was holding white-knuckle-tight the largest of their kitchen knives. 'Leave. You must go,' she said.

'Or you'll kill me?'

'Richard, it isn't safe!'

'Someone's been here?'

Her bottom lip trembled.

'Oh, Mother.' He took the knife from her and folded her in his arms. She gave a little sigh and he felt her shoulders relax – but only for a moment.

'He says he wants his money,' she said, pushing him away. 'Who is he, Richard?'

'He came here?'

'This evening. A little after nine.'

'He has a scar on his face?'

'He said you weren't going to get away with it: what did he mean?'

'Come,' he said, leading her by the hand into the kitchen. 'Will you make me some tea?'

'No, Richard, no. You must think of the children!'

'Mother, I am. I won't stay, but there is something I must do first. I won't be long.'

'Richard, it isn't safe!'

He took her hand. 'A lot has happened. I will tell you, only first . . . You'll have to trust me.'

She hesitated – goodness, she had the right to.

He unlaced his boots and climbed the stairs in his threadbare socks to the landing outside his children's room. The door was ajar and he was sorely tempted to slip inside and gather them in his arms, but, no, first he had to think of their future. That was how he saw the money – their future. The curtains in his own room were open and to avoid being seen from the street he sank to his knees and shuffled round the bed to the chest of drawers. The front right leg of the chest was chipped and scuffed and appeared to be made of the same solid oak as the others, but he had fashioned it from pine before the war to hide a few small pieces of his mother's jewellery. They were family pieces of no great value, but his bastard father had found and sold them all the same. Grandmother's wedding ring had ended up on the fat little finger of a barmaid at the Anchor.

The hollow leg was a decent hiding place and he hoped this time a lucky one. Flipping a plug from the back with a finger-nail, he dropped the key to his mission deposit box inside the cavity.

Florence was sleeping with the doll her mother gave her pressed to her cheek. He swept a damp strand of hair from her forehead and bent to kiss her. She was so very like his poor dear Connie: the same round face; the same sunny disposition; the same mischievous twinkle in her eye. Come what may, Florence would be okay. But *petit* Pierre . . . He lifted his son's hand from the covers and brushed it lightly with his lips. Pierre was too young to be without a father. 'My little boy,' he whispered and kissed his son again. It was up to the prime minister now.

Marguerite was waiting in the kitchen, standing with her back to the stove. She had pinned her hair up in an unruly bun. On the table, a pot of tea, bread and butter. 'Thank you,' he said, pulling a chair away.

'Then you must go,' she said in French.

He nodded.

'You know I never ask you – God forgive me, I should – but for the children's sake . . .'

'Yes, I know.'

She stepped up to the table and poured him some tea. She had given him her own bone china cup.

'Thank you, *Maman.*'

'Oh, Richard,' she sighed, resting her hand lightly on his shoulder. 'When will you stop!'

'Soon. You mustn't worry.'

'That man was so angry.'

He reached for her hand and turned to look up at her. 'I promise things will be better soon.' He hesitated. 'I will be better.'

She was crying.

He pushed his chair away – 'Oh, Mother' – and wiped the tears from her cheeks lightly with his thumbs.

'I spoke to the prime minister this evening,' he said, breezily.

'Richard!'

'Perfectly true. We spoke, oh, for half an hour in his study in Downing Street. I was returning some of his letters. He was very grateful.' He paused. 'That's what this is about, Mother. The man who visited you hates the prime minister.' From his jacket he took a wad of five-pound notes. 'I want you to put this somewhere safe. On your person for now.'

'Is this the money they're looking for?'

'Yes, it's payment for my work. Please, take it – for the children.'

'Why can't you have it – *if* it's yours to keep?'

'A precaution.'

'But you said you were working for the prime minister?'

He took her hands and folded her fingers around the money. How could he explain? There were more powerful people in the country than the prime minister.

'If anyone asks, say *nothing*. Promise me. You know nothing about my work or about the money. Do you understand?'

'No, Richard.'

No? No to what? Please, *Maman*: he was too tired to argue.

'I'm to blame too,' she said. 'It's my fault, and your father . . . I've never asked where your money comes from.'

'Not now, please. You must trust me this one time. You must. It's *my* money . . .' God! Who had a better claim to it? '*Maman*! You have to believe me.' She was crying. '*Maman*, for the children, please.' He held her hands tightly; held the money in her hands. 'I know I haven't been the best father but—'

He was interrupted by a mighty blow and a splintering of wood like timber tumbling from a crane on to the dock. So, it was too late. He felt his mother shudder, and the fear in her eyes . . . he hadn't seen her face like that since his father raised his fist to her. The time for pleading and explanations was over. Someone was beating down their door. Upstairs, the children were whimpering. They called in chorus to her, 'Grandmère, Grandmère, Grandmère.'

'Go to 'em, Mother. And hide that!' he said, gesturing to the money. 'Hide it!'

'Richard. Please leave. Go!' she said, pushing him towards the back door. Through the yard, over the wall: he had managed it before. But no, he was staying to face the music; he would have to some time.

'Upstairs, Mother!' It wasn't going to be pretty. He pulled out a kitchen drawer. A knife would be a mistake. He selected his mother's rolling pin and thrust it into the waistband of his trousers. Then he snatched a kitchen chair from the table and made for the door.

They were dithering in the hall: Joyce, with a couple of bully boys and a copper at his back. The copper was a surprise.

'Where's the money, Stewart?' said Joyce.

'The money, you cunt? I need the money for a new front door.'

'Are you intending to resist arrest?' Joyce turned pointedly to the law.

'Can't 'ee speak for himself? Hey, you,' he said, calling to the copper. 'Can't you speak for yourself, mate? I'm under the prime minister's protection, by the way.'

Joyce laughed. 'Oh Dick, you are a funny one. Ramshackle couldn't care less what happens to you. You're expendable.'

Perhaps that was true. 'Tell Knight the prime minister has the letters.'

'He doesn't care. He wants the money back. Where is it?'

'I gave it to a Jewish orphanage.'

Holding the chair like a lion tamer, he lunged at Joyce and caught him in the chest with a leg. The Irishman grunted with pain and rocked on to his heels. 'Out! Out!' Stewart wanted them out. Bellowing as he used to when he went over the top in France, he threw his weight behind the chair again and Joyce staggered back against one of his bully-boy companions. 'Out of my house!' The copper was shouting too. Fuck him! 'Where's your warrant? Get out!'

A bully boy tried to push past the chair; no hope in the narrow hallway. Dick was driving them back, back, out through the splintered doorframe, over the splintered door to the pavement, where his neighbours were gathering, a dozen or more. One-leg Billy Mason was there, Ned Bristow and Bob Proctor in their nightshirts, and old widow Buttle who loved a good 'bull and cow' and always had something to say. Doors and windows were opening up and down the street.

'What's goin' on, Dick?'

'These buggers broke into my house!'

The copper said, 'Richard Stewart is under arrest.'

One policeman on a three-policeman job? No. He was a fascist doing his fascist comrades a favour.

'What charge?'

'Theft.'

'Of what?'

'Money.'

'Not guilty.'

Did they have the balls to put him on trial in the street? Even cocky Joyce looked uncertain.

'You're resisting arrest,' said the copper.

Dick dropped the chair and drew the rolling pin from his trousers. 'Bloody right I am.'

That made his neighbours chuckle.

'Bugger off,' said Brown.

'Yeah. Bugger off,' said someone else. Bugger off, bugger off, sang the chorus. No one knew the constable, no one knew the bully boys, and for all his faults and the faults of his hoity-toity mother, Stewart was Rotherhithe, his poor dear wife too. So, go on, bugger off!

'I'll be back,' said the copper.

Joyce was twinkling with hate. 'Bugger off, Joyce,' he said.

What else could they do? Shouting their defiance, they turned and walked away, laughter and catcalls, the beating of pots and pans ringing in their ears. And when they had gone Stewart shouted, 'Thank you, thank you' to the street, which was his street, Clarence Street. With the help of a neighbour he picked up his front door and propped it in place. The Stewart family would get by.

The police came for him at six o'clock in the morning, a plain-clothes inspector from Special Branch with a sergeant and five constables. The inspector was an Ulsterman called Macdonald. Macdonald with a small 'd', he said.

'Just to be clear, Inspector, you're arrestin' me for . . .?'

'On suspicion of disclosing official information without lawful authority,' he replied.

Official Secrets Act. How convenient.

'No fuss now, Stewart.'

There was none – only the wailing of his children as they bundled him into their van. From the bench in the back his last view of the street was of his own front door lying across the pavement.

Epilogue

Conservative Head Office . . . played a shady game.
It saw its advantage and took it, and, unfortunately,
  the size of the victory has weakened me.
Once again, I record that no honest man should trust in too
  gentlemanly a way the conservative wirepullers.

Prime Minister Ramsay MacDonald,
Diary 29 October 1931

O<small>N</small> 27 O<small>CTOBER</small> 1931 a new national coalition of political parties led by Ramsay MacDonald won an overwhelming victory in a general election. His government commanded a majority in parliament of 554, of which 470 were Conservatives. The Labour Party he had led for twenty years and helped to establish was almost wiped out, retaining only 52 seats.

29 October 1931

1

WHAT A FOUL bloody day! *Dreich*, the new prime minister would call it, the old one too since he was one and the same man. A bloody day; a bloody man! Fletcher folded his copy of *The Times* and placed it on the passenger seat. Really, it was too depressing. Grim, grim reading. Ramsay MacDonald back in Number 10 with a new government and a majority of five hundred in parliament. What times! He fished his cigarettes from his coat pocket and lit one. He was hungry, he was bored, and the view of the prison through the windscreen of the Austin was as bleak as bleak could be. Most of all he was still reeling downcast by the general election result and he was quite sure he would be for months to come. Prisons were always dreary and forbidding places and Brixton was no exception, but gazing across the road to its gates he found comfort in the thought that, whatever else they might have done, the men inside were entirely innocent of the appalling crime so recently inflicted on the Labour Party and the country at the ballot box since they were unable to vote. No, responsibility for that rested squarely on the shoulders of one man – its erstwhile leader.

Only a few months ago he would have cheered another victory for Mac, but that was before he turned his back on his friends, comrades, everything he used to hold dear. To make common

cause with political enemies and engineer the party's humiliation
at the polls because he imagined it to be in the national interest
was nothing but sheer vanity. Some in Labour said he had been
seduced by his high-society friends, whose good opinion he
valued more than that of his comrades. He would have done
better to let his enemies force him from the political stage. That
was what they had hoped to do with his love letters. But now
his Conservative enemies were his allies – for as long as it suited
them. Topsy-turvy world. My God, Fletcher felt it, he felt it very
personally. Look at those poor creatures! Half a dozen women
were waiting at the prison gates for their men to walk free. To
what sort of freedom? To swell the ranks of the jobless and the
poor. MacDonald's new government was proposing to do nothing
to ease their lot since it was intent on cutting the dole.

Mrs Fletcher was going to give him hell for filling their new
car with cigarette smoke. 'You're taking *our* car to work!' she
had exclaimed. 'Why don't *they* give you one?' Why? Because
they didn't approve of his visits to the prison. *They* were discour-
aging him from taking an interest in the fate of inmate Richard
Stewart. *They* wanted to throw away the key. He had made no
mention of visiting a prison to dear Elspeth, of course, goodness me no, she was badly out of sorts already. She was furious
with Ramsay MacDonald. For a few months only, she had been
the wife of a member of parliament and she cherished the hope
she would be again. But not this time, and, honestly, the state
of the Labour Party – he didn't have the heart to tell her – it
was perfectly possible she never would be.

Opening the driver's door, he dropped his cigarette and
ground it beneath his shoe. To judge from the litter and the
horse shit in Jebb Avenue, its residents were not going to
complain. Was a sense of civic pride possible in the shadow
of a prison? The door to the left of the gates had opened and
an officer was speaking to the women.

Their men were late. First, slopping out, then breakfast, then the return of personal belongings: the governor had said 'expect him at half past six.' Fletcher glanced at his watch: it was almost seven. He could have waited inside the prison, only it was so degrading and inhuman one visit was quite enough.

That had been on the anniversary of their mission to Paris. Well, Stewart had made him look such a fool! The prime minister had his letters and his mistress had her money, but what was Commander Fletcher thinking, entrusting the exchange to a fellow like Stewart? 'The PM's very unhappy,' his go-between, Jimmy Thomas, had confided to him. ''Ee asked *you* to handle it, Reggie. It was *your* responsibility. You don't understand the trouble this 'as caused the Chief!'

Then there was Admiral Sinclair: happy that Stewart had paid 'the vamp' but very unhappy to hear 'the impertinent devil' had spoken to the PM in person. 'Bring down your government? Nonsense, Prime Minister, the man's a crook,' the admiral had said, and Ramsay MacDonald had found it convenient this time to believe him. It was in everyone's interests to bury the affair – and bury Stewart too. Six feet under would be best; Brixton Prison would do. A catch-all Official Secrets burial: on remand awaiting trial for a year, more than a year, for as long as possible.

And Fletcher had been in no hurry to rescue the awkward bugger. But when it became clear Jimmy Thomas's promise of a safe parliamentary seat was going to come to nothing, he had allowed guilt to get the better of him. Yes, he was disappointed – he felt badly let down – but what was that compared to Stewart's situation? He was mouldering away in a prison cell for his part in a prime minister's love affair! He had been charged with giving away secrets to be sure he kept one – the conspiracy. The Service wasn't going to risk taking him to trial. It would either cut a deal or kill him.

From what Fletcher could gather Stewart had understood that from day one of his incarceration. There was talk of a large sum of money. How much and from whom wasn't clear, and no charges had been laid against him. Morton and the new man, Knight, were involved in some way and an ugly Irish fellow called Joyce.

'I don't know who Stewart has upset, Commander,' the governor had said when Fletcher visited the prison, 'but there's been trouble almost every day since he arrived.' Beaten six or seven times, stabbed in the thigh, he had put four of his persecutors in hospital too.

'Why?' Fletcher had asked him when they met. 'Why?'

'They think I've got their money,' he said.

'They' were the newspaper and business conservatives who had paid thousands of pounds for Mac's letters. 'They' wanted their money back and there were Brixton screws and Brixton cons ready to help them. The Service had turned a blind eye.

No saint, Mr Richard Stewart, but he was charged with selling secrets, not theft. Cut a deal or kill? Fletcher had made it his business to broker a deal. His attempt to treat with Mac had gone no further than his monkey. 'The PM's very busy, Reggie,' Thomas had said. 'Don't you read the newspapers? The government's falling apart; the Party's falling apart.' Oh yes, 'Reggie' read the papers. He understood perfectly that the days of the old guard were numbered and their patronage in the party counted for nothing now. 'Those newspapers, Minister, I hope they don't start asking questions,' Fletcher had replied; 'imagine what they'll discover if Stewart dies in prison!'

'You threatening me, Fletcher!'

Shrewd fellow, Thomas. He must have spoken to the prime minister, who must have spoken to the admiral. Fletcher was summoned to what he imagined would be a stormy encounter, but not a bit of it. Sinclair had been in a very good humour. 'Well, Reggie, what a turn-up for the books, eh?' he said, a twinkle in his watery blue eye. 'Labour split and Ramshackle in national coalition with the Conservatives! Imagine? A fine result for the country, what?' In changed times he was sure something could be done for Stewart. 'He's got to keep his mouth shut. You too Reggie. The prime minister asked me, you know. I said, "don't worry, Reggie can be trusted."'

Ah, that twinkle, that wicked, wicked twinkle. The country was saved, the socialist enemy in headlong retreat, and Sinclair seemed to want to claim some of the credit. What a disagreeable notion! But as the split in Labour had widened to a gulf, Fletcher had begun to wonder if persuading Mac to seek assistance from the Service was the very worst thing he could have done. Maybe Mac was a prisoner too, a prisoner of his new allies, his old enemies. Fletcher had mentioned it to no one. He couldn't discuss it with his Labour contacts without revealing the prime minister's affair, and most of them knew nothing of the Service's ways and would dismiss his concerns as fanciful in any case. No, the only person he could talk to was the agent formerly known as Frenchie.

And there he was at last, standing at the door to the left of the gate, a prison officer at his elbow. Thinner. Paler. Threadbare civvies and a knapsack – probably the one he had stuffed a prime minister's ransom into. There was no one to welcome him but Fletcher. His children had been told he was working at sea.

Over here, man. Fletcher stepped out of the car and waved his hat. Over here, Stewart, and if you did steal Morton's anti-Mac money, for goodness sake buy a new pair of trousers.

2

'Thank you.' They shook hands. 'Thank you for coming.' Stewart was a bit choked. Grim, well-groomed sailor spy, you have saved my life, he thought. Why Fletcher had thrown him a lifeline

337

was a mystery. No one else had been ready to. What did it matter? He was free at last. Free! 'Thank you' was simply not enough, only a public display of emotion would embarrass them both.

'You must be glad,' said Fletcher. 'What a terrible place.'

Dick laughed mirthlessly. 'Worse food than the army and almost as dangerous.'

'The governor said you were assaulted.'

'It's no thanks to 'im I'm still breathing.'

'Yes, well . . . Look, I'm parked over there. The Austin on the other side of the street. Have you eaten? I thought breakfast, then I can drive you home.'

'I've had breakfast, Commander.'

'Then have another, Stewart. We need to talk.'

'Would you?' He presented Stewart with the starting handle. 'A couple of turns should do it.'

The Austin 7 pulled away from the kerb at a stately pace. 'You heard about the election?' Right hand on the wheel, he reached back with his left for a copy of The Times. 'Ramsay MacDonald's back in Number Ten.'

'Yes, I heard that.'

'Did you, did you? Labour won fifty-two seats. The Conservatives have four hundred and seventy. With the Tories on board Ramshackle's new coalition has a majority of five hundred! Front and page two . . .' Fletcher tapped the newspaper. 'Damn thing is, he doesn't have a clue how to save the country. Besides, the Tories are in charge now.' He paused for a response and when none came he said, 'You have every right to feel betrayed, Stewart. I mean you put your faith in the man, didn't you? We all did! That he should end his career this way.'

'Where are we going?'

'Not far . . . oh damn!' He braked sharply to avoid a car turning from a side street. 'Yes, it's bloody shameful – of Mac, I mean. So bloody ungrateful.'

They parked in front of Herne Hill station and crossed the road to the cafe opposite. Grimy windows, greasy food, cheap pine furniture, smoke-stained paper: Fletcher chose a table at the window. It was dripping with condensation, and there was a patina of oil and grease on the table. On the wall behind Stewart, the Great Northern Railway poster of a prancing sailor, eyes bulging, stomach bulging, arms out like a fairy. 'Skegness is *so* Bracing', was the legend. Stewart wiped a circle of condensation from the window with a finger. Bracing was for northerners. 'Do you have a fag?'

'Of course.' Fletcher took out his cigarette case.

'Thanks.' He took one and with a lazy flick of the wrist gestured to the other tables. 'You bring Mrs Fletcher here?'

'Of course not!' said Fletcher, 'only chaps like you.'

They both laughed. A cheerful waitress took their order: two bacon buns and two teas. The tea was the colour of the prison gates. They sat in silence waiting for their rolls, Fletcher gazing out of the window too, stirring and stirring his tea.

'Won't taste any better for stirring,' said Dick at last.

'What?'

'The tea. Never mind! There was somethin' you wanted to talk about?'

Fletcher placed the spoon in the saucer. 'What would Frau Forster say, do you suppose?'

'I suppose she would be disappointed, but I think she would say it changes nothin' because she did the right thing.'

'I wonder.'

'Do you? Well, she taught me somethin'.'

'Oh?'

'Don't sneer. I've done a lot of things I'm ashamed of and I came up with a lot of excuses. Don't get me wrong, I'll never be a saint, but I am goin' to try to hold fast to me.'

Fletcher smiled. 'Ah. Well, I expect the money you stole will help.'

'Now, there you are Reggie, that's the sort of cynicism I'm talking about.'

'All right, Stewart, I don't want to hear a confession. I'm not interested in the money.' He paused. 'What I want to say is this . . . in a way, we're to blame. We're to blame for what has happened. He's a prisoner, you see.'

'MacDonald?'

'Keep your voice down. Yes, of course, Ramsay MacDonald. The letters affair was where it began – the betrayal . . .'

Stewart laughed.

'Listen, man!' said Fletcher, tetchily. 'The blackmail plot . . .'

Whatever he was itching to tell Stewart had to wait for the waitress who was approaching the table with their bacon rolls. 'Sauce?' She was an impressively proportioned woman of middle years with a barmaid's bosom any of the local hostelries would have been happy to display. ''Ere you are dearies. More tea?'

Stewart averted his eyes. 'I'll try the coffee.' Hips swaying like a South Seas princess, she carried their cups away to the kitchen.

'It's like this,' said Fletcher, his voice urgent and low, 'the prime minister wanted someone to save his reputation. What did I do? I persuaded him to turn to the head of the Secret Service – you don't need to know his name – and from there . . . well . . . You gave Frau Forster the eight thousand pounds when there was no need—'

'She needed it.'

'That's not the point. You see, it was what the Chief wanted. The Service was plotting against the prime minister, you said so yourself, and by posing as his saviour . . . The Service paid his ransom. You paid it, and with taxpayer's money. My God, they had an even better story. Not just a sexual scandal, his affair with a German tart – no, no, don't protest, imagine the newspaper headlines – not just a sex scandal but a political scandal, and to cap it all, corruption – a corruption scandal too. Namely, thousands of pounds from the coffers of the state to save a prime minister's reputation. Don't you see?'

Stewart rubbed his right hand over his chin. 'I don't know what to think. Your breakfast, it's going cold.'

Fletcher lifted his eyes to the ceiling. 'I don't know why I thought you would—'

'You want me to agree it's *our* fault? You said you didn't want a confession – good, because you won't get one from me. Blame yourself, if you like. I can't give you absolution.'

'Ha! Imagine! No, Stewart. No.'

For a few minutes they sat in silence, fiddling with their cutlery, trying not to catch each other's eye. The air was thick with smoke and the smell of hot fat. The cafe's flat-cap regulars came and went with a stream of London banter, laughter, cursing, and to the chink of eating irons against heavy crockery. The waitress served Fletcher his coffee. Her name was Jean.

'Everything all right for you, dearie?'

'Perfect,' said Fletcher, lighting another cigarette. 'Absolutely perfect. I've never tasted better.' His bacon butty was sitting untouched in a puddle of grease, like a ship mine waiting to be made safe.

'Oh, good,' she said.

Stewart stared down at his own, half-eaten and oozing brown sauce. The sauce had been a mistake. 'What you're sayin' is, he's a prisoner.'

'Yes, I believe he is.'

'And that's why he's taken up with the Tories?'

'I think it's a factor, Stewart, yes. I expect he feels trapped by the reputation for probity and decency that he has gone

341

to such pains to cultivate over the years. He is held to a higher account – and he knows it. No, they have him over a barrel.'

Stewart pushed away his plate. 'I'm done.'

'Right, I'll get the bill.' Heads turned at Fletcher's cough and the click of his fingers; Jean's head wasn't one of them.

'Best pay at the counter, Commander.'

Stewart watched him weave between tables to the cash register. Strange one, Fletcher, he thought, choosing to share his disappointment and guilt with the likes of me. All right, he was Labour, but tweedy Labour; Secret Service, gentleman officer Labour; ex-Liberal Labour. Maybe he was right and they had played the part of Pilate. How could an ordinary bloke tell? In the end, the PM was responsible, because he was responsible for everything. Wasn't that the cross he had to bear? The lazy rhetoric of many campaign trails, preaching to the public of duty, civic and moral responsibility . . . fall short and the public would fall on you: 'Crucify him, crucify him.'

Fletcher was waiting for him at the cafe door. 'You'll want home.'

'I can walk from here.'

'No, you can't; I need someone to start my motorcar.'

'Job for a working man, I suppose.'

'I'm a working man too, Stewart.'

That made him laugh again – Fletcher too.

They drove north towards the river, past the gates of a jam factory and the Borough High Street nick, past a bronze Tommy, his fixed bayonet at the ready, past the grocers' vans queueing to enter the covered market and a shopkeeper rolling out his awning, past a Tooley Street tram that had tangled with a lorry, past the familiar, past the ordinary.

'Will you stay here?' said Fletcher. 'The money . . . You won't be safe.'

'We'll move. What about you? You goin' to stick with the Service? Doesn't seem like a place for you.'

'Oh, I think so, Stewart. The world is changing. There are new dangers. Herr Hitler and his Nazi Party in Germany.'

'Frau Forster was worried about him.'

'Yes. Ridiculous fellow, strutting about in a brown uniform. He was a corporal, you know. What with Mussolini in Italy . . . and I can tell you, that puffed-up popinjay Oswald Mosley is making plans for his own party. No, I'll stay in the Service because there is good work to be done.' He gave a short laugh. 'Not to forget a living to be made. And when this National Government fails, the people will turn to Labour again, and I'll be ready.'

'I hope so, Commander. I do.'

Fletcher dropped him in front of the Norwegian sailors' church. 'Goodbye. Good luck,' he said.

'Good luck to you too, Reggie,' he replied. Ha! That made the bugger smile. What would he say if he knew the missing money was only a stone's throw away? And that was where it was going to stay for now. No illusions, it wasn't going to be easy. What could an old spy do for a living? Carpenter? He had talked of it once. Farmer? His cousin owned some land near Liège. The children would grow up in the Belgian countryside. He would be sad to leave Connie, but it was time. There was a break in the grey sky at last, sun and a fresh breeze off the river. The wanderer was returning home from a voyage of many years to many dark places, returning contrite, wiser, hopeful. A prodigal, a sinner, glad of another chance, glad to be ordinary.

343

3

The prime minister had held on to Seaham, he had won the country and he was back in government at the head of his new national coalition. From his constituency he flew to London airport where he was greeted by cheering crowds. A reporter shouted, 'How does it feel, Prime Minister?'

Feel? It was impossible to explain how he felt in a sentence. 'To work!' he said, which was enough. Downing Street staff had gathered in the hall to greet him. Malcolm was there, and returning to parliament too, this time as new 'National Labour.' 'You've done it, Father!' he said, 'the papers are calling it a personal triumph for the prime minister!' And Jimmy Thomas: 'Business as usual, Chief! Business as usual.' Oh, Jimmy, how could it be?

But of course they were expecting him to put on a show, and turning on the stairs he repeated his defiant message to the electors of Seaham: 'Labour I am, and Labour I shall remain!'

In the small blue drawing room his family had made its own he collapsed in an armchair and shut his eyes. Conservative leader, Baldwin, had sent him a message: 'Rejoice! Rejoice!'

Rejoice with Baldwin? To think such a thing were possible. How had it come to this? That he should win an election against his own party! And there was no doubt about it, Malcom and the newspapers were right, the victory was his victory. Oh yes. 'The captain who stuck to the ship,' had been the slogan on his election posters. But what use a captain without a ship? He knew what his old friends and comrades were saying: 'It was you, Captain, who ran our ship on to the rocks!' National Government? Better say Conservative government.

'Father?' Ishbel had slipped into the room. 'Are you feeling well?'

'Yes, my dear. Resting.'

'Can I bring you some tea?'

He tried to smile. 'No thank you, my dear.' How like her mother she was in face and figure and in the love she showed her poor old father. 'What would *she* have said about all this, about me, my dear? A fine boorach we're in, are we not?'

Kneeling at the arm of the chair, she took his right hand and pressed it to her lips. 'Mother would thank you for having the courage to put the country first,' she said, 'for the sacrifice you've made.'

'Aye, but my heart is elsewhere. This is nae my ain hoose, I ken by the biggin'o't. I'm pulled up by the roots, Ishbel, and what I believe in, in these new conditions, seems dead. I'm worn out.'

'You must rest,' she said, squeezing his hand.

There would be no time to rest; the king, the country, his new Conservative allies, would not let him rest. In his election manifesto he had promised the voters he would consider every proposal likely to help solve the economic crisis.

'The cabinet will meet tomorrow. I must begin.' He leant forward to rise. 'Forgive your father's foolishness. One day I will rebuild *our* party – if they let me.' He raised her hand and was on the point of kissing it affectionately when there was a light knock at the door, then a firm one.

'You see, my dear, no peace.'

'It's Rosa.'

'Yes. Let her in, would you? No. Rosa, Rosa,' he shouted, 'come in!'

Miss Rosa was wearing her blood-red dress, the colour of the people's flag.

'Cheer up, Rosa, we've won!'

She made an effort to smile. 'I'm sorry to bother you, Prime Minister.'

'That's your job, Rosa, and you do it very well. What is it?'

345

'It's Admiral Sinclair, Prime Minister,' she said, 'the admiral is on the telephone. He would like to speak to you.'

Did she look embarrassed?

'All right, Rosa, then you better put him through to my study.'

Author's Note

'Porcupine through hairy bowers shall climb to paradise.'

*Reputedly from a letter by Ramsay MacDonald
to 'his little Austrian friend'.*

V ERY LITTLE IS known of the prime minister's affair with
the woman Oswald Mosley called 'his little Austrian
friend'. Mosley is the principal source for events at the heart
of my story, and, while almost everything he wrote about his
political and personal life was in some way exculpatory and
intended to present him in the best possible light, there is no
reason to doubt the veracity of his account of the affair. That
was certainly the view of one of his harshest critics, his son,
Nicholas Mosley, who included a passage dictated by his
father in a memoir of his parents, *Rules of the Game*. Mosley
senior describes meeting 'an old Viennese tart: faded blonde,
very sophisticated, very agreeable', and Ramsay MacDonald's
excursions to the galleries with her in Vienna and Berlin. At
MacDonald's suggestion she was included in a 'gay party' that
assembled the following year in Cornwall. 'It would be such
fun if she could come,' he remembered MacDonald saying; 'will
you explain it to the others?'

Then Labour won the election, MacDonald became prime

minister, and 'this old girl got very nasty'. According to Mosley she made contact with him in the autumn or winter of 1929 and persuaded him to visit her cheap rented flat on London's Horseferry Road. 'I'll come straight to the point,' she said, 'I was once a very rich woman. The prime minister, when I used to meet him in Switzerland, was a very poor man and I helped him a lot in those days. Now he's got the whole Treasury of Great Britain behind him.'

She told Mosley that she had visited Downing Street to ask her former lover for help. 'He saw me in the Cabinet Room and became completely hysterical and began to bang his head against the wall,' she said. 'Then Isobel (sic) came in in the middle of this performance . . . he took me by the shoulders and pushed me out in front of all the porters in Downing Street. I fall down, I break my lorgnettes, my eyes, they are blinded with tears.'

Then she turned to the letters. 'You know, he's a very innocent man and he wrote to me letters which were pornographic,' she said.

Mosley was in no doubt that she was threatening to blackmail the prime minister. 'The whole thing will blaze in the French press,' he recalled her saying. 'Very, very dangerous,' he replied; and warned her that if she attempted to publish them she would be arrested and thrown into prison at once.

Mosley thought he had done enough to intimidate her into abandoning her scheme, but he learnt later that she had made a second attempt, this time from Paris. A friend of Mosley's who worked at the British Embassy at the time claimed to have seen extracts including a poem by MacDonald to his lover. The only line the diplomat could recall is the one I quote in this note.

Mosley was more circumspect in his autobiography, *My Life*. Love affairs were both natural and necessary, in his view, and he despised what he characterised as the 'puritanism' of Labour Party colleagues and the hypocrisy of the press and the public. 'MacDonald was in principle a moral man of Puritan antecedent and instinct,' he observed, '[but] in company with many of his colleagues, he would regard a love affair as a fall from grace rather than a fulfilment of life.'

No mention is made of the prime minister's affair in the official histories of the Secret Intelligence Service (MI6) and the Security Service (MI5). Official historian of the Security Service, Christopher Andrew, believes secret files that might have cast light on the episode 'may have been destroyed'. Some details of the affair were revealed to the naval historian and former deputy director of naval intelligence, Captain Stephen Roskill, by a senior diplomat in the Foreign Office. Andrew concludes, 'it is probable, though not certain, that SIS (MI6) was used to purchase and retrieve the letters,' and that Lieutenant Commander Reginald ('Reggie') Fletcher was responsible for arranging the exchange. The Chief of the Secret Intelligence Service, Sinclair, had recruited Fletcher in an effort to build bridges with Labour after the bad feeling caused by the leaking of the Zinoviev letter. Fletcher appears to have believed that he was not sufficiently rewarded for his part in hushing up the affair. A friend and service colleague observed in his diary that Fletcher was 'very down on Ramsay' and claimed he was 'notoriously ungrateful to his friends'.

Ramsay MacDonald makes no direct mention of his lover in his diaries. 'Grand Easter holidaying at Fowey with a village of most pleasant companions,' he recorded on 12 April 1929. One of those companions was his Viennese mistress. Mosley took a photograph of some of the party but, pointedly perhaps, she is not in the picture. In the same diary entry MacDonald bemoans 'the misjudgements which my life puts in for me. Someone to share the duties would have meant that they would have been done and that smoothly. How often I think of the dead. Oh, had she been here these last years. I wonder if they know.' No doubt he was thinking of his late wife, Margaret. In the diary entries that follow he records that he is deeply troubled by 'personal concerns'. 'The debts of folly are the heaviest to pay,' he reflects.

MacDonald's biographer, David Marquand, was inclined to doubt Mosley's account of the affair until his attention was drawn to a passage in Harold Nicolson's diary. Nicolson was serving at the British Embassy in Berlin when the Mosleys visited the city with MacDonald in 1928, and it was to his friend, the diplomat, that Mosley first revealed details of the affair four years later. He claimed Ramsay MacDonald had first introduced him to an 'old friend' called 'Frau Forster' in Vienna. Mosley had dismissed her at once as an 'obvious vamp'. His account of her attempt to blackmail the prime minister the following year was in all essential points the one he shared with his son many years later. We can only assume Nicolson believed him since he took the trouble to record it in his diary. 'I now think that Mrs Forster was probably a real person,' David Marquand wrote in a revised edition of his biography. 'MacDonald probably had an affair with her; he probably wrote her compromising letters; and she probably threatened to give them to the press but was deterred from doing so.'

Since publication of the Marquand biography the National Archives in London has released letters that shed light on an earlier secret relationship between the Labour leader and a member of the British aristocracy. MacDonald met Lady Margaret Sackville, poet, society beauty, daughter of an earl, not long after the death of his wife. The letters they exchanged over fifteen years are full of passion and longing. 'Do you dream that I come to you?' he wrote to her in the summer of 1915. 'Do I come to you when you are not dreaming? Do I kiss you and lie on your breast? Give me all the news about yourself and your heart and tell me all about your love.' There is a playfulness to their correspondence that is echoed in the line of verse quoted at the beginning of this note.

MacDonald feared that newspapers hostile to Labour – most of them – would make much of the working-class illegitimate son of a ploughboy conducting a love affair with a member of the aristocracy; a Presbyterian member of the Free Kirk with a Roman Catholic; a devoted family man with a woman fifteen years his junior. And what would Labour's newly enfranchised working-class supporters think of their leader's relationship with Lady Sackville? His friendships with grand ladies were much remarked upon by his comrades and enemies alike. Mosley called him 'a great snob' and observed that his later friendship with Lady Londonderry was 'linked only by her curiosity and his snobbery'. The economist and social reformer, Beatrice Webb, recalled an encounter with MacDonald at the Trades Union Congress in 1926. 'He was evidently absorbed in the social prestige of his ex-premiership enhanced by a romantic personality,' she wrote in her diary. 'He went out of his way to tell me that he was going to stay with Mrs Biddulph near Cirencester – "The Hon. Mrs Biddulph," he added . . . Of course so long as he does his duty in public speaking and in attendance in Parliament, his social relations are his own concern . . . But MacDonald is not working at his job; he is not thinking about it . . . His thoughts and his emotions are concentrated on his agreeable relations with the men and women – especially the women – of the enemy's camp . . . he is becoming impatient with the troublesomeness of the working class.'

Webb's diary entry does scant justice to the complexity of the man. MacDonald took – in the words of his biographer, Marquand – a 'sneaking satisfaction' in being able to move up and down the English social scale, a privilege afforded to him because he was a Scot from a small town in Aberdeenshire and not from a working-class district of London or Leeds. A 'craving for solitude and peace went hand in hand with a love of colour and excitement,' Marquand observed. Harold Nicolson knew MacDonald and judged him 'a fundamentally simple man. Under all his affectation and vanity there is a core of real simplicity.'

Sixty years ago, Secretary of State for War John Profumo was forced to resign after an extramarital affair with teenage model Christine Keeler. Dozens of politicians have been 'exposed' in the press since. Parliamentary 'love cheats' have been pursued by photographers and pilloried on the front pages of the papers. The historian, Macaulay, a hundred and fifty years ago famously observed that there was no spectacle more ridiculous than the British public 'in one of its periodical fits of morality'. Well, that may have changed. Coverage of Boris Johnson's extramarital liaisons and the speculation about the number of children he has fathered did not prove a significant electoral obstacle. It may even have contributed to the image he cultivated of the fun-loving rogue.

Ramsay MacDonald was a faithful and loving husband and a devoted father. He was heartbroken when his wife died and for the rest of his long life she was never far from his thoughts. But he was a vigorous, passionate man and too young at 43 to forsake the possibility of another relationship. He asked Margaret Sackville to marry him three times. His proposals were probably made without any great expectation of success, since they both agreed marriage would damage his political career. MacDonald believed the Conservative press would use their relationship to undermine his position in the party and the country – and with good reason.

'We have implacable enemies who sleeplessly lie in wait to damage our reputation,' he confided to his diary in January

1930. It was not his political opponents in the House of Commons he feared but their supporters in the papers and the secret services. He had been scarred by personal attacks on him in the press during the war and the conspiracy to undermine the party's election campaign in 1924. For fifty years the British intelligence services denied any involvement in the production and publication of the Zinoviev letter and suppressed all evidence to the contrary. Historians now know the letter was a fake. Winston Churchill described the Labour government as a 'national misfortune such as has usually befallen a great state only on the morrow of defeat in war'. MacDonald's politics were hardly revolutionary, but that is how some senior Conservatives and their friends in the press and secret services chose to view them. The Labour government's opponents were, in the words of Foreign Office historian Gill Bennett, 'waiting for it to make a fatal mistake, but also working to undermine it in any way possible'. The Zinoviev forgery was intended to raise the spectre of a class war and an armed Soviet-style rising in Britain – and politicians on both the left and the right believed that it succeeded. Lord Beaverbrook, the proprietor of the *Daily Express*, congratulated Lord Rothermere, the proprietor of the *Daily Mail*, on his 'red letter' scoop. The *Daily Mail* had won the 1924 election for the Conservatives and saved the country from a socialist revolution, he declared.

When Labour returned to power five years later it was to meet the same 'implacable enemies' in the press and the secret services. MacDonald had good reason to fear his relationship with a 'continental cocotte' would be used to undermine him. The Zinoviev affair had exposed the many links between the Conservative Party and the intelligence services. Conservative Party leader Stanley Baldwin and colleagues Churchill and Chamberlain were honorary members of a secret dining club for those who had worked or were still working in the intelligence services. The founder and chairman of the IP Club was the serving head of the Security Service (MI5), Vernon Kell. Conservative Party chairman John Davidson was also a member of the club. 'Its members were a pretty odd lot,' he recalled in his political memoir, but the club 'provided a very convenient way for Baldwin to meet them informally'. Baldwin and his colleagues were on excellent terms with senior officers from both services, including those responsible for leaking the Zinoviev letter.

Davidson was able to recruit one of their number to Conservative Central Office. Major Joseph Ball was an experienced intelligence officer, the head of the Security Service's B Branch (Investigations). In 1927 he joined Central Office to help run 'a little intelligence of our own'. Davidson described his work like this:

'We had agents in certain key centres and we also had agents actually in the Labour Party Headquarters, with the result that we got their reports on political feeling in the country . . . We also got advance "pulls" of their literature . . . This was of enormous value to us because we were able to study the Labour Party policy in advance.'

Labour was 'the enemy', as far as Ball was concerned, because the 'revolutionary tail wags Labour's dog'. Among those he approached in 1930 to help him with his intelligence network was Maxwell Knight.

'M' – as Knight liked to be known – was to play an important role in undermining fascism in the 1930s and in breaking up Nazi spy rings during the Second World War. But in the 1920s he was an enthusiastic supporter of the movement. As a member of its paramilitary 'K Squad' he was involved in a campaign of violence against communist supporters, kidnappings, and in break-ins at the Party's offices. One of his closest friends and comrades was a young Irishman and adventurer called William Joyce. During the war, Joyce became the radio voice of Nazi Germany – Lord Haw-Haw – and was hanged as a traitor in 1946.

Knight provided information on 'subversive activities' to both intelligence services during the 1920s, but his closest contact was with Desmond Morton of the Secret Intelligence Service (MI6). 'I have only one enemy,' Morton declared: 'International Leninism.' For a time, he seems to have drawn very little distinction between international communism and democratic socialism, since he was one of those most intimately involved in the Zinoviev conspiracy.

In the summer of 1930 his covert activities in Britain and his relationship with Maxwell Knight in particular fell foul of the Metropolitan Police's Special Branch. Deputy Assistant Commissioner John Carter discovered Morton and Knight were flouting the government ban on undercover operations against the Communist Party. Carter confronted Knight: 'I can make things bloody unpleasant for you.' Morton was 'a worm', he said, and he accused them both of 'doing the whole of this thing for the Conservative Party, and presumably giving the latter official information when another Party is in Power'. Carter pointed out to Knight that the Labour government was against 'this sort of work' and that it was his duty to carry out its policy. The matter came to a head in the summer of 1931 when a committee of senior civil servants and intelligence officers decided responsibility for counter-espionage and anti-communist operations at home should be left entirely to the Security Service (MI5). Knight and his Casuals moved to MI5, where they became known as 'M section'.

For most of their history the British intelligence services have been more comfortable with governments of the right than of the left. Senior intelligence officers harboured the suspicion that socialist was another word for communist. One American intelligence officer posted to Britain recalled the reaction in MI5 to the election of the Labour government in 1964. 'I simply could not believe my ears when I heard the openly scurrilous and disloyal remarks,' he reported. Unbeknownst to Prime Minister Harold Wilson, MI5 had opened a file on him after the Second World War and for a time had kept him under surveillance. Wilson's colleagues dismissed his claim that Downing Street was bugged as paranoia, but a Security Service file examined by Christopher Andrew, suggested otherwise. Bugs were placed in the Cabinet Room, the waiting room and the prime minister's study in 1963, the year before Wilson's election victory, and remained in place until 1977. They were finally removed on the orders of another Labour prime minister, Jim Callaghan, who made a disingenuous statement to MPs denying that electronic surveillance had ever been undertaken in Downing Street.

I would like to acknowledge my debt to the following archives and authors. Christopher Andrew, *The Defence of the Realm*, and *Secret Service: the Making of the British Intelligence Community*; Baedeker's *Paris and its Environs*; Francis Beckett, *Enemy Within: The Rise and Fall of the British Communist Party*; Arnold Beichman, 'Hugger Mugger in Old Queen Street: The Origins of the Conservative Research Department' *(Journal of Contemporary History Vol. 13 No. 4)*; Gill Bennett, *The Zinoviev Letter* and *Churchill's Man of Mystery: Desmond Morton and the World of Intelligence*; Noreen Branson, *History of the Communist Party of Great Britain 1927–41*; J.C.C. Davidson, *Memoirs of a Conservative*; John Ferris and Uri Bar-Joseph, 'Getting Marlowe to Hold His Tongue: The Conservative Party, the Intelligence Services and the Zinoviev Letter' *(Intelligence and National Security Vol. 8 No. 4)*; Wal Hannington, *Never on Our Knees;* Henry Hemming, *M: Maxwell Knight, MI5's Greatest Spymaster;* Keith Jeffrey, *MI6: The History of the Secret Intelligence Service 1909–1949;* Nigel Jones, 'The Assassination of Walther Rathenau' *(History Today, 7 July 2013);* James Klugman, *History of the Communist Party of Great Britain 1925– 27;* David Lloyd George and Frances Stevenson, *My Darling Pussy: The Letters of Lloyd George and Frances Stevenson 1913– 41;* Ramsay and Margaret MacDonald/Jane Cox (ed.), *A Singular Marriage: A Labour Love Story in Letters and Diaries;* Ramsay MacDonald, Diaries and Correspondence (National Archives, Kew PRO/30/69/1753/3 and 4); Ramsay MacDonald, Correspondence and Related Papers (University of Manchester Archive, John Rylands Library (GB 133 RMD/1 and 2); David Marquand, *Ramsay MacDonald;* L. MacNeill Weir, *The Tragedy of Ramsay MacDonald*; Nicholas Mosley, *Rules of the Game;* Oswald Mosley, *My Life;* George Orwell, *Down and Out in Paris and London;* Harry Pollitt, *Serving My Time;* Kevin Quinlan, *The Secret War Between The Wars: MI5 in the 1920s and 1930s;* Wolfram Selig, *Organisation Consul;* Robert Skidelsky, *Mosley;* Howard Spring, *Fame Is the Spur;* The Times Newspaper Digital Archive; Steven Woodbridge, *Fraudulent Fascism: The Attitude of Early British Fascists towards Mosley and the New Party.*

Finally, a big thank you to all those who helped me write my version of the prime minister's affair. In particular, the British Library in London, my source for many of the articles and books listed above – an inspiring place, always – Nick Sayers, my editor at Hodder, who commissioned and helped me shape the story, agent and honest critic, Julian Alexander; my friends and family, to whom the book is dedicated.

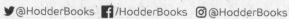